THE REMNANT

AN HISTORIC NOVEL ABOUT

THE JEWISH RESISTANCE IN WWII

BY
OTHNIEL J. SEIDEN

BABY BOOMER SERIES PUBLICATION

Cover Art
by Capri Brock

Proudly Published in the USA by

www.BooomerBookSeries.com

ISBN: 1519496346

To Jessica,
the DINH... the DINH

1

DOV...

This story I begin to put to paper now is an account of the Holocaust that has been largely ignored these past decades.

Of all the tales of this inhuman time, little has been written or spoken of the Jewish resistance against the Nazi forces. Much has been documented about the slaughter of our men, women and children, but too little is known of the heroic efforts against horrific odds by those few of us who were able to stay free enough to fight.

This is not really my story; it is the story of *"The Remnant."* Every Jew alive after the Holocaust is a survivor and one of The Remnant. Anyone having the least amount of Jewish blood in his or her veins is a survivor and as part of the Remnant is alive today not by any skill or intelligence of his or her own but because of luck. Actually, alive by more than luck, alive because of the will of God, for it is God who promised The Remnant. Jews of any nationality outside of Europe are alive today only because of the foresight or wanderlust of one of their ancestors. Had they stayed in Europe until the Holocaust, chances are these jews would be ashes today as are six million of our co-religionists.

This is *our* story and I must tell what I know of it before my earthly time is past. There are too few of us left to give testimony — to chronicle this horrific past. Tragically, there are those today who would rather avouch that this tragic time was myth and fantasy. These libelers must be exposed for the liars they are, their slanders refuted. As the Nazis slaughtered six million of us, these slanderers are trying now to destroy the memory of our martyrs. They too are Hitlers and must be confronted with the truth.

The anti-Semites love to say, *"They went to their deaths like sheep to the slaughter!"* I hope the story which follows dispels this insufferable myth. Those who died, died because they had no chance to fight back, had no place to escape to—but, those few who were able to escape fought and fought bravely, against horrific odds. Those few Jews who remained *"free,"* — less than 3% of the total population of Jews in Europe—made up a large percentage of the total resistance against the Nazis, perhaps as high as 20% of that battle.

They not only had to hide themselves from the Nazi forces, but also from the general population of most of the occupied countries, for that population would gladly have turned Jews over to the enemy or killed them outright from their own anti-Semitic hate.

Sadly, the lessons of that horrible time were poorly learned. Every decade in this intervening time has had its own holocaust. Indo-China, Cambodia, the Sudan, Rwanda, Bosnia, in Central and South America— millions of people have suffered inhuman atrocities—anguished deaths—because of ethnicity, race, religion or for being in the way of some maniacal ambition or agenda. Forgetfulness is no cure for man's inhumanity. These stories must be told and retold as often as possible to save the future races.

The story I tell I know from those who lived those terrible years in the forests with me. I know them from diaries left behind by those who didn't live to give confirmation on their own. In those long and lonely hours, days, years in the forests, we shared our most intimate thoughts, feelings and certainly our fears. And then there were the transcribed testimonies at **Nuremberg**—all to supplement what my comrades and I experienced in the forests.

Thus, in my 80th year I shall finally detail my account and what I know of the stories of so many others. I begin penning this story in the fall of 1998, 59 years after it began for me.

On September 1, 1939 I turned 21. I was born in 1918, as World War I drew to close. I was presented with the beginning of World War II for my twenty-first birthday. It was the day Hitler's forces invaded Poland to begin that conflagration.

My name is Dov, short for Dovid or David as you say in America. **Dov Malmed** was how I was known in those days. As a child I was called Dovy, but after I was about sixteen only my grandmother, of blessed memory—*Olov Hashalom*—may she rest in peace—continued to refer to me as Dovy. Dov is how I will refer to myself in this account.

As far back as anyone could remember, our family has always been Polish. For all I knew, my ancestors came to Poland in the year 1492 when Spain expelled all her Jews. Poland invited her refugees to settle there.

On my twenty-first birthday, the long history of the Jews in Poland was launched toward its conclusion. I recall my first image of the beginning of this holocaust. My attention was drawn to it by a strange thundering to the west. Our village was some seventy kilometers to the east and south of Warsaw. It was early in the morning and as the light strengthened we saw smoke rising high in the direction of the great city. It climbed steadily from the horizon, higher and higher into the morning sky, until it darkened the white clouds. The smoke would not cease for most of a month, as the thunder of bombs and cannons spread over the country. By October, the government had capitulated and all of Poland was in the hands of her German oppressors.

Most of Poland's Jews were trapped awaiting a fate too fantastic to anticipate or imagine. Less than two percent of us remained *"free"* in hiding, able to even consider saving ourselves or fighting back. It was the same all over Europe. Few of us were able to stay out of captivity. Those who were engulfed couldn't resist and had nowhere to escape to. We had little chance of survival.

My account is of those unfortunate and fortunate whose paths I crossed.

2

SOLOMON...

Solomon awoke in a small enclosure—the space under a stairway—dimly lit by a lantern. His eyes were not yet open and he sensed strangeness. It was that first moment when one awakens. Somehow he knew he was in an unfamiliar place. Horizontal boards slowly came into focus, as he opened his eyes, dimly lit boards about twenty centimeters wide, making up a wall not more than two hands from his face.

Unfamiliar. This cot—unfamiliar! The ceiling slopes down toward my head—the underside of stairs. "Oh! It hurts to move!" I'm sore—stiff. This wall on the other side of me is stone—cold stone. "Where the hell am I? How did I get here?" His voice was weak as a whisper, his throat felt dry. Am I a prisoner? I can't remember. I can't remember anything!

These sheets—clean sheets. I'm naked! Where am I? There's barely room in here for this cot. It's some kind of a cell. A prison cell? I don't see a door. No window? My God where am I? Only this cot and that lantern hanging under that top step—there's nothing else in here. Is that an entrance? It's almost too small. What's that? Sounds like a door opening—footsteps...

As the sound advanced down the stairs, terror filled Solomon. They were heavy steps on the stairs that made the lantern swing and caused eerie shadows to move on the walls. He could follow the steps along the other side of the board wall. They're coming for me! He heard wood sliding. A man came through the small opening at the foot of the tiny cot. A big man, he hardly fit through the small opening.

Strangely Solomon's first thought was, he doesn't wear a uniform; he felt a slight relief. He wondered, why did I expect a uniform? Why did I fear a uniform? The man straightened at the foot of his cot. Huge! He was huge. Massive! Powerful! He smiled.

"Well, it's about time. You've been sleeping like the dead ever since I found you!"

I've never seen him. Found me? What's he talking about. I can't remember.

"Don't be afraid. You're safe here." The man spoke calmly.

"I—I don't understand. Where am I? How did I get here? What is this place?" The words barely escaped his throat. He felt very weak, exhausted, his mind a blank.

"My name is **Ivan—Ivan Igonovich**. Don't you remember anything?"

Solomon shook his head feebly.

"Let's start with your name? Who are you?"

"**Solomon Shalensky**. I'm sorry, I don't understand — I can't remember anything."

"I found you two days ago, in a ditch along the road. I've never seen such a mess. Mud, blood, filth—caked all over you." Ivan was animated now, gesturing with his arms and massive hands, as much as the cramped quarters would allow. "I thought you were dead; but when I touched you, you opened your eyes and mumbled something. Then you fainted again. You've been mostly unconscious ever since."

Solomon managed, "I don't understand," some of his fear melting. The lantern light was too weak for Solomon to make out Ivan's features clearly, but the deep voice was gentle.

"You are safe," the stranger reassured him. "We have you hidden. We've gotten some broth into you. You've been delirious. Don't you remember anything at all?"

Solomon tried. He couldn't seem to focus. He had no memory to focus on.

"You spoke of a pit of death. German gunners ... piles of death ... you kept repeating we're all dead. What does it all mean? That is why we hid you here. Are you a fugitive from the Germans?"

Solomon's eyes widened in horror as realization poured in on him; a deluge of memory struck, grotesque memory. He uttered a muffled and hideous cry, "They murdered us! The Germans—shooting us. Killing us! All of us! Murdered us—in the ravine." He wept uncontrollably.

"What are you saying? Shot who?"

Solomon answered between sobs, "All of us—the Jews—all—all of us Jews of Kiev..."

"That's impossible. There are over a hundred thousand Jews in Kiev. You're trying to tell me the Germans shot all the Jews in Kiev?"

"All of us..."

Ivan felt sure the young man was mistaken but wondered how he could have imagined such a thing. "Solomon, where did this happen? You mentioned a ravine."

"At *Babi Yar* ... in the Babi Yar ravine. They killed us all, there in the ravine—near Kiev."

"But you are alive."

Solomon wept silently. Ivan watched, searching for words. Finally, "It is too dismal in this place. I'll get you some clothes and get you out into the daylight. I'll be back in just a few minutes." He ducked out the small opening with remarkable speed.

Solomon tried to put things into perspective. Where must I start? Mama, Papa, my sister and brothers—they must all be dead. Grandpa. "All dead." His tears came in a torrent now. "All dead but me. Oh God," he whimpered, "why me? Why not me?"

His face was damp with tears when Ivan returned with an armful of clothes. Solomon dried his tears on the sheet.

"Here. Put these on. They may be a bit large on you, but they're all I have. Belonged to our son. He was a big muscular boy. He's married now to a girl from the Eastern Ukraine. They live near her home. Thank God, they've been spared this insane war so far."

As Solomon dressed, Ivan gazed at his face. Could it be true what he told me? Is it imagination — exaggeration? Delirium perhaps. He was a horrible mess when I found him. He's sure been through something atrocious.

"I don't know how to thank you. These clothes — and for helping me. It's not usual for a Christian to help a Jew."

Ivan felt a moment of hostility, "Solomon, not all of us are like that. Besides, I wasn't sure you were a Jew; but, had I known — well, I'd have done the same."

Solomon heard the anger in Ivan's voice. "I'm sorry. I didn't mean..."

"That's all right. You've a right to be suspicious of us, Solomon."

"Please, call me Sol. All my friends call..." a pained expression crossed Solomon's face, "...*called* me Sol."

"When I was younger, Sol, I saw the aftermath of a *pogrom*. I saw the organized slaughter of Jews in their *shtetl* — their village. Sixty-three Jews were killed that Easter. I don't know how many were raped — maimed — injured. Their homes were burned — their shops looted. The so called 'good Christians' claimed it was vengeance for the Crucifixion." Ivan's gaze fell to the floor as a frown of disgust wrinkled his brow. His eyes closed. "Our priest put that idea in our heads. Rape, slaughter — all in the name of revenge for the Church... Since that day I have never set foot inside of a church."

Solomon was dressed now, but he sensed that Ivan wasn't finished speaking. He sat down on the edge of the cot.

"I worked for a Jew once," Ivan continued, still looking down at the dirt floor. "I was treated fairly and decently. That is why this room is here," he added, looking back up into Sol's eyes. "This was his place. He always feared a pogrom. It was to hide his family should a pogrom happen. He'd survived one as a child and never got over it. Several years ago he decided to leave here for Palestine. One night he and his family just left. They took only what they could carry. They planned to walk all the way. He left me all of this for my loyalty during the years I worked for him." Ivan looked about the little chamber. "I've a feeling it will get more use now."

Solomon broke a short silence with, "How will I ever be able to repay you?"

"Never mind that. Come on; let's get out of here into the daylight."

3

IVAN & SOSHA...

Solomon followed Ivan through the small opening in the wall into a fruit cellar full of vegetables, dried fruits and sacks of grains. Ivan pushed a box in front of the small opening. It was impossible to see or even guess that there was a room behind the wall supporting the stairs out of the cellar.

Solomon couldn't believe the amount of food he saw stored here. Sol was from the poor part of Kiev, where life was a hand to mouth existence; some days the hand never reached the mouth. Bread and potato soup were often all his family had to eat for days on end. Eggs were a luxury, milk a delight saved for the young. Tea was always available. Meat was on the table perhaps once a week and only on the first Sabbath meal, in very good times. Various vegetables were to be found steaming on the table when they were in season and so plentiful that their price was forced down or if they had been grown in the little garden his mother had labored over. But often the vegetables grown in the garden could not be eaten by his family. If they would bring a good price at market, like the eggs their few chickens laid, they would have to be sold and cheaper foods would be purchased for the household.

"Come on; my wife **Sosha** will have food ready for us." Suddenly Solomon realized he was very hungry. When had he eaten last? He had no memory of having had a meal. Why have I no memory?

They climbed the steps and came out into the light. Sol was temporarily blinded. The last daylight he could remember was the day he and his family were taken to

Babi Yar. Babi Yar and suddenly horrible images flooded his mind. He felt a weakness momentarily, thought he might fall, staggered slightly and looked up to Ivan who didn't seem to notice.

"See," Ivan said, "You should be safe here for the time being."

As Sol squinted his eyes slowly became accustomed. The storage cellar had been dug after the house was built. Its entrance was about three meters from the house, so in bad weather they didn't have far to go for supplies. It was located at the rear of the house, so if trouble came from the road, about two hundred meters distant, the family could enter the cellar without being seen; the house was between the cellar entrance and the road. Its location had been selected for security, not for convenience.

The house was small, built of native stone and wood. It wasn't a large farm he inherited from his employer. Jews weren't allowed to own much property and Ivan had not needed to add more land. In Solomon's eyes, Ivan was a man of means. He had two cows, several pigs, chickens and geese. Most of the land had been tilled and now the animals were free to wander in the field and eat what was left after the harvest. The land was surrounded on three sides by forest and on the fourth by a dirt road.

"I've never seen such a big place. Is it really all yours?"

"All that's been cleared. It represents years of hard work. We are proud of it, Sosha and me.

The Germans will confiscate all your animals and stored food I'm told. They obviously haven't gotten out here yet. We haven't even seen a German yet. Come, let's go in..."

"It's good to see you up," a woman said as they entered the house. "I am Sosha. Ivan tells me you are called Solomon."

"Please, Sol."

"All right, Sol. Now you two sit down here and start eating. I hope your strength will return quickly."

"I feel quite well. Hungry, but well. A little stiff. I don't know how to thank you sufficiently."

"Thank later, eat now," Sosha insisted.

Sosha was an attractive woman. Her blond hair, highlighted by the whiteness creeping into it, was pulled back and rolled into a bun. She had a round, full face, skin reddened from hours of work outdoors. Her skin would have been as brown as Ivan's had her complexion not been fair. Instead of tanning, her skin had a blush to it. Tall for a woman, she had a typically big-boned Slavic build. Though her hands were rough from years of hard work, next to her huge husband her warm smile made her look almost girlish.

She ladled out two wooden bowls of potato soup from a pot that constantly simmered on the wood stove and placed them on the large, rough-hewn timber table before Sol and her husband. In the middle of the table, she placed a large plate heaped with black bread and cheese. She took a glass of tea for herself and sat down to join them.

Sosha realized that she'd never seen Solomon in full daylight. His hair was light brown. When Ivan had carried him home that first day, he took him directly to the cellar, where the dim light made his hair look nearly black. I must have washed it a half dozen times to get the filth and blood out, she thought. Now she could see the uneven patches where she'd had to cut out some of the tangles.

"I'll trim your hair later this afternoon," she said to Solomon, "Ivan is due for a trim, too. I can do you both today while it is still warm outside."

"Thank you, but that's not necessary," Solomon answered, apparently surprised by her proposal.

"Nonsense, I enjoy cutting hair." I'll have to fatten him up a bit, she thought, though he's huskier than he appears in those baggy clothes. He's a rather handsome fellow. How penetrating his brown eyes are. Thoughtful. Even now they sparkle. We'll get the stubble off him too. It makes him look gaunt. He certainly doesn't have Slavic features. His ancestors must have migrated from the south, perhaps Italy, Spain or Greece — someplace Mediterranean.

"Tell us," Sosha said, "what do you recall now?"

Glancing at Ivan, Solomon replied, "It's all come back. It was horrible. I find myself wondering if it really happened. But it must have happened. I could not dream such horrors." Solomon paused for a moment, apparently trying to organize his thoughts, fighting the tears that welled up in his eyes.

4

KIEV...

"The shelling was almost constant in our part of Kiev, as it was all over the city and the surrounding villages. We lived with it day and night," Solomon began. "The earth shook. Many families dug trenches in their yards and moved into them. The city officials even recommended it. We stayed in our home. My father insisted that God would see to our safety, if He meant for us to survive. 'If we Jews have nothing else, we have faith!' my grandmother used to say, always." There was a sadness in his moment's pause as he sat remembering.

"We could hear the explosions from here," Sosha interjected. "But it never came here."

"That's because we're almost fifty kilometers from the city. It's a wonder you got this far, Sol," Ivan added.

Solomon took a deep sighing breath and continued, "I only remember part of that — getting here, I mean." He hesitated. A tear formed in his eye. He cleared his throat. "For several days, we began to see an increasing number of Russian troops running from the front. They occasionally stopped and begged for civilian clothes. Anyway, out of the growing retreat came rumors that in a matter of days the war would end for us and the front would pass us by. The Communists and their officials left the city along with the retreating soldiers. Most of us that remained felt that living under the German occupation would be better than life under the Bolsheviks. We certainly preferred it to the constant bombings! We were—if not openly, at least secretly—looking forward to occupation. Not that we weren't afraid, but only afraid as one is when he awaits a new experience that he knows nothing about. Afraid like children on their first day of school.

"I recall my father telling us about the Germans, 'They are the most enlightened civilization in the world,' he told us. 'The Germans have given the world the greatest scientists, writers, poets, musicians, philosophers — and in Germany, Jews could become doctors, lawyers, shopkeepers — they could go to the university.' He didn't make it up. He'd heard that from others. Everyone talked about it, on the streets, in stores, everywhere. Compared to life under the Bolsheviks, it sounded like a dream come true. And for us Jews, well, there was an additional incentive — perhaps the Germans would end some of the anti-Semitism we'd known here for so many centuries.

"On September 19th, everything stopped. The quiet was almost frightening. For the first time, I realized how relentless the explosions had been. For a long time we sat paralyzed by the silence. Was it a lull? Would it start again? Were the Bolsheviks gone forever? How soon would the Germans be here? Perhaps the Russians would counterattack. We doubted that, but no one knew."

Sosha looked to the 1941 calendar on the wall, "The 19th of September — yes, that was the day we noticed the shelling stopped. We could stand in our field and watch the smoke around and in Kiev. We saw the airplanes fly over the city. On the 19th it all stopped."

"Yes," Sol continued. "September 19th, 1941 — I'll never forget that day. Later that morning, we heard first one, then another voice and another, 'The Germans are here!' 'Bolshevik oppression is over!' 'Come out everyone — greet our liberators!' 'Hooray! The Germans are here!' We could hear people running outside. Everyone cheered as the Germans entered.

"Once outside, my family and I heard the noise of trucks. We ran toward it. The crowds grew as we approached the main road through Kiev. It was breathtaking! As far as we could see in both directions—trucks loaded with soldiers—none marching or walking. There were military pieces in tow and occasional motorcycles with sidecars. And, every so often, a polished, open roofed car with officers went by. How different from the Russians who'd retreated through Kiev over the previous days! This was an army. They didn't even look like they'd been in battle. We cheered our liberators." Solomon hung his head thoughtfully for a moment. He shook his head, then raised it and continued.

"As more and more of our citizens came to watch, the procession took on the mood of a parade — a circus parade. The soldiers waved and smiled, at first at the girls and children. The children cheered and the girls laughed, blushed and then waved back. Soon everyone cheered and called out words of welcome."

Sosha asked Solomon whether he wanted a glass of tea. He nodded and went on.

"It took a long time for all of the trucks to pass by and then the marching troops came. Then there followed enormous supply wagons pulled by the largest draft horses I'd ever seen. The wagons were loaded with food and ammunition. Looking up, I realized that this was the first time in what seemed like ages that no German planes were dropping bombs—no shells dropping out of the sky! It seemed a glorious day. My father kept saying it was the beginning of a new life." A sudden frown crossed Solomon's brow and his eyes began to water. He swallowed hard, then continued.

"Everyone was curious, the Germans included. I'd never in my life seen so many cameras! The Germans took pictures of everything—the people, our bomb damaged streets where houses and buildings still smoldered, of each other..." Solomon paused. "I still can't believe it all." He shook his head.

"It was fascinating. There was a feeling of wonder and freedom! It was as if we had been transported to a new and different world. Even the surroundings, those that weren't bombed out, seemed different. We were liberated — freed from our former existence. Now everything would be — was different and we felt it. We celebrated it.

"On Kirillovskaya Avenue, a number of buildings had Soviet flags waving in front of them and as the crowds moved past they pulled the flags down and trampled them into the ground. Some flags were burned and their burning cheered. Had the Russians counterattacked to retake the city, I think we would have all fought against them beside the Germans — and you know, I believe the Jews would have fought the hardest to keep them from returning." He took a long drink of his tea.

"Can I refill your glass?" Sosha asked.

"Yes, thank you. I guess I'm still very thirsty from the ordeal." He reached the glass across the table to her. "As the day passed, there was more and more activity. The Germans were busy establishing headquarters. They were all over the city now. Many went about fully armed, seeking out foolish Bolsheviks — partisans who stayed behind. They had help from the citizens pointing out Communists. I'm sure many who weren't Communists were picked up simply because they'd been pointed out. It was a bad time to have enemies. We had no idea where they took those people. They were rounded up and taken away — vanished. I suspect now they also went to the ravine, Babi Yar."

Sosha placed the tea back in front of Solomon and another glass before Ivan.

"As the fervor of the crowds grew, they became a mob." Now that Solomon was telling the story, he couldn't stop. It flooded out — a catharsis. "Mobs frighten Jews. They have a way of turning on us. Most of us withdrew to our homes at that point. I think it came with the pulling down of the Soviet flags, most of which were on stores and buildings owned by party members."

"Who else owned businesses but the Bolsheviks?" Ivan asked a sarcastic tone in his voice.

"Right!" Sol continued. "Soon the mob started breaking windows and looting. Then it didn't matter who owned the property. There were goods of all kinds to be had for nothing—for the taking—by people who were used to having nothing. In minutes, stores were stripped of goods, fixtures, equipment—everything. People fought over things they couldn't even use. It was insane. The Germans watched and laughed. If there was something they wanted they just took it from the looters."

Solomon sipped his tea. He couldn't keep his story from pouring out now.

"Not everyone who was in the city stayed when the Germans came. Over the next few days, a good number of people left with what they could carry, most in the middle of the night. Their abandoned property was quickly claimed by those who remained. Of course the better homes and buildings were taken over by the Germans, whether the owners abandoned them or not. If the Germans wanted a headquarters, they requisitioned it, meaning they kicked the owners out. The same happened with livestock and food. Cows, pigs, grain, chickens, ducks, geese—anything the Germans wanted, they took. If the owner argued, the Germans gave him a slip of paper telling what was taken, telling him to take the paper to the commander for payment. That usually satisfied the owners, until they found out the receipts were useless. Of course, by that time their property was long gone—probably in a German stomach. But no one was terribly shocked by this treatment. It wasn't really any worse or different from treatment we'd received from the Bolsheviks for years. And after all, 'to the victors go the spoils.' Everyone knows that.

"September 19th came and went. Most of us went to bed that night happier, full of hope. Before then, I think only party members might have known that feeling.

How soundly you can sleep when you go to bed with hope!"

How sensitive he is, Sosha thought. "Where were you educated? You express yourself so well."

"Yes, you speak as if you went to a fine private school," Ivan added.

"Very private," Solomon replied. "Since the government never saw it necessary to provide an education for the Jews who lived in the poor section, the **Podol,** we had our own school. It's as it has been for centuries, either by tradition or necessity, we are..." Solomon frowned as he remembered, "...we *were* taught by our own scholars. And my grandfather, blessed be his memory — that's the first time I've ever had to say that — my grandfather was a learned man." A sad, reminiscent look came to Solomon's eyes, "How many hours he spent with me, nights, weekends, reading, tutoring..." Solomon took a drink of his tea, wiped a tear.

"When we got up on September 20th, the German flag was everywhere. It too is red — only the swastika replaces the hammer and sickle. September 20th was a day of settling in — the Germans into Kiev and us into our new situation. That night we again went to bed hopeful.

"I think it was the next day that we saw the first notices posted. They announced that all property looted had to be returned to the Germans. All surplus foods had to be turned over to them. All radios, weapons, military equipment and supplies had to be given up as well. The disturbing part of the notice stated that failure to carry out the instructions, immediately, was punishable by death. 'Anyone not carrying out this order will be shot!' it said."

Sosha pushed the bread and cheese toward him. "Wouldn't you like to rest a while?" she asked.

"No, I want to go on. I must go on. I need to get it all out."

"What happened on the afternoon of the 24th?" Ivan asked. "Late that afternoon we heard some tremendous explosions from the direction of Kiev and that night the sky was aglow. We thought for sure the Russians were counterattacking — that the war had started all over again."

"Let me think — the 24th — yes, it was the 24th that Kreshchatik Street was blown up." Sol took a bite of bread, then a larger one of cheese. "The Germans had taken over the fine buildings on Kreshchatik, in the area of Proreznaya Street. They had taken over the Continental Hotel, the Doctor's Club and the party offices deserted by the Bolsheviks. The Bolsheviks must have anticipated the Germans' grand taste. After all, Kreshchatik Street was the finest area of the city — ideal for the needs of the occupation.

"As soon as the Germans were settled in the partisans blew them up. On the 24th, around four o'clock in the afternoon, there was a series of explosions at measured intervals."

"That's right, one after the other, a few seconds — maybe ten or fifteen between each blast — boom! — boom! — boom!..." Ivan interrupted, slamming his fist down on the table with each "boom" he imitated. "It was in the late afternoon and we heard explosion after explosion."

"You heard them blow up the Kreshchatik?" Solomon nodded vigorously. "The explosions continued through the entire night and all of the next day. In fact they didn't stop until the 28th of September. It looked as if all of Kiev would be blown up — burn to the ground."

"It must still be burning," Sosha said.

"Still burning?" Sol asked, surprised.

"Yes," Ivan answered. "At night the sky is red over Kiev — from the flames. They must not be fighting the fires, just letting it burn itself out. Probably too dangerous to fight — maybe nothing left worth saving."

Sosha studied Solomon. He seemed to be just under six feet, slim, but strong looking — athletic looking. Maybe he played soccer in happier days. I'll put a little weight back on him and he'll be as good as new. Even now he moves with grace and conviction—not the least bit clumsy. He still showed some weakness. The telling of his story must've be difficult for him. How horrible! He does have a handsome and sensitive face. He's pale now, but I can tell his complexion is normally dark. Goes with his brown eyes and his light brown hair. I wonder how old he was, looks nineteen or twenty. "How old are you, Sol?"

"Eighteen—I turned eighteen just last May. May 17th."

Those eyes—they want to say so much, Sosha continued speculating. He seems so well educated, in spite of the poverty he speaks of. People of the book... Yes, he looks Mediterranean, but not so much Jewish. Maybe among Jews he would look Jewish, but he could be Greek Orthodox as well. Among Italians he'd look Italian. He has a square chin and jaw, high cheekbones—a thin face. May not fill out even after I fatten him out a bit. He stands straight. Full of pride.

Ivan and Sol were still talking about the fire, which would indeed continue in Kiev for almost three weeks when Sosha interrupted. "Are you sure you wouldn't like to rest a while?"

"No, I feel quite strong. It is good to be out of that little room," Solomon said, "good to be alive." Sol fell silent a moment, wondering, then added, "But why me? All those others—why only me?"

Sosha refilled the tea glasses. "Are you sure you want to continue?"

"Yes, I feel I must tell it."

"When did the Germans single out the Jews?" Ivan asked.

"It was September 28th that the notice was posted. The Germans placed it all over Kiev. Its message spread like the plague. Little did we realize then that it would be far more deadly. Those who didn't see it themselves soon heard about it."

"What did it say?" Ivan prompted.

"As I recall, it said, 'All **Yids** living in or about the city of Kiev or in its vicinity, are to report no later than eight o'clock on the morning of Monday, September 29th, 1941, at the intersection of Melinkovsky and Dokturov. You are to have with you all documents, money, valuables. Bring warm clothing, changes of underwear. Any Yid not following this demand or who is discovered elsewhere, will be shot. Any civilian entering dwellings evacuated by Yids or looting their property will be shot.'

"Actually, the Germans had misspelled the names of both streets. They were supposed to be Melnikov and Deztyarev—but the message got across. The appointed location was near the old Jewish cemetery. The next morning, the intersection was a mass of humanity. Most people arrived very early. If they were to be deported, better to get there early and get a good seat on the train. Most of us expected we would go by train because the location was so near the freight yards, which would make loading easier.

"Some of us were very upset, assuming we were being deported because of the explosions of the Kreshchatik. Everyone knew that the partisans and the N.K.V.D. had planted those explosives in the basements of the buildings before the Germans arrived. Now, as usual, the Jews were being blamed. To be deported for acts of the Bolsheviks! But there was no arguing with the Germans.

"There was much speculation among us. The message had said to bring warm clothes. Did that mean a cold climate? It dispelled the hopes of some that we would be sent to Palestine—which most considered wishful thinking, at best. But that was just a rumor the Germans spread. How long would the train ride be? It did say to bring a change of underclothes. Why not more belongings? Well, obviously they couldn't expect to take all the belongings of a hundred thousand Jews. First they would move out the people, then the belongings. Besides, what did the Jews have worth taking? Most were poor as mice—in fact, mice lived better. The Germans allowed us to take what money and valuables we could carry. And it put many Jewish minds at ease that the Germans were not allowing homes to be looted. Of course, there were always the pessimists who assumed the Germans planned to loot the homes themselves."

They finished eating. Sosha suggested they continue their talk outdoors. "You need to get some sun and fresh air, Sol. Let's continue this outside." Before she left the hut, she picked up a comb and scissors and a small sheet.

Solomon shielded his eyes from the bright sun. He hadn't realized how dim the light in the two-room home had been. The main room was a living room, a dining room and a kitchen too. The cooking was done at a large fireplace which also served to heat the entire house. There was only one window and the outside door to the room. The other doorway in the room led to the bedroom, which was separated only by a curtain. It was a typical farm home in the Ukraine. Outside, near the back door, which provided an escape from the bedroom was the outhouse. The back door was an unusual feature, added by the Jew who had lived there before Ivan who feared for the lives of his family.

Ivan sat down on a tree stump and Sol on a bench next to it, tea glass in hand. Sosha laid the scissors, comb and sheet on the bench next to Sol and returned to the hut. A moment later, she came back out with the tray of cheese and bread and the *chinik* or teapot. Once more, she filled all the glasses, then wrapped the sheet around Ivan and began to cut his hair.

Sol went on with his story.

"We lived in the *Podol*—the poor, ghetto area of Kiev. It was early, still dark out when the noise of the first Jews to leave their homes woke us. It upset my mother. She was afraid all the seats would be taken—that our family might be separated. People who came late could not hope to be

28

seated together, she told us. She rushed us along, my brothers, my sister, papa, grandpa and me." Suddenly Solomon broke down sobbing.

Sosha handed her comb and scissors to Ivan and tried to comfort Sol. "Please, why don't you rest a while? You needn't go into any more..."

"No, I want to go on. I have to tell it all. You must know what these Germans are really like." He gulped down more tea, hoping it would wash down the lump that had risen in his throat. His glass emptied, Sosha picked up the chinik and poured the glass full again.

"Each of us carried a bundle we'd made up the night before. There was nothing of any value left behind — and nothing of any real value we took with us. We had only sentimental treasures with us. We certainly had no savings or jewels. All that we earned went to feeding our large family. We wore most of our clothing. Our furniture, the Germans or looters could have. Our home, I realized as we left it, had only been what our family made it. I mean, without us it was a terrible run down shack. When we walked out of it only an empty shell remained. I'd never seen it as the hovel it was. We all felt that if we could stay together..." he had to swallow hard to keep on, "...we could make as fine a home wherever they sent us." He paused and wiped an eye. "Except for me, they are all together now." There was a pause as Solomon sobbed again. Sosha, too, was silently crying. "I'm sorry," he said, "but I feel compelled to go on."

Ivan put his arm around Sosha. His left hand, in a gesture disguised to look like scratching, wiped away moisture beneath his left eye.

"The streets were terribly crowded. Everyone headed toward the designated intersection, slowly, because of the congestion. Not all were Jews. Many were just curious citizens. Others were neighbors and friends helping us carry our belongings. Some had their things piled high on wagons or pushcarts that jammed up the streets even more. There was no hope of reaching the corner by eight o'clock. Our only concern was to stay together. We selected points along the way where we'd wait for anyone who accidentally got separated.

"From the Podol, we had to cross the **Dnieper**. It was half past eight before we arrived at the bridge. After crossing the river, the crowd became even more impossible. There were often such bottlenecks that we couldn't move at all. Frequently, we just sat down on our bundles, waiting for the crowd to move on. Sometimes, it took thirty minutes or more. A hundred thousand people are a lot of people to move out. It occurred to us that there would be no way that all of us could be loaded on trains that day. We tried to think what other ways we could be moved, trucks? Walking in procession? We were perplexed. Others sat down, too. Many, out of frustration, ate food they had packed for the trip.

"The torment of deportation deepened and was made more terrifying by the acts of some of the citizens who came to see us off. What Jew has not been stung by the barbs of anti-Semitism? But that day! That day the bigots had no inhibitions. They spat on us from balconies. I saw several people empty chamber pots on the procession below their windows. Rotten vegetables, stones, bottles — insults, laughter — all plunged down on the stream of Jews. Now and then someone would dart into the crowd, grab an elderly or weak Jew's bundle and run off with it. At first, other Jews would tried to stop the thief, but the Germans stationed all along the route soon brought that to a halt. The pursuers were struck down with gun butts.

"It was late in the afternoon before we got to the appointed spot. A barrier had been placed at Melinkov Street and a number of Ukrainian police and German soldiers stood about to see that all traffic passed the barrier in only one direction. They didn't seem to care who went beyond the barrier, but they checked everyone who tried to come back. To come back, papers had to be in order. You had to have proof that you were not Jewish. All the Jews had their papers, as instructed by the Germans. But many of the other Kievites didn't carry theirs. Those who couldn't prove they weren't Jewish were detained. Non-Jewish men, of course, could show they were uncircumcised and were passed back through. Women had a more difficult problem."

Sosha blushed.

"I'm sorry," Solomon realized, "I shouldn't have been so blunt..."

"Don't be silly. You forget, I've raised a son and Ivan's no saint. Tell your story however you must."

"I guess there's no delicate way to tell it." He paused. "It only gets worse."

"Dusk came and we were stopped at the barrier. 'That is all for today,' a German officer shouted. 'The rest of you will be put on tomorrow's trains.' 'Does that mean we have to go back to home and start all over again tomorrow?' my mother asked papa, but before he could say anything the German officer went on. 'All you Jews will remain here, in the street, until we start again in the morning!' A mummer passed through the crowd. 'Here, in the street?' someone yelled to the officer. 'I am not used to repeating myself,' the officer shouted back to the crowd. 'You will all remain where you are until morning. Anyone trying to leave will be shot on the spot! This is your only warning! I suggest you make yourselves as comfortable as possible.'

"The streets were cordoned off and we spent the night there on the roads—thousands of us—guarded by hundreds of Germans and Ukrainians with dogs, clubs and machine guns.

"The night was cold and sleep was impossible. All night long dogs attacked those who tried to escape. Shots rang out all along the road, throughout the night. There was no way out—no way to resist. Old folks moaned—children cried. We shivered from the cold—and with fear, too.

"At dawn, the procession started again. We passed the old Jewish cemetery. Many of us wanted to stop and bid goodbye to the graves of our loved ones, but a German soldier blocked the gate, which was closed off with barbed wire. So, as we passed the long brick wall of the cemetery many stopped to pray. A last **Kaddish**, our prayer for the dead. The elderly knew they would probably never return to Kiev. 'Who will visit the graves? Who will care for them?' my grandfather moaned. 'We cannot even say goodbye. My children, promise me you'll return and visit the graves. Tell my dear Sara that I wanted to say goodbye. Tell her they would not let us.' He cried as I had never seen him cry before. Even when his Sara, my grand-mama, died, I did not see him cry as he did that day. Now they are together...

"He leaned against the brick wall and started to pray. 'Move on, you old Yid!' a German soldier shouted, giving him a shove that knocked him down.

"'You German bastard!' my oldest brother shouted, lunging between the soldier and grandpa. 'Keep your filthy hands off him. I'll teach...' He was felled by a blow from a club wielding Ukrainian. The German and the Ukrainian laughed. 'That'll teach the Jews a little respect,' the German said and walked away.

"My mother and father jumped to my brother's side. We all thought he was dead. He lay there, the back of his head bleeding. Grandpa stood up, too stunned to know what had happened. We had to struggle to contain my other brother from going after the German.

"Finally my fallen brother moaned and moved his head. 'He's alive!' my mama exclaimed. 'Oh, thank God, he's alive!' She took a handkerchief and pressed it over his wound. He hadn't fully come back to his senses when another German came along and herded us on. My brother and I had to half-carry him along, at first. Then enough strength for walking came back, though we had to guide him. He was dizzy and sick to his stomach.

"In the excitement, my sister had her bundle snatched. We looked about and saw a Ukrainian woman running with it toward the barricade. We had no hope of getting to her through the crowd. As she ran, a German soldier grabbed her. He demanded her papers, I suppose, for there was much animated conversation between the two. Apparently she had none with her. Carrying the bundle, she was even more suspect. A German officer was called over, but he didn't seem to believe her either. Finally she was dragged back into the crowd, swearing and shouting until one guard slapped her hard across the face. There was still no chance to get to her through the crowd, but we tried to keep an eye on her, hoping for a chance later.

"The crowd moved faster now. There was less noise and talking — more Germans stood about, aiming us in one direction. We assumed we were nearing the train. We wanted very much to get on board — to put all this behind us. Then perhaps we could rest. Mama could attend to my brother's injury. We could eat a little of the food we'd been saving. Though hungry and exhausted, we were happy we'd stayed together.

"But now, that there was less noise we could hear gunfire in the distance — machine gunfire. Not continuous gunfire interspersed with explosions, like in battle. It was intermittent, at almost regular intervals. There were perhaps twenty seconds of shooting, followed by a few minutes of silence, then another twenty seconds of firing. As we moved the gunfire got louder. We became nervous. 'It's just maneuvers,' the Germans told us. 'We are having troop maneuvers further up in the ravine. You need not be concerned about it. It's only a training exercise.' And we believed them. What else could it be?

"After we'd gone — I don't know how far — the crowd started to slow. And then we stopped. We stood for a few minutes then moved on again and stopped again and then moved on again. 'They're taking us a train car load at a time,' someone said. It made sense. And it excited us to know we were near the end of this—hardship. The rails were just ahead around the bend. We still could not see the train, but neither could we see the front of the crowd.

"We continued to move and stop, move and stop.

"At last, we came to a spot where the number of Germans nearly tripled. There was a bend we couldn't see around, where we'd have to go. We moved again and this time a German stopped us, letting the group ahead of us disappear around the bend.

"Germans and Ukrainians passed among us. They tried to take our coats, jackets, sweaters, our bundles. 'We will return them to you on the train... You must board quickly. These things will slow down the process. Give them to us now; you will get them back on the train.' At first, some people resisted—they were beaten until they relented. After the first few beatings, we realized it was stupid to resist. For most of us there was little in those bundles to fight for. What would the Germans want with them anyway? We probably would get them back. We had no choice anyway.

"They told us to move on. It was chilly now. The long late afternoon shadows fell over us. A brisk breeze had begun. Most of another day had been spent in this slow-moving mass of people. At least tonight we'd be on the train, not sleeping in the open.

As we approached the bend the breeze grew stronger, bringing with it the measured sound of the intermittent gunfire. The sound was much louder now. And then we heard music being played loudly over speakers, coming from around the bend.

5

THE GAUNTLET...

Solomon's voice lowered. He was silent. He put his head in his hands, closing his eyes. A very low moan came from his throat. He shook with sobs. Then he cried openly. Sosha came to his side and put her arms about him, pulling his head to her chest. "Please, Solomon, rest now. Don't try to go on."

Sol couldn't stop crying. Sosha sat with him for a long time. At last, she released her embrace. He wiped his wet face on the sleeves of his shirt.

"Please, Solomon, don't try to go on," she repeated.

"I must," Sol flatly insisted. "I must tell it all now!" He took a long drink from a fresh glass of tea Ivan handed him, wiped his eyes once again and cleared his throat.

"As we rounded the bend, we saw that there were even more Germans, Ukrainians also. Just ahead of us—a corridor formed by soldiers—perhaps two meters wide, through which we'd have to pass. As we entered the narrow passage, we saw Germans with dogs on short leashes, about every ten meters, on both sides. Between them, the rest of the soldiers and Ukrainian police—they had clubs, whips and some German officers held pistols in their hands. We had to pass between them. There was no way out, nowhere else to go. No way out! They made us pass over the empty tracks into the narrow corridor. Now the music was very loud.

"When we were into the gauntlet, we were made to run. 'Run, you Jews!' came the command. 'Run! Show us how fast you Yids can run!' Whips and clubs came down on us. We were stunned—but we ran. My God, we ran.

Children — elderly — women — we all ran to stay ahead of the blows. The whips hissed through the air and tore at our flesh. Clubs crashed down. The screams and cries pierced the ears and all the while they yelled commands at us — laughed at us. And the music kept our cries from those who would follow soon.

"Many fell. One would fall under a blow or slip on the sandy ground, toppling others who would trip over him. The dogs were set on those who went down. Many couldn't get up and the dogs ripped at them, ripped them open. There was blood on everyone.

"We ran as hard as we could. Some were trampled to death, I think — small children and the old. Some parents carried their children through. We tried to pick up separated children as we ran, but they beat anyone who tried to help. It was impossible.

"A few tried to break out. They were shot in the attempt. By the time we were a few meters into the corridor most of us were dazed. The run seemed endless. Once I tried to look back. It was horrible. Bodies lay the entire length. Dogs biting, whipping, clubbing, shooting, I think a third of us never got through.

"I don't know how long that corridor was, but at the far end we stumbled into a large clearing. Stunned beyond pain — and worse, beyond any chance for resistance — we stood in that clearing, bewildered, bleeding, uncomprehending — like cattle.

"'Take off your clothes! Off! Everything off!' Again the command came, 'Take off all your clothes! Everything off, now!' Not one of us moved. Soldiers came and started ripping clothes off. Someone resisted. A shot rang out and she dropped dead to the ground. It began to sink in. 'Everything off, Jews! Your shoes, your stockings, your filthy underclothes. Take off everything, you filthy Jews!'

"We took off our bloodied rags, ripped by the whips. We dropped our things where we stood. In a few minutes, we were all naked. Children sobbed. Women wept. We all looked at the ground, not wanting to see each other. I didn't want to see my mother and sister naked.

"I remember a small child crying near me. I picked her up. She pointed toward her father and I took her to him. He held her close. We bled and shivered and stood helplessly while the Germans and Ukrainians laughed and amused themselves.

"When everyone was naked the Germans passed among us taking any rings or jewelry, eyeglasses — then they herded us together. 'Now move, fast! Go through that opening!' Ahead of us were two high mounds of earth. To get through we had to go single file. We were still too dazed to understand..." Solomon paused and then added, "And if we hadn't been dazed, I still don't think we'd have imagined what was to come next.

"If I live to be a hundred, I will never forget what we saw when we passed through that opening."

Solomon stared vacantly.

Sosha wondered whether he remembered they were there in the yard with him. He began to speak almost without emotion, as if the voice were not even his.

"We entered a ravine. It looked to have been a sand quarry. To the left was a very narrow ledge, which ran along a sandstone cliff. To the left was a flat plateau and on it aimed at us across the ravine, were a number of machine guns.

"They marched us out. I was still somewhat dazed. We all were. Didn't really focus on what was happening. Someone up front who refused to go farther was immediately shot with a pistol and pushed into the ravine. My eyes followed him down — it was the first moment I realized the ravine was full of bodies. Thousands of bodies piled there. They weren't deporting us. "My God, they're killing us!" I shouted.

"My eyes came back to the path. It was covered with blood — puddles — very slick, some sticky. We were walking barefoot in the blood of our people. Then we stopped. I still didn't fathom it all.

"A machine gun started to fire, then another. They moved toward me from both ends of the line and I saw people fall into the pit — like dominoes, one after the other. I suddenly realized — my family — and I called out, "Mama! Papa! Where are...

"As I turned to look for them I slipped on the blood underfoot. I fell into the ravine — struck my head. As I drifted into unconsciousness, I recall, wondering if I'd been shot — wondered if I was dying..."

6

BABI YAR...

Sosha and Ivan sat speechless.

There was no doubt in their minds that Solomon had lived through it all. How could it have happened, they each wondered. They'd all heard of pogroms, but that was mob violence. As awful as pogroms had been through the ages, this was worse. This had been planned — arranged — orchestrated...

"How did you get away?" Ivan finally asked to break the silence.

"The next thing I remember — it was dark — very dark. I became aware that I was shivering from the cold, something cold and damp on my back. I tried to move, raised my head. Bits of dirt fell from me. Dear God, I'm buried, I realized. I lay my head back down. I can breathe. I'm alive. I must be alive...

"The machine guns were silent. Now I heard another sound, shoveling, men talking, dirt falling. They were burying us. But it was late, dark and apparently they were just throwing a thin layer of dirt over us; leaving room for tomorrow's victims. I looked again. There they were, several, maybe twenty meters past me. Flashlights were showing workers where to throw the dirt. I heard a loud moan. One of the flashlights picked out the spot where the moans were coming from. A shot rang out. The moaning stopped. I bit my tongue to keep from crying out. The stench of blood, urine, excrement and vomit reached my nostrils, the smells of death."

Solomon was silent, head bowed. A pained expression crossed his face. "I gave thanks to God for my life," he looked almost ashamed, guilty, "while below me and all around me my people were dying, had died, lay dead." He could only whisper the words.

Sol took a drink of his tea, not noticing it was cold. Tears were heavy in his eyes.

"God was with you, Sol," Ivan said, "God was with you that day."

They were words that could only have been spoken in retrospect. Surely, few there, at Babi Yar that day could have thought God was with them — anywhere near them. More likely their thoughts cried out, God why? Why have You turned against us? Why do you let them kill us? Even the children! And me — why me? And then Sol thought, Yes, God, You were with me that day. But were you with the others? What of the tens of thousands of others? "Why only with me?" he asked out loud.

"You must rest now," Sosha said. "I insist."

7
ESCAPE...

Sosha carried in the tray of leftovers. Ivan followed her with the chinik and glasses. "I think I'll hitch up the wagon and drive toward town," he said.

"Today?"

"Now."

"Why?"

"Close to Kiev, I might be able to find something out. We must know more about these Germans. I still don't understand how all this could have happened. I have to ask some questions."

"Ivan, be careful. If you reveal that we are sheltering Sol..."

"Don't worry, Sosha, I'm no fool. I think I'll go talk with **Retski**. He lives near enough to Kiev—and he's always arguing politics. If anyone knows what's going on, he'll know."

She watched her big husband hitch up the horse. After all the years of marriage, she still admired his huge stature. He stood well over six feet and weighed well over two hundred-fifty pounds, but solid, muscular pounds. She often teased that his hands were like shovels and loved to put hers up to his and be amazed at the difference in size. His hair was still red, only streaked with a little gray. Bright brown eyes peered observantly out of his rounded, typically Slavic face. His voice was deep but gentle, as was the rest of him. He'd been a good father, she thought and a better husband.

Ivan was gone for almost four hours. The early October sun set as he returned. Sosha had begun worrying. Sol slept for two of the hours and then waited anxiously with Sosha. She put supper on the table. Ivan related what he'd learned that afternoon.

"Retski confirmed that people are being slaughtered every day at the ravine. He said it still goes on, from dawn to dusk. He says it hasn't stopped since the 29th of last month. But what I can't believe is that he's in sympathy with the shootings. 'Good riddance with the Bolsheviks and Jews,' he kept saying."

"Are his sympathies with the Germans?" Sosha asked.

"You know Retski … his sympathies are with no one. He calls them fascist pigs, whatever fascists are. He is against all political groups."

"What does he say about all that's happened?" Sosha asked.

"Retski, as usual, had a long explanation, but it's probably mostly true."

"Do you think he had any idea that we are hiding anyone?"

"Believe me, Sosha, when I tell you I was very careful, especially after I learned of his feelings about the ravine."

"Go on with what he told you," Sol prompted.

"Well, according to Retski this all had its beginnings when Stalin and Hitler made a secret pact in 1939."

"And how does Retski know about secret pacts?" Sosha asked skeptically.

"If it has to do with politics, Retski finds out. And you know, in these matters, he's usually right. Anyway, he said it was a situation of one tyrant dealing with another tyrant and as usual the people pay the price.

"Hitler and Stalin had agreed that if Russia did not interfere with the Nazi invasion of Poland, they would divide the country up between them after Germany's victory. Stalin would get the eastern half of Poland; but more important to him, he felt he was bargaining for time and security on the Western border of Russia. Some bargain, huh? The only problem, Hitler is even less honorable than Stalin. His forces invaded Russia on that entire front. And Poland is now all under Nazi rule."

"What does *Nazi* mean?" Sol asked.

"I asked that same thing of Retski. He just spoke of Nazis when he referred to the Germans. He explained to me that we in the Soviet countries knew only what Stalin and the government wanted us to know. Stalin did not allow the Soviet Press to reveal much about Hitler's activities in Europe. What we heard about or read was praise for the secret ally. That is why, Sol, that your father praised them so. But in 1933 the Nazi political party, Hitler's party, took over the German nation that had been at the pinnacle of civilization, as your father said. Little news of what Germany has done since the Nazi takeover has gotten through to us.

"Now the German war machine turned against the Soviet Union. As the Russian troops clog the roads, most of the people feel relief, as you did. For those who have not felt the heavy hand of the Germans yet, the prospect of 'civilized German' rule holds more promise than what we've known under the Bolsheviks."

"And they are still shooting in Babi Yar?" Sol asked.

"That's what Retski says." Ivan bowed his head as he continued, "I am afraid he confirms what you have told us. All the Jews are killed. He says that the many Ukrainian people watched..."

Sol interrupted, "Yes, I saw that the next day. They watched us..." Sol choked, "...die. I must tell you about that, too. He confirmed that all are dead?"

"Yes, Sol, I'm afraid so. By the end of the second day, when you — went through — 36,000 had been — shot. At the end of the third day, about the time I found you — 56,000 were dead. Yesterday, at the end of the week — in just five days — they had murdered the last of the Jewish population of Kiev." Ivan looked up at Sol, "I'm sorry.

They doubt that very many escaped. Only those who got away before the round up." He paused, then, "Sol, you are possibly the only person who got out of the Babi Yar ravine alive. Retski says over 100,000 Jews died there."

"He's in sympathy with that?" Sosha asked with disgust.

"Worse, he thinks most of Kiev is in sympathy."

"I don't doubt that at all," Sol said casually.

"You're not surprised?" Sosha was astonished.

"No. We Jews have never been loved here — or anywhere, I guess. And when I saw how the people reacted when we were rounded up. I know they could not have done a thing to help us, but they taunted us, spit on us, had to get in their last bit of hate."

"Do you feel up to telling the rest of your story?" Ivan asked as they neared the finish of their dinner.

"Yes, I'd like to get the rest told, if you're ready for it. There isn't much more to tell. I think I told you we were being buried. Anyone who moved or made a sound was shot. I lay very still for a long time, afraid to move — afraid to breathe. I was only under three or four inches of dirt and sand. My face was mostly uncovered. I was naked and cold. I listened. Finally silence. It was time to escape.

"I raised myself up, constantly fearing I might be seen — waiting for a bullet to tear into my back. As cold as I had been, the dirt must have been protecting me, because as it fell away the cold bit deeper into me. My eyes couldn't adjust to the dark. If there was a moon, its light wasn't falling into the ravine — an advantage, I guess, if there was a guard about. I groped my way over the bodies. The thin layer of dirt could not hide the carnage. My hands touched now a thigh, now a face, a hand, now a riddled chest — all chilled and sticky with blood. I was afraid I might vomit and some soldier would hear. But my stomach was empty. I crawled.

"At last, I came up against one of the sandy walls. Which, I couldn't tell. My sense of direction was gone. I stood up. I felt for the top but couldn't reach it. Then I tried to walk across the bodies, using the wall to balance and guide me. At every step, I reached up for a handhold. Loose dirt fell into my face. Nowhere could I reach the top. My feet pressed down on the soft bodies. Soon the cold, disorientation, despair and fear all gripped me. I could find no way out!

"Then I had an idea. I bent down and reached into the earth and grabbed a body. Limp and heavy, there was no lifting it. I got down on my knees and dragged it onto the body beside it. For the moment, I was thankful for the blackness of the night. I felt, grabbed and dragged another body onto the first. Then another and another each on top of another. Another. Another... It took a long time. It was exhausting, gruesome work. I cried as I piled up my dead..." the words choked off. Neither Ivan nor Sosha could say anything to interrupt the silence that followed. They could hear Solomon's quiet weeping. At last he calmed himself and continued,

"Finally, I climbed on top of the pile and reached for the top of the pit. I could reach it. It took all my strength, but I pulled myself out of the grave.

"I discovered myself to be on the narrow ridge off of which we'd been shot. The blood was still not dry. It felt cold, thick and sticky. Again I felt the urge to vomit. I had to drag myself up on it and could feel it coat my stomach, my chest, my legs.

"I remembered the drop-off had been to my right when we marched in. Now it was at my left. I began to crawl slowly, stopping often to listen. At last, I reached one of the large dirt mounds. I crawled to the opening between the two and dared to stand up. Again I listened. Silence! I looked back. I couldn't see into the dark pit. I realized I was totally alone in the world. I thought, my God, everyone, my family, my friends the only people I really know and can trust are in that pit... I can only be sure of enemies out there... I've just been reborn out into a

hostile world — naked — without anything — anyone…
Alone!

"I escaped into the field where we'd been made to undress. I could see a little better, but that brought with it the fear of being seen. I stayed in the shadows and looked around. There was no sign of life. Then I saw what I hoped were piles of clothing. I rummaged through a pile near me putting on anything that looked like it might fit. I found two shoes, not a pair, socks, trousers, I put on two shirts and found a coat. I felt warmer.

"I crossed the field toward where I remembered some woods being. Passing under the branches, I could feel the terrain steepen. I didn't dare stop climbing. Fatigue pulled at me and the climb was slow. Many times I fell, ran into trees or tumbled into brush that tore at my skin, but I had to keep climbing.

"Finally, I was out. A clearing let me look back. From where I stood, I could see across the ravine. On the other side, the entire sky was lit by the fires of the Kreshchatik. Babi Yar was a deep black hole. There were a few fires below where, I assume, German and Ukrainian soldiers camped or maybe other Jews waited for tomorrow's *'deportations.'* My fatigue caught up with me. I found some underbrush, crawled beneath it and fell into deep sleep."

Sosha interrupted, "Perhaps a little more tea?"

Sol nodded.

Ivan picked up the chinik and felt it. "This has cooled off." He walked to the *samovar* and filled the chinik from it. The hot fluid steamed as it ran from the spout into the teapot. After all the glasses were refilled, Sol drank and then went on to tell how he awoke with a start the next morning. It was the sound of machine gun fire that brought him back from sleep. He couldn't see the pit, but knew what was happening. Twenty seconds of firing, a few minutes of silence and more machine gun firing. How many would die today? He peered out of the bushes. No one was in sight. He crept out and stood up.

Looking across Babi Yar toward Kiev, he could see people sitting on the other side, looking down into the ravine. Some had picnic baskets and blankets; many had families with them.

"They had a wonderful time watching the slaughter of the Jews of Kiev." Solomon said with bitterness.

Sol ran across the small clearing at the top of the ravine and into the woods. He ran until he was exhausted. He tripped over stones and stumbled through the underbrush. Finally, he fell headlong into the wild growth. He lay there breathing deeply for a long time, while his senses returned. This would not do. He had to move with caution. What if he ran into Germans? He would be right back in Babi Yar. Maybe they would shoot him on the spot. He decided that if he were captured he would try to escape and force them to shoot.

Getting up, he leaned against a tree. From the sun and shadows and the distant sound of shooting, he determined which way he wanted to go. Babi Yar was surrounded by Kiev and farms. The least habitation was to the west. He put the sun to his back and started to move with caution. He stayed in the woods as long as they lasted. He came to a sparsely populated area. He avoided the roads by cutting across fields or gardens. Soon he had passed through the only populated part of his escape route.

Now he had large, uninhabited areas to cross. Again he took to the forests, to ditches. When there were fields, he crossed only unharvested ones so the crops could offer him protection from view. He followed hedgerows and windbreaks. Occasionally, he would glean potatoes, onions or beets from the edge of a field.

Thus he traveled into the night.

Suddenly a realization came to him. Where am I escaping to? Where is there for a Jew to go? In all directions — there is no refuge... Exhausted, thirsty and near shock, he fell into a deep ditch. It was the second time in two days he was knocked unconscious by a fall into an opening in the ground. There he lay until Ivan found him at dawn the next morning.

8

BORIS, MOSHE & URI...

The three men were Ukrainian soldiers, Jews who had been conscripted into the Soviet Army. They'd come from various units captured by the Germans. The first thing the Germans did was separate the Jews from the rest of the prisoners of war. They were loaded onto trucks, under guard, to be taken to an execution point. All three had been on the last vehicle of the death convoy, along with about fifty other Jewish prisoners. Suspecting they were headed for execution, they decided unanimously to try escape if an opportunity presented.

There was a motorcycle and sidecar with a machine gunner following the convoy. Each truck carried four Germans: two in the cab and two armed guards, one at each rear corner of the truck where the prisoners were packed in. The captives had been told that anyone talking would be shot, but there were too many in the truck for two soldiers to watch. In very discreet whispers, they made their plans. Approaching the Kiev vicinity, headed for Babi Yar, they passed through a series of forests. The road twisted and curved quite severely. It was probably the best chance they would get. At a predetermined signal, they made their move.

Their actions were lightning swift. They hit the two guards who had been lulled into carelessness by the long, boring ride. Stripping their weapons from them in seconds, they threw the flailing bodies off the back of the vehicle into the path of the motorcycle, which had been following too closely for a long time. In the reflex swerving and braking of the motorcycle to avoid the bodies, its riders were sufficiently distracted to let the prisoners get off the first bursts of gunfire killing the cyclists and fallen guards. At the same moment, the other prisoners jumped over the sides of the truck, slowing to make the sharp curves of the road. Most of the prisoners were off and into the woods before anyone up front had a chance to know what happened. As the truck bed emptied, a burst was fired into the cab.

The first fugitives off the trucks ran to the dead cyclists and guards and confiscated the rest of their equipment, weapons and ammunition. In all, the whole escape took less than twenty seconds. By the time the convoy got stopped, the men were out of sight and the Germans couldn't go after them for fear of losing the rest of their prisoners. The getaway was very smooth.

Most escapees separated, but thirteen stayed together. The weapons and munitions were in their possession — three machine guns, two pistols and a small supply of bullets. With those, they decided to carry the war to their enemy.

For the next three, days they moved continuously through the forests. In running from the Germans, they came across a band of Ukrainian partisans. Their paths crossed purely by accident and both groups considered it extremely good fortune. The partisans numbered about thirty and the thirteen Jewish escapees wanted to join forces with them.

The Jews were still in their Soviet Army uniforms and the partisans realized these men were probably well trained — battle seasoned men. Many questioned the Jews — over and over — about their escape and all they had gone through before and after. They were finally satisfied that the fugitives where what they claimed — escaped prisoners of war, Jews, who wanted to join in the fight against the Nazis.

Not until they convinced the Jews that they believed their story did the partisans ask them to turn over their weapons. "We would be proud to have you with us, but we must ask that you turn over your weapons until we return to our camp. It is a precaution we must take. And beside that, we will distribute weapons when you go out on raids."

Overjoyed that they had been accepted into the organization, the Jews did not hesitate to relinquish their arms.

They were taken to the encampment.

"Now," the leader of the partisans began, "we must get you out of those uniforms — what's left of them. Follow this man to our supply cache. He will get you other clothes and show you where to bury your uniforms."

They were led off into the woods.

Moshe Pinsker, an orthodox Jew who had been the brunt of Christian anti-Semitism all his life and was sensitive and skeptical of all non-Jews and strangers, told his companions, *Boris and Uri*, "I feel uneasy, don't ask me why. I kept the pistol and bullets I'd taken off the Germans. The further we walk with that partisan, the less I liked it. I feel the pistol under my shirt. I'm glad I kept it. It has a full clip of bullets in it and I have one extra clip in my pocket. It makes me feel a little better, but not enough."

They'd been near the front of the group when starting into the forest; but as the feeling got stronger, they started to slip further back, whispering Moshe's fears to others as they passed. Most paid them no mind. After covering a little over a kilometer only these two, Boris and Uri had lagged back with Moshe. Now at the rear of the group, they turned off the indistinct path. They followed the sounds of the others, but at about thirty yards to the rear and side, Moshe repeated his fears, whispering, "I tell you there is something terribly wrong here. I would think the trail to their supplies would be frequently traveled. That path shows no sign of heavy traffic. And I cannot believe they would keep their supplies so far from their encampment. I don't trust them, but I don't know how to convince the others."

Boris interrupted, "'I think you are overly suspicious, Moshe. I think we should catch up with the others."

It was at that very moment that the three heard voices. The others had come to a clearing and there found three more partisans waiting for them with the automatic weapons they had taken from them earlier. Creeping closer they heard one say, "All right, you Jews, get your asses over there. Men, let's make this fast. We have their equipment. There's no reason to burden ourselves with these Yids any longer." If there was anymore said, it was drowned out by the noise of guns. When the firing stopped, all they heard was the laughter and joking of the Ukrainians.

Moshe, Boris and Uri ran.

9

RACHEL...

Rachel was from **Minsk**. She was the only child of a third generation rabbi of that city. Her mother had died in 1939 of cancer; and though the orthodox tradition encouraged a widower to seek a new wife after a reasonable period of morning, her father had not been able even to consider it. Rachel ran his household and filled in the duties of *rebbitsin* for the congregation whenever she could.

When the war broke out between Russia and Germany in June of 1941, Minsk had a Jewish population of 90,000 — about one third of the city's population. On June 28th, 1941, just three days after Rachel's nineteenth birthday and the announcement of her engagement to a young local merchant, **Avraham Rakitch,** the Germans occupied Minsk.

Within days, the city's commandant ordered all males between the ages of 15 and 45 to "report and register." Both Rachel's father and Avraham were included in that group. Since evasion was punishable by death, an estimated forty thousand men reported. The mass of humanity marched to a field at **Drozdy,** just outside the city. There the forty thousand men were divided into three groups: Soviet military men caught up in the occupation, Jews and non-Jewish civilians. For five days, they were kept in that field for processing, during which time Rachel had no news of her men. On the fifth day, all the non-Jewish civilians, who could prove they were neither military personnel nor Communist party members, were allowed to return to their homes.

After release of the non-Jews, the Germans commanded all of the Jewish lawyers, dentists, physicians, educators, rabbis and professional men to make themselves known. Several thousand men qualified, among them Rachel's father. From that group only the physicians were taken aside. The rest were marched to a nearby forest where they were machine-gunned to death—but not before they were made to dig their own mass grave.

The remaining Jews were crammed into Minsk prison. It took several days before news could be smuggled out to Rachel and the other Jewish mothers, wives and daughters as to the fate of their loved ones.

Rachel set aside her own grief, comforting many of the hysterical women in her murdered father's congregation. Not until August 20th did the Germans release the imprisoned Jews. Thousands had already died. Upon his release, Rachel's fiancée, Avraham Rakitch, went directly to her and demanded she prepare to leave the city with him. Earlier that day, the city commandant had issued an order establishing the **Minsk Ghetto,** declaring that all Jews had to move into the confined area.

"These Germans are not human. They are not the civilized people we have been led to believe they are. Get together what you can carry — take nothing you don't absolutely need. We are getting out — now! Tomorrow may be too late. You can't believe how they treated us in that prison. They hate us Jews worse than the Russians do!"

"But, Avraham, I have a responsibility to..."

"Your responsibility now is to salvage your own life, Rachel. It will do no good for you to die with those foolish enough to stay. And believe me, many are going to try to escape. It's all we talked of in prison. Now get your things together. We leave as soon as it gets dark."

Rachel and Avraham fled the city that night and became forest people—a new, growing society of Jews.

They traveled through the forests by night, heading south in hopes of finding some partisans to join. After five nights of travel, they crossed the border into the Ukraine. Though still behind German lines, they were getting closer to the front. But the front was now moving to the south and east faster than they were.

After two days travel into the Ukraine, they finally came across a partisan band. The couple was in the forest, lost—exhausted. She was falling asleep when Avraham shook her awake. He hushed her before she could speak. "Someone is coming," he whispered. She could hear footsteps through the dry brush on the forest floor. Avraham motioned her to follow him into some high weeds. There was no trail. If these were Germans the only hope was to be under cover. It sounded like a whole army approaching. No effort was made to quiet their steps. Certain that they were the Nazis, the couple was frightened.

But then they heard talk among the men. It turned out to be Ukrainian. Still, they maintained silence. The group passed by. Rachel and Avraham waited, then Avraham signaled her to follow him again. He headed in the direction they had gone, led by their sounds. "I want to be sure they aren't Ukrainian collaborators before we make ourselves known," he said in hushed voice. In almost the same instant they were grabbed from behind — arms about their throats — knives pressed into their ribs, "Resist and you're dead!"

She could feel the sharp point cutting through her clothing—biting into the outer layer of her flesh. The arm choked off her air until she thought she'd taken her last breath. Not until strong hands secured both her arms did the choking grasp free her throat. The fresh air rushed in. Her heart drummed wildly and she thanked God it hadn't stopped. Apparently she and Avraham had been following between the main body of men and a rear guard.

"Search them!" one of the guards shouted.

"We are friendly!" Avraham cried.

"Shut up! We decide who's friendly. Search them!"

Rachel was too terrified to speak. The thought struck her that they had indeed run into Ukrainian collaborators. There were now seven of them, two more coming out of the trees when they heard the commotion the first five made. Two held Rachel, two held Avraham. They didn't struggle and she could feel their grips on her arms ease. She realized they had cut the circulation to her hands.

One of them stood perhaps two meters in front of her, leveling a rifle at her head. Another pointed his weapon at Avraham. He was the one who shouted all the orders at the other men. Again he shouted, "Search them!"

One walked to Avraham and looked directly into his eyes. "Don't struggle. It will go easier for both of us." His hands slid over Avraham's entire body seeking the bulge of a hidden weapon. "He has nothing," the man finally announced.

"Look for identity papers!" the leader replied.

The man pushed his hands into each of Avraham's pockets. They were empty. He opened Avraham's shirt. He loosened Avraham's belt and opened his trousers to make sure nothing was hidden there.

"This one's a Jew!" he laughed. In his search he saw Avraham was circumcised. His tone was terrifying! "But there are no papers."

"Search the woman!"

All eyes but Avraham's turned toward her. His head hung tearfully toward the ground. Rachel swallowed back her own tears as she awaited her fate. Avraham felt her anguish and was defeated by the knowledge of their helplessness.

As the searcher approached her, he looked directly into her eyes, as he had into Avraham's, but a sickening smirk twisted onto his face. She looked around at her captors with pleading eyes, hoping for a sympathetic look—someone who might intervene. They all had those eager grins—waiting. Only their leader was without expression. No help would come from him either.

Fear rushed through every cell of her body ahead of his hands as they slipped over her clothing, slowing at her breasts, then going down...

She thought she might faint and then she heard, "She has no weapon." A reprieve!

"Look for papers!"

The reprieve was short lived.

She felt her blouse open—heard snickers. His foul breath penetrated her nostrils and a wave of nausea ran through her stomach as he stepped closer to reach around inside her clothing. His rough hands felt inside Rachel's tattered brassiere. She broke into uncontrollable tears and she heard Avraham whimpering.

"No! Please, no!" She screamed, as his hands probed inside her other undergarments. "No! We are not your enemy! We have nothing for you."

"Enough!" the commander said. "Bring the man to me." His words seemed heaven sent.

He had been putting questions to Avraham for some time before Rachel could pull herself together to notice what he was asking.

"Are you alone?"

"Are there more of you in the woods?"

"Do you have anything hidden?"

"Are you both Jews?"

"Why were you following us?"

Avraham answered all his questions, convincing him that they were who they claimed to be.

"You say you want to join us to fight the Nazis? I've never known a Jew to fight!" He laughed and his men responded in kind. "Besides, our mission is to kill Nazis— not save Jews."

A shot rang out!

Rachel screamed, "Avraham!" as she saw him slump to the ground.

After the echo of that shot died out she heard him tell his men, "Use her as you like!"

She heard her clothing rip, felt the hot, smelly breath of the first man as he grabbed her. Now God was merciful—for she would remember nothing else. She fainted into unconsciousness and hours later her ravaged body was left for dead in the forest next to Avraham's corpse.

10

DOVKA...

Dovka, at twenty four, had earned a law degree, unheard of for a woman or a Jew in the Ukraine. Her father was a judge, also very unusual for a Ukrainian Jew. Her family had been one of the first to be wiped out by the Nazis.

She had not been home at the time of the roundup, but her father, mother and two younger brothers were hanged in the public square as reprisals for an act of resistance. Dovka saw the terrible execution from a window overlooking the square. The town was in the northwest, one of the first overrun by the Germans.

Her neighbors warned her before she returned home, when her parents and siblings had been rounded up by the Germans; and they hid her in an attic overlooking the square.

As she watched the executions in horror, she decided she would extract revenge on the Germans and any Ukrainians who were in sympathy with the atrocities against the Jews. Right then she decided she would have to go to the forests. All her life she had thought that disputes were best settled with reason in the courts. But that was for civilized societies. These Germans and the Ukrainians who cheered as the executions were carried out were not civilized.

She told her rescuers that she was leaving after dark. Several asked to go with her. She agreed. A natural leader, they followed her. When she let herself out into the cover of darkness that night, seven Jews accompanied her into the forest, five men and two women. Dovka fell into the undisputed role of leader in the effort to escape certain death. As they picked up others who had independently fled to the forests, she remained their leader.

11

YORGI...

Exhaustion overtook **Yorgi Tzarof.**

Sleep claimed him right there on the dusty ground where his German captors threw him. He was unconscious of the search of his clothes by other prisoners. He had nothing of value on him except his shoes, which were quickly removed while he slept. Now he was completely ignored by other prisoners who wandered aimlessly or just sat around in the vast compound.

Yorgi awoke after four and a half hours of motionless sleep. He had to think a moment before he could recall where he was — **Darnitsa!** He opened his eyes very slowly, but still didn't move. Finally he raised his head cautiously and looked around. There were thousands of prisoners in the compound and to Yorgi's relief none seemed the least concerned with him.

He had been in prisoner of war camps before. He knew the other prisoners could be as dangerous as the guards — more dangerous. He sat up. Damn it, they got my shoes, he realized. He made no outward sign of emotion or recognition of the fact. Oh well, I'll get others. At least it's warm weather. But I'll need a pair before I escape. All in its time...

Darnitsa was across the Dnieper River from Kiev, a suburb made up mostly of working class people. During World War I, the area had hosted an enormous prisoner of war camp. At that time, it had been the Germans who died inside the barbed wire by the thousands. Now, the Germans had turned the tables on their former keepers.

These Russian prisoners could not complain that they were being treated any worse than they had treated the Germans nearly a quarter century earlier. In those days, hundreds of Germans died daily in Darnitsa, from hunger, exhaustion, exposure and disease. If more Russians died now, it was only because there were more of them detained in the same area.

As Yorgi looked about him, he saw a mass of wretched humanity. Most had dull, unseeing, emotionless expressions. They'd soon be reduced to spiritless animals. Draining them of all hope and ambition made control of them easier. Yorgi wondered whether most cared if they took another breath.

He'd been in other prisoner camps, but none like this. Sixty or seventy thousand men were enclosed by barbed wire in this place. The ground was hard, dry and dusty. There had been an abundance of plant life here before it had been reclaimed as a prisoner compound, but all of that had been picked and eaten by starving men — picked clean, down to the last blade of grass.

There was a stench common to all such camps of urine, vomit, feces and the odor of bodies not cleaned in days or weeks. At least here it appeared, they removed the dead quickly, so the horrible smell of death did not add to the other disgusting odors.

Officers, political prisoners and Jews were put into a separate enclosure where their life expectancy was even shorter than in the main camp. Yorgi had made every effort to keep two facts to himself since the Germans had occupied the Ukraine: that he was an officer and a Jew.

There had been a relatively large number of Jews conscripted into the Russian army. It was a method by which the Russians had tried to assimilate the Jews out of existence. For a Jew in the Russian army, it was almost a matter of assimilate or die. They weren't too eager to assimilate them into their society, but into the military, that was acceptable.

Few of these Jews had become officers, but Yorgi was an exceptional Jew. He had an appetite and an aptitude for survival. Even now, as he looked around Darnitsa compound for the first time, he thought escape.

He got up. The warm, dusty ground felt good to his bare feet. From past experience, he knew it wouldn't be too hard to get another pair of shoes. The death rate in such camps was so high that many pairs of shoes would become available every day. Right now, he enjoyed the feel of the earth against his feet. It reminded him of the dirt roads of the village of his youth. A million years ago, he thought. He was a little concerned about the night when it would cool, but that was several hours off, according to the sun.

Yorgi started a walk around the Darnista camp. In a few days, I'll be like all the other prisoners — unable to help myself — and not caring. I have to escape before they drain my strength.

Walking, he memorized everything. The entire enclosure is barbed wire. Guard towers at intervals of two hundred meters. It's amazing that most of them are unarmed. Those have Ukrainian guards. Germans don't quite trust them with weapons. Just lookouts to yell an alarm if someone breaks. Armed Germans and unarmed Ukrainian guards walked outside the wire. They joked with each other more than they attended to their business. But if someone made a try for it, they'd have him full of bullets before he got through the wire. But they obviously expected no escapes from these broken spirited creatures.

The guards were bored.

It was an ideal situation for escape — when the time is right. Yorgi wondered if he could find anyone here to help in an attempt? "It's got to be soon... Maybe it's better if I keep my plans to myself; don't know who I could trust," he mumbled to himself.

He walked on and observed, while doing his best to be unobserved.

There were two single fences around the camp. No electric barrier, no mine fields that he could sense, not even large clearings to cross. Along one area a road passed right by the outside barbed wire. Lines of women stood there on the chance they might catch sight of a husband, brother, father or son taken prisoner. They knew if a loved one were there, he'd be dead in a week or two. Many carried a basket or small bag from which they threw potatoes, turnips or onions over or through the fences. Like feeding animals in a zoo. When the camp first opened the Germans had shot at women for throwing food, killed them, but in time they stopped. They'd come to find it entertaining to watch the starving men fight each other to get at the food. Often one would kill another for a small morsel. It was one of the few times anyone in the camp showed signs of life.

It was along this section of fence that Yorgi thought he might find a few comrades still interested in and capable of escape. He also knew he would probably have to join that scramble for food to maintain his strength.

There were no buildings in the compound. Men slept, relieved themselves, lived and died wherever they happened to be at the time. There were a few trees, but their bark had been picked off as high as men could climb — picked off to be eaten. Starvation was everywhere. Here and there Yorgi saw men chewing leather belts and shoes. Men picked lice from their own bodies and popped them into their mouths. If a mouse or rat or squirrel or rabbit happened into Darnitsa, it would be captured instantly and eaten raw — bones, entrails, skin, all — but not before it had caused a near riot. It was so entertaining that often the Germans would catch them and throw them in. Even stray cats and small dogs had been thrown in, but now there were few of them left because the starvation in the city had made them a delicacy there, also. It was commonplace for those who died during the night to be discovered in the mornings with areas eaten out of them by starving humans.

Disease was rampant, especially dysentery. The smell of urine and excrement was everywhere. A rubbish heap was near the German military kitchen where they threw their garbage into the compound. Here, also, there were always a large number of prisoners rummaging through the refuse, picking out anything edible. Onion and potato peels, apple cores orange rind—delicacies all—could be found. "Slop to the pigs!" the Germans laughed.

Yorgi continued his walk. At the back of the compound, an area was fenced off and under guard. Inside the wires were building materials. The Germans planned to build barracks in which to keep some of the healthier prisoners. They would be worked while they still had some strength left. But the work programs would come too late for Yorgi. If he stayed in Darnitsa he would be dead long before the program began.

He continued around until he was back in the approximate area from where he'd started. After dark he made another round of the camp to see what the nighttime security was like. Also, at that time he'd knew he'd find a pair of shoes.

He lay down and went to sleep.

Yorgi slept longer than he'd intended. When he awakened, a quarter moon hung high in the sky, but a layer of clouds diminished its light. Without sitting up, Yorgi carefully looked about, scanning the camp while his eyes got used to the darkness. There was no movement, only a few moans and snores could be heard.

Several searchlights intermittently swept the entire compound, but they covered it sloppily. Yorgi correctly assumed that the night guards were as bored, probably more bored with their work as were those on the daytime shifts. In addition, they had sleep to fight, a more difficult fight than they'd expect from these prisoners.

Quietly, he got to his feet and started around the compound. As a sweep of a floodlight approached him, he'd lie down and feign sleep until it passed, then get up and go on. An important difference between the day and the night was that now each watchtower was manned by armed Germans. Each had a light and swept the area between the two lines of barbed wire.

Slowly, carefully, he continued on until he reached the area of the building materials. Not many prisoners were sleeping in that area. Three German guards were stationed inside the wire around the supplies. Yorgi lay down so he could study the area a little longer in safety. One of the lights swept over him without pause and went on. Now Yorgi focused his attention on the lights from the towers sweeping between the two lines of barbed wire fence. It took about fifteen seconds for the lights to make a complete sweep. Too short a period for me to dig under a wire, run across the alley between and dig under the second, he thought.

He moved on.

At about fifty meters beyond the building materials, Yorgi came to a sudden stop and fell to his stomach. He was among some sleeping prisoners. Something had caught his eye. He had to check it further. He watched a sweep of light between the towers at this area. He watched a second and third time. "Damn!" he mouthed.

Each light swept the area between it and the next tower to its left, but the light at the tower directly in front of him didn't make a complete sweep. It swept out to the next tower, but when the beam came back, it was three meters short of where the light from the tower to its right reached.

Yorgi watched through several more sweeps. In each sweep, there was an area of at least three meters which was never illuminated. He crawled to the area on his stomach. When he got to the spot he dug at the earth under the first fence. It was loose, sandy dust. It came away easily. Before he realized what he had done, there was an opening under the wire large enough to pass his body through.

In a completely unplanned and spontaneous move, Yorgi slid his body under the first line of fencing. He was in the alley between the two fences, looking up at the base of the guard tower. In a few seconds he knew he would either be dead or free.

The two searchlights were converging on him, one from the right, the other from the left. He held his breath. They stopped at the end of their sweep, leaving Yorgi still in darkness. He bounded across to the second fence. The ground was loose there, too. He dug in a panic now. Two more sweeps of the lights came and went—and a third. Yorgi remained in the darkness. And then he was out.

He ran. His heart pounded feverishly, his chest a kettledrum. Finally, in the protection of some woods he fell to the ground. It was a miracle! He was out almost by accident; when he realized, he was still barefoot. He got up on his bare feet and ran some more. He wanted to put as much distance between himself and Darnitsa as he could before morning.

All night Yorgi forced a rapid march on himself. He first headed due north until he reached another suburb of Kiev, **Sotsgorodok.** Keeping in the outskirts of that district, he turned northwest to the Dnieper River. Reaching the eastern bank of the river, he headed back south in search of a crossing.

In a short distance, he found a road with a bridge. It was guarded by two Germans. A sign near the bridge disclosed that this was not yet the Dnieper, but the **Kesenka,** a tributary that paralleled it. The water was low at this time and to avoid the guards on the bridge, Yorgi crossed the tributary in its shallows, keeping to sand bars. He stayed in the water to the edges of the sand isles so as not to leave footprints or scent that could be followed by men with dogs.

He crossed the narrow land strip between the Kesenka and the Dnieper and found himself due east of another subdivision of Kiev, a district called **Kurenevka.** Now he had the Dnieper to cross. There were no narrows or shallows on the Dnieper and all the bridges crossing were sure to be heavily guarded against saboteurs and contraband traffic.

Yorgi hoped he might find a deserted boat along the bank, but there wasn't one. For awhile he contemplated swimming, but decided the risk was too great. He continued his search upriver, taking him several kilometers above the city. No solution offered itself on the bank.

It will be dawn in less than two hours. I've got to put this river between Darnitsa and me. If the Germans search for me in the morning, it will be east of the rivers. He was about to change his mind and make a swim for his life when he came across a log floating with the current of the river. His decision was almost a reflex. He plunged after it, fearing the rapid current might carry the big log beyond his reach. "I've got it!"

He let the log carry him along for a few moments. Then he started the slow sidestroke that he hoped would force the log and him out into the center of the river and to the other side. He furnished the power to cross the current while the river furnished the force to carry them back toward the city. He stroked, rested, stroked again. Though not attempting to fight the current, Yorgi was very fatigued a half hour later when he found himself less than thirty meters from the west bank of the Dnieper River. It was still dark. He rested briefly, clinging to his log. Now he could see the outline of a huge bridge crossing into Kiev, perhaps two hundred meters ahead.

"Hell, I've got to be out of the river before I drift to the bridge."

Gathering together what strength he had, he began stroking vigorously. By the time he had stroked twenty meters closer to the bank, he was less than a hundred meters from the bridge. He let go of his log and swam the last distance. It took him only a few seconds, but also all the strength he had left.

Yorgi Tzarof pulled himself up onto the western bank about fifty meters from the bridge. Drenched and breathing painfully, he lay there trying to regain his strength and his bearings. He figured he had to be northeast of the city. Directly west of him was a totally unpopulated area. After a short rest, he started across it. Five minutes later, he came to another body of water, which struck fear into his heart.

"I don't have the strength to cross another river!"

Despairing, he began to follow the water's edge. After a few hundred yards the bank turned due east. Yorgi realized he'd just come across a cove in the Dnieper River that extended a finger of water inland.

The water fell away behind him and he could see the first buildings of Kiev's Kurenevka district ahead. Aware of the curfew, Yorgi hesitated to enter the city before daylight. He was still barefoot. His ragged clothes would not raise too much suspicion in the city where German occupation had brought poverty to a majority of the citizens, except that they were soaked. But the bare feet bothered him. That would draw the most attention. That, with his lack of identity papers, would be fatal.

He decided it would be best to get through the city as soon as possible. With caution he might get through before the day advanced too far. If not he'd find a basement to hide in until night. The eastern horizon held a hint of daylight.

Looking in every direction, he entered the city, avoiding main thoroughfares. He hadn't gone too far when he stumbled upon a body in the street, shot through the neck and head.

"Poor bastard," Yorgi said under his breath, "caught out after curfew."

The man's misfortune was Yorgi's good luck. The corpse still wore shoes, not only that, but a threadbare suit coat with which Yorgi covered his tattered shirt. He also had papers that, though they would not withstand close scrutiny, might increase Yorgi's chances a little. The shoes were tight on Yorgi and hurt his feet, but they'd have to do until a better pair became available.

"Thank you," Yorgi mumbled solemnly to the corpse and hurried on his way.

As he made his way through the back streets, he became aware of the risk he was taking. In the brief time he'd been in the streets of Kiev, he'd seen no less than three bodies—all, he presumed, shot for curfew violations. After sighting the third, Yorgi decided not to press his luck. He hid in an alleyway behind some trash containers to await the rapidly approaching daylight ending the lethal curfew.

He rested but could not sleep.

Soon the sun was up and with it the activity in the street increased. He hoped he would be able to lose himself in the gathering crowds. After six in the morning there were a good number of people on the streets. Yorgi fell in with them, continuing constantly westward.

As he walked, he was aware of a constant, repeating sound of gunfire.

It took him only twenty minutes to get through the west edge of the city, which led to the cover of woods— the same woods that had hidden Solomon Shalensky on the day he'd escaped the death pits of Babi Yar.

12

FATHER PETER...

The Roman Catholic Church came to the Ukraine and Russia by way of Poland. Its greatest influence was, therefore, in the Western Soviet Union. Though not a large population, most of the Roman Catholics in the Soviet Union now fell under German occupation.

Father Peter Rochovit's parish was in the countryside surrounding Kiev. It was a poor parish, his congregation mostly peasants. The economy was hard on them, as it was on every non-Bolshevik Soviet, but in the Ukraine the Roman Catholic Church was a minority church. The Bolsheviks discouraged religion and the Vatican considered communism its most dangerous enemy.

Father Peter was the second of six sons born to a peasant who came to the Ukraine in 1897. He was born in 1910 in the parish he now served. The Church was central to Peter's family's existence. Peter had been attracted to the Church at an early age, finding it an escape from the harsh life of the Ukraine. He became a favorite of the elderly priest of the parish, who encouraged Peter to pursue a life of service to God.

Because the parish was poor, the church school provided only a basic education. It was adequate for most, since most peasants considered formal education a luxury and frankly, a waste of time. Education didn't plow, plant or harvest. If a child learned to read, it was a great accomplishment. Literacy did little to help provide for the family. If one member of a family could read, then that family was no longer illiterate and it did not seem important for more than one member to learn the skill. In the Rochovit family, Peter had the greatest aptitude, so he'd been chosen to get the education.

After Peter finished his education at the church school, the old Priest arranged a scholarship for him at divinity school in Poland, with the understanding that he'd return to his district and follow in the footsteps of his old mentor.

Peter went to Poland at age seventeen. At age twenty two, in 1932, he returned as assistant priest to his parish. When the old priest died in 1935, Peter took over the parish and served the people he'd known and loved since childhood.

Father Peter believed in what he preached and lived by his teachings. In spite of his youth, he had good judgment, wisdom and compassion. An avid historian, he was an insatiable reader. His knowledge of other religions was vast. His interest in political philosophies was deep and he felt, as did the Vatican, that communism was a great threat to the Roman Catholic Church and to all other religions.

Even though Father Peter kept up an active correspondence with several priests in Poland, with whom he'd gone to school, he had no idea what German occupation would mean to the people of the Ukraine. His colleagues in Poland did not write of political matters. That was too risky since government perusal of the mail was common. He was a victim of the same news censorship that kept all Soviets uninformed. When the Germans came to occupy Kiev, which included his parish, he too saw them as liberators, believing they would lift the yoke of religious persecution off all the faithful, but especially from the Roman Catholic Church, since Hitler and most of his top officials were Roman Catholic.

He believed that the industrious, cosmopolitan Germans would bring his people new opportunities to throw off the heavy burdens of poverty and ignorance. But after the Germans entered his parish on September 19, 1941, he heard only the distant sound of machine gun fire, carried on the wind from Babi Yar.

13

DECISION...

"What are your plans?" Ivan asked Sol on the morning of Tuesday, October 7th. Solomon's restlessness was becoming quite apparent. Rest and Sosha's cooking had restored his physical health and strength. Each day his grief and mourning gave way to deeper anger and need for retaliation.

"I don't really know."

"You're welcome to stay with us until you decide," Sosha reassured.

"Thank you. I appreciate all you've done, but I'm endangering you by staying here. If the Germans found me here, they'd shoot us all. I can't put you to such risk."

"We haven't even seen a German yet. I don't know when they'll come this far from the city," Ivan said.

"Oh, they'll get here. As soon as they have the city secured, they'll come," Sol emphasized.

"We'll see," Ivan said. "Anyway, until you decide what your next move will be, you'll stay with us. We're safe enough for now. You'll sleep under the steps and during the days you can help me with the chores. We'll keep our ears open and an eye toward the road."

Several more days passed and still the Germans didn't come near the farm. They were fighting the Russians on an enormous front and couldn't stretch their ranks enough to put soldiers into rural areas. They concentrated their forces in cities and strategic villages.

Sol decided he would join the resistance and do what he could to avenge, in some small way, those who died at Babi Yar.

14

AWAKENING...

It wasn't until the middle of the first week in October that Father Peter found out what all the gunfire was about. He couldn't believe it.

The Germans were, after all, a cultured people. Even the Bolsheviks would not have dreamed of killing a hundred thousand Jews! That, plus captured communists, resisters, political prisoners, was it possible?

Pogroms had killed more than a hundred thousand over the past centuries—but that was not the same as shooting that many men, women and children and heaping their bodies in a mass grave.

On the other hand, he thought, it wasn't all that different.

As a priest, how could he confront these atrocities? By Saturday, October 4th, he had not yet found the answer. What stand would he take at mass tomorrow?

On Sunday, the words came.

Father Peter stood tall in his pulpit. Determination showed on his thin face. He was taller than his husky frame looked. He brushed his light reddish blond hair from his brow. Piercing blue eyes looked out over his congregation and he began to speak in his soft deep voice. But there was a crescendo in his voice that Sunday morning. He pounded his podium furiously as he gave a scathing sermon condemning the German atrocities at Babi Yar.

His parishioners were shocked. No one stayed after church to talk to Father Peter about his sermon, as was usual on Sunday mornings.

On Monday morning, a German staff car pulled up in front of the church. The officer got out and entered the church. It was empty. He went out and walked around to the back. There he found Father Peter pumping a bucketful of water.

"Good morning. You are Father Peter Rochovit, I assume."

"Yes. I am. Can I help you?"

"I am **Major Hans Oberman**. Mine is a rather delicate mission today. May we talk?"

"Of course ... please." Father Peter pointed to a bench and the two sat down. He wondered which of his parishioners had reported his sermon.

"Several of your parishioners have remarked to us about your sermon yesterday. I must say that we are surprised and disturbed by what we have heard."

"Surprised? Disturbed? I do not understand why this should surprise you!"

"Because, Father, your remarks go against official Church policy."

Father Peter was taken back by Oberman's words. "I do not believe so."

"Please," Oberman said, "the official Catholic policy is well known. It was clearly set out in 1933 by the Vatican, in an agreement with our Fuhrer. It is only because of that agreement that you have not been arrested." The German paused for effect. "We do not give everyone a second chance."

"I am not aware of this agreement. I'd like you to give me the details about it." Father Peter said the words to sound like a challenge. He was sure there was no such agreement.

"You priests amaze me!" the German said arrogantly. "Here we are doing efficiently what the Roman Catholic Church has been doing piecemeal for centuries and you all seem so astonished."

Father Peter sat speechless.

"Why do I shock you? I'm told you are an historian. You must know the Church has been trying to rid the world of Jews long before there was a Germany. The Crusades were blessed by several Popes—anti-Semitic policy was built into Catholic doctrine by Paul—the founder of our faith. You know as well as I do that the ghetto was not an invention of the Germans. We have just improved on that Christian concept."

"Surely you can't compare..." Father Peter began.

"If you will recall," Oberman interrupted, "the first ghettos appeared in Venice, toward the end of the fifteenth century. After that, the Church established ghettos for Jews everywhere that it had sufficient influence over local governments. And it was the Church that passed ordinances that Catholics could not work with Jews or deal with them, driving them out of many professions and occupations. We have just borrowed these ideas and methods. The Roman Catholic Church has reminded the world for centuries that the Jews are nothing but tyrants and congenital enemies of Church and state.

"Understand, Father, I have no argument with those facts. What I find disgusting and hypocritical is that you speak out against your own policies when someone else carries them out for you." There was a humorous sarcastic tone to his voice as he grinned at the priest.

Father Peter was stunned. He was well-versed in history and knew he could not argue these facts with the German. They were facts not openly discussed by churchmen—delicate matters, best left undiscussed. Well then, thought Father Peter, what of this agreement? "Tell me of the agreement you mentioned."

A smirk crossed Oberman's face, "I thought perhaps you wouldn't ask." He paused for effect. "The fact of record is that on July 20th, of the year 1933, our **Pope, Pius XI**, signed a concordat between the Fuhrer and the Vatican. The Roman Catholic Church agreed to keep its priests and influence out of our politics. Your sermon yesterday certainly did not uphold your Church's side of that agreement. I think you will admit that it is your obligation to support the policies of the Vatican. Am I wrong?"

"No, you are right. I must uphold the policies of His Holiness. I do, however, seriously question your interpretation of this agreement—if it exists."

"Oh, I assure you, it exists. Without question it exists. I would suggest you contact your superiors and make yourself familiar with your obligations in these matters. The Vatican knows that what Hitler and the Reich do are for the best. You should have faith in the wisdom of the Church. When the Vatican agreed to keep out of our politics, our Fuhrer granted complete freedom to the educational and religious policies of the Church." Oberman paused, studied the expression on Father Peter and then continued. "We have certainly lived up to our end of the bargain. We are very understanding people, however and we understand that your comments were probably provoked by a lack of insight. We felt that this dialogue would help you to understand the situation."

Father Peter looked at Oberman. He had nothing to say.

"I am sure, Father, that after you have had a chance to consider all that I have told you, you will find it in you heart to give your parishioners a better sermon next Sunday. Admit that you spoke hastily! They will have nothing but the deepest respect for you then. We are, after all, doing what is best for the world. The Vatican understands that ...surely you cannot doubt that wisdom."

Father Peter remained silent.

The German seemed satisfied.

"It has been a pleasure to meet you, Father. Remember, we are in this struggle together—the Reich and the Church—to rid the world of the Bolsheviks and the Jews. Both are a threat to civilization. Both are a threat to the Church."

Oberman got up, bid the silent priest a good day and walked back to his waiting staff car. He breathed deep of the fresh fall air, satisfied with the way the morning went.

On the wind, the sound of gunfire from Babi Yar continued.

15

HELP WANTED...

Solomon's decision to join the resistance was the easy part. How did one make contact with the resistance? Resistance organizations did not make their whereabouts generally known. Who were their contacts? How could Sol make his intentions known? He couldn't even make his existence known. He asked Ivan if he knew how to contact the underground.

"What do I know of such things?" Ivan replied. "But there must be a way. Perhaps I could ask in the city."

"And just who would you ask?" Sosha interjected. "You ask those types of questions of the wrong person and the Germans will come to arrest us all."

"She's right," Sol agreed. "It's my problem. I'll find a way."

"Maybe we'll hear something," Sosha said. "There's a lot of gossip in the market places. Maybe we'll hear something without asking risky questions."

"Good idea," Ivan added. "We should go into town. We'll go today. I want to see some of those Germans anyway. If they won't come here, well, we'll go there, Sosha and I. On the way, we'll stop at some neighbors. We'll get a feel about their sentiments on the occupation. Maybe we'll be able to get some leads. Who knows?

"And in Kiev—well, the marketplaces are troves of gossip. Sosha will be of more value there. Those women can talk..."

"Oh and your cronies don't have a thing to say?" Sosha inquired sarcastically.

Sol laughed.

"And we'll try to learn more about Babi Yar," Ivan added.

It was agreed that while the Igonovichs were at Kiev, Sol would stay out of sight. He decided to hide himself exploring the woods around the farm. Sol departed for the woods and Ivan and Sosha left for Kiev. Sol had wanted to explore the woods for some time. He'd thought it would be wise for him to know his way around the area. Sol wasn't looking just for an escape route, but also an alternate hiding place. He thought he might even be able to build one taking the risk away from Ivan and Sosha. It was just a matter of time before he'd be discovered if he remained at the farm.

The day was warm for autumn. This was the first time since his recovery that Sol had ventured away from the immediate surroundings of his hideaway. It was like a holiday. It had always relieved the drudgeries of the Podol when he had a chance to go out into the woods. It was much the same now. The few birds not yet migrated chirped and were answered by the chatter of squirrels. Sunlight trickled through the trees, making bright patches on the forest floor. Dry, fallen leaves rustled underfoot, releasing a strong scent of fall.

He'd walked about a half-kilometer when he came across an old trail. In days past, trails led from village to village, but when the villages were deserted, victims of urbanization, trails fell into disuse. The layers of leaves on this trail were thick and undisturbed. "This path is obviously seldom used," Sol said to himself. "I doubt the Germans will ever know about it." It might lead to an abandoned building or village. Might be perfect for me...he thought. He decided to follow it to his left as far as it would go. North, he reckoned. The morning sun was to his right and a little to his back. It threw a long shadow of himself toward his left and a bit in front of him. It amused Sol to have the company. "Okay, if you want to lead the way, I'll follow."

"They" walked about a kilometer and came upon a small stream. The ancient footbridge was in disrepair, the left railing gone and three-quarters of the planks missing or broken through. Solomon balanced his way across on a mostly exposed log that was the left support of the narrow span. A slight turn in the trail had put his shadow behind him. Looking around and seeing it Sol said, "Ah, on this rickety bridge you let me go first. Fine friend..."

On the far side of the bridge, the trail took a sharp right and followed the stream. Shadow was directly behind him now. Every once in a while he would look over his shoulder to see it still following him. "We must stay together, you and I. You are my only remaining *mishpocheh.* I fear I've no other family."

Sol followed the trail along the stream until it ended at a small ravine. He could see where a bridge had once been, but it had long since collapsed. "Perhaps it was washed out by a flood," he suggested to his shadow. "I'd wager it carries a real torment in the spring, with the rains and snow melt."

The ravine was perhaps seven meters deep and as many wide. Its sides were steep, but not too steep to negotiate. Sol could see where the trail continued on the other side. "It's an ideal place to explore for a refuge," he said to himself as much as to his shadow. "It's obvious no one ever uses this trail anymore. Certainly the Germans would have no idea of its existence.

He climbed down the steep walls and at the bottom looked back up. It didn't look as steep from here. Instead of climbing back out the other side, he decided to explore the ravine. As he looked around, he saw he was in complete shade. The deep sides kept out the sun. "I'll have to pick you up later, Shadow, when I come back up. Wait for me up there in the warm sun!" I must be going nuts, he thought, but it did help the terrible loneliness he felt since... Ivan and Sosha were wonderful—but the shadow was—from before... As a child he'd had a little stuffed bear and he remembered having talked to it the same way. When he had his stuffed bear—he always had a friend. Now, aside from Ivan and Sosha, he was totally alone. And as far as the world was concerned, "I, too, am dead."

If the trail on which I've just come ran north—then the turn that would have crossed it faced me east. Then this ravine must run north and south, also. I should explore the ravine to the south first. That will be nearest the farm. "Better I should know the terrain nearer the farm first. I can spread out, to the north, later..."

He estimated he'd traveled one or two kilometers north and about one kilometer east of the farm. If he traveled south now, he'd be staying within a two-or three-kilometer radius. "If I could find a good hideaway in that range, it would be perfect." I'll be near someone I can trust—near a place where I can get provisions—yet far enough away to hide without jeopardizing my friends...

This creek bed I'm walking in is probably one that runs full only with the winter runoff or when occasional heavy rains cause flooding for a few turbulent hours.

As he made his way south in the ravine, he wondered where the stream that the trail had followed went. It now occurred to him that stream and this ravine must both empty into the same body of water—"Perhaps the Dnieper River. It would be behind me, to the north." How far? It would be good to know. Someday that might be my escape route...

He pushed on to the south. At about a kilometer and a half he saw something that brought a bright smile to his face. "A cave—it looks like a small cave..." He ran to the spot. It was at a curve in the ravine, along the outside wall of the turn. Its entrance was under a shelf cut into the sandstone by centuries of rushing water. It was a hole about one meter high, five or six meters wide. "It should give excellent protection—except from floods. Then it could be a death trap..."

Stooping down, Sol went under the sandstone shelf to the low entrance. Crouching even lower, he crept inside. Inside he could stand up. It was a rather large chamber — a geological bubble, hollowed out by wind or water. When his eyes became used to the dim light streaming through the entrance, he noticed something else. At one end of the cavern — a rise, the floor at that spot was about a meter and a half above that of the rest of the chamber. Perhaps it would be safe there even during high water. The thought excited Sol. He went back toward the entrance where the light was better. There he looked carefully at the walls. His excitement increased. The water line appeared to go no higher than a meter. It went only a few centimeters higher than the cave entrance.

"Of course — it's like submerging an inverted glass into a bucket of water." As long as the glass remains inverted the air can't escape and holds the water out...

Sol emerged from the cave with a wide grin on his face. The sun was higher in the sky now and it could reach the floor of the ravine. Sol was happy to see *Shadow* had rejoined him. Together they went back down the path he had followed alone before, to a spot he remembered where it would be easy to climb out of the little gorge. In a short time, he was back on top, at the edge of the forest. He sat down by a tree and took two turnips from his pocket. "Lunch time," he told his shadow. As he sat eating, his mind raced. I'll come back here with provisions — store them in the cave. After I eat, I'll cut through these woods — find a more direct route to the farm. I must have traveled five or six kilometers to get here. "If I could go directly through the woods..." it might not be more than one or two kilometers. The farm must be almost due west.

He got up and started through the forest. His shadow shortened by the noon sun walked abreast of him now, to his right. It dodged in and out, disappearing and reappearing in the shadows of the trees. But as the sun started its journey west, Sol could notice his shadow starting to fall behind him. "Too bad you can't keep up," Sol laughed over his shoulder, "but I'm in a hurry now. You'll have to do the best you can."

Sol came across the path in the woods after only about twenty minutes. He saw no landmarks. I must be south of where I found it this morning. He turned right on the trail. He'd gone about a half a kilometer when he saw something he recognized — a large stone he'd had to veer around that morning. "I've come too far!" He backtracked about a hundred meters. "The farm can't be too far." He turned back into the woods, to his right, west. "It should be just ahead of me. At least if I miss it I should come out on the road that runs in front of it. He marked the trail at the spot and turned into the trees. Moments late he found himself at the edge of the woods, right behind the farm, almost exactly where he left the property that morning.

He was just about to cross the field when he heard someone shouting in German. He dived back into the woods, crawling behind a tree. He held his breath and listened. Again he heard German. He didn't understand the words, but knew there were at least three persons. His heart pounded fiercely. What can I do?

"Compose yourself. Relax. You're safe here in the woods. They have no reason to suspect you're here," Sol mouthed. He crawled on his stomach to a small clump of brush at the edge of the trees. Hidden there, he made a surveillance of the farm. No one, but the voices continued. Three, then a fourth voice ... no, a fifth — all in front of the house. One by one, five soldiers came around from the other side of the hut. They were looking in the window, annoyed to find no one there. At the back of the house, they saw the cellar's entrance. One man opened the door, pointed his gun down the stairwell and called into the empty storage room. He listened, then slowly started down, pulling a flashlight from his belt. One of the other Germans stayed at the door with his weapon ready. After a minute, the first emerged again. They both went on, leaving the door open.

Now a few more soldiers appeared — eight all together. One was obviously an officer. He barked commands left and right and the others made themselves busy. They searched the house with the same caution as they'd used in searching the cellar. Then the officer pointed out the few animals that were grazing, pecking and wallowing about the farm. As he did an aid at his side made notes on a clipboard. Probably they'll send a truck out to get them, Sol thought. They all went around to the front of the house, out of sight and in a few minutes, he heard motors start, vehicles driving off.

Solomon remained where he lay for the rest of the afternoon. Not until Ivan and Sosha came home, after dark and he saw the light go on in the house, did he come out of the woods. Even then he looked into the window before he knocked.

He told them first about the search of the premises. Then he told of his exploration. He warned that the Germans would probably be back to confiscate the livestock and food stores. He insisted that he move to his new home, the cave in the ravine. Ivan agreed. They decided to move much of the foodstuffs from the cellar to the cave where the Germans wouldn't get at it.

"But how will you explain that to the Germans when they come? They took notes on what they saw!" Sosha reminded.

"I'll think of something." Ivan replied, hoping he could find a reasonable answer. He didn't want to let the Germans have a thing of his.

The day had been exhausting for everyone. They decided to retire and plan more in the morning. Sol went to his bed under the steps for what he hoped would be the last time.

16

SEE NO EVIL
HEAR NO EVIL
SPEAK NOT...

Father Peter could not get the German Major's visit out of his mind. Over the next several days, he became more and more disturbed. Each day, he heard the intermittent gunfire from Babi Yar. At each silence, he pictured a line of humans being marched out in front of the guns — imagined the anguish they felt as they faced their last, horrifying moments. Then he heard the gunfire again.

The only respite was when the wind occasionally blew toward Babi Yar; but Father Peter knew they were still busy with their loathsome work.

"Dear God," he would murmur, "how long can they keep that up? How many people are they killing? People! They killed all the Jews of Kiev in the first week. Who are they killing now? Will it ever stop?"

The questions haunted him. He could not reverse his stand in his next sermon. Memory of the German's words assaulted him day and night. Father Peter knew the historic facts about the Church were true. Anti-Semitism was a product of early Christianity and it had been kept alive by the Church ever since. These were facts he and the Church had to accept but preferred to sweep under the rug. As an historian, he could not deny the truth, but he did not like having these facts pointed out to him by Major Oberman. And, in spite of all, he would not believe his superiors expected him to sit silently while human beings were being slaughtered like so much livestock. He would write to his bishop for advice.

For two nights he lay awake, composing the letter he would send. Over and over he wrote it in his mind. But before he had a chance to put his thoughts to paper, he received a letter from the bishop. Word of the sermon had gotten to his superior churchman. The letter didn't contain the history lesson the German presented, but it did express an unquestionable reprimand for the stand Father Peter had taken. "It is not our place to mingle in politics. Our place is to teach the words of our Lord, Jesus Christ. Political matters are to be left to those who govern and now that is the occupation force of the German Reich. They are our allies in the Church's struggle against Bolshevik oppression."

He knew he could not bring himself to reverse the stand of his last sermon. The words of the Lord, Jesus Christ did not condone the political slaughter of men women and children. He struggled with his conscience. Finally, he decided that his next sermon would be on a subject completely divorced from the problem, a simple commentary on a Bible reading in no way connected to the events and the times.

Since his bishop had left no doubt about the position he was taking, Father Peter decided to take unprecedented action. He would write directly to the Vatican for guidance. He would not say more on the subject until he heard from the Holy See or his representative. That was as far as he could make his own conscience bend. The thoughts he was going to put on paper for his bishop he now wrote to His Holiness, Pius XI.

Father Peter wrote and rewrote that letter, perhaps twenty times, until he thought it was just right. He wrote of his sermon in great detail and his defense of it. He also wrote all the details of his encounter with the German, Major Hans Oberman. And he wrote of what he'd heard about Babi Yar. Then he asked for enlightenment on all agreements and policies of the Vatican and the Roman Catholic Church in regard to the activities of the German Reich. He closed his letter asking for specific guidance: "How should I advise my flock, my parishioners to behave under the occupation? How should I behave toward the occupation? And what must I do about the activities at Babi Yar?" His answer would be long in coming.

17

A CHANGING INSANE TIME...

The next morning, after breakfast, Sol and Ivan went to the cave. Following the landmarks Sol had set, they had no difficulty finding it. The jaunt took them only about twenty minutes. They estimated that, if pressed, it could be done in half the time. They decided which provisions should be taken to the cave. Sol suggested they make a small enclosure in the woods to keep some of the livestock hidden.

"The Germans will surely be back to confiscate the animals. Why let those bastards find them all? You could say some were stolen. I'm sure they are being stolen all over."

On the way back, they selected a spot by the stream that the trail followed, so the animals would have water. They returned to the spot with tools, cleared an area and made a makeshift fence. This done they herded a few of the animals from the farm to the corral. They hurried, knowing the Germans might be back anytime—certainly in a few days.

The next day, they made several trips to the cave, each time carrying supplies until they had provisions to sustain a person for weeks without having to leave the cavern. All the time they worked, Sol wondered if he would be the only person needing the sanctuary of that little cave.

Ivan and Sosha told Sol all about their trip to Kiev. They had no leads on how to contact a resistance group. People in Kiev were all extremely cautious—afraid to talk openly of their feelings. No one trusted anyone. The city was completely without Jews now.

People said, "All have been killed at Babi Yar!" "If any escaped, it had to be before the roundup." "If there are any left they aren't in the city. Maybe a few are hiding in the woods." "It's no loss, really. The Germans did a good job of it."

Whomever Ivan and Sosha asked, they confirmed what Sol had told.

"But if they killed all the Jews in the first week," Ivan asked an old acquaintance in the market, "then who are they shooting now? I can still hear gunfire!"

"Oh, Bolsheviks that they find or bring in on trains from God knows where, captured Russian soldiers — anyone who doesn't follow their edicts..."

There was a curfew in Kiev now. Anyone on the street after the appointed time was shot on sight. Each morning, women, children and men were found where they'd fallen, killed only because they were on the streets after dark.

The people who in the beginning greeted the Germans as liberators now feared them — hated them.

"How foolish the Germans are to make potential allies into staunch enemies," Sosha said.

"No one speaks of resistance," Ivan said. "If such a movement is already under way, no one admits being part of it. Too many are willing to sell information to the Germans."

"I can imagine," Sol said.

"Sosha did hear one bit of gossip that might be a lead. In the marketplace, she heard some women talking about a sermon that had been given by a Roman Catholic priest, a Father Peter. It seems he condemned the Germans in his sermon. The gossipers said he was sure to end up in the ravine for his comments, but so far the Germans had only reprimanded him."

"Perhaps he's changed his views to save himself," Sosha suggested.

"Anyway," Ivan continued, "It would be dangerous to see the priest at this time. He might be under surveillance. A visit could endanger him..."

"Or the visitor," Sol interrupted.

"Yes. But if I can't find another way to contact the resistance and if the priest is not put in custody — and does not change his sentiments — perhaps he might be a lead in the future. We'll have to wait."

Two days went by. Ivan and Sol moved some stones to a corner of the field near the woods at the back of the property. Ivan suddenly stood straight. "Listen!"

"What is it?"

"Listen! A truck!"

It was very near. Sol ran into the woods. There wasn't time to run to the cellar. He dived to the ground and found himself near the same brush from which he watched the Germans the other day.

"Stay hidden," he heard Ivan say. "I'm sure it's the Germans. I'll deal with them." He walked toward the house.

There was a squeal of worn brakes. A door opened and slammed shut, as did another. German and Ukrainian voices sounded. The motor idled. Now Ivan could see the truck on the road in front of the house. Sol could not see it, but all the sounds reached him.

Two Germans had gotten out of the cab and three Ukrainians jumped from the open rear of the truck. They had been riding there with several animals apparently picked up at other farms.

Ivan met Sosha as she came out of the house. They walked together toward the approaching men.

The Germans spoke neither Russian nor Ukrainian. The German who was not the driver, a corporal, spoke to one of the Ukrainians who acted as interpreter. He, in turn, spoke to Ivan.

"We are here as representatives of the German occupation forces. We came to collect your livestock, as decreed by the commanding officer of the occupation forces of the Kiev area."

"But I do not understand," Ivan said. "The Germans picked up my animals just yesterday!"

Sosha's heart skipped several beats. She had no idea what Ivan was going to say to the Germans, but she never dreamed he'd tell a lie like that.

"What are you saying?" the Ukrainian asked.

"A truck came by here yesterday. Several Germans came on my property and just took my animals. I protested. It did no good."

The Ukrainian repeated the story to the German who screamed questions back at him.

"They had a German truck?" the Ukrainian asked.

"Nicer and bigger than that one. They were all in German uniforms. No Ukrainians. All were Germans. An officer and four in uniforms like his."

Again the confused Ukrainian spoke to the German corporal, who also became confused. More questions in German.

"He wants to know why they left some animals."

"I begged. I told him they were my livelihood. The officer finally agreed to leave me my horse and a few ducks. They emptied out my storage cellar."

Again the Ukrainian talked to the German. The German answered, very animated and final.

"I am sorry," the Ukrainian said, "there can be no exceptions. We must take all that you have left. Our list shows you had five pigs, three cows, a horse and several chickens and geese."

"All they left us was the horse and a few chickens. Surely you won't take them. What will we eat? How will I work the fields? If you take everything now there will be no production next year. What will they eat then?"

Sosha was terrified. What if they didn't believe Ivan? Did he have to tell such a preposterous lie? Well, it was too late now.

The Ukrainian spoke in German again. They both looked at Ivan. Sosha looked at Ivan. She couldn't believe the ignorant expression he had placed on his face. Had she not known him, she'd have believed him too. Stupid to have made up such a story. Maybe the German would believe. She had a sudden impulse to laugh. God, no! If I laugh now we're all dead. That thought was sobering enough that the impulse faded.

The German yelled something to the Ukrainians and turned, walking back to the truck with the driver.

"We must take the horse and all but three of your chickens. And you must show me that the cellar is truly emptied."

Satisfied, they drove off to the next farm.

Ivan turned to Sosha as the sound of the truck dwindled into the distance and chuckled.

18

PAIN IF CONSCIENCE...

His church was full on Sunday.

Father Peter didn't know quite how to interpret it. Were they there because they were in sympathy with him? More than likely, they were there out of curiosity. Would he speak out against the Germans again? He wondered who in the gathering had reported to the Germans last week. His eyes picked out a stranger in the crowd. He's too well dressed to be a Ukrainian, Father Peter thought. They're not going to depend on my congregation to tell them. German! Well, if they want fresh material for charges and arrest, they'll all be disappointed today.

The sermon was no more inflammatory than the mass itself. As the worshipers departed the church, the traditional line of parishioners formed to compliment the priest on his service.

The well dressed man was in the line. He spoke Ukrainian, but with a German accent. "A fine service, Father. I especially enjoyed your sermon. I want to continue attending your services while I am stationed here. It will be wonderful to hear such a sermon each week!" He tipped his hat and departed without waiting for an answer.

Father Peter was relieved. He had feared the Germans would demand a public retraction of his stand. He could not have done that. He hoped the German's superiors would be satisfied. But all this was only a stall. Sooner or later, he knew, the matter would arise again. The Germans were not going to change. Every day the wind carried their message. He could not continue to ignore that sound.

He'd eventually be forced to restate his feelings. He would have to do that much, regardless of Church policy.

Days passed. No reply came to his letter. The gunfire continued. He could not escape it. From dawn to dusk Father Peter heard each report as a life snuffed out. How many shots could be fired in a single day? "Thank God the days are getting shorter," he mouthed, crossing himself. If each day is even a few minutes shorter, how many lives will that save? How many times can a machine gun fire in twenty to thirty seconds? How many march out in front of those guns each time? Ten—twenty—fifty? Yes, even a few minutes less light each day would be significant. And if a few minutes less daylight can save fifty lives—for another day—then how many are dying each day from dawn to dusk. "Oh dear God, no! This can't be happening! We can't close our eyes!"

But it is happening and I am closing my eyes. He began feeling responsible for the deaths of all the people who died each day of his silence. "Silence condones the crime," he said to himself over and over. But what good will speaking out do? It will only add me to those in the pit.

Still there was no reply. How much longer could he continue waiting? If he didn't get answers soon, the pressures of his conscience would force him to act. If the Church did not show him the way, perhaps God would.

19

GREGOR...

Three days later, God replied.

A man appeared at Father Peter's door. It was **Gregor Kirtzof**, a congregant for as long as Father Peter could remember.

"Good morning, Gregor. How pleasant to see you."

"Father," Gregor interrupted, "I must come directly to the point. I heard your sermon two Sundays ago."

"It seems the whole world did!"

"We all know your sentiments. I want to tell you there are a number of us who feel as you do. We realize you are in danger from the Nazis if you speak out again. You must say no more than you have. We implore you not to speak out again. There is a small but growing group of us who intend to act against the Germans. If there is any way we can serve your cause—I will be happy to be your contact—so you are not endangered further."

Father Peter was so eager for a sign—some approval to act—something that could free him of his guilt. He was sure this was divine guidance, but, he had to be careful. It could be a test—a trap! How could he be sure the Germans weren't setting him up? He knew the consequences of trusting the wrong man. Arrest would be immediate. This could be one way the Germans could find out his true intentions...

But Father Peter was at the limit of his endurance. Here was a chance to act. If it was a trap, then let it spring.

Father invited Gregor into his personal chamber.

Gregor lived at the edge of Kiev proper. He was the eldest son of a blacksmith and had apprenticed to his father. He was about four years older than Father Peter. The family business had made a meager living, but by Soviet standards they lived well. The family was large. Gregor had four brothers and two sisters, so the forge had nine to feed. The Kirtzof's were a religious family. The few Sundays they didn't show up, the church seemed more than a little emptier, especially when hymns were sung. Father Peter had known the family since he was a child.

He closed the door to his humble apartment, two rooms attached to the rear of the church. He poured two glasses of tea and they sat down at a small table.

"Tell me, Gregor, what is it like in the city?"

"Terrible! Much worse than under the Bolsheviks. The Germans are not what we believed them to be. How can cultured people be so uncivilized? They have no regard for human life."

"I hear shooting every day. Are they really killing so many?"

"Yes, in the first two days they killed over thirty thousand Jews and since then, all the rest. They've killed ten percent of all Kiev, Father Peter, over a hundred thousand Jews — all dead."

"But surely some escaped."

A few may be hidden, but they would be very few. Any Kievites discovered hiding Jews are also killed. Their bodies are also stuffed into Babi Yar, but they are publicly shot first — in town where everyone can see. It sets an example. And always after a public execution, a number of Jews turn up, deserted by their benefactors." Gregor paused. "Who can blame them? Who would risk their entire family being executed to save — to save anyone else?"

"So it is true. I can't believe it," Father Peter said.

"It's not only Jews they kill. They take prisoners of war to the ravine, partisans, communists they discover, ex officials of the previous government who did not escape the city. And worst of all, the insane, lame people, severely ill—and people they round up at random."

"You mean to tell me they just pick up people?"

"Reprisals for breaking the rules!"

"No questions? No trials?"

Gregor laughed. "Trials? The nearest thing they have to a trial is interrogation and torture. That is reserved for partisans who might have information the Nazis could use."

Father Peter sat stunned. He had heard it was terrible, but, like many, he had hoped that much of what he heard was rumor.

"Once they swooped down on the Kreshchetik," Gregor continued, "and arrested the first hundred men they found on the street. They took them off to Babi Yar and shot them to pay us back for a German soldier who was found dead one morning. They might drive to an area at night; arrest all the people in an apartment building or in several houses. The sound of motor trucks and brakes terrifies people."

"Terrible," Father Peter murmured.

"It's not just the fear," Gregor continued. "What little food there is, is rationed. For a few ounces of flour or stale bread, we stand in line most of a day. All food stores and livestock, if we had any, were confiscated during the first days of occupation.

Father Peter frowned as he wondered if his few chickens and food stores had not been claimed because of that same agreement between the Vatican and the Reich.

"And food is not all they have taken. Radios, weapons, tools, good clothing and blankets—all have been confiscated." There was a short silence. "And there is the curfew. We must be indoors between six p.m. and five in the morning. If you're caught out on the street, bang! You're shot! I think the Germans consider it sport, like hunting squirrel or rabbit."

"It is truly a wonder that I wasn't arrested for my sermon. Why did they have such patience with me?"

"That is why you must not say more. You cannot know whom to trust. A great many people would sell information to the Germans for an extra ration of bread. Besides, there are far more important things for you to do."

Hearing those words, Father Peter couldn't contain himself. "What? What can I do?"

"In time, Father, when we can be sure it is safe, when they don't watch you so closely."

"Gregor, do you have any idea who spoke to the Germans about me?"

"I don't know. But you were the talk of Kiev that day. The Germans may have heard it from a second or third party."

"I see."

"The Germans will watch you closely, but I don't think they will move against you if you keep your course! It is said they do not try to interfere with the Catholic Church. Hitler is a Roman Catholic, you know. Apparently he made a pact with the Pope."

The priest was shocked to find the Nazi Vatican pact was such common knowledge. If it were so well known, why had his superiors not yet replied?

20

DOV...

Before we get too far afield telling the stories of others as I learned them, let me get back to my own experiences in Poland. By the time the Germans came into Kiev on 19 September, 1941 and began murdering the Jews in Babi Yar on 29th September, 1941, we in Poland had already been living and dying under their persecution, oppression and murder for over two years.

As I mentioned before, on my twenty-first birthday, 30th September, 1939 the invasion of Poland began. To everyone's surprise Russia, whom we thought would be our allies, invaded Poland's eastern borders on 17 September. By the 28th of September, 1939 the Polish government capitulated and the German occupation began.

I had finished my studies in Warsaw just three months earlier and had been conferred my medical degree. At the time the bombings of Warsaw began, I was in the village of my birth where I intended to practice my profession among people I knew and loved. But on 6 September, an announcement was heard on our radio by a **Colonel Umiastowski,** asking all men capable of bearing arms to report and help defend the city. Most of the men of my village and I complied.

Our village became a community of women, children and a few old men.

At first, we were ordered to leave the city, but then we were ordered back to defend Warsaw. The bombings were relentless and again we were ordered to the outskirts to await invasion. After the Russians invaded eastern

Poland, there was total confusion. Most of us thought they crossed our borders to help us fight the Germans. We didn't know much about the Nazi-Soviet Non-aggression Pact of August 1939, signed by **Ribbentrop** and **Molotov.** When we were ordered to that front, it caused real chaos. By that time, the futility of our defenses became clear to many and they laid down their arms without ever seeing action against either Russians or Germans.

During the long days of waiting, I volunteered to work at various dressing stations about the city, treating wounded civilians injured in the bombings and rubble. After the government capitulation, a number of us decided to cross the borders out of Poland to reorganize and continue the fight against the Germans. There were rumors that life behind the Russian lines was quite normal and we could regroup there. We just could not comprehend that the Soviets and the Germans had really made a serious pact. We'd heard that the borders were open and that we could cross them in either direction.

On the 7th of October, several friends and I did indeed cross the lines and found ourselves in **Bialystok.** In the next weeks, thousands of Poles came to this city, many from Warsaw and eastern Poland. At the end of the second week, the Russians passed out questionnaires to most of the Poles asking them if they intended going back to Poland. Of course, virtually all of us stated we intended to eventually return to our homeland. Little did we realize that this obvious answer would lead to disaster. Within weeks the Russians began arresting Poles who answered positively to returning home and sent them to the **Gulag** where they vanished. By sheer luck, I was gone when the roundup took place in the rooming house I shared with several others. It became so dangerous in the Soviet territories for Poles that many of us decided to return to the German-occupied sector where we at least knew the territory. After all, we knew the Russians were never kind to Jews and that they invented the pogrom and would have no aversion to deporting us to **Siberia** or perhaps just killing us. And we still thought of the Germans as a civilized people with their poets, scientists, musicians, writers, professionals. We still thought of them as perhaps the most civilized people on earth. We began to wonder why we had left Poland in the first place. It had been a nationalistic thing, thinking perhaps we could continue our fight to make our Poland free.

It was decided that my companions who had not been rounded up and I would return to German-occupied Poland and determine what life in that occupation would be like. We would keep our options open and carry on a clandestine resistance from territory we knew. The trip back was considerably more difficult and dangerous than our crossing into the Soviet sector.

We soon discovered that the borders were closed to traffic trying to return to the German sector. Of course, as soon as the borders closed the smugglers went into business. A lively business it was, too. They took those who wanted to escape the Russians into the German sector, just to turn around and take those who wanted to escape the Germans back into the Russian zone. For a sum of money, they would take us across. It was a sum greater than we could muster.

"If they can cross, so can we!" we reasoned. It was decided that we would send one of us to learn the way, then that person would return to lead the rest of us out. It was a naïve idea, but those were naïve times and we knew no better. I first voiced the proposal, so somehow I was appointed to the task. We put together all our funds and covered my fee.

I was given instructions to go to the region of the **Bug River**, which at that time was the border between the Soviet and German zones. This was an area known as **Byelorussia.** I was forewarned not to speak Polish since the Byelorussians were not at all fond of Poles and especially not of Jewish Poles. Fortunately, because of my medical school training I spoke reasonably good German; since the Russians and Germans were then allies, I traveled as a German. My major fear was that I didn't have papers to back up my charade.

My first rendezvous was a place called **Malkinia Station**, a small railroad terminal swarming with Russian patrols. There I was met by a peasant whose name I never learned, who took me to a small farm outside of nearby **Czeremcha**. Everyone there spoke Byelorussian. Fortunately, German was so foreign to them that they couldn't tell that mine was heavy with a Polish accent.

I stayed at the farm that night and was hidden all the next day. The following night a "caravan" was to cross. Seven other Poles and I were to cross over. We were only part of the merchandise being smuggled. Tobacco, food, liquor and small arms also were being taken. Of all the merchandise, we were surely considered the least important or valuable. I had no doubts that if it came to saving the goods or us we would be quickly sacrificed.

The date of the crossing was not randomly picked. These smugglers knew the habits of the German and Russian border guards. They had picked a cloudy moonless night. "Guards and patrols do not like to be out on very dark nights and if they are, their hearts are not in their work!" one of the smugglers informed me.

It was indeed a dark night. If a guard were right next to us we couldn't see each other. The guards considered it great sport to shoot people out of boats on the Bug River who foolishly crossed on moonlit nights. This was indeed an ideal night for us to cross, but it was so dark that I was afraid I'd never be able to learn the landmarks I'd need to get back and lead my comrades out of the Soviet zone.

Luckily, the crossing was not far from the farm which bordered on a narrow strip of forest which ran between it and the Bug River. It was on a turn in the river that protected us from view at a narrow just after the turn. We crossed in some flat bottom boats that were hidden in the forest and were rehidden in a forested area on the other side. It was an ideal area for smuggling and I'm sure it had served that or some other illegal purpose for centuries. The next morning I found myself on the German side of the Bug.

I spent the entire day in the woods near the crossing point for fear I'd not be able to find it again. That night, under the same moonless sky, I crossed back to the Russian side, but this time wading and swimming. The water was ice cold. When I got out on the other side, the chill made my bones ache. My soaked clothing drained what little heat was left in my body. I knew that I was in danger of going into hypothermia. I had to get dry. The forest floor was covered with dry leaves. I couldn't make a fire; I had no matches. If I had I think I would have set a fire even if it would have given me away. I was freezing, shivering painfully. I piled up leaves into a huge mound. I stripped off my wet clothes and crawled into the mound. It didn't warm me, but at least it let me conserve what little heat I still had in my body. I shivered and that warmed me a bit. I fell asleep and slept well into the next day. The sun was high and warmed me through the leafless trees. More important it had nearly dried my wet clothes. "Once more God has spared me," I mouthed to myself.

It took me three more days to get back to the "benefactors" who paid my way with the smugglers and it took us all five days to get back to the German sector. We spent almost a full night searching the woods for the boats the smugglers used. Just before dawn we found them. They were wet. We then realized we hadn't found them earlier because the smugglers had been using them to transfer their booty. We all crossed in one boat. There was more light on the river, but the border guards must not have expected crossings so near dawn. We were home.

That first winter of occupation, 1939 - 40, was bitter cold. The streets were inundated in rubble, snow and ice. Almost all the houses were damaged from the bombings. Some were no more than grotesque skeletons, burned out, damaged beyond repair. Others had their windows boarded up against the wind and precipitation. Food was still quite available; but the money had little value and most could not afford to buy it. Barter replaced currency and as people traded off their possessions hunger began to replace their resources.

When we arrived back in Warsaw we found that in October barbed wire had been laid around the major Jewish neighborhoods, creating makeshift enclosures. We could still pass in and out of these enclosures, but it was obvious we were being separated. Many of us still lived outside these "Jewish districts."

In November the *Judenrat* was formed, a Jewish Council of Elders to administer our affairs. Naïve! Oh, were we naïve. The Germans actually had us believing all this was for our own good. After all, we'd been living under Polish and Russian anti-Semitism for centuries and these Germans were supposed to be a more civilized breed.

Then there came the decree that all Jews would have to wear the yellow Star of David when outside the impounded Jewish districts. In December, the Germans placed signs around the Jewish districts stating, **"Epidemic Area Danger!"**

Then other perils threatened. The persecutions began, first of the Jews, then of anyone displeasing the Germans. Jews were beaten and kicked, insulted and degraded, humiliated and demeaned in the streets for no reasons at all. Too frequently our own Polish countrymen chimed in with the *"fun."* But to the Germans, all Poles were considered subhuman and more and more non-Jewish

Poles were oppressed in the streets for minor provocations. The Nazi bully took his "pleasure" at will — from a Jew if available, from any other Pole if necessary.

Naïve! We still had no comprehension of what was to come. With every new indignity we thought that was as bad as it was going to get. How often we would say, "Things can only get better."

21

MENOCHEM...

In the spring of 1940, restrictions were gradually imposed on movements between the Jewish areas and the rest of Warsaw. With these restrictions, forced labor was imposed on the Jews. While the rest of us tried to delude ourselves that things couldn't get worse, my good friend **Menochem Marek** tried to convince everyone he could that we were destined for disaster. "Can't you see what's happening? At best we will be enslaved, at the worst, annihilated!"

Perhaps a period of forced labor, a form of "enslavement," true, but how long could that last? "Annihilation, who would believe such a crazy thing as Annihilation? Unimaginable!" When did we start to listen to him? In November of 1940 when the ghetto was closed some of started to believe. The barbed wire had been replaced by walls. Most Jews who had lived outside the "Jewish areas" were now herded into the walled ghetto. Over half a million of us were behind those walls. We had to wear *yellow armbands* with the **Star of David** anytime we were outside the ghetto walls, now less and less frequent; and everyone had to be inside the walls at nightfall.

In December, large signs went up at the entrances to the ghetto declaring, **"Danger: Epidemic Zone!"**

Conditions became harsher with each day that passed. Crowding became worse. Every day more were crowded into the space that encompassed a few dozen square blocks — over half a million jammed into an area meant for perhaps a few thousand. One family apartments were forced to house twenty to forty people, several families in every room. People slept in halls and stairways. And more would be forced in daily.

In the spring of 1940, activity and movement between the ghetto and the rest of Warsaw, the outside world, was severely restricted and forced labor was imposed. We were thrown into slavery to the **Third Reich.**

I went to work at the **Bersohn and Bauman Children's Hospital on Sienna Street**. As crowding got worse, diseases increased to almost epidemic proportions. As more and more people died from diseases, exposure, malnutrition, stresses, suicide, our hospital became as much an orphanage as an infirmary. We had minimal medications and equipment. What we had we smuggled in from outside the ghetto. The Germans surely didn't care for us to cure or save lives. Supplies, food and equipment had to be bought or bartered on the outside and sneaked into the ghetto at risk to our sources and ourselves.

Conditions over the next month worsened when we thought conditions could not get any worse. But we were thinking in terms of a civilized world at first. Until we fully realized the Germans were a totally uncivilized, barbaric and brutal people, did we come to understand that there was no limit to their cruel, sadistic savagery. They delighted in our suffering. Even the deaths of infants and children didn't disconcert them.

In November 1941, the ghetto was closed and traffic between it and the outside was punishable by certain death.

The ghetto actually consisted of two parts, the **large** and **small ghettos,** connected by a bridge that passed over **Chtodna Street**. Now hunger and disease really took their toll. Hunger, disease and the bitter cold of the harsh winter killed hundreds daily. Each morning, the dead were placed on the sidewalks to be picked up in carts for the burial details to place them in mass graves. There was no other way to manage the enormous problem of putting our loved ones to rest. There were no coffins, no services, no interment among family and friends. We could only place them outside for pickup like refuse, like trash, like garbage — and grieve in private. But in that terrible time, everyone had losses and we understood each other's heartache and it made an abominable routine — barely sufferable.

On 22 July, 1942 my friend, Menochem Marek's warning and prediction came true. Though by now there were fewer doubters and even with all the suffering and inhumanity the Germans had shown, what came next was still unimaginable. On this infamous date the **mass deportations** from the Warsaw Ghetto were ordered. **"All Jews with the exception of those employed by the *Judenrat* (the puppet governing body inside the ghetto), the German workshops, Jewish police, Jewish hospital and their immediate families will be resettled to the east."**

"What a relief!" many thought. "At last we'll get out of these horribly overcrowded conditions. It can't be any worse than this!" People were frantic to get on the first trains out. Indeed they went to less crowded conditions. They went to **Treblinka.**

We remained naïve. Who could conceive that even the brutal Nazis could invent what was planned for us. From the end of July through September 1942 The Judenrat was to deliver from 6,000 to 10,000 Jews *daily* to the *Umschlagplatz*, the switching point, where cattle cars were filled to bursting with human cargo, to be sent for *"relocation* to work camps" with better, more humane conditions. By the end of September, there were only 60,000 of us left in the Warsaw Ghetto and it was now designated as a work camp. Now we understood that Menochem Marek was right. The truth had finally filtered back. Treblinka was a fact we all understood. Unbelievable as it was, we knew what our intended fate was to be.

We formed **ZOB**, the **Jewish Fighting Organization.**

I knew time was getting short when they closed the **Children's TB Hospital** on **Stawiki Street,** near the *Umschlagplatz.* Instead of transferring the children to our hospital, they were deported; hauled off in cattle trucks. We knew it was just a matter of time now until they would "relocate our children." A drastic decision was made. We would try to smuggle out those children who were healthy enough to escape. Those who weren't would be given as much treatment as possible to get them into shape to be taken out at a later date. Those too sick to escape would be mercifully given morphine just before the Germans could take them away.

For many months, others and I had been making trips to the outside to barter for food and supplies with our contacts. Now I would lead out the first group of children able to make the journey. Under the cover of darkness, we let ourselves into the sewer system under the ghetto, our smugglers' route in and out of the ghetto and ... walking and crawling through the waste water and excrement ... made good our escape. Quietly we crept from shadow to shadow hoping we'd not be seen by patrols eager to make target practice of curfew breakers.

At long last, we got to a farm at the edge of the city from where the children would be taken to a convent for safekeeping. We doubted that these children would ever be raised as Jews or would find Jewish homes at some time in the future, but at least they were being given a chance to survive.

I made this same trip with three more groups of children, each less healthy than the last, but the nuns insisted that they would take them with their illnesses and hoped to heal them back to health. After the last group, I decided I would not return to the ghetto. I knew the last of the children could never make their escape and I didn't want to be there to have to administer the morphine. I have had to live with the fact that it was an act of cowardice that I left the responsibility of mercy killing of those gravely ill children to others, while I turned to the forests in hopes of killing Germans.

22

HIS HOLINESS, PIUS XII...

His Holiness, Pius XII, was born **Eugenio Maria Giuseppe Giovanni Pacelli** in 1876. In 1901, after his education was completed, he entered the **Secretariat of State in Rome**. He was appointed professor of ecclesiastical diplomacy at the **Pontifical Ecclesiastical Academy** in 1909, holding that post until 1914. During that time, in 1911, he was also made **Under Secretary of State in Rome**. In 1917, he was appointed **Archbishop of Sardis** and **Apostolis Nuncio to the Bavarian court at Munich**. In 1920, he became **Nuncio to Germany.** In 1925, he moved to **Berlin.**

He became **Cardinal Pacelli** in 1929.

In 1930, he became **Rome's Secretary of State**. It was in that capacity that he negotiated the concordat between the Holy See and the Third Reich. That agreement was signed by him and Hitler's **Vice Chancellor von Papen** on June 20th, 1933.

In that concordat, then Pope Pius XI, the Church and its priests agreed to stay out of Hitler's politics. In return, Hitler, himself a Roman Catholic, would not interfere with the policies of the Vatican and the Roman Catholic Church.

Though Franz von Papen signed the concordat with Cardinal Pacelli, he was cordially welcomed by His Holiness, Pius XI, who took the opportunity to express how pleased he was that Hitler and the German government were so uncompromisingly opposed to communism. The Vatican considered itself a full partner in Hitler's battle against communism and all enemies of the Church and the "civilized" world. He blessed the Third Reich—even while the first concentration camps were being outfitted to receive "political prisoners." The Vatican's prayers went out to bid the Third Reich, *"Godspeed in attaining your goals."*

The Vatican ordered its bishops in Europe to "support and swear" their allegiance to the Reich. *"In performing my spiritual duties, I will endeavor to avoid all acts which might be detrimental or dangerous to the Third Reich"* were the concluding words of *the churchmen's oath.*

In 1939, Cardinal Pacelli became **His Holiness, Pius XII.** He supported the agreement he had negotiated and signed for the Vatican six years earlier. The great majority of bishops and priests supported the agreement. There would be no public condemnation of the acts of the Nazis from the Roman Catholic Church.

When Father Peter Rochovit finally received his letter, it came from a secretary at the Vatican. "It's impersonal," he muttered, frowning, frustrated. "It gives me no specific guidance for my situation." There was enclosed a copy of the June 20th, 1933, concordat. A brief cover letter declared that the enclosure would explain the position of the Church. It emphasized that the Third Reich was doing what was best and necessary in the common struggle against communism. Father Peter was reminded, "...and your duties are to be concerned with spiritual and not political matters of your parish."

Father Peter Rochovit decided. "I will not be able to support the dictates and position of the Church."

23

A FATEFUL GATHERING...

Four days had passed since the Germans came to confiscate Ivan's animals. No more Germans had been seen in the area since. It was nearing dusk and Sol entered the woods behind the farm. He was headed for the corral to prepare the hidden livestock for the night. He'd just gotten to the trail when a sound stopped him in his tracks. A mumble, hushed, but it had a strangely familiar ring to it. Again he dived into the underbrush.

He listened. The sound continued. It came from deeper in the forest, somewhere between the trail and the cave. Cautiously, he started toward the sound. Creeping, the sound got louder as he neared, becoming more familiar but still too low to identify.

He found himself at a small clearing. What he saw was too unlikely. "I must be dreaming," he mouthed.

In the clearing were three men dressed as peasants. Ukrainians! Two silently rested against trees, while the third man produced the sound that had brought Sol there. It was not quite night, but the forest held out much of the fading light. It was properly dark for the evening prayer — the evening *Amidah, Maariv* — chanted daily at this time by all Orthodox Jews.

Here in the forest, Sol had found another Jew. Another Jew! Probably three Jews! He thought, at least one of whom is orthodox, saying the three *Amidahs* each day — *Sheehrit* in the morning, *Mincha* in the afternoon, *Maariv* at evening time. Sol had to restrain himself from running into the clearing, but he didn't want them to flee before he could identify himself. More important, if they were armed and on the run, they might shoot before asking questions. At that moment, he thought of the safest way of making his presence known. Softly, Sol started chanting the Maariv as he had done daily with his father, grandfather and brothers.

The two men sitting came to their feet. Suddenly to hear evening prayers coming from the trees! The *davening* Jew almost choked on his words. They all stood, dumbfounded, as Solomon walked, chanting, into the clearing. Without stopping his prayer, he walked to the side of the davening Jew and they continued their chant to its completion together.

They embraced like brothers who hadn't seen each other in years.

After introductions they told each other of their recent plights. The three men, Moshe, Uri and Boris, seemed half-starved. Sol decided the livestock would just have to wait while he took the men to his cave. "Stay here 'til I come back. You'll be safe. There is food stored inside— and candles. Eat all you need. I'm going back to the farm now; I'll be back after dark.

That evening Ivan and Sol checked on the animals, then went to the cave together. No glow from inside the cave was visible. The three men had eaten their fill of turnips, carrots, cabbage, potatoes and dried fruits and were resting, feeling somewhat safe for the first time in weeks.

Moshe woke his two companions and introduced them to Ivan. He seemed to be their spokesman, their leader. Formalities done, the five of them got down to business.

"I suppose Sol has told you our story?"

Ivan nodded, "Yes."

"We wanted to join a partisan group to fight the Nazis," Moshe continued, "but it appears we will have to do that on our own. We were almost killed with the rest of our companions trying to join a group we crossed paths with. It's not safe for a Jew among gentiles here in the Ukraine."

"Perhaps another group would have welcomed you," Ivan speculated.

"We're not about to take the chance to find out," Uri said. "They are only interested in our weapons. They rationalize their hatred of us by claiming they will all be killed by the Nazis if they are caught harboring Jews. The fallacy in that reasoning is that as resistance fighters, they would all die regardless if they have Jews among them or not."

"I think the anti-Semitic Ukrainians are as big a threat to us as the Germans," Boris added. "Why should they change now, after centuries of hating us? I'm staying clear of them. I only trust Jews from now on."

"I can understand how you feel," Ivan said. "I hope you'll trust me. Maybe I can earn your trust."

Boris was a little embarrassed that he'd spoken so candidly. "I'm sorry—but many of my friends died out there—trusting. Perhaps I shouldn't have..."

"I understand how you must feel," Ivan interrupted. "No apology is necessary. Perhaps with time... Anyway, for now you will have to trust me. Unless you move on."

"Enough," Moshe intervened. "It is a mute subject. If we are to form a Jewish resistance group, there is much we have to do. Winter is coming and survival in the coming weather is our first priority. It will not be easy."

The words excited Sol. "I will be your first volunteer!"

"Good," Boris exclaimed. "What success! We have increased our ranks by twenty five percent!"

In that moment, Sol felt for the first time since Babi Yar that he belonged somewhere. It didn't matter that his future was no more secure than moments before. He was no longer alone. Kind as Ivan and Sosha had been to him, it was not the same. Now he was among his own people. He was with mishpocheh—family—his tribe.

"How do you plan to recruit?" Ivan asked.

"I don't know," Moshe replied. "But if need be, we will be a four-man army."

They decided that for the time being the cave would be their home and headquarters. It was the safest place and could be easily winterized. Sol spent the night with his new fellow partisans.

He would be go between from the farm to the cave. It would not be wise to have too many strangers moving visibly around the area.

Ivan volunteered, "I will be the eyes and ears for you in the outside world — if you want me to be, that is."

"Good," Moshe replied. "Better that we have gentile eyes and ears in the gentile world."

Ivan didn't take offense but suddenly became a little more aware of what they were up against, how they felt. It was not just the Nazis and certain Ukrainians they had to fear. They had to be wary of the entire European Christian world. Anti-Semitism was not a Nazi invention — it was an invention of Christianity.

In this part of the world, Jew baiting and Jew killing had never been looked upon as such big crimes.

Sol continued working around the farm for Ivan and Sosha. In time, the neighbors who occasionally passed would think him a hired hand and not think him out of place. That way he could move freely about the area.

The Germans were still not a common presence in the rural areas. When Ivan and Sosha went to Kiev, however, he could not accompany them as hired hands often did. It would be too risky. Dressed in peasant clothes he could easily pass for a Ukrainian non-Jew, but he had no papers. And in Kiev he might be recognized.

The four Jews used morning and evening twilight to become familiar with the entire area. They explored their ravine from end to end. At its northeastern end it did empty into the Dneiper River, as Sol had suspected, at a point about twelve kilometers above Kiev. There the ravine widened and became heavily wooded.

At the cave, the ravine turned and they explored its southwestern reaches. It deepened as they followed it. But when they approached that end, in about three kilometers, the sides lowered again and widened until they found themselves on some rolling, hilly pastures.

Cautiously they pushed on until they worked their way to the top of one of the highest points and the only one that offered some trees for cover. From there they saw a paved road leading to a sizable town perhaps a kilometer north.

Sol reported their findings to Ivan later that day.

"That town would be **Irpen,**" Ivan told him. "It is not too important a town, except that it is on the major route — the road you saw — across the Ukraine. It leads to Kiev if you follow it on east."

Sol frowned and speculated, "It's bound to be a major supply route for the Germans." He paused, thinking more, "How far would you guess Irpen is from Kiev?"

"Ten or twelve kilometers, I'd say."

That evening, all four of the partisans and Ivan followed the ravine to the south again. After dark ,they descended to the road and made their way to the outskirts of the town. There was little activity there, but plenty of Germans. They appeared to be using the town as a storage depot. Sixty to seventy trucks were lined up in rows on a large field that had been turned into a huge parking lot. A number of storage buildings had been set up. There seemed to be only enough armed troops to guard the equipment. The rest of the Germans were probably drivers.

"These must be supplies to be used in Kiev." Uri suggested. "They probably store them here because it's easier to protect them from sabotage."

"That sounds reasonable," Moshe agreed. "What do you think they store here?"

"I doubt there are weapons," Boris said. "Weapons

would call for more security. My guess they have clothing, food — supplies for maintaining their troops and occupation government in Kiev."

"Well, I think we should try to find out for sure," Ivan suggested. "Maybe I can find out by a visit here tomorrow. I'll figure out an excuse to come here — some business maybe."

"Good idea," Sol added. "Let's get out of here and make some plans. No reason to press our luck."

They returned to the ravine and started back toward the cave. A kilometer into the ravine they were suddenly stopped by voices. Each man froze. The voices came again. Moshe touched his index finger to his mouth. It was unnecessary; no one was going to make a sound. Then he pointed to the top of the ravine at his left. The walls were steep and high. Moshe signaled the men to follow him. He headed on toward the cave. After a little more than a half kilometer he stopped, listened, heard nothing.

"I think it's safe to speak now, but quietly," he whispered. "As we came up along here earlier I saw a way up to the top of the cliff."

"That's right," Sol interrupted. "I noticed it this morning. It can't be too far. Maybe a hundred meters north of that rock outcropping we just passed." He pointed to the landmark about thirty meters behind them.

"Good," Moshe replied. "Uri, come with me. We will double back on top of the cliff. The rest of you go back to the cave and wait. We should return within the hour. If we don't, do not — *do not* come after us! It would be pointless for all of us to be wiped out in one operation."

An hour passed; an hour and a half. Ivan had gone back to the farm. He didn't like leaving Sosha alone. People were getting desperate for food and clothing, anything that could be sold or traded. More and more reports were circulating about robberies throughout the area. People who lived outside the cities were easy prey to drifters. It was all part of survival.

He'd left the cave with great trepidation. He feared the worst for his new friends. Boris could see his concern. Before Ivan left he said, "Ivan, about what I said the other day—I want to set it straight. You are a friend. I've no worry about you. The others—well, that remains the same. But you, Ivan, you're to be trusted. Thank you."

Ivan put his massive hand on Boris' muscular shoulder. "Boris, I thank you. I think I understand your feelings."

"Ivan, I'll come to the farm later and let you know if — when they've returned," Sol said.

24

BIRTH OF A COMMUNITY...

Finally after two hours, Moshe and Uri returned. With them were two Jewish families and seven other unrelated Jews. Theirs had been the voices on the cliff. They'd been living in the woods, migrating from the northwest of the country. Their intention had been to escape the occupation ahead of the German front. They had to restrict their movements to nighttime and through the forests. It was very difficult. By the time they reached this area, they realized that to reach unoccupied territory was almost hopeless.

The refugees had a meeting to decide what to do when Moshe and Uri came upon them. The two partisans had only to listen for a short while to become convinced they were escaping Jews. It took a little more convincing for the larger group to believe Moshe and Uri were what they claimed. Again, a demonstration of Moshe's davening became the "password." Recruitment was easy after that.

The partisan band now numbered twenty, twenty one if Ivan were included. And if Ivan were to be included, then Sosha had to be counted. Twenty two!

The two families contained five children between the ages of three and seven. Their fathers were twenty three and twenty seven, their mothers, twenty four and twenty five. The unrelated Jews among the new group were four men and three women between the ages of nineteen and twenty nine.

There were no elderly or sick among them yet, but one of the first things they decided was that no Jew would be turned away from the group. The partisans committed themselves to saving Jews as well as destroying Germans.

Their new growth was not without its problems. To accommodate the number of people now in the group they would need to reorganize. The cave was certainly too small to house them all. Maybe it could still be used for storage, but a new encampment would have to be found. And they would have to get more food and supplies. Irpen was the logical target.

For the present, Moshe was appointed leader. He picked his next in command from those he knew best; Sol, Uri, Boris and one of the new partisans — the one who seemed to be spokesman or rather spokeswoman, for them. Dovka was her name — an attorney from Minsk. Several of the newcomers had followed her in an effort to escape their town after the public murders. As they picked up others in the forests she remained their leader.

Rachel was another of the unrelated. At nineteen, she was next to the youngest of the girls. Shy and sensitive, she had developed a close attachment to Dovka, finding security in the woman's strength.

Moshe felt they had the manpower to carry out a raid against the supply depot at Irpen, with some training, but their entire armament was the gun which he'd not yielded to the Ukrainian partisans and its two clips of nine bullets each, plus an old rifle of Ivan's with a few rounds of ammunition. Among the new arrivals were three knives and these were kitchen utensils.

He called the group together early the next morning. Ivan was with them. He asked Ivan to go into Irpen to reconnoiter and report back. Ivan took Sosha with him. They were the only ones who had identity papers. That made them the intelligence arm of the band.

Sol and Boris were sent out to find a site for a new encampment. It would have to be a place where they could build shelters that wouldn't be seen from the air. Time was short; winter would be upon them too soon.

Late that afternoon, Ivan returned with his information. "The Germans are storing supplies in the trucks themselves. It eliminates the need for handling and more storage buildings. When the trucks come in they merely park them; then as the supplies are needed they drive the trucks on into Kiev. Seldom does a truck remain at the parking more than thirty six hours."

"How did you find that out so fast?" Uri asked.

"It doesn't seem to be a secret. Anyone can see what's going on. Everyone in Irpen knows the routine."

"Are you sure you didn't arouse suspicion—asking about..."

"I'm sure. It all came out in casual conversations."

"Do you have any idea what is stored there?" Sol asked.

"Apparently everything from canned food to office supplies. Few weapons, a little ammunition, small stuff, maybe. Clothing. I tried to find out more but no one but the Germans know that and I didn't want to ask them," Ivan said with a chuckle.

"Could you tell how the trucks are guarded?" Moshe asked.

"I walked around the area..."

"They didn't mind?" Dovka asked.

"I didn't try to walk in. Several people were walking there. No one seemed to care. There is a makeshift wire fence around the area, but no gate at the entrance. A guard was there, more to direct traffic, I think. A few more Germans were about the entrance; four or five at the most. They, too, seemed to direct trucks in and out of parking spots. They just don't seem too concerned about theft."

"It seems too good to be true," Boris countered.

"I don't know," Moshe said, thinking, "Perhaps because there hasn't been any type of resistance yet, their guard is down. They're complacent. If there were weapons stored there maybe it would be different. Anyway, I think we should take advantage of the situation—as soon as possible—before things change."

"There didn't seem to be many guards there last night either," Sol reminded them.

"No, you're right," Moshe agreed. "I think the way to do it is simply go in and drive out as many trucks as we can."

"It sounds too simple." Boris said.

"Let's hope it will be." Moshe said.

"There is one problem that may make it more difficult," Sol said.

"What?" Moshe asked.

"Who can drive?"

"**Oy!** A good question. That will dictate how many trucks we can steal," Moshe said. "I drive. Uri and Boris learned in the army."

"I drive," Dovka said, to everyone's surprise. "But I've never driven a truck."

Of all the others, only one of the men, the oldest of the parents, had driven before. Not only could he drive, but he'd been a mechanic. He taught the others how to start the trucks without their keys. At best, it looked as if they'd be able to steal five trucks and they'd have no way of knowing what their contents were until after the job was done.

Easy or not, it would be a risky mission.

Ten partisans would enter Irpen. Five would take care of the guards while the drivers would go to work wiring the trucks to start. The remainder of the band would wait at an appointed place to unload, should the mission be successful.

The supplies would then have to be carried to the cave for storage. The empty trucks would then be abandoned, far away, to mislead the Germans. The drivers would have to walk back.

Moshe, Uri and Boris gave the others a quick lesson on how to kill a guard silently. The plan seems simple, Sol thought, but there are so many ways it can all go wrong. "Dear God, don't let me panic..."

One hour after darkness, the ten left for Irpen. It took them about two hours to get to the parking area. They were amazed to find only six Germans guarding the trucks. Uri decided to make his way clear around the area, to make sure there weren't one or two more in the vicinity. He was back to the others in less than five minutes. They turned to the unpleasant task of eliminating the enemy. Moshe changed the plan. He appointed one German to each of four groups of two partisans. He and Boris would take care of the remaining two guards, one each. Each team crept off into the darkness. They had learned well. Only one of the Germans had a chance to cry out and fortunately he was the last to die. No one heard his brief yell except the other partisans, who had already dispatched their victims in silence. So far the mission had gone perfectly — too perfect, perhaps.

They dashed to the trucks. Within three minutes all five had started. They pulled out on the road without headlights and proceeded to their rendezvous. Dovka's truck lurched a few times as she tried to coordinate the clutch and gears, giving her passenger, Sol, a jolting ride. It was the first time he'd ever ridden in a truck or a car.

There was no traffic on the road. No one followed them. The raid had not yet been discovered. Six Germans lay dead, stripped of their weapons and ammunition.

"Beginner's luck!" Moshe confided to his partner.

A few minutes later, they were at the rendezvous with

the rest of their comrades. Quickly they emptied each truck. When they got to the last truck, the one Dovka had driven; they came across their first bit of bad luck. In retrospect, it was humorous. Dovka and Sol had risked their lives to take a truck loaded with condoms.

From the time they had stolen the trucks until they were emptied had taken only thirty five minutes. The raid had gone so well, in fact, that Uri suggested they go back and steal five more.

"You're crazy!" Moshe exclaimed.

"Sure it's crazy," Uri agreed. "It was crazy the first time too. But when will we have a better chance than right now? After tonight the security will be ten times heavier."

"He's right," Sol said. "If we go back, cautiously, we can do it. If they've found out about it we'll know it. There will be activity. They would never think we'd try again tonight, so they wouldn't be setting a trap."

"Let's take a chance on it," Boris added.

"It is crazy," Dovka confessed, "but I think it might work. If these five trucks have not yet been missed we can surely get five more."

Moshe considered, then said, "All right. But only the five drivers go this time. I'll not risk ten lives for this insanity. Maybe God has given us this night. Let's make the most of it."

"I should go with Dovka," Sol interjected. "She should not go alone."

"I don't need any help," she said, a little insulted.

"Probably not, but I need a ride."

Moshe gave the okay.

Thirty minutes later they were back with five more trucks. Twenty minutes after that, those trucks stood empty behind the first five.

Now they realized a blunder. With only five drivers they would not be able to take the trucks to a distant place to throw off the Germans. "Let's take them back to nearer Irpen." Dovka suggested.

"I guess that's better than leaving them here," Moshe agreed.

They took the trucks back to the edge of Irpen, including the truckload of condoms.

Dovka said, "I only regret having taken back all those condoms. If we'd have only destroyed them, maybe the whole German army would get syphilis!"

25

INVENTORY...

They carried supplies all night. They couldn't begin to get everything back to the cave, but what had to be left was hidden for transport over the next few nights. An hour after sunrise and about ready to drop, they finally heard Moshe's order to rest for a few hours.

While the others slept, Moshe, Dovka and Sol started taking inventory. From the guards they had taken six automatic rifles with twenty rounds of ammunition for each. They had taken one pistol with three clips of bullets. Five knives and six bayonets were also obtained. But when they started through the other supplies they realized the full measure of their success.

Moshe made an inventory list in the order the items were discovered:

- ❖ Blankets, wool #260
- ❖ Canned field rations #50 cases of 96 tins each.
- ❖ Dynamite #50 boxes of 24 sticks each.
- ❖ Lentils #50 bags 50 lbs. each.
- ❖ Bullets, 5,000 (wrong caliber)
- ❖ Oil lamps, 48 (no oil)
- ❖ Medical supplies #8 cases, assorted
- ❖ Pencils #1 case of 1,000
- ❖ Typing paper #10 cases of 12 boxes of 500 sheets.
- ❖ Shovels #1 case of 24, short handle.
- ❖ Emery boards #1 box of 1,000
- ❖ Soap #5 cases of 48 bars.
- ❖ Handkerchiefs #6 cases of 60
- ❖ Dinner bells #1 case of 60

- ❖ Table salt #10 bags 50 lbs.
- ❖ Light bulbs #10 cases of 48 bulbs.
- ❖ Coats, winter #70, all medium size.
- ❖ Flour #6 bags 100 lbs each.
- ❖ Coffee beans, #4 bags 60 lbs each.
- ❖ Soup ladles #60
- ❖ Shoe polish, black #4 cases 60 tins each case.
- ❖ Mouse traps #3 cases, 100 per case.

Moshe was disappointed there were no weapons. There were neither blasting caps nor fuses for the dynamite, but he thanked God they'd lost no lives on the mission. And they still had the hidden supplies to go through. He was grateful.

26

THE CHILDREN...

The children had been asleep in the cave while the adults worked the night away. They awoke to find the grownups in exhausted slumber. Rachel chose the entrance of the cave to lie down. She was awakened by the children as they came out into the day. To keep them from waking the others, she decided to take them for a walk in the woods before their breakfast. Quietly, they slipped away down the ravine until they found a place where they could get up the side easily. Once on top, they walked into the woods on the side of the ravine away from Ivan's farm. She pointed out the different trees she could identify. They'd gone only a little way when they came across thousands of chestnuts lying all over the ground. It was an abandoned grove. Rachel told the oldest child to run back to the cave and bring some empty boxes.

An hour later, the triumphant children and Rachel returned to the cave with two boxes filled to the brim with chestnuts. All day long the children went back to the grove with one adult and then another, until by mid-afternoon they had brought thousands of nuts from the forest floor to the cave. The children were little burden to the partisans.

27

CAT & MOUSE...

As head of the intelligence arm of the small group, Ivan started to look for sources of information. He decided to talk to "the priest" who had spoken out against the Germans. There had been no more inflammatory remarks since the first, but Father Peter Rochovit was still one of the biggest topics of gossip in Kiev. Ivan thought something might be gained by carefully opening a dialogue with him.

During the last week of November 1941, almost eight weeks after the slaughter began at Babi Yar, Ivan made his trip to Father Peter's church. There had been no let-up in the gunfire from the ravine. Ivan had put off this inevitable visit because of concern that the priest might be under surveillance. Furthermore, many of the Jews indicated they did not trust any gentile. "Isn't it possible that the priest might have made that first sermon just to attract partisans and Jews for the Germans?" some asked. It was not a majority opinion, but it had to be considered. "The first sermon was probably legitimate, but what if he takes the opportunity to reingratiate himself with the Germans by turning us in? What do Jews mean to a Catholic priest? Instigators of pogroms ...they hate Jews as much now as during the Crusades and the Inquisition!"

There was much and continuing discussion. The consensus leaned against contact. Finally, Ivan decided to go on his own. He would make the visit. His concern was not that he'd reveal too much to the priest, but if he were arrested for the meeting, the Germans might extract information from him by torture.

Early on the last Friday in November, Ivan made his way to the church. He left his home before sunrise to get there by eight. He didn't go directly, but walked past it on the road for about half a kilometer. The church was surrounded by fields. The priest's garden was in the rear. To one side was the cemetery; in front, the dirt road.

At a half a kilometer, he turned around and scanned the entire area. There was no sign of surveillance. "It must be safe," he said to himself. They have made a paranoid out of me, too. "It's Boris." He's convinced me that every eye in the Ukraine is looking out for us.

He walked directly back to the church, found the door to the sanctuary open and went in. Ivan sat down on a bench and wondered — what should I do next?

Father Peter had watched Ivan walk past the church. He watched him walk up the road, turn, observe, return. He heard him enter the sanctuary. Now he sat by the window of his quarters, wondering — what should I do?

There was really no alternative. He would have to go see what this stranger wanted. It certainly was not the first time a stranger had entered his church. It isn't so strange for a troubled person to find it difficult to seek help he thought; to walk past while gathering courage — then return... "But this man disturbs me..." I must be cautious.

Getting up, he entered the sanctuary.

"Good morning! You are a stranger here. I do not recall seeing you before — but please feel welcome." He studied Ivan carefully, yet trying not to be obvious. "I am Father Peter Rochovit."

"I know, thank you. I am Ivan Igonovich. It is true, I am a stranger to your parish, but I do not live far from here. I have a farm to the north, about eight kilometers." As he said it, he wondered why he gave away the location of his home. But this priest put him at ease almost immediately. Careful, he reminded himself.

"You must have started out very early. Can I offer you some tea?" Be careful of this Father Peter. Maybe he did start out early, before daylight — on the other hand, maybe the Germans let him off on the road just out of sight.

"Yes, thank you. Tea would be good."

"Let's go to my chamber and you can tell me, Mr. Igonovich, what important matter brings you here so early in the morning." Could he be sent by Gregor? If so, he will tell me.

Ivan was obviously uneasy. But his uneasiness made Father Peter more comfortable. Insecurity did not fit the German personality or that of their collaborators. He was not reassured enough to let down his guard. When Ivan couldn't find words right away, the priest continued, "Are you a Catholic, Mr. Igonovich?"

"Please, call me Ivan. No, Father, I practice no religion. At one time — Well it was long ago — I was raised Russian Orthodox — like most around here."

"Yes, we are a minority religion in Russia and the Ukraine." Strange, Father Peter thought, this puts me more at ease. It's because I think the Germans would try to trap me with someone who, at least, professed to be Catholic. "Well, then, you are not here for confession. Tell me, are you seeking sanctuary?" The question was out before the priest realized it and now he was sorry he'd asked it.

Surprised at the bluntness, but pleased at it, Ivan answered, "I am not seeking sanctuary, but I understand that if I were, I would do well to come here. If I, too, may be frank, Father, I understand your heart is in the right place."

Father Peter suddenly felt very uneasy. He'd placed himself in a vulnerable position. "I refer to sanctuary of the soul," he said. "I — I ..." he tried to find words, "I do not mean to get involved politically."

"Father," Ivan said, "I am going to gamble my life on the hunch that I've heard the truth about you. Then I'm going to leave. You will either turn me in to the Nazis, which I doubt — or you might completely ignore what I tell you—which I also doubt. I think you will find some way to react that will help my friends and me fight this oppression."

Father Peter was aghast at the sudden candor. He tried, but couldn't completely hide his shock.

"Father, I suspect that since your impassioned sermon several weeks ago, certain people have or will in the future, seek you out. There are certain of those people I am interested in.

"I don't understand," the priest said in sincerity. "What certain people?"

"Jews!"

The priest had expected almost anything but that reply. Why does this man want Jews? Is he indeed a collaborator? Is he asking me to turn Jews in to the Nazis? "Jews? Why do you want just Jews? How do you expect me to get you Jews?"

"Because the Jews have a very special problem; they cannot trust non-Jewish partisans." Ivan related the story of Moshe and the Ukrainians. "They feel—and they are correct, I'm afraid—that everyone is their enemy; but I think Jews might try to contact you. They have nowhere else to turn. And if they do, you cannot direct them to non-Jewish partisans. It would be too risky. They might end up dead after being stripped of all they own. With us they will at least have a chance."

Father Peter did not commit himself.

Ivan did not ask for commitment. He suddenly rose and started for the door. Turning back to the priest he added, "Father, I have placed my life in your hands. Please consider carefully what I have said." He told the priest how to find him at his farm. "I hope you will contact me and not the Germans. Thank you for your time."

It took several days for Father Peter to absorb all that Ivan had said. He went over and over the events of the morning, trying to find flaw, some clue that would tell him whether Ivan's message was truth or treachery. He weighed all the possibilities. "If Ivan is a collaborator..." even inactivity could be interpreted as treason by the Germans. They would expect me to report such a meeting as we had. To ignore it would be shirking *my duty* to the occupation. "Well, if that's their game, then be done with it!" There's no way I'll turn Ivan or anyone else over to the Nazis. "My decision's made for me!" On the other hand, maybe they are really trying to use him to capture Jews... "How can I be sure?" I know, I can talk to Gregor Kirtzof about it. But what if his partisans would also kill the Jews for their possessions? I don't think that possible! But listen to the gunfire from Babi Yar—that, too, I didn't think possible.

28

HILLEL..

During the second week in November, about an hour before sunrise, a knock on the door woke Ivan and Sosha. They both sat up quickly. Sosha immediately thought something was wrong at the encampment, that the knock was a partisan. Ivan thought first of Father Peter—could he have sent the Germans?

There was no chance for escape. Ivan got up, went to the door and opened it. A tall, thin man in clothes too light for the cold fall night, stood framed in the doorway.

"You are Mr. Igonovich? Mr. Ivan Igonovich?"

"Yes. And who are you? What do you want?" Ivan looked him over for any visible weapon and then looked into the darkness behind him, for accomplices. Would this turn into a robbery?

"The priest Peter Rachovit sent me; I am a Jew!"

Ivan stepped part way out the doorway, looking about more thoroughly. There was no one else. "Quick, step in!" He closed the door behind the stranger.

"You say Father Peter sent you? How did he happen to send you to me?" He was flustered, unprepared. He doubted it to be a trap, but now it was not just his life, but the lives of all the others—and Sosha's, too.

"He said you would know about it. He told me you would know what to do."

"You say you are a Jew. How can I know you are a Jew? What is your name?"

"To the Germans I can't prove I'm not a Jew and to you I have to prove I am a Jew. How do I prove either? My name is Hillel. I'm named after a famous rabbi from the past."

"I don't know — say something Jewish." Ivan felt like a fool.

The stranger looked at Ivan as if he were mad, but went ahead and said a few words in Hebrew and a few more in Yiddish. "There, does that mean anything to you?"

"No. It sounds Jewish, but I can't know for sure. I must know for sure."

Sosha watched from the darkness of the other room.

"Wait here while I get dressed."

Ivan went into the darkened room and returned moments later. "Follow me!" Ivan wanted to get the man out of the house. He would think about his next steps as they walked. He felt better when they got away from the farm. If this were a trap, getting away from the house would not alter anything; nonetheless, he felt better about it. False security is better than no security, he thought.

"Is anyone else with you?"

"No. I'm alone."

They walked toward the road and along it for about a kilometer. Ivan kept looking about to see whether they were being followed, but it was still too dark to see very far. This darkness is making me all the more paranoid, he thought. What the hell am I so afraid of? I asked the priest to send me Jews, so what did I expect? This is all making me crazy. He must think I'm crazy. I think I'm maybe crazy. So I'm crazy. Too much caution can't hurt me — us.

"I'm sure you understand my caution. If you are who you say you are, it's best for both of us."

The Jew said nothing, just followed.

Finally they came to a sharp turn in the road. As they rounded the corner Ivan led his companion abruptly into the woods. Five meters into the trees Ivan stopped. "Now we will wait quietly. Not a sound from you. If anyone is following us we will see them when they round that curve."

When no one came, Ivan began walking again. The sun started its rise, lighting their way dimly through the woods. They turned and doubled back and made circles, retraced tracks. Ivan thoroughly confused his companion. The whole time he looked and listened for followers. None appeared.

After almost an hour in the woods he started toward the new encampment. It took almost another hour to get there. When they finally arrived, Moshe and the others took a few minutes to satisfy themselves that the newcomer was indeed Jewish, a *landsman.*

"Did Father Peter warn you that you might be walking into a trap?" Ivan asked the man.

"Yes. He told me you contacted him, but that he couldn't be sure it was not a trap to uncover his activities or capture Jews in hiding—or both. I knew the chance I was taking."

"Ivan," Moshe said, in the presence of all the others, "you had no right to go to the priest on your own. We all decided that it would be too risky. You had no right. You can gamble your own life, but not ours. This time it appears to have worked out well, but it could have led to a catastrophe."

"I took every precaution..."

"You could have made a mistake," Boris interrupted. "You know our whereabouts. If they tortured you and they would have, you'd have told all."

"That's not to say you're weak," Moshe added. "Anyone can break under torture. If everyone here would go off on their own and do what they thought was right, it wouldn't be long before the Germans would have us."

Ivan realized they were right. "I'm sorry. I see what... It won't happen again. It won't."

"I for one thank God you did it," the stranger said, "and the others will agree with me."

"What others?" Moshe demanded.

All eyes were on the Jew. Ivan's eyes were wide with

surprise.

"We agreed, the priest and I, that if I found Jews, I was to return and inform him that Ivan was what he claimed. If I do not return, they will assume that I met with Nazis."

"They? Why do you say 'they?'?" Ivan insisted.

"The priest and the other Jews."

"There are more Jews?" Moshe asked.

Seventeen of us. We have gathered over the weeks, in the forests. Survivors from villages and cities all over the Ukraine—some from Poland." He paused, looked at Ivan and continued, "We didn't know where to turn for help. One of our group had heard about the priest's sentiments. We thought perhaps he could help us. Thanks to you, Ivan, he could." He looked at Moshe, "If you will have us, I will report back to the priest and get the rest of my group."

They worked out a safe way. Ivan and Sol accompanied the stranger back to bring the others. This, too, could still be a trap. If it were, Ivan, Sosha and Sol would be sacrificed. If they didn't return with the Jews by day's end the new encampment would have to be moved.

The Jewish band now numbered forty-nine. They would have to build some more huts and it was time for another supply mission.

29

ILYA...

Ilya Chuikov was a small man in his early thirties. He wore thick glasses. One lens was cracked and the metal frame held it precariously. The crack caused him to squint — and to remember. The lens had been cracked by the Nazis when they broke into his home months earlier. They'd arrested him, his wife and two children — a boy three and a girl two months old. They were immediately separated and he never saw his family again. He cherished no illusions about their survival.

The Nazis took him to the school building where he had been a mathematics teacher and threw him into the basement lunchroom where he was detained with about a hundred others — all men, all Jews. He never found out why he had been spared his family's fate. No one in the room knew why they were there.

They'd remained in the room for about an hour. There were no windows, only a ventilator shaft on one wall, about three meters up from the floor. There was only the one door he and the others were pushed through. Rather than risk being rushed by the prisoners, the Germans guarded from the outside. After a while, a few of the men started talking about the possibilities of escape. It seemed hopeless until someone suggested the vent.

"It's too small," one noted.

"Perhaps some of us could get out," countered another, not wanting to give up all hope.

"The only one who could get through there is that little man," said a third, pointing at Ilya, who was totally preoccupied with worry about his family.

"Hey! You, you, with the broken glasses!" the same man tried to get Ilya's attention. "You there, come here!"

Ilya looked up, squinting through his newly broken lens. Without the glasses he was as good as blind. The man who had called to him was motioning for him to join the group.

"What do you want of me?" Ilya asked.

"If we can get that screen off that vent up there, you think you could get through it?"

Ilya looked up at the screened vent. "Where does it go?"

"Who knows? But what do we have to lose? Maybe it leads outside. Maybe you can get out and figure a way to help us. On the other hand, you may get caught in there." He paused and then shrugged. "Will you try?"

Ilya agreed without hesitation. If he got out he might also be able to help his own family. He realized his chances of even fitting through the ventilator were slim, that he was probably crawling to his death. But what choice had he?

"Like you say, what's to lose?"

Two of the larger men lifted his frail body easily. He tugged at the screen covering the vent, which popped loose, bringing dust down on him and those below. He handed the screen down and the two men all but heaved him into the small opening. He fit, easily. After he was in, they lifted another man, small, but too large for the vent, who snapped the screen back into place.

It was cramped and dark in the shaft. As he slid along, dust flew into his nostrils. Struggling to stifle a sneeze, Ilya Chuikov snaked his way on. He came to an elbow turn in the duct. He could get his head far enough into the elbow to see the shaft's outside screen. Daylight showed through and Ilya knew freedom was probably just beyond; but he could not get his shoulders past the elbow turn. With escape not two meters away, Ilya would be forced to return to the basement room.

As he started backing down the duct, he raised more dust. It penetrated his nostrils and he sneezed before he could stop it. He was over a seam in the duct, at a point where the thin sheet metal was poorly supported. The convulsing motion of his body was more than the duct could withstand. The seam gave way and dumped Ilya into a shallow crawl space.

Stunned and sore, Ilya found himself in darkness pierced only by a sliver of light off to his left. He crawled in the loose, cool dirt under the building. The light came through a crack between two boards in what felt like a small, wooden access door.

He put his eye up to the crack. Beyond there was a German standing by a car. Probably its chauffeur waiting for his officer, Ilya thought. He knew right away where he was. The little door was one he had often seen from the outside as he walked to and from the school. He'd never paid much attention to it. Now it was his doorway to escape.

It opened, he knew, onto an alley at the side of the building, next to the faculty entrance to the school. The stairway to that entrance would give Ilya protection from the view of anyone on the street. On the other side, he would be kept from view by trash bins. Now if only that damn German would leave!

For four hours, the German remained at his spot. He kept getting in and out of the car, yawning and talking to himself or anyone else who came by and would pause a moment. He must have smoked a complete pack of cigarettes. Doesn't he have to go to the toilet—or eat—or get a drink of water? Ilya wondered. But he never left his post. Finally, after dark, Ilya heard the officer return to his car. After exchanging a few words with someone in German, which Ilya couldn't understand, the car started and drove away.

Alone with his thumping heart, Ilya waited several minutes before trying the door. It moved easily. He slowly, carefully opened it. The alley was empty. He slipped out and followed the shadows to where the trash bins stood in the alley. He saw no Germans.

Now he paused. How could he help his fellow Jews? No sooner had he started to ponder the problem than he heard a commotion at the rear of the building. The Germans were moving the Jews he had been imprisoned with into trucks. If there had been any chance to help them, it was too late now.

He could not help his family either. He couldn't even find where they'd been taken. Dejected, despondent, overcome with grief, Ilya blindly — dazed, escaped to the countryside. He made his way into the forest, like a ghost, empty and in despair.

30

PARTISANS...

By mid-January of 1942, Solomon's partisan band was a community of more than a hundred Jews. Between November and mid-January, the encampment was moved three times. Moving was a precaution Moshe thought would reduce the chances of discovery or betrayal. It happened each time a partisan disappeared, to assure the Nazis couldn't torture the camp's location out of him or her if he or she'd been captured.

As the group became larger, moving became more difficult. Sol came up with an idea that would provide maximum security without constant disruption of their community life.

"What if there were three camps. The first camp, a very mobile one, would be where supplies would be gathered for and from missions," he explained to Moshe. "We wouldn't use it for more than two or three days. New members could be brought in through it, be observed, not being told about the other camps. If there were a betrayal or if someone followed newcomers or a returning raiding party — only a few of our number would be jeopardized.

"Returning from a mission, we'd stay at the first camp for at least twelve hours; maybe more. Long enough to make any followers think it was our headquarters." Sol paused, waiting for Moshe's reaction.

"Go on, what about the second camp?"

"Camp two would be a temporary camp, too. It would house mission eligible partisans and newcomers from camp one. The new people would remain at camp two until their loyalties proved unquestionable. We'd make it look to them that this was the main camp. The second camp would be moved only if there were a capture of one of our people. However, if someone is captured, we would know that he would disclose the first camp—to minimize the torture. We would move the first camp right away, leaving enough evidence to convince the Germans he wasn't lying. It may buy him or her a less painful death.

"Unless a major mission was planned, camp two would never house more than a fourth of our number. This would reduce the chance of a crippling raid on us."

Again Sol paused. "Any question so far?"

"No. It's clear. So far I like the idea. Go on."

"Camp three would be the main camp, permanent community. It will be deep in the forest. Somewhere in an area of wilderness, far from any civilization … at least a day's travel from the nearest road or village. All routes to this camp would be posted with lookouts. A warning system would give us at least three hours to prepare for defense or evacuation. All the children, elderly and non combatants would stay there permanently.

"Those scheduled for a mission would leave camp three and set up a new camp one. Camp three would be far too remote to be a staging area for any mission."

"Where do you envision the camp three being?" Moshe asked.

"I have no idea. The site will have to be carefully chosen and very remote. These forests around Kiev are vast. People have been lost in them for weeks. We must find a place deep—hours deep into the wilderness— where we can build a permanent community—a secret community—under tree cover so as not to be seen from the air. And it must be defensible. Such a place might be hard to find, but it will also be hard for the Germans to find."

31

A VILLAGE IN THE FOREST...

As soon as the site had been selected, the number one priority was to build shelters. Every person, man, woman, child, was pressed into working at whatever tasks capable. Snow was already in the air. Nights were cold but not yet freezing. Days were chilly. They thanked God that this winter of 1941 was beginning later than usual, but they also realized that late-starting winters were sometimes the bitterest when they finally did strike.

In four days, they had enough shelters built to house everyone in an emergency, should a storm strike. Over the next few days, they completed the rest of the necessary buildings.

Shelters at both the first and second camps would be makeshift, temporary, usually lean-to type structures made of cut tree limbs, fallen leaves and evergreen boughs. Sometimes trenches were dug and lived in, covered over by the same materials, but as the days and nights became colder digging trenches in the more shallow frozen ground became impossible. Any natural shelter, such as a cave, was utilized when possible. Once in a while, they used deserted farm buildings and villages for the first and second camps.

The main camp was another matter. Everything had some sign of permanency. Houses were built among the trees to give added protection from the weather, but more important, protection from observation of men in overflying aircraft. Built simply, the houses were like those used by Ukrainian peasants for centuries. The average building was about five meters by three meters and more underground than above. It could be put up in a day or two by several men, before the ground was too frozen.

First, a hole was dug about four feet deep by the dimensions of the building to be constructed. The hole looked like that dug for the foundation of a house, but empty of the foundation itself. Then logs were built up on the ground at the edge of the excavation, to a height of about a meter or a little less. From outside the structure looked like a short log cabin. A thatched roof was added. The earth, which had been excavated, was piled outside the logs for added insulation and protection. When finished, the houses looked like low mounds of dirt with thatch in the middle. There was a vent for smoke from a fireplace at one end of the room. Inside it was dark. The distance from the dirt floor to the roof was about two meters, with the roof having just enough slope to carry off rainwater or melting snow.

The primitive structures gave excellent protection from the cold of winter blizzards. In the hot summer months, if the Jews were still there, the huts would be cool. Unmarried men and women would live dormitory style, eight to ten per building. The goal was to eventually have a shelter for each family. Until that was possible, young children stayed in dorms with their mothers and older boys lived in men's dorms with their fathers. They built huts at a feverish pace to house all the families before the ground froze for the winter.

There was one hut built and designated as headquarters, another synagogue and school. Supplies for the camp were kept in three other buildings. There was a common kitchen, though it was used mostly by the single partisans. Families usually preferred to cook for themselves. There was also a hospital building—as yet seldom used. By Chanukah of 1941, December 24th, all was finished.

A short time after the three camp system was established Solomon started to keep a diary. Events demanded documentation. Certainly the Germans wouldn't keep honest chronicles of their atrocities. If there were no survivors, how would the world ever know? It was a common fear among the Jews that the world would never learn the truth about their extermination. Many besides Solomon started diaries, hoping they would be found later, should the worst happen.

The new life in the forest, the daily chore of survival, the inhumanity of the situation, all produced changes in the partisans. The times made changes in Sol, too. He now wore a beard. The warm sparkle in his eyes didn't disappear, but he developed a bitterness common to those who had lost so much. His humor often turned sarcastic. It was never directed at individuals, but at the world outside the encampment. The hard work of survival made his body strong and sinuous.

By the beginning of 1942, he matured remarkably. People respected his opinions in spite of his youth, but then much of the activity and leadership was carried out by the young.

For most of the Jews, camp three was the first place they had ever been free of the constant abuses of the Christian world. And in those first few months of forming the Jewish community in the forest, Rachel became an increasingly important part of Solomon's life.

32

BUILDING A COMMUNITY
REBUILDING LIVES...

Now that there was a mutual trust between Father Peter and Ivan, the priest started to send him many escaping Jews. It was a dangerous situation for the priest, one he could do nothing about. When refugees came to him, because they had nowhere else to turn, he took every precaution but could never be really sure he wasn't being entrapped. Fortunately, the Germans had so many other problems that they only watched one facet of the priest's activities, his sermons. Each Sunday, the same German came to the worship service, sat attentively through the sermon and then reported back to his superiors that the priest was being cooperative with the occupation.

Father Peter watched the man during prayers and was impressed that he took the services seriously, participating sincerely in the service. But the priest never thought for a second that the "good" Christian would not turn him in for the least infraction.

The reports temporarily satisfied the Nazis. However, Father Peter and the partisans had no way of knowing whether the Germans considered the Churchman a threat or not. To them, every shadow hid an enemy observer.

Security and suspicion were problems shared by all resistance groups. But there was one matter unique to the partisan Jews, the policy of accepting all Jews into the community. There was no exception. Age, sex, health, disabilities or handicaps were not even considered. If a refugee was Jewish, that refugee was welcomed. Other groups could select only those capable of fighting, but the Jews could not, would not refuse refuge to any Jew. To do so would mean a death sentence. Outside the partisan camp was enemy territory, inhabited by Nazis and anti-Semitic Ukrainians.

This policy actually became an asset rather than a liability to the Jews. Others had a single objective in their activities, the disruption and destruction of the German war machine. The Jews had not only that goal, but the goal of survival—both for the individual Jew and for Judaism at large. This difference was reflected in the Nazi attitude toward their enemies. Gentiles were executed because of political philosophy or military action against the Reich. Jews were executed because they were Jews. Hitler had singled out only one other group for the final solution, for genocide—the Gypsies.

The policy of accepting all Jews kept the Jewish partisans more human, more humane. The permanent camp with its children, old people and families was a cross section of society. It constantly reminded the fighters what they were fighting for and provided a civilized place to go after they'd finished their missions. For the refugees, it was an unbelievable blessing—alone in a hostile world—having lost everything and with little hope for escape or survival, suddenly finding themselves in a community of other Jews, functioning with relative security deep in the Ukrainian forests. It was a community free of non-Jews, anti-Semites and few of them could remember ever feeling so free of the abuses and barbs they had suffered daily in the Christian world.

"Strange," Sol said to Rachel one day, "how under these conditions, I feel a peace and a freedom I've never known before. Not until I got away from the Christians did I realize what bastards most of them have been to us. Besides Ivan and Sosha and that priest, Father Peter, I can't think of but two or three that didn't cause us grief."

Rachel was thoughtful a moment, "That's a horrible

thing to say, Sol, but I can't see that my experiences have been that different. I wonder if it's that way everywhere?"

"It wouldn't be if we had a Jewish nation."

"Now you sound like one of those Zionist workers that used to come to our village before..."

"I heard them speak a few times, too. Didn't impress me much then; makes more sense now."

When refugees finally reached the family camp, they were taken into the community and made to contribute in some way. Many had begun to doubt their self worth, some on the verge of suicide. The Nazi program of dehumanizing the Jews by verbal and physical abuse worked well on its victims. Their new responsibilities in the family camp reversed this process. It helped them to feel their lives were worthwhile — necessary.

Early in the formation of the family camp, a group of Jews came to the band. They had started out in Poland ten months earlier. At that time, they had numbered twenty-nine. Their original destination was Palestine. They were a Zionist youth group and they had intended to walk to Palestine, as many Jews had done before them. For ten months, they eluded the Germans, forced farther and farther south and east, until they were found by Solomon's Jews. Twenty of their number had perished.

These young Zionists intended to form a **kibbutz** when they finally reached the *Promised Land* and had trained for years in pioneering techniques. Their training was invaluable to the establishment and survival of the community. It would be even more valuable in the spring when their agricultural skills helped grow their food. Now, in the winter they were already planning their crops.

33

GRANDPAPA
PAPA & SON...

Three Men of Letters...

About the same time the nine Zionists arrived, there came to the camp three Jews from Kiev. These three were very orthodox, a grandfather who was nearly ninety, his son who was well past sixty and his grandson who was forty six. They had escaped the city before the Babi Yar roundup and miraculously survived living in the woods until Father Peter directed them to Ivan. They'd sought the priest when they'd heard some peasants speak of his still-famous sermon.

When they first arrived, no one realized what extreme importance these three, elderly orthodox Jews would have. Though he hadn't known them in Kiev, it was Sol who discovered their great talent—printing.

These men represented three generations of printers and had run a family-owned printing shop in Kiev. When the Germans occupied the city, the shop was immediately confiscated—the written word being the greatest threat to any occupation force.

The old man was retired and spent his time at his first love, reading. He retained much of his old skill, however. His son, being a master printer, was capable of the finest reproduction work anywhere. But the greatest talent had surfaced in the grandson. He was not only a master printer but also a master engraver. Solomon's first question was, "Can you reproduce official-looking papers—papers like passes, identity cards, documents and letters?"

The youngest of the three, the grandson, answered with a chuckle that was almost arrogant, "It would be simple if we had the equipment and proper paper—but we are here and it is there."

"Are you certain you had everything in the shop that you would need?" Sol asked eagerly.

This time the father answered, "Our shop was the finest in Kiev. It was set up most efficiently. The Germans would be fools not to use it. If I'm right, there will be plenty of official paper, ink and engravings of official letterheads and seals."

A mission was immediately planned.

The next day Ivan and Sosha went into Kiev to the address of the printing shop. It was still there, not open to the public. The Germans ran it for the occupation. It wasn't a big plant. Ivan guessed that one truckload could move everything out of the building. He reported their findings back to the planning committee and the mission was put into operation.

Winter operations were dangerous business because tracks were easily followed in the deep snow. Most partisan groups chose the best defense—to wait out the winter in hiding. But Solomon's three camp system allowed his group to function year round. Even during the winter, they averaged one or two missions a week.

Stage one of this latest operation was to obtain a German truck. Four men waited along the road to Irpen and selected the first solitary, large truck which fit their needs to come along. The Germans didn't send many trucks without convoy, but there were always a few. With this truck, they got a bonus of three rifles, several rounds of compatible ammunition, three uniforms from the occupants, two grenades and a truckload of barbed wire. They had no immediate use for the barbed wire, but it was stored away. Everything was kept, no matter how unlikely. Improvisation was a key to survival. And if they couldn't find a use for an item, well, everything had a value on the black market. They could always trade for things that were needed.

As soon as the truck was captured, four other partisans initiated stage two by dressing in German uniforms from the growing captured military wardrobe. One played the role of officer, the others became enlisted men. Four others dressed as Ukrainian workers — collaborators. Within the hour after stealing the truck, the masqueraders drove it to Kiev.

They entered the city at dusk. With all the *chutzpa* they could muster, they drove the main streets across half the metropolis, turned and rumbled three blocks up the proper side street, then steered into an alley behind the shop.

Hans Geller, the partisan dressed as the officer, spoke perfect German. Before escaping the advancing Nazi front, Hans lived in Berlin where he'd been a chemistry teacher. Now, Hans hopped down from the high cab of a German military truck behind a Ukrainian print shop full of enemy military men. He strode to the alley door and gave it three authoritative knocks. When it opened to reveal a German corporeal, Hans mustered all the arrogance he could.

"I am Major Strauss. We have been informed that this print shop is a target for a partisan raid tonight!" He hoped that only he could hear the nervousness in his voice. To cover his anxiety he spoke even louder, more arrogantly. "Quickly — we must prepare a trap for the swine!" As he spoke, he motioned his crew into the shop. "There are only three of you in the shop now?"

"Yes. That is all we ever have here."

"I will have to do something about that. It is a wonder those bastard partisans haven't hit you during the day."

Hans Geller began to enjoy his role now, all anxiety dissipating. If these three Germans gave them any trouble they'd be eliminated; if not they'd be used. He strode through the plant, thankful that none of the occupants were officers. It's easier to intimidate enlisted men, he thought thankfully.

"First, men, move out everything that they could find helpful to them! Nothing useful must fall into the enemy's hands."

Overwhelmed by the invasion, the three Germans began helping to move equipment. Outside, the last man to enter the building cut the telephone wires. Hans Geller played his role well and did none of the work. He just kept yelling orders to keep the real Germans rattled.

With ten men working, they had everything they wanted and more, in less than ten minutes — everything but the presses. There were two of them — one large and a second smaller, hand operated proof press. In another five minutes, the small proof press was on the truck.

As quickly as they had entered the building, the partisans left; but not before they dealt with the three Germans. Hans, who'd lived all his life in peace and two others, who'd also never expected lives of violence, skillfully cut the soldier's throats. There was no hesitation. They knew it was necessary to insure success of the mission. There was a lot of German territory to drive through before they were safe. Any alarm or identification of the band and truck could spell disaster.

The Germans had no weapons, but the partisans took their identification papers and uniforms, leaving the three bodies clad in underwear.

Bolstered by the success of their raid, they drove back out of the city with twice the chutzpa with which they had entered. Only for a moment did Hans dwell on the thought that he had to take lives to make the mission a success.

Seven days passed before the printing press and equipment reached the family camp. Thus, the three *"men of letters,"* as Sol called them in his diary, busied themselves. They had all the tools of their trade and the paper stock from the print shop proved to be official German paper. It took them a day to set up and on the second day they were busy forging identity papers and all the documents necessary to allow them more freedom and safety in their movements about the occupied country.

34

A ROMANCE...

"I think I love her!" Solomon wrote early on in his diary this day. He meant Rachel. Now, in February of 1942, he no longer had any doubts.

Rachel had a simple beauty. She was fair and blue eyed with black, full and naturally curly hair. The combination was stunning. Her tall, slim body made her looks more frail than she really was. She seemed at first a shy and dependent person, but was, in fact, quite self reliant. Though not a leader of people like Dovka, the leaders could rely on Rachel too.

When Sol and his three new friends first found her group in the forest and brought them back to the cave, she was attracted to Solomon and he recognized it. He encouraged her, but thought of the relationship as one of protector and friend.

As time went on, though, he found she was giving at least as much as he was. Stable and attractive, Rachel was easy for Sol to talk to. Like most survivors of atrocities such as Babi Yar, Sol had denied himself the necessary grieving. Rachel recognized his tenseness and undercurrent of depression and forced him to talk of his past, his loss, his guilt, his hate.

Her own past was no less tragic than Solomon's, of course. No Jew at that time, in those places, had any special claim on tragedy. As they shared their stories with one another, a bond grew and love followed.

35

MAJOR HANS OBERMAN...

Major Hans Oberman sat in his office, irritated because his superiors had warned him to curb the growing guerrilla activity in the area.

At first, there were only isolated incidents, the enormous explosions and fire in the Kreshchetik, a few minor thefts and killings. Then there was the incident of Father Peter's sermon which he'd put an end to himself. That's probably why they dropped all the rest of their partisan problems in my lap, he speculated.

Anti-occupation activity was discouraged by severe penalties to the perpetrators—death to them and their entire families.

Then organized activities began.

There was the raid on the supply depot at Irpen, which cost six German lives and nine truckloads of goods. For that action Major Oberman rounded up six hundred Kievites and had them shot as reprisal. "One hundred civilians," he made it known, "will be shot for every German soldier who is killed!" Surely that will deter the partisan activities, he thought. He was wrong. After that sabotage, raids, killings and disruption of troop and supply movements steadily increased. Heavy reprisals don't seem to disturb these partisans. Surely they are the Bolsheviks.

"Reprisals are not enough, Major," Hans Oberman's Colonel explicitly pointed out. "I suggest that in addition to your reprisals, you start measures to capture the scoundrels. The only way to stop these partisans is to exterminate them. They are just like rats, Gypsies and

Jews. We have plenty of room for all of them in Babi Yar. But Jews and Gypsies are easy to catch—rats are more difficult." He looked to see what impact his words had on Oberman. Then he added sarcastically, "You might even have to get out of your office or your mistress's bed to capture them!"

"Yes sir."

"I suggest you make it your *first* order of business! Do you understand me?"

"Yes sir!"

"Good. You are dismissed."

This was not the way Oberman was used to being talked to. He was deeply humiliated, especially since he considered the Colonel a boor and imbecile. He knew the Colonel was passing on to him what he, himself, had gotten from his superiors. It had probably been passed down the entire chain of command. But it ended with Oberman. Failure to get the job done would be borne by him alone.

Yes, Major Hans Oberman was very irritated as he sat in his office mulling over his problem. Ordering six hundred people to their deaths is easy. I can do that with a signature. I can do it before breakfast and have the rest of the day to myself. Why don't those inhuman bastards learn that their deeds are costing their countrymen's lives? Don't they value the lives of their own people?

Now he would have to be inconvenienced. It would have been so much easier to raise the reprisal rate to two hundred to one, but the Colonel would not hear of it. "Capture those scoundrels!" he'd ordered.

Oberman decided he would have to set a trap for these partisans. Once they were out of the way he could return to the simpler task of executing civilians. This had been for him a safe and comfortable war until now. Get this problem over with and it would be again, he thought.

Hans Oberman had come from an old, aristocratic German family. He'd been to the finest schools, wanted for nothing. No deep interests led him into no profession. He'd always hunted new pleasures and because of that, he'd developed a broad and perverse body of knowledge. His delightful conversation made him wonderful company.

All this, in addition to his totally amoral nature, made Hans Oberman an ideal candidate for promotion within the SS.

Three hundred Kievites had just been rounded up and executed in reprisal for three Germans found dead the night before in a gutted print shop. As furor over those reprisals started to die down, word spread about a special troop transport train due to pass through Kiev in about two weeks. Fifty new pilots were to pass through the city on their way to airfields near the Russian front to relieve or replace veterans killed, injured or furloughed.

These men, a special squadron, entered flight school on a day when **Herman Goering** made a formal inspection with heavy news coverage. In his honor the group had been named the **"Goering Squadron."** Publicity followed them all the way through training and Herman Goering took a special interest in them. The replacements would spend one night in Kiev. To pay Herman Goering homage, preparations were being made to satisfy "his favorites" every pleasure while in the city. The exact date, time and train were to be kept secret for security reasons.

Ivan was in Kiev two days after the story of the squadron broke. The next day the family camp held a conference.

Moshe began, "Ivan has gotten word to us of a train coming through Kiev with a special squadron of pilots headed for the Russian front. They are known as the Goering Squadron. If we could sabotage that squadron, wouldn't that be a fitting present for that egomaniac Goering?"

"So what is to stop us?" Boris asked.

"Blowing up the train will be no problem," Sol replied. We're very proficient at that. The problem will be to get the date, route and time."

"That's right," Moshe agreed. "Without that information, our skill is useless. So I will appoint two teams. Those of you who can move about Kiev with relative safety, I'll send to gather information. Sol, you can't go into the city for fear you'll be recognized. You'll move down to camp one and gather the information the others bring back. Boris, Dovka, you go into Kiev with three others and gather what intelligence you can.

"In the meantime, my group will plan the actual mission which will depend on the information you return to us."

Sol had the proper papers made up for the team going into Kiev. The three men of letters had them in hours; identification papers, food coupons, work papers, all necessary to pass a sidewalk inspection at any soldier's whim.

They went into town with Ivan. He arranged for them to stay with Gregor Kirtzof and his family. Ivan met Gregor through Father Peter. Now an opportunity arose to use Gregor's facilities and contacts. It was not a step taken lightly. It was the first time the Jews depended on a non-Jewish partisan, other than Sosha and Ivan, for their own security. They were very nervous about their vulnerability.

Once in the city, the Jews spread out into various crowded sections to watch and listen. Before they parted, Gregor warned, "If military vehicles come, get off the street immediately. Go into a building, down an alley, up a side street—somehow vanish. It could be a roundup." He paused a moment. "And be off the streets by six thirty curfew every night or you may be shot on sight. I remind you that it is not just Jews that have to fear the Germans now."

Gregor was nervous, too. These Jews were not the only ones vulnerable. He knew that if even one of them were caught, torture would probably bring forth the information that he was involved with them. Then he and his entire family would end up in Babi Yar. He knew he himself was no threat to the Jews, but he doubted anyone could stand up forever to the tortures of the Nazis. He was at great risk, too.

Dovka went into the marketplace with Ivan. There they split up. She double checked her forged papers, indistinguishable from Ivan's real documents. She carried very little money. No one had much money. What she carried was real. The partisans had considerable amounts of coin and currency taken from Germans they had killed. Compared with the citizens of Kiev, they were well off.

She moved once around the marketplace, first to fix in her mind escape routes. Then she passed through it slowly, purposely heading into the biggest crowds. That was where the conversations were and like flocking birds there was security in numbers. There was hardly anything to buy. People sat about hawking their belongings to buy food. But little food was available, even if they did have money. Long lines huddled in front of the few food stores still open. Dovka happened by a bakery at the moment the baker tried to close his door. The line to his shop was still long; people had been waiting for hours. Those nearest the door, who had been waiting longest, protested loudly.

"What do you mean you're out of bread?" cried the closest man. "It's not yet two o'clock! We've waited three hours and now you tell us you're out of bread?"

"Don't complain to me!" the baker shouted back, showing no sympathy for the unfortunate shoppers. "I only have what I can make. Complain to the commandant! Maybe he'll listen. We've had our supplies cut for the next eight days because of those damned pilots. We're rationed so they can have their fancy party! So tell your troubles to the Germans. Maybe they'll invite you to the affair." He laughed in the man's face as he slammed and locked his door.

"Eight days," Dovka said under her breath.

She was filled with excitement. About four forty- five, she met Ivan again. She could hardly wait to tell him what she'd heard, but he spoke first.

"A week from tomorrow," Ivan exclaimed!

"Yes," she said, surprised. "Eight days."

"How do you know?"

After hearing her story, Ivan added, "That's much the same way I found out. I overheard two women complaining of a cut in their meat supply."

"Everyone in town seems to know the day."

"That's when they are celebrating the pilots. They'll be coming in during the twenty four hours before. Now, if we can just piece together the other details as easily."

In the basement of Gregor's home that evening, everyone compared stories. Each confirmed that the Goering Squadron would arrive in seven to eight days. Ivan went back to Sol with the information while the rest stayed in the city. Ivan was anxious to get back to Sosha.

For four days, the Jews risked their lives on the streets of Kiev. But they found out nothing new. On the evening of the fourth day they were depressed and frustrated. It was then that Gregor's father came in with a newspaper.

"I have it!" He was waving the newspaper excitedly over his head. "It's right here!"

"What? Let's see," Gregor said.

"A soldier threw it away and I picked it up," Gregor's father explained. "It's their armed forces paper. They all read it. It's written in German, but someone told me what it says."

"Let me see that," Dovka demanded, "I read German." She looked at the article. "Goering Squadron in Warsaw," she translated aloud. The Goering Squadron was being sent through Poland to boost morale there. It took a few seconds to sink in. "Of course, now we know the route. There's only one train that runs direct from Warsaw."

"Now we know the day and the track!" Gregor announced.

"I don't think we should stay to discover the exact time," Dovka said. "That information won't be on the street. We can assume they'll arrive in the early morning if they leave Warsaw in the evening or arrive here in the late afternoon if they leave Warsaw in the morning. It's narrowed down to a twelve hour period. The mission will be a little more risky, but I don't think we should waste time trying to get more accurate information. It will just put us all at risk."

The Jews thanked Gregor and his family. It was early morning by the time they arrived at the first camp. After the Jews left Kiev, all the local papers carried the story of the Goering Squadron being in Warsaw.

36

A PARTY FOR THE GOERING SQUADRON...

The morning the Squadron was to leave Warsaw, Major Hans Oberman awaited his Colonel's call. He remembered how uneasy he'd felt at their last meeting. But today would be different. He'd give his report, put his plan into action, accomplish his task and in a few days things would be pleasant again. The call came and Oberman strode into the Colonel's office.

"Well, I assume you have a plan to trap those partisans!" the Colonel said expectantly.

"Yes, Colonel, I have a trap, part of which has already been implemented. The wheels are already in motion," he said looking at his watch.

"Don't you think you should have cleared it with me first?" There was anger in his voice.

"You can stop it if you like, but I had to take care of the preliminaries. There was no time to check with you. If you like the plan," Oberman said confidently, "and it works, I will gladly let it be known that you were instrumental in it. If you don't like it, it can still be scrapped."

The Colonel's tense face slowly relaxed. He motioned Oberman to go on.

"As you know, sir, there has been a security leak regarding the Goering Squadron."

"I am aware of that—painfully so." He squinted and sourly pursed his lips.

"Colonel, I am that leak."

"What?" The Colonel flew to his feet. "Are you crazy?

Are you trying to get us all demoted ... shot?"

"I hope not, sir," Oberman said, a smug smile on his face.

The Colonel sputtered and growled. "Explain yourself! This had better be good!"

"As of now, they are not coming." Oberman said quietly. "Instead—unless I change the orders in twenty minutes—a trainload of Jews will leave Warsaw."

"Jews?" cried the Colonel in disbelief. "We're receiving a trainload of Jews? What do we want with more Jews?"

Oberman just waited a few seconds, letting the Colonel settle down. He knew he'd have to explain it all, point by point, to the old fool. Stupid old fart, he thought.

"Colonel, I doubt we'll ever get them here. When the Goering Squadron's arrival became public knowledge, I thought, surely every partisan within a hundred kilometers would be after the train's route and schedule. So I rerouted them—but not their train. My guess is the partisans will sabotage that train and when they do, we'll have the bastards. Now," he remarked acidly, "if you think the partisans will not try something, we can still let the Squadron come by the original route."

The Colonel disliked Oberman's sarcasm, but he liked the plan.

"Go on, Major."

"Well, these partisans have always worked a fifty kilometer area north of Kiev. There are five excellent places there to sabotage the train. Right now we have lookouts at each of those places. As soon as one of them reports partisan activity, we will converge and wait. Either the partisans will kill a trainload of Jews and we'll take them; or if the train gets through, we still may get the partisans; and the Jews go to Babi Yar."

The Colonel was smiling now but still had a few questions.

"What about the train crew?"

"All Poles," Oberman returned the smile. "Even the guards are Polish collaborators. We can afford to sacrifice three dozen Poles for this plan."

"But what if the partisans have spies in Warsaw? What if they're warned?"

"They may well have a spy system in Warsaw," the Major conceded. "But the spies will see what they think are pilots boarding the train. The Jews have been on the train for twenty hours already. They were put on before the train entered the station." Oberman again looked at his watch. "Right now, thirty Polish collaborators in Luftwaffe uniforms are boarding that train to guard it en route."

Satisfied with himself, Oberman continued, "We will have our party tonight." He chuckled, "But we will be celebrating something more than the Goering Squadron!"

The Colonel joined him in laughter.

37

A DOUBLE SURPRISE...

While Major Hans Oberman and his Colonel toasted *their* plan, the partisans left camp one, led by Boris, who had been chosen to command this important mission. They headed for the spot selected to sabotage the train, a trestle about thirty kilometers north of Kiev. If the explosion didn't kill the Squadron, they reasoned, the long fall would. Traveling with caution through the area took several hours. As soon as they arrived at the appointed spot they set the charges on the bridge, unaware they were being watched.

Just before dusk, an ear shattering explosion shook the earth. The trestle and train just steaming onto it fell into the deep, narrow gorge. When the dust finally settled there was silence. Each witness was momentarily transfixed. Finally Boris broke the spell.

"Down to the train; let's finish our job and get the hell out of here! Gather weapons and anything else we can use."

They came out of their hiding places. It was difficult climbing down into the steep gorge. It took them several minutes. The watching Germans didn't reveal themselves. A major was enjoying his view of the scene. Hans Oberman took charge of his operation. "Not a sound until I fire my pistol," he passed the order along from man to man. They'd been told it before, but he wanted to make sure. He was savoring. "I can't wait to see their faces when they find those dead Jews," he whispered to his Lieutenant."

Now the Lieutenant understood why Oberman had let

the guerrillas blow the bridge. They could have taken them before, left the bridge intact, saved the train. "Won't this disrupt our transportation for days?" he asked the Major.

"We have plenty of Ukrainians to put to work on a new trestle. It's worth a little inconvenience and rerouting to teach them a lesson. Besides, they have no hope of escape from that deep gorge. We'll be able to pick them off like target practice."

The Lieutenant dropped the subject.

When the first men reached the bottom and looked into the broken rail cars, at the carnage, they realized something was wrong. "Boris," one called, "These men are tied to their seats—those not torn loose by the fall."

"These aren't pilots," another called. "They look like prisoners. My God, I think they're Jews!"

Then another voice called down, "Halt! Do not move! You are surrounded! Drop your weapons!"

Boris and his men looked up from the bottom and sides of the gorge. Confusion gripped them as they looked into the muzzles of fifty two automatic weapons trained down on them.

A long second passed. Then Boris yelled, "Run for cover!"

At the same moment, the Major who had screamed the commands fired his pistol.

There was little cover to run for. Most of the Jews were still on the walls of the cliff, climbing down the difficult face when the Germans opened fire. Most were unable to return a single shot. The few men who reached the bottom were able to duck into the wrecked train for momentary protection. In a few minutes, when all their comrades had been shot off the wall, they found themselves the target of overwhelming odds, four men and a woman under the guns of fifty two Germans.

For the next few minutes, high caliber ammunition showered the remnants of the train—the remnants in the train. Most devastating were the grenades dropped into the wreckage from above. When the partisans tried to return fire, they only disclosed their positions and invited a new barrage.

Finally, no gunfire returned from the wreckage.

There were nineteen dead partisans and one severely wounded. Then a single shot rang out—Boris Spovinski finished what four German bullets had not quite accomplished.

That evening, in the officers' club, the Germans celebrated the deaths of a hundred Jews from Warsaw, thirty six unfortunate Polish collaborators and train crew and twenty partisans.

No one knew, yet, that all the partisans were Jews.

38

GRIEF & GUILT...

The exact facts did not get back to the family camp until Gregor took a newspaper from Kiev to Father Peter, who took it to Ivan, who in turn carried it to the family camp. Until then, the partisans knew only that their brethren had not returned to the second camp.

Moshe, Uri, Solomon, Dovka, Rachel, Ivan and several others sat in the main meeting hut, mourning. Twenty of their friends were dead—among them Boris.

"God has given us good fortune until now," Uri said.

"Yes," Moshe agreed. "But that makes this all the more painful. We've had few injuries and only three deaths. I guess this was bound to happen sooner of later."

"But how did it happen?" Dovka asked. "They were waiting. We stepped right into their trap. Do you suppose Gregor informed on them?"

Ivan dreaded this question. He'd asked it himself. After all, it was *he* who persuaded the Jews to take another gentile, an entire gentile family, into their confidence.

"But how did they know where we would strike?" Sol asked. "That decision wasn't made until after our people returned from Kiev. Gregor knew nothing of that. No, this was more than simple betrayal. We betrayed ourselves by forgetting our enemies aren't fools." He paused thoughtfully, "If it wasn't a trap from the beginning, why did the train have no pilots—only Jews on board? It's like the newspaper says..."

"They could have changed their plans after finding out," Dovka interrupted, arguing, "and Gregor could still have been in on it!"

"I know how you feel about gentiles," Ivan said, "and especially Gregor. But I think he was not involved. Gregor has no idea of how many of us there are or that we have more than one camp. Father Peter and I and Sosha would all have been arrested already. The Germans were clever, yes — but I think they acted without Gregor's help."

The others were not convinced.

After a short silence, Sol spoke, "We are not victims of Goering's ego, but our own. Our motives were stupid. This was a mission of vengeance, not necessity."

"In these times, vengeance *is* a necessity," Rachel angrily interjected. "And would we feel any better if they had died for another reason? We have a right to grieve, but let's keep a proper perspective. The world has condemned our people for centuries of not fighting back — now you would condemn us for our retaliation. You have no right to add guilt to our grief!"

"And what of the Jews on the train; are we to feel no guilt over plunging them to their deaths?"

"May I ask you, Solomon," Rachel replied, "where do you think they were headed. Yes, I grieve for them, too. But we did not kill them! The Nazis could have trapped us without filling the train with Jews. That was their sick little joke! They probably made wagers on whether they'd make it to Babi Yar. Think of the terror and pain we saved them. Sol, you know what that trip into the ravine would have been like for them. Would you wish that on anyone? Would you go through that again for an extra few hours of life? Do you have any doubt that they were headed for the same thing?"

Rachel was being purposely brutal. Everyone in the room was headed toward the same depression as Solomon. They had been shocked into it — they would have to be shocked out of it. Rachel was sensitive to the complications of grief turned on one's self.

Dovka went around the now silent room, pouring fresh tea.

Sol sat looking into his cup. The perplexing, haunting thought returned to him as it had frequently in the past... Why me? Why me? Why was I chosen for life while all those others were murdered? Why me at Babi Yar? Why me instead of the twenty on the mission? Why me instead of those on the train?

Dovka poured tea into his empty glass, snapping him back from his thoughts. He looked up at her.

"Thank you, Dovka."

She smiled back at him briefly and went on to the others.

Solomon's eyes scanned the room. Did anyone else feel guilty? As his gaze traveled the room, he realized that almost everyone here was a remnant. No one in that room had any family left. All of their pasts had been annihilated, murdered, buried or burned by the Nazis. Not because they had been enemies. Not because they had been hostile to the Germans; only because they had been Jews.

Why have we been spared? Why has God done this to us? No answer came. Where is God? Can it be He doesn't know? No answer. His thoughts rambled. And as usual with such thoughts, some were logical and some were not; some were realistic, some not; some made sense, most did not. Are we, the survivors, the fortunate or the unfortunate? Have those who died earned the right to go somewhere better? Must we earn the right to die? Is *that* God's plan? The faithful would say we have to earn a better world. How hard it is to keep faith in these times! Perhaps God is testing our faith. Will we ever pass the test? My parents, grandpa, my brothers and sister—did they pass the test—or was it failure? Why them and not me? If the reward is after death, why does the **Torah** tell us, *"Choose Life"*? God gives us the Law, *"Choose Life."* Is that why we cling? Are we too obedient to die—or do we lack the faith to die well?

He found no answers.

Someone's sighing brought Sol back to the reality of the room. Everyone was silent with thought — looking into cups, gazing into space — asking themselves their own questions... Were they finding answers?

Why do we choose life? But *I* didn't choose! It was chosen for me! Thrust upon me! Some of these people are here because they chose and acted. They escaped by their own cunning and action. But all I did was slip. They were killing all of us — and only I slipped. Pure luck! Pure luck? To be one in a hundred thousand — was it chance or was I chosen?

The last thought overwhelmed him.

How presumptuous! How can I think that?

But the thought was there...

39

MESSAGE ON THE WIND...

It was an overcast day.

A constant, chilling wind blew through Babi Yar, biting hard at the naked bodies of the "enemies of the Reich" still being marched to the pit.

The same wind carried its persistent message out of the ravine, over the woods, to the church of Father Peter. He, too, sat in deep depression, distraught over the catastrophic mission. He wondered if the Jews felt they had been betrayed. He had faith that neither Gregor nor his family had betrayed them, but how could the Jews be expected to believe? He'd come to understand why Jews doubted the good will of Christians. He could not escape the sound of gunfire that drifted to his ears daily.

"Dear God, let that sound drift to the ears of the Holy See... Let the Vatican hear, Dear God. They are silent enough, so they should be able to hear. Let them hear, too! Then, perhaps, they will not be so silent," he muttered through clenched teeth toward the icon hanging on his chamber wall.

He could hold back no longer. Again he wrote to his superiors.

40

SURVIVOR'S GUILT...

The same wind that plagued Father Peter brought a violent storm to the area. It was nearly the end of the winter, but twenty inches of snow fell on the family camp and the wind drifted it to several feet more in places. It made travel impossible. Ivan was stranded at the family camp. The total isolation depressed the partisans further. A mission would have diverted their thoughts, but the weather kept them confined with their torment.

Solomon was preoccupied with the ghosts of all those who he'd lost. The thoughts drove him deeper and deeper into thoughts of death. *Perhaps I've not given the Angel of Death a fair chance to reach me. Have I unconsciously avoided hazardous situations? Have I volunteered often enough? I've never hesitated to go when called on... Why have I been so lucky? Not even a scratch... Or is it more than luck? Death seems to ignore me. Does Death only want those God loves?*

Rachel felt his melancholia, his total immersion in survivor's guilt and torment; common among those whose loved ones and friends had perished leaving them the only remaining.

"Solomon, we have an obligation," she said one day. "We've an obligation to those whose lives were stolen from them. I do not believe God has forgotten them — or us. And we must never forget them. We must survive to make sure the rest of the world never forgets them. And believe me, if we are not there to remind the world, the world will forget as quickly as possible. We must survive to be the conscience of the world. Our lives have gained meaning through their deaths. We cannot shirk our responsibility now."

Sol heard but did not answer.

There was sadness in Rachel's eyes. She put her head on Sol's shoulder, her arms about him.

"Poor Solomon, my poor Solomon. It's all hitting you at once. You've put it out of your mind all these months and now it's pouring over you — drowning you."

41

TEMPTING FATE...

The storm came and passed.

Sol's depression persisted.

A path was finally cleared to the second camp, but they had to wait to send out a mission. It would have been too easy to follow them back in the snow.

Sol volunteered for the first mission and for as many missions after that as he could. By April of 1942, he was a seasoned guerrilla, having gone on almost every operation since the train incident. At times he wouldn't reach the family camp for two weeks, coming in from one mission and volunteering for the next one, waiting to go out.

At first, Rachel and Moshe and the others were concerned. They feared that he didn't care whether he survived, but then they saw that he always acted with caution. On the fifth mission after the storm, he had to kill. It had been a routine operation. He and two other men had been out on reconnaissance when they were surprised by a German coming around a curve on a motorcycle. He was alone, the sidecar empty. He almost ran into them, swerving out of reflex and running his cycle into a ditch. His reflex action proved to be his last. Sol leaped into the ditch and onto the German before either realized what had happened. On top of the cyclist, pistol in hand, Sol pulled the trigger.

Afterwards, Sol trembled. He'd killed before, but always felt some remorse. This time he felt nothing. He did it without hesitation. He didn't like it—nor dislike it.

Do others kill so coldly, he wondered?

What happened to the boy, Solomon Shalensky?

42

PARTISANS OR GUERILLAS...

By the end of April, much of the snow started to melt in the forests. The weather was much warmer. It was easier to move about now. Missions were easier to carry out. The Jewish guerrillas attacked supply convoys, sabotaged troop trains, plundered and burned warehouses; they attacked small German patrols whenever and wherever they ran across them. They also took heavier losses themselves. Losing ten to twenty percent of their force became common. But they took comfort in the motto, "At least we die fighting the Nazis." They didn't think about the future. The Germans were winning in Europe and Russia; and if the Germans were victors, there would be no future for them. It was only a matter of time before the Jews were wiped out completely.

At least these Jews had the opportunity to strike back on behalf of themselves and the millions who had no chance to resist.

As the missions became more frequent and more hazardous, Sol and many others began avoiding close relationships. The injury or death of a comrade was painful enough—the injury or loss of a close friend was devastating.

Rachel recognized Solomon's withdrawal and fought against it. When he tried to go off by himself she forced her company on him. "I'll not let you walk off and brood alone. Sol, you have no special claim on tragedy, so stop feeling sorry for yourself." At first her behavior angered Sol, but she knew that even hostility was better than self pity.

Rachel's actions were not all benevolent. She needed this close relationship. Though it seemed an eternity, it was only a few months since she and the others had lost their loved ones. In many ways, Sol reminded her of Avraham, her fiance'. Perhaps that was what attracted her to him in the beginning. Both were sensitive, considerate and respectful. Now he tried to suppress these characteristics to protect him from further hurt. She was determined to keep them alive in him.

Sol didn't have the formal education Avraham had, but he was well read on his own. He had a practical "street education" so necessary for surviving the poverty of Kiev's Podol. Physically, Sol was taller, slimmer. His facial features were more distinctive. Sol was more thoughtful, less impulsive, but both had a determination to see things to completion. Both were highly principled, intolerant of injustice.

As was the ancient custom, Rachel's betrothal had been prearranged by their parents, but she had fallen in love with Avraham. That love had now, very naturally, transferred to Solomon.

When Sol was away from the family camp, Rachel was busy at the infirmary. They had limited medical supplies, no trained medical personnel and a growing number of patients. Rachel did the best she could for the injured and sick. With the help of God and her nursing care, most survived. Those who did not survive did not die alone.

Sol, for his part, never pursued her aggressively. Not only had she recently lost her father and fiancé, but also she was orthodox in her upbringing, the daughter of a great rabbi. Solomon was not experienced in the ways of love. Having turned eighteen shortly before the invasion, there had been no real opportunity. And now, in his depression Rachel realized that if their love was to develop, she would have to be the aggressor. Her physical and emotional needs were strong and awake.

His, she decided, needed awakening.

It was now mid May. For the first time since the Germans had occupied the Ukraine, the weather was becoming warm. The long dreadful winter was over. The forest life was renewing. Freshness was in the air—a wonderful fragrance. During the days, the guerrillas could abandon their heavy clothes and greatcoats. They referred to themselves as guerrillas now rather than partisans. It had come from a casual discussion one evening in the meeting hut. Several of the Jews had been talking and one had spoken of their partisan activities.

"I'd rather consider myself a guerrilla fighter," Sol interrupted. "Partisans have a country to fight for. I'm not fighting for Mother Russia or the Ukraine. I'm fighting for us; for our survival. Russia and the Ukraine don't want us any more than the Germans do. When we have our own Jewish nation I'll be a partisan."

From that time forward they all spoke of themselves as guerrillas.

At night, it was still quite cool. During the days they could bathe in a nearby lake. It made them shiver, but still it was such pleasure. Until the spring thaw they hadn't known the lake was there, but thought the white expanse a snow covered clearing to be avoided at all costs, lest they or their tracks be seen from the sky. The lake's discovery was a pleasant surprise to all, not only for its beauty, but also for the abundance of fish, which added a variety to the otherwise limited and boring diet they'd tolerated.

Much of the depression, which had been suffocating them, melted away with the winter snows.

43

THE GOYIM...

Sudden excitement, tinged with panic, spread through the family camp.

Ivan came from the second camp with news that he had Father Peter, Gregor, his entire family and seven other Kievites hidden in the forest. He wanted permission to take them to camp two. All were gentiles.

The catastrophic events of the Goering Squadron came to mind. Many wondered if the *goyim* hadn't betrayed the Jews. How could they be sure this wasn't another Nazi ploy? A command meeting was called immediately.

"Let me bring you up on all the facts," Ivan began. Father Peter came to me in the middle of the night—three nights ago. He had the others hidden in the woods near my farm. He told me they and he were all being sought for immediate arrest by the Germans. When I heard him out, I had no choice but to help them. For two days, I've kept to the woods. I backtracked a hundred times. I think if we'd been followed I'd have found it out. I'm asking your permission to bring them in."

"Let's say you weren't followed," Sol said, "how do we know they don't plan to signal the Germans somehow? I'm not too worried about the priest or Gregor's family, but what about the seven others? This is a hell of a departure from our security policy!"

"I know that," Ivan agreed. "I would never suggest we bring them in here. Camp two. Watch them there." He paused and then added, "I think Father Peter has earned your trust. A lot of these people would be dead now if it weren't for him. I know how some of you feel about

Gregor and the mission he helped in, but I still feel if he had been a part of that disaster, the priest and I would have been arrested by now. If for no reason other than to be tortured to tell all we know."

The Jews considered.

"By the way," Ivan continued, "they've brought some valuable equipment with them. Three radios! For a change you won't be cut off from the rest of the world."

"Radios!" Moshe exclaimed. "That would be a godsend. How did they get radios?"

"Yes, how did they get radios?" Dovka asked suspiciously. "How can we be really sure one of them isn't working for the Germans? It would be a small price for the Nazis to pay to get us. Just give a collaborator a radio to gain our confidence, follow the goyim to our camp — and carry out the slaughter. I believe Father Peter is safe — I even think I trust Gregor and his family — but how do we know they haven't been fooled, too?"

"We can't be sure," Moshe said. "That is why we have to watch them closely and be on our guard. They could be a great asset to us if loyal. If not..."

"I think it better to watch them under our control," Sol interjected, "than have them fending for themselves in these woods. If they did something to bring the Germans down on themselves it might accidentally bring them across our trail, too."

"If it will add a little confidence," Ivan said, trying to add to the argument to bring them in, "I must tell you that Gregor warned that we could listen to the radios anywhere, but that we must never transmit messages from the proximity of our camp. He warned me that the Germans could locate us by our signals with a method called triangulation. Now does that sound like the warning of a Nazi collaborator? If he wanted to give our location to the Germans, sending messages from our headquarters would have been a perfect way."

Most agreed it was a favorable point, but skepticism

still ran high in the group. "How do we know one of them won't radio the Germans directly of our positions?"

"Why are the Germans after them? How did they get the equipment and supplies? How did they get the radios? I think we need the answers to those questions before we make a decision," Solomon insisted.

"Father Peter told me he recently wrote to his superiors of the German atrocities," Ivan replied. "Especially of those carried out at Babi Yar. He pointed out that mass murder is going on there and that the Church in its silence is condoning the crime. He wrote that he could no longer sit by as if deaf and blind. Not to condemn the Nazis, he told them, is a sin of omission. He closed his letter by asking direction—asking direction for the second time, by the way." Ivan looked about at the still skeptical faces in the room. "Well, his reply came, opened by the Germans. Censored! But they let it go through to him. Father Peter realized that his letter to his superiors must have been opened, too. But the Germans had not yet made a move against him. Possibly they also were awaiting the Church's reply. Because of the reply ..., which pleased the Nazis, I'm sure—the Germans decided to hold off a little longer. After all, the priest's arrest might incite the members of his congregation."

"What was the reply?" Sol asked, hoping to get Ivan back to the subject.

"The gist of the letter was that Father Peter had already been informed of Church policy. They reminded him that his job concerned the religious needs of his parishioners, not the nation's political problems. As a crowning blow, it pointed out that deviation from policy might lead to German retaliation, from which the Church could not protect him. Also, his superiors threatened that if he deviated sufficiently from Church policy, he might be subject to punishment by the Church — even excommunication, if his actions warranted it."

The Jews understood what excommunication meant to a priest or any devout Catholic, for that matter. Ivan could see that the hard expressions of doubt were softening. He pressed his argument.

"I'm sure the reply satisfied the Nazis. I'm sure they decided just to watch Father Peter more closely, avoiding the problems his arrest might initiate. Anyway, Sunday the die was cast. In his sermon, Father Peter condemned the Nazis as murderers, not only of human beings, but also of civilization. He condemned the Church and the Holy See for disassociating themselves from morality and humanity. He called the Vatican 'the seat of world hypocrisy.' He called on his parishioners to strike out against the Nazis or be damned with them, for to be silent was to condone the horror."

The listeners felt Ivan's conviction and one by one they were swayed from their fears.

Father Peter told me he was awaiting his arrest when suddenly Gregor and several other of his parish came to his chambers. They'd met after the service, waited until the rest of the congregation left — and most left in one hell of a hurry! They then spirited him away before the Nazis returned to arrest him. To give themselves more time, one of them killed the German who sat in the congregation to watch each Sunday.

"Without waiting for his consent, they took him from the premises and hid him in the forest. It was then that Gregor, his family and the others decided they would try to find a partisan group to join. Each went to get what things he had that might be of value in the forests. They met back in the woods with their belongings to begin their new lives. Two days later, Father Peter contacted me to see if I would lead them to you."

"How did they get the radios?" Dovka questioned again, to keep the group from lowering their defenses.

"Yes," Moshe asked, "how did they come by those radios? It's an important point."

"Gregor and his father have—had the biggest blacksmith shop and foundry in Kiev. You who were hidden by them saw it. You'll also remember the Germans took some of their heavy equipment there for repairs. They've done it since the beginning of the occupation.

"When they decided to leave for the forests, Gregor and his brothers stripped the radios and generators out of three half track trucks that were in for welding. When they took all that they could carry, they put a torch to their home and their shops. A lot of German equipment and everything they owned went up in flames."

"Well, what do we do?" Moshe asked.

"I'm not convinced," Dovka announced. "What an opportunity for the Germans to get a spy to us. We must be very careful! We might be condemning those of us who move into camp two with them to death!"

It was a sobering statement.

"I trust them," Sol said. "But I agree we must be very careful. I would bring in Father Peter. I would bring in all their equipment and supplies. I would keep the rest of them in a new camp one, under tight surveillance. Supply them with what they need to live in camp one while they prove themselves to us. Then we bring them in to the family camp as we have always done with newcomers in the past. I will volunteer to live in camp one with them. All should be volunteers. There need to be enough of us to make it look the real camp to them."

It seemed the safest and most reasonable plan. The Jews agreed on it.

44

Love Breaks Through...

Solomon believed the newcomers were what they claimed, but still he wanted to devise a way to prove them safe. In two days or as soon as a new camp one was established, he would have to go along with a few others to spend a test period with the strangers. A camp one was always uncomfortable, primitive and unpleasant to live in. It was a frustrating dilemma that troubled him all day. After their evening meal, Rachel tried to distract Sol.

"You're trying too hard," she told him. "The solution will come to you if you relax and let it. It's a beautiful evening for a walk. Why don't you take me down to the lake? Let's forget the war and the Germans and all those other people for a while. Please, Solomon."

He agreed. She picked up a blanket and they walked.

The night was cool. A light breeze ruffled the small lake. There was neither moon nor clouds in the sky. The stars shone brightly. Sol pointed out the various constellations. He'd learned them as a boy from his older brother. It saddened him. "I guess as long as I can recall the stars and their names, a little of my brother will live on."

"Solomon, all of our past lives on in our memories," Rachel said softly. "It's an age old proverb that as long as you are remembered by someone, you have immortality."

"I guess that's so."

He lay flat on his back looking up, recalling nights many years past when his brother would show him the stars. He could always see the big and little dippers, but he could never even imagine all the other constellations.

He distinguished the grouping said to be a bowman—he could find the stars, but no bowman.

Rachel lay on her side watching him. Suddenly, impulsively she rose up on her elbow, leaned over to him and kissed him on the lips.

Surprised, Sol lay rigid a moment before responding.

"There," she said. "I think that was long overdue!"

"Very long overdue," Sol agreed.

He kissed her and held her to him for a very long time. "Rachel, Rachel, is it possible that you feel as I do?"

"Only if you love me," she said almost teasingly.

Again there was a long silence as they held each other and kissed.

"Solomon, these are unusual times," she finally said. "It isn't good that we keep our feelings to ourselves. In our lives, where there is so much tragedy and terror—we *need* to express our love. We can't live on fear, hate and vengeance alone. When everything is so indefinite, we need to hold on to our love. It gives us one more thing to hope for."

"Oh Rachel, I do love you. God, I've wanted to say it a thousand times—but—well, I didn't know if you were ready to. After Avraham, I mean."

"We mustn't suppress our desires. The times do not allow us the luxury of long courtship. Time is too precious!"

"God knows how I've wanted to hold you, Rachel."

"We must express ourselves fully and without inhibition, Sol—my dear, dear Sol."

He wanted her, but he was shy. He pulled her very close again and held her.

"I want you, too, Sol. Want you—intimately."

She sensed his uneasiness. She took his hand and put it to her breast. Solomon felt helpless, almost terrified. He felt the fool. He'd heard other men and boys talk boastfully of their exploits with women, but he'd never had any experience like this himself. He'd always felt self conscious about it when among braggarts. Now he felt almost ashamed. What will she think of me? What am I to do now?

"Solomon, please don't be nervous. You're so tense! Have I offended you? Don't you want me?"

"Oh God, Rachel—yes, I want you. And I love you. I just don't want to do the wrong thing. I'll be clumsy. I'll disappoint you."

"I assure you, Solomon, I'm no expert. I have no sordid past to judge you by. We'll learn together. Solomon, I love you. Please be at ease with me."

For the first time, he relaxed enough to feel the warmth and smoothness, the firm softness of her breast. He could feel the erection of her nipple. He moved his fingers slowly, lightly, over the breast, exploring all its contour. "You'll tell me if I hurt you. I've heard it can be very sensitive."

"*It*, I have two of them, Solomon." She giggled at him.

He slid his hand to the other, his own embarrassed chuckle smothered by a warm, tender kiss.

"Oh, Solomon, I do love you. More than I've ever loved anyone." She felt suddenly very sexual. Having found and explored her own sensitive parts at an early age, Rachel knew her needs well. But never had those needs been stronger than right now, here, with Sol. "Have you ever had a woman, Solomon?"

"No. I've never even kissed anyone outside my own family before. I'm afraid I'll be a disappointment to you."

"Don't you think I have fears? After all, I'm a rabbi's daughter. My courtship was very proper."

His excitement rose. Bravely he started to move his hand downward. He reached her smooth, slim stomach. There he froze. His courage failed him. When it didn't return, he started slowly to move his hand back.

"No," Rachel whispered. "Please go on. I want you to. Please."

Sol was hesitant.

"Please, please, Solomon." She took his hand and moved it slowly and gently down. She felt she had waited this moment all her life.

"Please make love to me. Make love to me now!"

45

THE GUNFIRE CONTINUES...

Father Peter and most of the equipment were brought into the family camp the next day. Two radios were brought up, the third left in camp two. Gregor's tools were brought up. If only the blacksmiths themselves would check out as *safe*, they would be invaluable to the guerrillas.

"Kiev is an unbelievable place to live," Father Peter told the news starved Jews that first evening after dinner. "Starvation, looting, disease, reprisal roundups, shortages of everything—people are living in constant fear.

The Jews were unimpressed.

True, they ate well, but they knew cold and the threat of discovery and death. And they knew that much of what was being sold and traded in the marketplace had been stolen from the hundred thousand Jews who had lived in Kiev. Still, no one interrupted the priest.

"People had to destroy all of their books under threat of death. Most used them for fuel to heat their houses. All the books from the public library were thrown out of the windows to be burned. Schools are closed."

Finally someone asked about the ravine—Babi Yar.

"Babi Yar..." He hung his head. "Babi Yar is the shame of the world." It obviously pained him to talk of the ravine. He spoke, eyes to the floor. "It is inconceivable what the Germans do at Babi Yar, but everyone knows they do it. It's inconceivable that no one speaks out against them, but I know the world is silent. Babi Yar is everyone's sin. In just two days at Babi Yar, over thirty thousand people were murdered — all Jews. Perhaps a few escaped. But they had no chance! Those who tried were shot on the spot. Many invited death by running just to end the torture of waiting."

The room remained hushed as the priest paused. Even Sol, who had lived through it all at Babi Yar, found the tale crushing when told by someone else.

"By the end of the week, no Jews could be found in Kiev. There had been over a hundred thousand! No one raised a protest. It is a sin shared by all the world."

The priest was still for a few moments, still gazing at the floor. Then he continued. "But the ravine is not full yet. The gunfire continues. From dawn to dusk, I hear the deadly report of the guns. Trains come with thousands of new victims. I cannot recall a day when I've not heard the terrible staccato from Babi Yar. I've prayed for the wind to change directions — blow toward the ravine — and a few times my prayer has been answered. But too briefly and I would hear it again!

"And several times each day, I've heard enormous explosions. What they mean, I don't know. I fear to think what new device of death the Germans have come up with."

Again he fell silent. Rachel handed him a cup of tea. He thanked her and continued his morbid account. "Only the efficient Germans could invent the *gas wagon*. I first heard of it when one of my parishioners came to me distraught over the death of his mother. The mother had been a patient at the **Pavlov Psychiatric Hospital**. In mid October of 1941, a German doctor came there and announced that the patients were to be sent to another facility to free up the Pavlov Hospital for 'more important needs.'

"The patients were put into the back of a truck; the doors were closed and the truck driven off. Only the Germans knew that the trucks exhaust was piped into the sealed compartment—that their destination was a pit at Babi Yar.

"Now one can see gas wagons daily, driving their dying load toward Babi Yar. They save time and bullets for the Germans." He paused to wipe tears from his eyes.

"And even with the gas wagons, the sound of machine guns continues from dawn to dusk!"

Father Peter took a long drink from his glass. His throat and mouth were dry. No one of his audience spoke. Dovka refilled his glass, which he acknowledged with a nod.

"Sadly, the German character rubs off. The people of Kiev—too many of them—have learned hate from the Germans..."

"Or perhaps they have learned nothing from the Germans," Sol interrupted. "Perhaps they *were* what they *are*. Perhaps they just needed the German occupation to show their true character. Perhaps the Germans will show us the true character of the whole world."

Father Peter looked at Sol thoughtfully. "Perhaps, perhaps you are right."

"Father Peter, I am from Kiev. Believe me when I tell you Christians, there had no love for us before the Germans came. I've been spat upon for all of my life. I think you'll hear the same from every Jew here. Regardless of where he came from," Sol added, bitterly. "I'm afraid the righteous Ukrainians are the exceptions. Ivan, Sosha, Gregor and his family and you, you are, I'm afraid, among the exceptions."

"Yes," the priest said sadly, "perhaps the Germans will show us what *we* really are. Our own people turn in their neighbors to the Gestapo for an extra ration of food or worse, for money. In the black market, our own people prey and profit on the need of their neighbors. And no one protests, no one. No one!" His thoughts turned to his disappointment in the Vatican.

The Jews in the room didn't think about the Vatican or

the rest of the world. They had long since learned to expect inhumanity from the non-Jewish world. The only difference now was that they were fighting back. "Is our effort being felt?" Dovka asked, breaking Father Peter's introspection. "Do our activities hurt the Germans?"

"I'm sure you hurt the Germans. There's no way to know how much. We get no news of the actual acts, but only of the Nazi reprisals carried out because of them. There are several partisan groups around Kiev, I think and no way for us to know which is doing what. One thing is certain; however—no one knows there are Jewish guerrillas at work in the area! The Germans might know it, but if they do they haven't made it known publicly. I'm sure their propaganda wouldn't allow it. They would never let it be known that the Jews would do anything but go to their deaths like sheep. What would people think if they knew Jews could hurt the Germans?"

"Do they really take reprisals for every act against them?" Sol asked. "We've heard they do."

"They have reprisal roundups almost daily. People are picked up at random, usually ... hundreds every day. They just pick up the first one, two or three hundred people they find on the street. Men, women, children—it doesn't matter. They are executed either in the street or at Babi Yar."

"Then our acts cause the deaths of innocent people," Sol said almost inaudibly.

Rachel retaliated with fury in her voice. "Solomon, you are not going to carry the burden of the Nazi's guilt! If the Germans were to take reprisals, which they may well do, when the Russians stage a counter offensive, do you think they would or should call off their war so the Germans would not execute civilians? We are fighting a war, too. A war for our very survival! Maybe if the Germans take enough reprisals, maybe the citizens of Kiev will also rise up against the Nazis! If we curtail our activities because of their inhumanity, then we justify it!

"And at least this time, it is not our brethren being slaughtered in reprisal. They are already dead! Now they slaughter those who cheered openly and in their hearts when the Jews were rounded up. Those who were glad when the Jews went to their deaths 'like sheep' can now go to *their deaths* because *we* resist!

"Father Peter, you are right when you say the German atrocities are the sin of the world. Anyone who does not resist in some way must share the guilt. That is a course we must refuse!"

There was a long silence until Moshe said, "She sounds more like a rabbi than a rabbi's daughter."

Laughter purged the somber mood of the room.

46

YOSEF...

Sosha walked at the rear of their property near the woods when she heard a rustling in the underbrush. At first, she thought it a rabbit or squirrel but when she heard it again it seemed too heavy a tread to be a small animal. It frightened her and she cautiously went closer to the edge of the forest. "Who is there?" No answer. Another few footsteps rustled through the underbrush and then a small boy stepped from behind a bush. He was in tattered clothing and was filthy with dirt from head to foot. He looked fearful and prepared to run.

"Don't be afraid; I won't harm you. Please, let me help you. Who are you?"

The boy remained silent. Tense.

"Are you hungry? I'll fix you some food, something to drink. Please, tell me who you are—where do you come from?"

He said nothing, but seemed to relax a little.

"Please, what is your name?" Sosha coaxed. When he didn't answer she had a hunch about his concern. "Are you Jewish? I will still help you. Please, you must trust me. You can't hope to survive alone. Trust me, please. Start with telling me your name, please." She smiled sympathetically.

"I—I'm **Yosef—Yosef Dukowski**. Please—help me—I'm very hungry—very tired—please..."

Tears flowed from Sosha's eyes. She felt his fear and pain. His plea was so forlorn. She got him to follow her to the house. She heated water for him to clean himself, gave him soap. Gave him some clothing, from when her son was small, which was far too large for him, but at least clean. She had to cut off the leg and sleeve lengths and tied the waist with a rope. He looked ridiculous but less afraid as he ate cheese, bread, cabbage and tea. She didn't think him trusting enough to question him. She would have Ivan take him to the Jews in the forest.

Ivan took Yosef directly to the main camp via camp two, not fearing him a security risk. Rachel took him over, getting him some clothing that fit him better and feeding him. He could hardly believe that he found himself among his own people. After a few questions by Rachel his story poured fourth.

When the Germans announced that all Jews were to leave their homes for deportation his parents decided to escape before the roundup. He was an only child, fourteen years old. They were fairly well off and his father took all the money and jewels they had. They left the city during the night, almost getting caught twice by patrolling Germans and Ukrainian guards. Finally, they escaped into the country to a farm that sold produce to his father's vegetable store. They hid the family in a small pit they dug under the floor of their barn.

The hole was dug out two meters by two meters by a meter deep. Boards were placed across the top and hay was stored on that. His father paid the farmer for the protection and what food they would need. For the first few weeks it wasn't too bad because the Germans didn't go too far out of the city. They could get out as long as they stayed close to the barn.

The Germans became more numerous in the area and they had to stay in the pit all during the day. The farmer fed them twice daily. If they had to relieve themselves of bladder or bowel during the day it had to be in the little pit. They could only come out during a few hours after dark. It was difficult and barely tolerable but necessary.

The winter was miserably cold. They had only their clothes, hay and huddling together to keep them warm. Occasionally, the farmer would let them come into the house for a few hours to warm up, but only on the coldest nights for it was a risk that could have cost them all their lives. Spring finally came and they thought it would get better, but his mother got sick, her chest, pneumonia his father thought. They could not risk a doctor. After three days she died in the pit with them.

All day they stayed in the pit with her body until they could bury her under cover of darkness. Yosef and his father could no longer tolerate sitting in the pit that took their wife and mother's life. They decided to take to the woods.

His father became deeply depressed and could hardly function. His health deteriorated and one morning Yosef awoke but his father didn't. He found a board and dug a shallow grave with it. It took him all of a day to bury his father. Three days later, weak, hungry and terrified, he found Sosha.

47

LIVERY...

Days passed. Father Peter operated the radio, having been taught by one of the newcomers still out but now in the second camp. No messages were sent. They had no one to send to; and, heeding Gregor's warning, they didn't send between the camps. All day long, people would drop into the radio room, which had quickly been added to the headquarters building. They listened to the signals, dispatches and newscasts that the priest continually monitored. Of course, all messages of importance were sent in code. The Jews had been starved for news. Now they could hear not only local transmissions but also broadcasts beamed into the area from unoccupied Russia.

The news from Russia was not good. The Germans were beating the Russians on every front with superior weapons and crack troops but the Russians were fighting hard. The thing that most heartened the Jews was that the Russian broadcasts often referred to the damage being done to the German war effort by guerrilla activities.

By June of 1942, the Germans moved troops and supplies at a feverish pace. They made every effort to advance on the Russian front before the hard winter returned. On the radio came appeals to sabotage the German effort. After the first appeal, Moshe sent out scouts to determine which roads and rails carried the most military traffic. They'd disrupt as many of those routes as they could.

The new gentile arrivals were relied upon heavily in the scouting missions. It was an opportunity to further test their loyalty. On their return from one of the surveillance missions, six of the gentiles came upon three German soldiers grazing horses in a field. Two trucks were parked on the road to Kiev that bordered the field on one side. A fourth German was in one of the vehicles. He was skillfully and silently killed by a knife-wielding guerrilla. His weapon, ammunition, papers and money were taken. The other three Germans sat near a fence at the edge of the woods. They were in full view of the trucks, so the partisans had to crawl along a ditch on the far side of the road. They crawled until they were opposite the woods and out of sight of the three relaxing Germans. Then they crossed the road, entered the forest and came through the trees to where the soldiers sat.

Their weapons had been set against the fence. They were smoking, talking and laughing. At a signal, two of the guerrillas went for the weapons while the other four went for the unwary Germans. Before they died one of them got out a horrified scream, but no one who could help would hear him. Each met death at the sharp edge of a blade.

It took them awhile to round up the horses. Only one of the six was experienced with the animals. Once rounded up, they tied the horses in tandem. They made a quick search of the trucks and found saddles and other equipment. Papers in the trucks showed the horses were being brought to Kiev for the pleasure of the officers. They took their booty through the woods to the second camp. Two of the men covered the tracks the horses left.

Horses would make it possible for the guerrillas to expand their area of operations. They were kept at either camp one or two, never at the family camp. The animals would leave too distinct a trail; and if camp two was discovered by the Germans, it was feared they could easily track them to the family camp.

By the end of the first week in June, Gregor and his companions were approved to be residents in the community.

48

DOVKA...

In the weeks following the acquisition of the radios, horses and the first non-Jewish residents, the guerrillas carried out numerous raids on German troop movements and supply lines. Roads and rail lines were sabotaged and blown up daily by the many resistance groups operating in the Kiev area. The favorite method was to place homemade mines under roads and railroad bridges or tracks which detonated under the weight of a train or vehicle. When possible, the guerrillas scavenged for supplies and weapons.

Dovka returned to the family camp from one of these missions. She had been out nearly a week, staying at camps one and two, doing several missions before returning *home*. It was typical for the groups to go out that frequently now. The Germans sent troops and supplies to the Russian front at a feverish pace. Another winter would follow this summer and the Germans knew they had to have their troops supplied and at full strength before the snow fell. The resistance groups knew this too. They felt that every convoy or train that got through lengthened the war. They received radio broadcasts daily and were encouraged that there would soon be a Russian counter-offensive.

The pace was exhausting.

No one thought much about Dovka's exhaustion. Everyone was exhausted when they came in. They took a few days of rest in the family camp before going out again.

Dovka went to bed with a chill despite the warm summer temperature. She complained to Rachel of feeling cold but was fast asleep, unrousable, before her friend returned with a blanket.

Rachel covered Dovka. As she did she noticed her skin was hot. She wondered if it would be better not to cover her, but Dovka shivered as she slept. Rachel placed the cover over her loosely. She wanted to give Dovka some fluids to drink and some aspirin, but she could not be awakened. Still concerned, Rachel decided to let her sleep. Maybe in an hour or two fatigue would relinquish its grip.

Rachel checked Dovka several times over the next two hours. Her body would not cool. She awoke Sol, who had returned to the family camp with Dovka. They tried to wake her. Dovka was a little more responsive now and tried to resist their attempts. Together they moved her to the infirmary. Dovka winced with pain as they carried her, especially when her head moved. Her neck seemed rigid. Because of her fever they assumed she had something contagious. Fortunately there were no other patients in the infirmary.

With Sol's help, Rachel got Dovka's clothing off and covered her. She was moaning and mumbling now, her fever rising. Rachel started sponging her hot skin. Half an hour later, Dovka felt a little cooler to their touch. The shivering stopped. She was more responsive. Rachel doubted that Dovka knew what was being done for her. They did get her to take three crushed aspirin tablets dissolved in water. They also got a little tea down her before she again lapsed into slumber. After another hour, Dovka felt much cooler to the touch and Rachel was relieved. Her main problem seemed to be a very painful stiff neck.

She asked Sol to go to each of the others who had returned to the family camp with them that afternoon. If anyone else had a fever, she wanted to know it. When Sol returned, he reported that no one else showed any symptoms. Most of the returnees had napped an hour or two, but none was ill. It appeared only Dovka came back sick. Probably her resistance was down from all the stress of the raids. She would have several days to rest and get over it.

49

YORGI...

Yorgi struggled through underbrush, after his escape from Darnitsa, crawled across fields and sloshed through irrigation ditches. He traveled any route that offered him cover. In spite of aching muscles and blistered feet rubbed raw by his tight shoes, he refused to stop. Distance was the key to his survival. He maintained a pace he knew he could keep up steadily. Until dusk, he continued his torturous, self-disciplined trek.

During that quarter hour between day and dark when eyes adapt and visual acuity is poorest, Yorgi rested. He came out of the woods and found himself near a road. Across the way was a small farm. The house was well back from the road. A dim light shone through a window. Someone had just lit a coal oil lantern.

"I wonder if they'll be friend of foe?" he asked himself." I'd love a warm meal — some fresh clothing — a chance to clean myself up — to rest. "Oh — just to rest!" It was no time to cast caution aside. Yorgi advanced carefully across the road. Odds were he'd find someone more than happy to turn a Jew or an escaped Russian officer over to the Germans. Even if they didn't know he was either — assuming the worst... he'd settle for whatever he could glean from the field. It wouldn't be the warm meal he dreamed of, but it would fill the emptiness that gnawed at his gut. How long had it been since he ate a warm meal? He couldn't remember. Would he ever have another except in his fantasies? He couldn't imagine it. He climbed the rail fence fronting the property.

The greater part of the land was planted in grain,

probably wheat. He crept over the property looking for the vegetable garden that most farmers planted for their personal use. As usual, it was near the home. *If I can get to it without arousing the chickens or the dog, if they have one,* he thought. *If only they don't have a dog!*

Hunger drove him. He was only a few feet from the house now. Circumventing it quietly, he found a surprisingly large garden at the rear. *This garden must raise more than this family can eat,* he thought.

Staying at the edges furthest from the house, he started digging at the plants. First he found potatoes. Pulling up a plant he started to eat, dirt and all. The fruit was not yet ripe, but he wasn't eating for taste. Ending his hunger and surviving was his only purpose. As he ate one, he slipped two into his coat pocket, all the time moving on to find some other foods to vary his diet. He did not see the man quietly approaching him, rifle cocked, finger poised, pressing on the trigger.

"Fall flat on your stomach or I'll blow your head off!" Ivan Igonovitch barked at the trespasser.

Yorgi Tzarof fell flat, as commanded, the cool soft dirt in his face.

"I'm unarmed! I mean no harm! I'm taking only what I need not to starve! Let me go and I'll move on." Yorgi exclaimed rapidly.

"Who are you? Where do you come from?"

Yorgi's intuition prompted him to try the truth. "Yorgi Tzarof. My name is Yorgi Tzarof. I've escaped from Darnitsa. Last night. I escaped last night—and I was hungry. I'm trying to get as far away from there as I can."

Sosha had now come up behind Ivan. She too held a gun.

Ivan's rifle was pointed directly at the base of Yorgi's neck, between the shoulders. Yorgi sensed it, the hair at the back of his neck bristled.

"Sosha—hand me your pistol and search him. Make sure you don't get between him and the end of my gun. If he as much as takes a deep breath, his head's coming off with one blast!"

Sosha approached Yorgi from the side opposite Ivan. Keeping away from his extended arms, she swept her hands skillfully over his body.

She's trained, Yorgi thought as he felt her search.

Her search disclosed only the papers he'd stolen from the corpse that morning. Handing them to Ivan, she lit a match to reveal their message.

"These papers do not say you are anyone named Yorgi Tzarof!"

"Those papers came with these shoes and this coat, neither of which fit Yorgi Tzarof!" Yorgi said, trying to make a point. "I took them off a dead man in the city this morning. I tell you I am what I said I am."

Ivan was satisfied with the answer. Had the man intended to deceive, he would have given the name on the papers. But he kept the gun trained on Yorgi. Taking the pistol from his belt and handing it back to Sosha, he told her to keep the man covered. He stepped back a few paces and told Sosha to do the same and move to her left a few meters so the prisoner couldn't lunge at them both at the same time.

"All right, get up very slowly and move toward the storage cellar — that mound outlined by the moon — to the left of the house."

Yorgi did as he was told.

When Sosha opened the door, she lit the lantern that hung just inside and went down the stairs ahead of the two men. Inside, the captors and captive got their first good look at each other.

Yorgi was every bit as tall as Ivan, but not as massive. He was muscular but trim. Whereas Ivan had the build of a wrestler, huge — Yorgi looked more the part of a discus thrower, his muscles more defined. The stranger was filthy, not only from his travels this day, but filth accumulated over weeks of being a war prisoner. His shoes were wet with blood from his feet. His hair and beard were matted and dirty, giving no revelation of its reddish brown color. The lantern light did reveal the deep brown of his eyes. His face was square, handsome, but with an expressionless set. He had thick eyebrows and thin lips. His nostrils flared slightly as he breathed; otherwise little about his face moved except for his eyes, which moved constantly, quickly. Sosha thought him extremely observant and acutely alert.

After considerable interrogation, both Sosha and Ivan were satisfied that this man was a safe guest. Yorgi's fantasies were to be realized. He had a warm meal, a bath and received some clothes and shoes from Ivan. They were at least too large rather than too small. Best of all, he slept that night on a cot. It was the nearest he had come to sleeping in a bed in the ten months since the German occupation. He slept free of fear for the first time in as many months, on a little cot in a secret room under the stairs of a storage cellar.

50

QUARANTINE...

Dovka's fever started to climb again. Her sleep changed to delirium. She thrashed and threw off her covers. They tried to force fluids down her. It was impossible. Again they dissolved aspirin, but she spit them out. They tried again with better success. Her temperature dropped a little and she settled down. Her breathing was noisy, though, as she had fluid in her chest. They wanted to make her cough to clear her lungs but couldn't. Every move seemed to cause her severe pain. Her fever spiked again and her breathing became labored.

And then she was dead.

Before the sun set, she was dead. Dovka was dead. The whole course of her illness had taken less than six hours. Dovka was dead and no one knew why. The Jews were prepared for sudden death in battle. That they could understand. That they could accept. It was painful but understandable, acceptable. But this was an unseen enemy...

Was Dovka's illness contagious? Would there be an epidemic? If so, how could they fight it—defend against it? If only they had a doctor.

Sol decided to do several things immediately. Dovka would have to be buried. Two men were sent to dig a deep grave. Since he and Rachel had already been exposed, they alone would take Dovka to the grave and bury her. It was a horrible task, but they could not risk anyone else contacting the disease. Secondly, everything in the infirmary would be burned. Since the infirmary was a dugout, everything was piled at its center, doused with coal oil and ignited. All of Dovka's possessions were also burned. It was done that night so smoke would not be seen over the trees. They prayed there would be no flyover aircraft to see the flames which they tried to keep low with sprays of water from buckets, balancing the amount not to put the flames out, just to keep them low.

Then Sol and Rachel quarantined themselves by going together to a hut apart from the others where they would stay for a week. They could leave the hut and go to the woods or walk outside the camp, but they dared not mingle with the others. Each day supplies and food were brought to them, left outside the hut. Rachel cooked their meals.

They were isolated and they mourned.

The days passed. No one became ill. Ivan brought a new man into camp—a soldier, a Jew, an escapee from several German prisoner of war camps.

Solomon wrote in his diary, trying to bring it up to date.

Rachel was grief-stricken. She kept wondering what she should have done differently for her friend. She played the events over and over in her mind and each time the end was the same—Dovka was dead. For a change, it was Rachel who had to rely on Sol's strength and comfort.

It was after Dovka's death that I came upon the community of Jews in the forest or should I say they came upon me. I had been in Poland ever since the War began in September of 1939. Most of time I'd been in the Warsaw ghetto. I was brought into the camp months after Rachel's and Solomon's self-imposed quarantine. From what they described to me it sounded as if Dovka had died of meningitis. Had I been in the camp at the time she became ill I could have done no more than Rachel had done, this having been before the advent of antibiotics and the camp not even having sulfa or most other drugs.

After the sterilizing fire, they rebuilt the infirmary and I began my forest medical practice with Rachel my able assistant. My patients referred to me as *"Dr. Dov"*. It was through this practice that I learned the details of so many heartbreaking stories.

51

A NEW LEADER...

When the period of isolation was over, Yorgi had already been indoctrinated. Daily he regained the strength that had been sapped from him while in the various prison camps. He was eager to go out on missions. It felt good to strike back at the Germans. Vengeance burned in him. Meanwhile, he'd been placed on the general staff to replace Dovka. His military background was very valuable.

Dovka's death had as devastating an effect as the Goering Squadron incident. Being an outsider, Yorgi recognized the seriousness of the situation first and knew that something had to be done right away to take everyone's mind off the tragedy. Something spectacular, all consuming had to happen. Perhaps a mission that would hurt the German effort beyond anything they'd yet carried out.

To Yorgi nothing was impossible. That was why he was still alive. When others wrote off an idea of escape as impossible, Yorgi started to look for the weaknesses in the prison. Now those same qualities would be turned to offensive instead of defensive efforts. No sooner had he decided what was necessary to change the self-destructive mood of these battle weary guerrillas than he planned the operation.

Yorgi referred to this village, this *shtetl* in the forest, as a community of Jewish guerrilla fighters. It was only a name, but Yorgi made an important implication with it. "Heretofore," Yorgi pointed out, "you have been opportunists. You've attacked the enemy when the enemy came through your territory. Many of your actions have been spontaneous. Like when you found the horses. The opportunity presented itself and you acted.

"If you needed horses, you should have planned a mission to get them. As it turned out, you were lucky and you got them accidentally. But this type of an operation is dangerous. I think you will have fewer casualties and do more damage to the Germans if your missions are planned specifically to their purpose. I am amazed that you have had such good fortune."

He saw frowns on the faces looking at him.

"One of the best ways we have of hurting the enemy is to disrupt their supply lines," Yorgi went on, speaking to the crowd that gathered in the community hut. "Now you're hitting as many trains and convoys as possible, using anywhere between twenty and thirty people on those missions. And you're taking ten to twenty percent losses. No doubt the enemy has felt the sting of your efforts, but they have been more annoyances than crippling blows."

The frowns didn't go away. The furrows seemed deeper. Who was he to tell them that they risked life and limb just to be an annoyance to the enemy?

"What I have in mind should make the Germans sit up and take notice. With about the same risk as a raid on one convoy, I think we can have the effect of hitting a hundred convoys!"

The frowns and furrows were replaced by looks of skepticism and interest.

"Let me tell you my plan."

Everyone in the room listened to Yorgi. He was a big man and spoke with authority. "We know one thing — and that is that the traffic beyond Kiev is not as great as it is going *to* Kiev. That can mean only one thing. The Nazis are storing their supplies somewhere in the vicinity. It makes sense. Kiev is near enough to the front to get supplies to the fighting forces, yet far enough away to protect them if there was to be a brief counter-offensive. Now we must find out where these storage depots are. We need only to follow a few of those convoys. Once we know their whereabouts — we'll destroy these depots! One depot must contain the supplies from hundreds of convoys and trains."

There were doubts, but no one voiced them. They never considered themselves important enough to take on such a mission. Such a target seemed a major military objective. Yorgi saw it that way, too. The difference was that Yorgi saw the guerrillas as a major military unit. They still considered themselves as refugee Jews who were fortunate enough to be able to carry on some sabotage against the Germans. They didn't realize that their experiences of the past ten months had molded them into a top caliber fighting force. Most had seen far more action than any of the Germans they were going to go up against.

"Do you honestly think we can carry out such a mission?" Moshe asked.

"And why not?" Yorgi replied. "If I had my old army unit here, I would not hesitate to pick such an objective and you are better equipped and far more experienced than they ever were. Our war against the Germans was a catastrophe and lasted only a few days before we were routed. We were using outdated Russian arms against the most modern military equipment in the world. You now have an arsenal of that same modern equipment — the best in the world — and you know how to use it! Moshe, with the proper preparation, we will deal the Germans a blow that will set them back months!"

The renewed enthusiasm in the room soon spread throughout the encampment.

The next day, they had scouts out on all the major roads and rails into Kiev. They found out the major traffic was not even entering Kiev, so they tracked back on the roads and found a large percentage of the trucks were turning toward the city of **Zhitomir**, directly west of Kiev at a distance of a little more than a hundred kilometers.

Two days later, they converged on the Zhitomir area, six men on six horses. Much of their trip had been through flowing creeks to hide their tracks. There they discovered that the trucks turned east toward Kiev again. Now they followed that road. At some distance, they came to a small town called **Rozvazhev.** It was little more than a village, but the Germans had turned it into a major storage depot. Its warehouses were being filled with supplies and equipment. Trucks stood in long lines waiting to discharge their loads into the storage buildings. It seemed that the entire German army was there, too. But on closer observation, it became evident that most of the military personnel were truck drivers and crews. Obviously, they didn't trust the Ukrainians with these supplies, for only German soldiers unloaded the convoys.

Two of the Jewish guerrillas remained in Rozvazhev with their forged papers to get more detailed information. The rest returned to take their information back to headquarters. The two who stayed behind spent the rest of that day memorizing everything they could about the town and that evening they drew a detailed map of the entire area. At the same time, they also discovered the majority of the Germans were gone with the trucks.

The Germans who had unloaded the trucks were barracked at the edge of the town. The warehouses were heavily guarded. They estimated the guard force at any one time to be around fifty men, also some dogs. An electrified fence surrounded the entire compound.

It was after midnight before the two left Rozvazhev. Ten kilometers from town, they turned into the woods for the long trip home. They had horses hidden in the forest. Even by horseback, the trip back took them all night and most of the next day.

52

WELL LAID PLANS...

The news from the scouts created excitement. All information was put before the general staff and planning begun. As it turned out, Rozvazhev was a major supply depot for the Germans. Yorgi was ecstatic over the thought of the crippling blow this might be to the German war effort. "My friends," he started, "this mission should stagger the Nazis — and I see no reason why it should not be a tremendous success."

"When shall we hit them?" Uri Bolnik asked.

"Not until we're ready," Yorgi answered. "Everything must be right. We can afford to take our time with this operation. If we bumble it up, we will have missed our best chance. It must be right on the first effort."

Then Solomon interjected, "The longer we wait the better. We do not want to strike too soon and give them the chance to re-supply. The later we strike the less time they'll have to bring in new supplies before the Russian winter."

"What do you mean?" Moshe asked.

"Just this; the Germans have been bringing supplies in for months now, much more than they need for the occupation of Kiev. We saw trucks going into Rozvazhev full. Coming out they were empty. They are stockpiling. What for? For winter! They were putting up new warehouses. That can only mean they intend to stockpile even more. The later we hit them, the more of their equipment we destroy. The nearer to winter that we strike, the more it will hurt them. It's just the first week in July. Destroy Rozvazhev now and they have three or four months to resupply."

Yorgi smiled, "Spoken like a real strategist! It will be hard to wait, but it would be foolish not to. If we destroy the depot in September, they won't have a chance to re-equip themselves before winter."

"But I think we should watch them very carefully. We must be ready to strike immediately if we see that they start to ship out their supplies before the fall," Sol added.

There was a brief silence in the room as everyone absorbed what had been said.

"Well," Yorgi finally said, "you're right, Sol, we'll have to keep observers around that town. If they change their routines, we'll have to know it. They are likely to make all kinds of changes over the next few months. We'll have to work out an intelligence system specifically for the Rozvazhev operation."

It was hard to muster excitement for a raid to be carried out in three months. Sol felt he'd thrown cold water on their enthusiasm. He thought of a more immediate problem and suggested it.

"These summer days make it easy to repress the memory of last winter with all its sufferings. Now is the time to plan ahead for next winter. We have over two hundred people now to think of. To feed and clothe and shelter them will be far more difficult than last winter."

The more they discussed the matter, the more they realized they had little time to prepare.

52

CHANGE IN MODUS OPERENDIE...

September came, September passed. This first week in October, the eve of the raid on Rozvazhev, was already unseasonably cold. In the months between the conception of the mission and its execution, the guerrillas had prepared for winter. Under Yorgi's command, they carried out only those missions that would supply them with food, clothing, equipment they would need and shelter. And they prepared for Rozvazhev.

Yorgi's philosophy proved sound. Instead of hitting convoys randomly, they planned each action with specific aims. If food was needed, they struck where food was known to be. If weapons were to be obtained, they planned a raid that would get them. If by luck other supplies and equipment fell into their hands, it was a bonus. Sabotage became a secondary motive for the time being. Now they were primarily concerned with supplying themselves for the approaching winter and preparing for Rozvazhev.

To make such a change in their mode of operation, a very superior intelligence gathering system had to be developed. The radios were monitored twenty four hours a day. Members of this resistance group with false papers were in all the towns, villages and cities of the area. The money they had taken from victims and hoarded for the past year now became extremely valuable. With money, one could buy remarkable things in the black market. Information was no exception. In fact, black marketers survived and supplied themselves with goods by using the same information that the Jews needed.

Blackmarketeers knew schedules of convoys, what they carried, where they were going and how they were defended. Once the guerrillas made contact with the proper people and the black market was not hard to contact. They could buy any information they needed. At first money, large amounts of it, was the tool of exchange. But after a mutual trust was developed between the guerrillas and the Blackmarketeers, an agreement became mutually beneficial. The guerrillas took only what they needed out of a mission. Now instead of destroying what was left so the Germans couldn't use it, they left it intact for the Blackmarketeers who waited like buzzards to scavenge the remains.

The Blackmarketeers, of course, bought their information and protection from the Nazis themselves, so in effect, the Germans were selling information to the guerrillas via the black-market. Everyone seemed satisfied with the arrangement. It was risky, but everyone had much to lose. The Jews took their chances.

The raids that grew out of the information they gathered and bought turned out to be excellent training missions for the upcoming Rozvazhev action. Because of their new methods, the guerrillas didn't attack convoys and trains as often. With their information, they could strike at points in the chain of supply that would offer greater rewards for less risk. It was far safer to get food where and when the shops were being supplied; it was easier to obtain equipment at a rural transfer point, less populated with military personnel; it was more efficient to obtain weapons at small arms depots than to take them from randomly ambushed soldiers.

These new methods supplied the partisans richly with food and equipment for winter and for the impending raid. It also honed them into a topnotch fighting force—a fine army. And their casualty rate was reduced to an average of three percent a raid.

Still, they anticipated much higher losses on the Rozvazhev action.

53

THE ROZVAZHEV ACTION...

Never in the past had so many of the guerrillas been committed to a single action. Sixty three made up the total force. Even at that, they expected to be outnumbered four or five to one. The number of Germans stationed at Rozvazhev had been increased since the warehouses had been filled to near-capacity. The number of guards had been enlarged to sixty on each shift. The rest were inventory personnel and workers. All were potential adversaries once the fighting started and the partisans planned to keep as many as possible out of the battle.

For once, the guerrillas went into battle 'in style.' They had a small convoy of stolen German trucks and military vehicles hidden. They'd drive to the vicinity and then separated into groups, each with its own objective. The three men of letters had worked diligently to prepare the proper orders, should the drivers be questioned. The drivers and those visible in the vehicles wore captured German coats and caps. The four-hour drive to the separation point went without incident.

It was 11:30 p.m., just ten minutes before the first shot in the twenty-five minute raid would be fired. The first group to go into action cut telegraph and telephone lines at two designated places, isolating the town except for the wireless transmission station, which two dynamite blasts destroyed fifteen seconds later.

The second group stationed machine gunners around the barracks. When the transmission station exploded, the guerrillas threw dynamite into each of the buildings, blowing them up. A huge fire erupted and lit the entire sky. The few Germans who escaped through windows and doors were cut down by gunfire. In the first seconds of the battle, more than a hundred and seventy Germans died.

Almost simultaneously, the police station housed in an old church and the few Ukrainian policemen inside met the same fate. An officers' club and one for enlisted men were also leveled. After the first two minutes of battle, other than those men on duty, nearly all the Germans in town were dead or dying. This left sixty or seventy guards at the warehouses without replacements or reinforcements.

Two groups carried the main attack to the warehouses. One was to attack the main entrance first, drawing as much fire as possible. The second group would then attack the rail gate, after which the Jews' secret weapon would be brought into action.

At several points near the main entrance, dynamite blasted out large sections of electric fencing. The attackers immediately cut down a number of guards with machine gun fire. The remaining guards took cover and trained their guns at the gaps in the fence, waiting for the attackers to rush through the breach.

None came.

The Germans were puzzled. The attackers would have to come through there to reach the warehouses!

Suddenly a gigantic explosion behind them brought down the front wall of one warehouse, crushing twenty sequestered Germans. Then another explosion rolled flames into the sky at the next storage building. The Germans scattered into gunfire as they broke into the open. More explosions followed and flames licked at the stars from several areas in the buildings. Now there were secondary concussions as volatile materials stored in the buildings exploded.

As planned, many of the guards were drawn to the action at the front of the buildings. But minutes later, at the rear, the guerrillas set up their secret weapons. They'd made giant slingshots out of forks of small trees and rubber truck inner tubes. Two men held each trunk firmly while a third drew the sling, which cradled a packet of six dynamite sticks. A fourth man lit the short fuse and at the first sign of sparks the payload was let go.

The device lobbed dynamite nearly a hundred meters. The first charges dropped on the warehouse roofs blowing gaping holes. The next payloads soared inside where they destroyed the entire compound and stored supplies.

Secondary explosions and wind driven flames were destroying the whole warehouse complex. The guerrillas withdrew. The entire operation took fifteen minutes. It was not yet midnight when the guerrillas raced out of Rozvazhev. They had not yet counted their casualties but few were missing from any of the vehicles.

The group at the rear, led by Moshe Pinsker, fled, having done their job perfectly and without loss of a man. They crossed a clearing and unknowingly entered a minefield. A sudden blast tossed the truck onto its side, igniting its fuel. Before the stunned passengers could crawl free the extra dynamite they carried exploded. When the smoke cleared no one survived of Moshe and his group.

54

MAJOR OBERMAN'S PROBLEMS...

Major Hans Oberman was livid with rage, but only because his superiors were livid with rage. That created unpleasantness for Oberman. As his superiors did, so did he pass the unpleasantness down to his subordinates. "I want a complete report on Rozvazhev!" he roared as he stomped through the outer office. "I want facts and figures — and quickly!"

The lieutenant cowered and nodded.

All day long bits and pieces of information filtered into Oberman's office. "Total destruction of the warehouses..."

"Destruction of the communications center..."

"Destruction of Ukrainian police facility..."

"Two hundred seven German military personnel known dead, seventy nine injured, most serious to critical, ninety six unaccounted for..."

The figures changed as the day drew on; the injured joining the dead, the unaccounted uncovered in the rubble. The one figure that remained the same all day was, "Eleven enemy dead, none captured or known wounded."

The next day Oberman reported to his superiors, "Gentlemen, it appears our troops were the victims of a very well planned raid. They obviously knew our entire routine and layout at the Rozvazhev complex. How they came by this information is not yet discovered."

"And just *who* are *they*?" one of his superiors demanded.

"Partisans," Oberman stalled. "An army of partisans; our estimates indicate a minimum of five hundred!"

"An army of five-hundred partisans?" he sputtered. "How can that be? Where would they operate from?"

"Perhaps this force was made up of several groups joined for this specific action. We know that many groups operate throughout the Ukraine. We would be naïve to think they could not work together on major projects. Until now, they've carried out only minor raids on trains, convoys, isolated patrols and small storage depots. Never before have they ventured a major military action." He paused. "We think this was directed and organized out of unoccupied Russia."

"Out of Russia?" the Colonel barked in surprise.

"Yes. We have monitored almost daily broadcasts into occupied territories from the Russians. They encourage resistance. They could have sent leadership, even troops, to participate in the action."

"You have evidence to support these ideas?" one officer asked.

Major Oberman looked down at his hands, "We have no hard evidence yet. It is evident, however, that this raid two days ago was a superb military effort—not what we expect from loosely disciplined guerrilla gangsters."

"Well, let us hear some facts now," the Colonel insisted, pointing impatiently at Oberman's papers. "Continue with what is black and white."

"Very well," the Major said with a shrug. "Our latest figures and these are still not final, indicate that of our total military force of three hundred eighty two men assigned to Rozvazhev that night, three hundred forty eight have died, twenty three are on the injured list, eleven are still unaccounted for."

"And what price did the enemy pay?" inquired one of the officers.

Oberman's eyes lowered. His voice weakened. "Only eleven of their dead have been found. But we do not know how many of their dead or wounded they took with them."

"I have heard enough!" the Colonel exploded. "I want no more speculation! I want no more excuses! Oberman," he said, his voice dangerously quiet, "I want action. I want the forests of the Ukraine purged of partisans. I want every guerrilla rotting in Babi Yar!" He sprang to his feet and stomped from the room.

During the silence that followed, while each officer digested his commander's orders, one by one each gaze turned to Oberman.

55

THE MISSING...

It looked as though the entire town of Rozvazhev went up in flames as the group looked back, waiting for the truck with Moshe and his men to come. When it did not appear as scheduled, they grew concerned.

"They should be here by now." Sol said anxiously. "Even the extra time it would take them to come from the back of the depot..."

"I'm afraid they've had trouble," Uri interrupted, "maybe we should send someone back..."

"No one goes back!" Solomon insisted. "We can't risk more lives to their unknown fate. We agreed to that from the very beginning."

"But its Moshe—his whole group, Uri protested as more and more of the concerned group gathered, awaiting a decision.

"I know it's Moshe's group. No one loves Moshe more than I, unless it's you, Uri." He paused. How has this come to fall on my shoulders, he thought? Why doesn't Yorgi speak up? He just watches me struggle with the problem. Then without thinking further, spontaneously Sol said, "It's not my decision that we not go back. It's Moshe's. He made the rule long ago—and wisely. We all agreed long ago! And each of us knew we might one day be the ones left behind."

"How much longer can we wait?" Uri asked.

"Not long," Yorgi finally answered, stepping before the group. "Sol's right! We have no choice but to go on," he looked at his watch, "and right now."

He looked back down the road toward Rozvazhev.

They could all see the sky brilliantly lit where the town had been.

"I'm afraid the illumination can be seen clear to Zhitomir. Even with communications down—especially with communications down, that glow will bring Germans. They must be on their way already."

Yorgi looked at his watch again, a fine German timepiece captured several weeks earlier on another mission. He thought a moment. He, too, was fond of Moshe and the others, but as a soldier and commander he could not let emotion cloud correct judgment.

"If they are well, they'll make it back. If not, we'll not be able to help. Let's go home! Now!"

Yorgi gave his next command, "Set off two dynamite charges in those vehicles!"

They set long fuses and plunged into the forest with their wounded. The journey by foot to their base was expected to take them two days. They carried seven seriously wounded comrades. Twelve others had minor injuries and could travel without help. Before the night was over four of the seriously wounded had died. Their friends could not stop to bury them. That was understood before the operation began. "It is difficult to leave friends alone, even in death. Final farewells are not meant to be so abrupt and unceremonious," Sol commented.

Father Peter and Rachel were in charge of the wounded. The council would not let me go to the rendezvous point because they were not willing to risk the only physician the camp had. I could not change their minds to let me go. The best I was allowed was to wait for the wounded at camp two. Not even would they allow me to go to camp one. Father Peter and Rachel weren't allowed to accompany the combatants into the town during the raid but waited the long minutes for the fighters on the road at the meeting point. Each explosion they heard conjured up fears for their friends. Father Peter and Rachel had become close companions since Dovka's death. Along with Sol, the young priest had helped Rachel regain her strength and objectivity. In turn, Rachel understood better than anyone else the torment and personal anguish that plagued Father Peter. When he wasn't busy with the radios and she not occupied with the hospital or alone with Solomon, she and the priest spent many hours together, trying to fathom this ungodly world.

As each vehicle came to the meeting point, Rachel and Father Peter assigned people to help with the wounded. Makeshift bandages were checked and changed, but little more could be done for the seriously wounded. They continued to bleed and writhe in delirium. There was nothing to reduce their pain. They knew their efforts with the most critically injured were futile and that carrying them was a tremendous expenditure of energy, but it was difficult enough to leave their dead behind — impossible to leave their wounded.

By noon the next day, the last of the critically wounded had died. The group had traveled many kilometers but could not stop long to rest. They knew the Germans would start out with dogs from the point where the trucks had been destroyed. At best they had a five-hour lead. Hampered by their wounded, that lead would be reduced to three hours. The first six hours did not lead them toward home. Instead they headed west past Zhitomir, about five kilometers south of that city. By dawn, they had passed by the city and then they continued twenty kilometers due west, until noon when they came to the **Teterev River.**

The river flowed northeast at that point. There, they entered the river and doubled back, walking in the water to confuse the dogs. They waded for three or four kilometers, a slow and dangerous route because the Germans were searching by air also. Every so often a plane would drone in the distance and the party would scatter for cover along the bank until the aircraft passed, almost skimming the water. While the others waded, backtracking in the river, two of the group stayed on land, going the opposite direction. Alone, they could move fast and it was hoped they would lay a false scent for the dogs, giving the main party more time.

When the raiders finally left the river, they headed north toward home. They plodded in silence, each person weighing in his mind the successes and losses. Eleven were missing. Seven had died since the raid. The remaining injuries fortunately were minor. Moshe was among the missing—all probably dead. Except for those missing with Moshe, their comrades had been felled and injured by small arms fire. What targets they'd made, silhouetted against the flames! They'd probably been shot by Germans roused from the beds protected by their mistresses when the dynamite blasts shook them.

When they reached camp one, the two decoys waited for them. They waited two days at camp two. Their lookouts saw no sign of either their friends or the Germans.

Finally, the survivors started back to the family camp.

56

OBERMAN'S SECRET...

When Major Hans Oberman was asked by his superiors who the attackers had been, he'd kept one bit of information, a startling fact, to himself. He knew it would have only added to their rage. He himself didn't want to believe it. The seven dead found in the woods the day after the raid proved it though—beyond a doubt—all circumcised.

Do I dare tell them, he wondered? A band of Jewish partisans operating under our noses! More insulting is the fact that these Jews have probably been operating in the area for more than a year—have been responsible, in fact, for most of the resistance activity in and around Kiev. To be outwitted by these sub-human Jews!

Oberman did not want the responsibility of suppressing this new information, but he decided against making the facts known at that first meeting. Better to tell only his Colonel who would share the brunt of the wrath if the facts came to common knowledge.

"What do you mean, Jews?" the Colonel exclaimed. "Jews are not capable of bravery. Are you mad? We will be committed as lunatics if we expound such a theory!"

"It's not a theory," Oberman said. "I have substantial proof."

"Proof, what proof?"

"Their dead, my proof is their dead. Whenever dead partisans have been left behind they are examined lest they carry hidden information. It is at once clear if they are Jews."

The Colonel had a blank expression on his face.

"They are circumcised, Colonel. Only the Jews mutilate their penises!"

"You mean to tell me all those dead were cut?"

"Every last one and in certain actions all the dead have been — as you say, 'cut.,' in others, none. To me that means there are non-Jewish and Jewish groups out there. Rozvazhev was all Jews. And many of the other operations of the past year have been all Jews. There is at least one very active Jewish resistance group out there. I've suspected it since the Goering Squadron event, but waited to make sure. This raid left no doubt in my mind."

The Colonel was silent a moment, his face scarlet. "Who have you told of this, Oberman?"

"I've only mentioned it to you and no one else, sir."

The Colonel took a long, deep, shaky breath. "For the time being, keep it that way." He pondered a long moment, then continued, "Have any ideas of how to wipe them out, these Jews?" He looked at Major Oberman with a stern expression and wrinkled brow and almost whispering added, "Before the information gets out?"

"I have some ideas. If you will come to my apartment tonight, I will show you what I've gathered."

"Your apartment?"

"Yes, Colonel. I want no one around here to see what data I've brought together."

"I see your point, Major. I'll be there."

"At nine."

"Nine."

The Colonel had never been to the Major's apartment. The Major greeted him at the door dressed in a smoking jacket. The Colonel was disturbed. He owned no civilian clothes. The military was his life. He had no room for anything else.

"Come in, sir," Oberman said graciously.

"Thank you," the Colonel replied uncomfortably. In the Colonel's office, Oberman was a subordinate to be belittled at whim. Here, the Colonel felt ill at ease, off balance.

"May I offer you a drink, sir?" Oberman asked with a smile. He'd registered the Colonel's discomfort and knew he would be listened to with greater respect.

"Schnapps, thank you."

"Excellent! I'll have the same." He poured the drinks slowly, giving the Colonel plenty of time to take in the opulence of the room. The apartment reflected both Oberman's flamboyant private life and his family's wealth. In one corner of the living room was a large credenza, which served as Oberman's bar. Other fine furnishings — those he had not confiscated from previous owners — he had bought at a fraction of their value or traded for favors. Several fine oils hung about the room. There was a beautiful floor to ceiling window that overlooked a park across the street below. The parquet floors were covered with fine oriental rugs. Nowhere in the Ukraine, under the Bolsheviks, could rugs such as those have been found.

The Colonel noticed a woman's coat hanging up in the corner on a large brass coat stand. He wondered whether it had been forgotten there or whether the owner was behind the closed door at the far end of the room. Ordinarily, it would have bothered the Colonel that his subordinate lived so much more luxuriously than himself, but he was too overwhelmed to brood about it now.

Bringing the drinks, Oberman asked, "Cigar? They are fine Dutch imports. In my opinion, no one makes better cigars than the Dutch."

The Colonel helped himself. He rolled the cigar between his fingers and sniffed its fragrance. He was impressed with the freshness and scent, but not nearly as impressed as when he looked at the black and gold cigar ring which displayed a family crest and the words, "Major Hans Oberman."

Oberman grinned with satisfaction, struck a match and held it to the Colonel's cigar. "I think you will enjoy it. I have them specially selected, wrapped and sent directly from Holland. If you like it, I will take the liberty of ordering some for you — with your name on them."

The expression of 'pleased surprise' on the Colonel's face was not lost on the Major. The Colonel nodded his approval as he drew in the first mild wisps of smoke.

"Well, shall we get down to work?" Oberman asked.

"Yes. What do you have to show me?"

Oberman brought a map over and rolled it out on the coffee table in front of the Colonel. Taking a seat on the sofa next to his superior, something he could never have done in the office, Oberman began.

"This is a map of Kiev and the countryside surrounding it within a hundred kilometer radius. I have made three separate markings on this overlay, you will notice. The 'X' marks represent acts of hostility against the occupation. Where there is a circle about the 'X' mark — like this one — circumcised dead were found. Now that information was not reported in the accounts of guerrilla actions. I had to go to the individual medical reports for that information. Those two groups of information were never filed together. But when I brought them together, these facts appeared." He pointed to a cluster of circled "Xs" on the map overlay.

"And what do these circles without the 'X's mean?" the Colonel asked.

"Those are points we have been fortunate enough to triangulate in on radio transmissions. Oh, they're smart, Colonel! They seldom broadcast for long, leaving us no time to fix on a location. But in a few instances we have been able to pinpoint them. Of course, they're never there when we search the area. They're too smart to transmit from their camps.

"Still, we have collected some information — and now it will tell us part of what we want to know!"

The Colonel leaned closer, studied the markings on the cellophane overlay in silence and finally said, "This is quite impressive, Oberman. Now just what do you conclude from this information?"

Major Hans Oberman smiled and raised one index finger. "First of all, if we take into account the dates of the actions represented by the circled 'X's, then we must conclude that these Jews have been active against us from almost the beginning of our occupation. I have to admit, I find it difficult to believe the Jews are capable of such actions, but I cannot come to any other conclusion. I fear we have become victims of our own propaganda. We underestimate what 'sub-humans' are capable of. We must change our attitude of them a bit."

"Is it possible others than Jews circumcise among these Ukrainians?" the Colonel asked.

"I assure you, Colonel, only the Jews do that. It's the same all over Europe and especially in the east. I understand that some non-Jews do this in America now, but here—they are Jews."

Oberman paused a moment to find his train of thought again. "Secondly, there are many guerrilla groups in the forests around Kiev. The wide range of territory in which these activities have taken place precludes there being only a few. They could not travel freely enough to cover such vast areas. I think there are many groups, which work independently, perhaps within a radius of fifty kilometers of their camps. Now, if that is true, these vast forests around Kiev could easily hide up to a hundred different resistance groups."

The Colonel was stunned. "Up to a hundred?"

"Absolutely and many wouldn't even run into each other. If they were in remote areas they could keep as isolated as they wanted. There are thousands of square kilometers of forests around here.

"Our best hope is to totally overpower them. We could be risking many lives and even then they might escape. To go into those woods blindly, with less than a hundred well armed men—that would be inviting disaster!

"Now, a second method might be more productive, but it would require knowing their exact locations."

The Colonel pondered Oberman's assessment of the situation.

"If we concentrate on circled 'X's,'" Oberman continued, "We see that they are concentrated in this area to the west and north of the city. Incidents have occurred outside this area a few times, but seldom to the east of Kiev — and seldom beyond this radius. The Rozvazhev raid, the Goering Squadron train and a few others are exceptions. I'm sure they're encamped in this large forest northeast of us.

"Of course, that area covers two thousand square kilometers. We must narrow it far more than that. If we assume that the radio transmissions in that same area are from them, then that will narrow it some more.

"Admittedly, there are very few transmissions from that area. We only have three to go by. But if we assume they would go less than twenty kilometers to transmit, then we've narrowed the camp location to within sixteen hundred square kilometers. That's still a large area but much less than the original."

A pleased expression crossed the Colonel's face.

"Now, Colonel, let me pose a question to you. Do we want to go after those Jews or shall we go after one of the other guerrilla groups?"

The question took the Colonel completely by surprise. "I don't understand you, Oberman. One minute you are brilliant and the next you ask a question like that — and I'm convinced you are completely mad! Why would we spare those Jew bastards, especially since they are responsible for Rozvazhev?"

"Not only Rozvazhev, but many other major actions," Oberman added. "But remember, you and I are the only ones who know that. And since I have these files it is unlikely that anyone else will find out — unless *we* make it known."

"Oberman, I still do not understand."

"Let me pour you another drink, Colonel and I will explain." He filled the glasses.

"Prost!"

The Colonel raised his glass in a silent salute. "Please explain yourself, Oberman."

"As I see it, Colonel, there will be great repercussions if it becomes known that the Jews have been operating under our noses in Kiev. You and I will bear the brunt. The high command will not be pleased to hear that Jewish sub-humans have been carrying on a guerrilla war against the finest army in the world for over a year—and undetected! Who do you think they will lay blame on for such a humiliation?

"Colonel, you and I will be made out to be fools, inferior to the subhuman Jew. I hate to think what our reward for such stupidity will be."

The Colonel saw Oberman's point. The wrath of the Reich would be upon them.

"What shall we do?" His voice was edged with fear.

Oberman was calm. He drew on his cigar and savored the smoke, which he exhaled slowly through pursed lips.

"It is simple. If we keep all this to ourselves, we can still be the heroes. I will see to it—with your permission, of course—that these medical reports never reappear. Without the corpse descriptions no one will ever know *what* they were. Germany's propaganda will go unquestioned. The Jews will be remembered as cowards who went like lambs to slaughter! And we will not be seen as fools and failures."

"How, how can we save the situation? What must we do?"

"As I said, it is simple. All our superiors want is to get the guerrillas. With this information, all we have to do is go after one of the other groups—from another area— where dead Jews have not been found. In fact, it will be easier to go after a group that's been careless about its activities and that resides in a smaller, more accessible forest."

Again there was silence as Oberman let his Colonel ponder. Finally, a smile crept over his face — a smile where strain had been moments before.

"Fate plays many strange tricks, but none of those partisans would ever believe that they're being saved because they are Jews!" Oberman grinned.

The irony was wasted on the Colonel. "Major, not *'saved'* only *'reprieved.'*"

A few days later, Oberman staged a raid on a small wooded area south of Kiev. His calculations indicated that a small guerrilla band was working out of that area. He sent an overpowering force, which annihilated the entire group. He'd ordered, "No prisoners!" The ruse worked. Their superiors were satisfied.

For Major Hans Oberman, however, the matter was not closed. He knew that the Jews were operating in the area and they would eventually come back to haunt him. As far as he was concerned, the decoy operation only bought him time. Sooner or later he would have to destroy the Jewish resistance fighters. Now he could take his time and do it quietly. He set about developing a plan to accomplish his own final solution.

57

REORGANIZATION...

After the Rozvazhev mission, the Jewish resistance fighters had to reorganize.

Moshe was dead.

Solomon and Yorgi became joint heads of the general command — Yorgi leader of all military matters, Sol to be responsible for all non-military matters. The rest of the general command was made up of Rachel, Uri, Father Peter, Ivan and Gregor. Ivan still lived on his farm with Sosha, but took part in many of the decisions of the community. He was their link to the outside world. During this reorganization Sol suddenly realized that he, Rachel, Uri and Ivan were among the few survivors of the original group. Time and battles had taken their toll.

And again Solomon found himself asking, "Why? Why me? Why not me?"

58

OPERATION
BARBAROSSA...

The winter of 1943 made an abrupt and ferocious debut. Autumn of 1942 had hardly arrived when snow began to fall on Russia and the Ukraine. By the end of October, the forest floor was carpeted white. The Jewish community's attention narrowed to problems of food and shelter.

Elsewhere in the Soviet Union, nature was about to play a decisive role in world history. A year earlier, she saved a nation under siege; now she would strike a blow that would eventually bring down the aggressor nation.

"Operation Barbarossa" began on June 22, 1941, when Hitler hurled the most powerful army the world had ever seen against Stalin's ill-equipped, poorly trained and ineptly led troops. He attacked the Russians on a front that spread from the **Black Sea** to the **Arctic Ocean**. An enormous force of more than two hundred and fifty divisions was set in motion to race for **Moscow, Leningrad, Kiev, Stalingrad** and all territories between. Barbarossa's objective was not just to gain these territories, but to destroy, totally, the Red Army. Had nature not sided with the Soviets, Barbarossa would have succeeded.

It was Hitler's idea that Barbarossa would accomplish all its objectives within eight months, putting the Soviet Union at the mercy of the German Reich. His timetable was delayed from the beginning. Barbarossa was to be launched in May of 1941, but because of misfortunes on other fronts — especially **Mussolini's** problems in **Greece** and at **Belgrade** — the starting date was postponed. When the Germans began their move on Moscow and Leningrad, winter entered the battle on the side of the Russians. The first snows of the Russian winter were falling.

The modern and ferocious German war machine bogged down in snowdrifts; men and animals froze. Supplies couldn't keep up with the advancing armies; men and machines became stranded without fuel, ammunitions, warm clothes or sufficient food. For the first time, the Germans found themselves at a disadvantage. German losses became heavier and harder to replace. By the time winter had set in at the end of 1941, Hitler had lost more than three quarters of a million men to the Russian campaign. That was only about a fourth of the original force he had thrown into the campaign. Seven hundred and fifty thousand Germans dead and the fury of the Russian winter brought the momentum of the Nazi advance to a standstill. An age old Russian strategy was to work again. They had traded space for time, strategically retreating over vast wastelands while they equipped and trained men for the eventual counterattack in their heartland.

Now the Russians could start trading lives with the Germans. They were willing to do it because they knew they were fighting for their very survival in their own homeland. Under these circumstances the Germans stood no chance. They had difficulty transporting replacements to the front now, while the Russians had endless replacements, taking them right out of the population as needed. The Russians could trade five lives for every German if need be and still outnumber them.

While the German mechanized divisions stood with their radiators frozen and fuel tanks empty, the Russian cavalry, six hundred thousand strong, galloped out of the forests to surprise and slaughter the Germans, paralyzed by the weather.

By the third week of October, 1941, the German Army was within one hundred kilometers of Moscow. It was probably the worst moment of the war for the Russians. Stalin himself directed the battle for the defense of Moscow from the **Kremlin**. It was Russia's moment of truth. If Moscow fell, the Kremlin would fall and with it the entire Soviet Union. Barbarossa would be realized. The retreat of the Russians would have to end at Moscow's doorstep.

Every war has many miracles — events decisive in their timeliness. Such was the first heavy snow of the winter which began falling while Germany was preparing to make its final assault on the heart of the Soviet Union.

First the snow came, then a melt and a rain, which left the Germans wallowing in mud. Then there came a freeze and ice and then more snow. Suddenly, the great German Army found itself frozen in its tracks to the west, north and southeast of Moscow.

Through the long and cold month of November, the German army tried to regroup and salvage what it could. The generals wanted to withdraw to a point where they could dig in and resupply, but Hitler would not hear of it.

The Russians spent this time productively, building forces and supplies at the points where they were needed. And they waited for their ally; winter, to unleash its full force against the Germans. Now the Russians would decide when and where the next offensive would take place — the Russian offensive.

On December 6th, 1941, **General Georgi Zhukov** dispatched his one hundred divisions in a counteroffensive that shattered the German lines.

The myth of German invincibility was destroyed.

To the north of Leningrad, the Germans were also stopped before they could enter that city. But there the story was quite different. The Germans were indeed stopped, but the city was surrounded on three sides with its back against the **Baltic Sea**. And across the sea was **Finland,** a small but determined enemy of Russia and an ally of the Germans against the Soviets.

When Leningrad was first cut off, surrounded, there was only a few days' food supply in the city. It led to a ghastly and deadly siege. By the height of that winter 1941-42, up to five thousand people were dying daily of starvation. That blockade lasted until 1943. Never did the Germans or Finnish armies penetrate the boundaries of Leningrad, but they shelled and bombed the city to rubble. A few supplies were smuggled in or dropped by parachute, but they were a mere pittance compared to what was needed. Still, those people of Leningrad held on. By the time the blockade was broken in 1943, more than six hundred thousand men, women and children had died there.

As the summer of 1942 approached, it became increasingly clear that the German takeover of Russia had ended. It was obvious to everyone but Hitler and a few of his closest confidants who shared his madness and unshaken belief in their own propaganda.

Hitler issued his directive that **Stalingrad** and the **Caucasus** were to be the objectives of the 1942 German offensive. On September 13, 1942, a German division broke through the defenses and entered Stalingrad. What they found was a bombed out city, but not a relinquished city. Every foot of that metropolis cost the Germans dearly in lives. Every deserted building was mined, almost room by room. Snipers, marksmen, were everywhere. Each overhead window was an opening through which death could be hurled in the form of a **Molotov cocktail**. The German advance was no longer measured in kilometers, blocks or even meters. It was measured in corpses.

Miraculously, **General Vasili Chuikov** and his troops,

reinforced by civilians of Stalingrad, held the besieged city. For more than two months, they dealt death to the Germans who shared their city with them, while they themselves suffered terrible casualties.

Then, on November 19th, 1942, **Zhukov**, the General who saved Moscow, launched a counterattack at Stalingrad. In four days, he had the Germans trapped. Hitler would not allow his generals to surrender when they realized the struggle was hopeless. They continued their futile effort until January 13, 1943. By that time, **General Freidrich Paulus** had no choice. He was forced to surrender his **German 6th Army** to the Russians. He and ninety thousand emaciated, ragged, half frozen men were all that was left of the once proud three hundred thousand soldiers who had planned to take Stalingrad.

The series of defeats that started at Moscow continued to plague the Germans along the entire Russian front. What the winter of 1941-42 started, the winter of 1943 finished.

59

SNOWBOUND...

As hard as the winter of 1941-42 was on the Jewish community in the forest northwest of Kiev, the winter of 1943 was far more difficult—even though they were better prepared for their second winter in their family camp.

This winter of 1943, the snowfall was heavier and the sub zero winds made going out impossible for days at a time. The very first storm dropped on the family camp more than a meter of snow, which fierce winds drifted, here and there, to three meters in depth. An elderly woman who'd led a young child to the latrine lost her way in the blizzard, disoriented by the blinding snow. They froze to death not twenty meters from their dugout. When it was over, the dugouts looked like white burial mounds among the trees. No sooner did the Jews clear out their entrances and chimneys than the snows began to fall and swirl again. The second storm brought another half-meter of snow to the guerrillas' problems.

Fortunately, Ivan and Sosha had been at their farm when the first storm broke and the only fighters caught out in it were five at the second camp. When the blizzard ended, the five made their difficult way to the cave Sol had found the year before. It was still used as a warehouse and emergency hideaway.

There was sufficient food both at the family camp and at the cave, but feeding the horses became a real problem. The five men from the second camp led their horses to the gully where the cave was, but once there they found no hay. The animals could not graze the snow covered ground. There wasn't enough grain stored to last the horses even two days.

The men had but two choices — to shoot the horses or let them go free in hopes they would be claimed by someone who could care for them. But merely to let them loose would not work. The animals would starve among the deep drifts. They decided to try to get the horses to the vicinity of Irpen and let them go there, though they'd probably fall into the hands of the Germans. Still, the Germans treated animals well — it wasn't like turning Jews over to the Nazis. And if Ukrainians did get hold of the horses, they would probably be eaten.

The day after they reached the cave, the second snow storm hit. The horses were tied together and under cover of the snowfall one man led the animals out of the gully to the road that led to Irpen. Two kilometers from the village, he released the animals and returned to the cave, letting the new snowfall cover the fresh tracks.

In the family camp, they remained snowbound. The days turned to weeks, the weeks to months. The many kilometers of waist to shoulder deep snow they'd have to struggle through made guerrilla actions impossible. And if they could make it out, the deep tracks they would leave could never be entirely erased by snow. The Germans would surely find them and slaughter would follow. So the Jews became prisoners in their own community from November 1942 into March of 1943.

The radios were the only link to the outside world. Without them, their morale would have dwindled. They couldn't get far enough from camp to transmit safely, but news coming in was tremendously uplifting. Each day brought news of more and greater disasters befalling the Nazis. The Russians beamed news of their victories over the now starving German army, into the occupied territories so that in the midst of their white prison the many resistance groups could gather hope for the future.

When Father Peter was not busy with the radios or helping Rachel and me with the sick or in philosophic conversations with his other new comrades, he sat brooding on his own future. What does it hold for me? Will the Church accept me when this is all over? I've rebelled on behalf of my own conscience, but did the Church really condone the acts of the Nazis? Each time Father Peter asked that question the answer wounded him. "If the Church didn't condemn the Nazi atrocities — it condoned them. Anyone who didn't cry out against the crimes is guilty of the sin of omission."

Father Peter wondered, in fact, whether he could ever, in clear conscience, return to the pulpit — should the Church accept him back. In his mind, the Vatican had lost its purity, its mystique, its holiness.

But why did it take the Nazis to make me see? I'm an historian. Did I simply close my eyes to the facts? Yes — this has been my sin of omission... He knew his Church's history of torture, anti-Semitic teachings, war, inquisitions, crusades — but had never questioned it — never questioned the hypocrisy of it. "I can no longer deny the one shattering fact — that the Nazi success is the outcome of nearly two thousand years of Christian ideology and hatred of the Jews."

He continued the mental chastisement of himself. When Paul of Tarsus could not convert the Jews of his time, he introduced anti-Semitism into his teachings for those who *would* listen. In the **Gospels of Matthew and John,** a major anti-Semitic mythical theme appears — that the Jews killed Christ and should therefore be identified with the powers of evil.

Father Peter recalled that the early Christians had renounced the Jewish rebellion against Rome, had minimized the role of **Pilate** in the crucifixion to pacify the Roman authorities. He recalled the two centuries of Crusades in the Middle Ages during which hundreds of thousands of Jews were raped and murdered with the Church's blessing. "Why have these facts never disturbed me before?" he asked himself bitterly.

In more recent years, there have been the pogroms. How many churchmen have preached hatred of Jews — encouraging their flocks to lash out, maim, plunder, burn Jewish villages? He sat downcast as he thought. So much anti-Semitism has been so deeply ingrained in parochial education, it is no wonder the Germans found it so easy to slaughter Jews without Christian resistance.

That winter was one of anguish for Father Peter. He felt the weight of his own and his Church's sins building up all around — like the snow.

60

HOPE FOR A FUTURE...

That winter, Solomon and Rachel, for the first time since the occupation, allowed themselves to think of the future. Since the news of the Russian victories and the changing tide of the war, many of those in the resistance started to think that there might be a future for them after all. The group of young Zionists, who had joined earlier in 1942, spoke constantly of their plans to continue on to Palestine after the war. Their plans influenced many others, including Solomon and Rachel.

"There is no place left in Russia or Europe for Jews," was the contention of the young Zionists. "The survival of our people depends on a homeland for the Jews. Now is the time to re-establish our **State of Israel** in the Promised Land!"

It had been recognized almost a century earlier that for the Jews to ever have their just dignity and freedom, they would have to have their own nation. The Jews were a nation in *Diaspora.* That fact and Christianity's refusal to allow Jews equal status in any nation under its influence, made Europe and Russia a hostile environment for the Jews.

These young Zionist resistance fighters, under the influence of the founder of their movement, **Theodor Herzl**, organized before the war with the intention of settling on land in Palestine purchased by the **Jewish Agency**. There they would form a community, a kibbutz. They would be one of the many settlements with the dream of joining to become a new Jewish State — the State of Israel.

The training for the hardships they would face in Palestine stood them well here in the forests of the Ukraine. But all the time they fought against the German occupation, they kept alive their dream. For the Zionists, this was just one of the difficult steps to the Promised Land.

Rachel and Sol decided they would make their way to Palestine with the young Zionists and start a new life after the war. Their families had been exterminated. There wasn't even a grave marker for them to visit in Europe.

61

OBERMAN'S
FRUSTRATIONS...

Major Hans Oberman spent much of the winter seeking out and destroying guerrilla groups. Using his clever map and tracks left in the snow, he established an impressive record for his superiors. In a few short months, he rid the Kiev area of a dozen partisan groups not as cautious as the Jews. Forced to move out of their camps to obtain supplies, many groups were easily stalked by the Germans. Oberman still suspected Jewish partisans of headquartering in the vast forest but was unable to detect their movements.

Frustrated, Oberman decided to fly over the forest personally with an experienced reconnaissance pilot. For two days, they flew over the area northwest of Kiev and found nothing. On the third day, they spotted deep tracks in the snow. They followed them from the air for several kilometers to a small herd of deer. Oberman swore at the animals and cursed the pilot. "Damn it, find me some tracks or some smoke or some lodges! Those bastards are down there someplace. Why the hell can't you find them? You're supposed to be the best we have!"

The pilot answered meekly. "I'm sorry, sir. That is an enormous area down there. We could fly over it for a week and not find them. They're probably smart enough to put out their fires on windless days. When it's windy the smoke dissipates before it clears the trees. And to see tracks among those trees from above is near impossible. We only found those deer because they crossed a clearing.

I doubt the guerrillas ever get out from the cover of the trees."

Oberman fumed in silence. When they landed back at Kiev, he canceled any further overflights. He would find another way.

62

A WELCOME SPRING...

When spring arrived in 1943, everyone was ready to welcome it.

Major Hans Oberman was disgruntled that he had not yet pinpointed the location of the Jews. The advent of spring would let partisans all over Eastern Europe and the Ukraine move about freely and resume their activities. Oberman had been unable to track the Jews in the snow; perhaps he could get at them through their activities now.

The German army was, of course, also overjoyed at the end of winter. Winter had been their mightiest foe so far. Now they could retrench, resupply, reinforce their starved and frozen troops. What they did not realize was that during the long winter the Russians had built up their forces and supplies and had modernized their equipment. The Russians were also ready for spring.

During the long winter, while Father Peter monitored the radio, he began to suspect another resistance group had moved into the area. They didn't broadcast often, but when they did their transmissions were always clear. Also, though most of what they transmitted was brief and in coded conversation, they occasionally made references to familiar things—to a fierce blizzard, just after the family camp had also been hit by a fierce blizzard, for example. A few other transmissions had raised Father Peter's suspicion—also his fears. He had maintained radio silence to avoid detection by the Germans and now another group was sending messages that might bring the Nazis down on them all.

The rest of the group was also concerned; they

considered breaking radio silence to warn the others not to transmit so frequently and freely. Father Peter was sure they were in the immediate vicinity. "Now that we can move out of the camp, let's carry a radio and our hand generator to a safe distance and radio them."

"And what if they are a group hostile to Jews?" Uri suggested. "We have a lot of supplies and weapons that another group would love to get their hands on. If they are a large force it would not surprise me to have them turn on us. Believe me I've had experience with another resistance group. We'd be smart to know who they are before we give knowledge of ourselves away to them."

"How can we contact them without inviting the Germans also?" Sol asked. "A meeting I mean. Arrange to find them without jeopardizing ourselves. If they are hostile to Jews, they just might decide to attack us."

"A definite possibility," Yorgi agreed. "If only we could locate the new group without revealing ourselves. That would give us a chance to look them over before risking our own security."

Everyone feared too long a wait. If the group increased their transmissions or did something else to bring the Germans this deep into the forest, they might also be found. They didn't just want to transmit a warning, but agreed it was the wisest move. Just before the vote, Rachel asked, "Just how do the Germans locate a radio transmission?"

Yorgi explained, "Radios have directional aerials. They receive the best signal when the aerials are trained in the direction from which the transmissions come. That being the case, all the Germans need to do is draw a line on a map from their receiver in the direction of the signals. Then they know the transmitter is somewhere on that line. To pinpoint the spot, they have another listener at a different location draw a second line from his receiver to the signal's direction of origin. Where those two lines intersect on the map is the location of the transmitter.

That's why we go far from camp to transmit and why we never transmit from the same spot twice."

"We have two radios. Can't we do the same thing to locate the other camp?" Rachel asked.

"If we had a map," Yorgi concluded. "But then we would only be locating the point they transmitted from. By the time we got there, we'd find only empty woods — if we were lucky — Germans with the same idea if we were unlucky."

"I'm not so sure," Sol said. "I have an idea. It has some problems, but I think we can work it out. Wait a few minutes while I get Ilya." He jumped to his feet and ran out of the room, leaving everyone wondering what he had in mind.

Ilya Chuikov was a small man in his early thirties. He'd been a mathematics teacher. He wore thick glasses. One lens was cracked and the metal frame held it precariously. The crack caused him to squint — and to remember. The lens had been cracked by the Nazis when they broke into his home months earlier. They'd arrested him, his wife and two children — a boy three and a girl two months old. They were immediately separated and he never saw his family again. He'd been arrested and made good his escape. He couldn't help his family. He couldn't even find where they'd been taken. Dejected, despondent, overcome with grief, Ilya blindly and dazed, escaped to the countryside. He made his way into the forest, like a ghost, empty and in despair. Three weeks later his path crossed that of the guerrillas and he joined their ranks.

Sol explained the problem to Ilya when they got back to the room where the general staff tried to chart their actions. "Ilya, what information would you need, would we have to give you for you to locate another resistance group somewhere in these woods? We can pick up their transmissions from two different locations and can tell the directions from which the transmissions come. But we have no map to plot their locations."

Ilya didn't even have to think before he answered. "That's a simple trigonometry problem. If you can give me the directions, I can convert them into the degrees of angle of two sides of a triangle. If you can give me the exact distance between the two receiving sets, I will have two angles and one side of a triangle. Given that bit of information, I can easily construct the rest of the triangle and tell you exactly how far you have to go and in what direction to find them."

"Then there's the answer!" Sol exclaimed.

"There are still a few problems with that," Yorgi pointed out. "First, we will not find their camp, only a transmission point from which they will have fled by the time we get there."

"I have that figured out, too," Solomon smiled triumphantly. "We'll send out two men with a radio for a known distance. The men will send an emergency message to the other group, which I hope they will return. That will give Ilya his two angles and the distance. He'll point us in the right direction and tell us how far to go.

"Our reconnaissance will observe them. If they look safe we'll make contact. If not we'll get the hell out of there and warn them by radio to stop sending before the Germans get them — or us!"

"Do you think they'll be foolish enough to transmit a reply from their camp?" Yorgi challenged.

"I have a theory about that group," Solomon explained. "I don't think they have a permanent camp like this one. I think they are mobile and move about, every few days. If they have a permanent camp, I don't think they'll transmit. Anyway, that decision will be theirs."

"Why not just warn them by radio to keep their transmitter quiet and leave it at that?" Uri asked, still uneasy about making themselves known to another resistance group.

"Because if they're moving around out there," Sol replied, "I want to know who they are before they perhaps, happen onto us. They are a greater threat to us than we to them if they *are* mobile. It's worth a try to find them. Our security may depend on knowing where and who they are."

The most difficult problem was measuring the exact distance between the two radios. They tied together and measured out two hundred meters of rope. One man walked with his end of the rope until it was fully extended, then the other walked past him until it was once more extended. They repeated their tedious process forty times, making the distance eight kilometers. It took them over twice as long as traveling that distance usually would. When they reached their destination the two men set up their radio and transmitted, using the other group's code name, picked up from monitoring transmissions.

"White Rabbit — White Rabbit — Please respond. White Rabbit — brothers in arms share your woods — please reply — we have an emergency. White Rabbit..." They transmitted the same message five times, once every minute. Then suddenly a reply came.

"Brothers in arms — this is White Rabbit. Transmit your message."

"White Rabbit — brothers in arms need to make contact with you. Can you make transmission appointment for tomorrow?" Please give time and frequency — we will stand by..."

The Jews were not really interested in establishing a time for the other group to transmit to them the next day; they just wanted them to transmit an answer that they could beam in on. The reply came.

"White Rabbit will transmit on this frequency tomorrow at 1400 — Will stand by for one minute now if there in any further message."

As soon as the message started to come in, the Jews at both receivers moved their aerials to determine the direction of best reception. Two minutes after the transmission from the other group ended, the Jews at the family camp changed to another prearranged frequency and received the exact directions from the other radio. Ilya took less than one minute to figure.

"They are exactly thirty one kilometers north of here — about five degrees west of due north."

In minutes, a contingent of five set out in that direction. It would be a torturous journey through virgin forest, with no roads or trails to make travel easier. In thirty kilometers, an error of one or two degrees could cause them to miss the other camp completely. They took one of the radios with them. If they had not made contact by transmission time tomorrow, they could use that broadcast to give them a new fix.

The trip proved more difficult than anticipated. It took more than twenty hours to travel what they estimated to be the proper distance. It was three hours before White Rabbit was scheduled to transmit again. The Jews decided to rest for the remainder of the time rather than go blindly through the woods. When the transmission came, they would get a new direction.

Of course, the Germans had monitored the transmissions of the day before and had pinpointed both parties. Their locations were marked on a map for Major Hans Oberman.

63

CAPTIVE OR FRIEND...

While four of the Jews rested, sleeping under the trees, one got up to explore the immediate area. He went one direction, then another. He found nothing, nor did he expect to, but he couldn't sleep and this kept him occupied. He'd been wondering for about twenty minutes when he found himself looking down the barrel of a German machine gun. It was in the hands of a bearded man in civilian clothes. He'd crossed paths with that of a sentry posted by the partisan group they'd been seeking.

It had been the intention of the Jews to observe the other organization before making contact. Now as he eyed his captor, the Jew wondered what he should do next. He assumed the man he faced was a partisan, but he made a split second decision not to reveal his four companions. Certainly he was not about to reveal himself as a Jew.

"Who are you? What do you do here?" the captor demanded.

"I'm a refugee. I escaped arrest in Irpen," the Jew answered, making up what he thought might be a believable story.

"Irpen? That's a hell of a long way from here. How long have you been in this forest?"

"Five days, I think. I'm no longer sure."

"Why were the Germans after you?"

"They suspect that I was involved in partisan activities."

"Were you?"

"Nothing organized."

"Why are you in this part of the forest?"

The Jew noticed that the man was relaxing a bit, lowering the weapon from being aimed at his head to his stomach. A blast there would still be fatal, but he took the gesture to mean he was being believed—perhaps. He wondered whether he should say he was lost, just wandered here or should he test this man.

"I heard in Irpen that a guerrilla group was active in these woods," he said at last. "I was hoping I could join and fight the Nazis properly."

The captor said nothing for a moment but looked his captive over carefully. Then he motioned with his weapon saying, "Lie down on your belly!"

The Jew went down.

"Now spread your legs and arms to their full reach."

The Jew stretched.

"Make one move and you're dead!"

The Jew froze.

Carefully the captor searched him. Inside the Jew's shirt he found a German pistol. "How did you come by this?"

"It's a long story. It has to do with why the Germans are after me."

"Okay, get to your feet. Put your hands behind your neck and grasp your wrists. If I see you let go of either wrist, you will have taken your last breath. Now walk." The captor pointed out the direction with his captive's gun.

The Jew walked.

One of the other Jews awoke and noticed that his comrade was gone. He'd gotten up to look for him. Hearing the captive and captor talking, he followed the sounds until he saw what was transpiring. He, too, assumed the captor was a partisan, one from the group they sought. He didn't make his own presence known. If he captured the partisan he'd never lead them to his camp. Better to wait and follow.

When the Jew and his captor started away from the spot where the confrontation took place, the observer followed unnoticed. They only had to go about two kilometers before they came to a temporary encampment. As soon as the follower saw where the camp was, he returned to his three companions and led them back to their objective. To their surprise, they saw their captive comrade coming out of the encampment with three of the other partisans. They were coming to get his friends. They couldn't understand what could have gained each other's confidence so rapidly. They had no chance to duck for cover.

"Don't be afraid! Put down your guns!" the Jew called to them as soon as he saw them. "These are Jews. This is the group of the famous **Diadia Misha.**"

64

DIADIA MISHA...

Diadia Misha was a name well known over the partisan radio network in Eastern Europe and the Ukraine. The exploits of his guerrilla group were transmitted into the occupied areas by Russian radio as a morale booster and as an encouragement for other resistance groups. What **Radio Russia** didn't publicize was that Diadia Misha's band was made up mostly of Jews.

Misha Gildenman was the name he was known by when he was an engineer in the town of **Koretz**. He'd been a peaceful man — a family man. He'd never been a leader, nor had he ever been inclined toward military matters. He would have been only too happy to live out his life as an average citizen in his town.

Life in Koretz could have been described as simple and Diadia Gildenman was content living there with his wife, son and daughter. He was approaching his middle years with satisfaction, looking forward to the future.

As had been the case in Kiev and most towns and cities where the Germans came, they were greeted as liberators when they entered Koretz. The welcome was short lived. Almost immediately after occupying Koretz, the Germans rounded up all the Jews in the area. The elderly, children, women, the weak and ill were taken to a pit twenty meters long, twenty meters wide and three meters deep. They were made to undress and were thrown in, six at a time. The Germans found great sport in shooting those stunned by the fall or the others who made futile attempts to climb out. The Nazis had set up picnic tables laden with food and drink to make a holiday atmosphere for the *sporting event*. By day's end, the Germans had slaughtered two thousand two hundred Jews. Misha's wife and thirteen year old daughter were among them.

Those Jews not murdered were herded into a makeshift ghetto. There was a synagogue where many went to say the *Kaddish*, the prayer for their dead. Many were oblivious in their grief, it had all happened so fast! So fantastic were the horrible events of the day that many of the survivors felt mainly disbelief. Some time after the Kaddish, the full impact and gravity of what had happened began to sink into Misha's mind.

Those who did not die today will surely be chosen for death tomorrow, he suddenly realized. He looked at his son, **Simcha,** sitting dazed by it all, staring into space. Misha concluded that to prevent his son's and his own murder there was but one course of action—to get away from the Nazis—escape to the forests.

"We must go, Simcha! We must get out right away! Tomorrow will be too late!"

"Go? Go where?" Simcha asked, still in a state of shock.

"To the forest," Misha answered as he rose up to face the others in the synagogue. "Listen! Listen to me, all of you! You condemned Jews, hear me!" He saw bowed heads, blank stares and tearful eyes turn toward his voice.

"Be assured," he continued, "we have no hope other than escape to the forests. That is, if it is not already too late. If we can still make it to the woods—then from there we'll take our vengeance on these Nazi pigs! Who is with me?"

Most of the unfortunate Jews in the synagogue were still too stunned to understand what Misha was saying. Many did not really hear him. Misha was, after all, one of the luckier in the sanctuary for he still had his son. Almost all the others had seen entire families butchered. Suddenly, they were alone in the world. It was too much for them. It was hard for them to think of their own escape. It was too much to ask them to care about their own lives.

When all the talking was done, sixteen men fled the ghetto in small groups, evading the German guards under the shelter of darkness. They decided to meet in the forest where they would regroup as a single band. Between them they had one pistol and five rounds of ammunition.

"Our most immediate problem is weapons, Misha said. "We now live in a world where the currency is bullets."

"I know where we can get more weapons," Simcha said. "There is a house not far from here, at the edge of the forest, where the district forester lives with his wife. I know he has several guns. He used to burst with pride showing them off to us when we played in the woods near his home. I don't know if he ever used them, but he always carried one under his arm as he inspected the woods for traps and poachers."

"He still lives there?" Misha asked.

"I suppose so," Simcha shrugged, "Unless he also has fled from the Germans."

"Or the Nazis may have confiscated his guns," another interjected.

"Let's go and see," Misha said.

"We won't have to hurt him, will we," Simcha asked. "He was always a pleasant fellow."

"I hope not," Misha replied. "I hope not. I don't even know how I'd react if violence were required of me."

It was past midnight when the Jews got to the forester's hut. Misha—in possession of the one pistol they had, its cylinder short one bullet—knocked at the door of the little house. Guns were completely foreign to Misha. He had never fired one before; now he was about to threaten a man's life with this pistol.

The dim glow of a kerosene lamp came on, its light penetrating a window at the front of the house. A voice came through the bolted wooden door. "Yes, who is it? What do you want at this hour?"

"I am told you are the forester in this district," Misha answered nervously. "I was sent to report a fire to you. It is burning in the forest about three kilometers from here!"

They could hear the bolt of the door slide back. Misha's throat tightened and his heart pounded. As the door swung open, Misha thrust the pistol forward. In his excitement, he miscalculated the distance to the man who stood closer than he'd expected. The barrel of the pistol jammed right into the left nostril of the flabbergasted forester.

"Don't move!" and seeing what he had just done, Misha added, "This is a gun I have up your nose!"

The error in judgment was quite effective. The poor man stood speechless, looking down with crossed eyes at the pistol barrel. One of the other Jews shouldered past the terrified forester and in a moment brought the forester's wife out from the only other room in the house. Both were clad in nightshirts, speechless with fear.

Simcha and two others went in and searched the premises.

"You have guns and ammunition?" Misha demanded, overcoming his own anxiety sufficiently to get the words out.

"Yes! Yes! Please don't hurt us! I'll give you anything you want. Please, trust me! Please!"

Misha began to feel sorry for the poor devil, but he was struggling for his own survival, for his son's, that of his small band. "Get them. All of them! No tricks! Get all of the ammunition, too."

The forester went to a locked cupboard in a corner of the room and took down a key hidden above the door. He fumbled with the lock nervously trying to get the key in. Before he could get it opened, one of the men shoved him aside, got it open and emptied the cabinet of four rifles, a shotgun and enough ammunition to last quite a while—if they were frugal.

Simcha and the other searchers found a few other supplies that would be helpful in the forests. They then abandoned the house as quickly as they'd come, leaving the forester and his wife safe inside.

Their first action was a success. But as they left the hut, Misha felt pangs of guilt. He was not yet used to bullying his fellow human beings.

Diadia Misha was the name by which Misha Gildenman became known. His group grew and remained predominantly Jewish. They were mobile, in spite of the fact that they had families and elderly Jews with them. Their activities against the Germans from the forests of the Ukraine soon became legend.

65

BROTHERS IN ARMS
MEET WHITE RABBIT...

The five Jews who had come to make the rendezvous were welcomed into the camp where they were introduced to Diadia Misha, his son Simcha and his entire general staff. They told them of their own group and of their activities, several of which the Russians had attributed to Diadia's men.

It was decided at that meeting that Diadia Misha would move his group to the vicinity of the family camp. They had no intention of merging the groups, but perhaps they could exchange supplies, equipment and weapons. Perhaps they could also coordinate a few missions. So mobile was this resistance group that they broke camp and were on the way in less than two hours, in spite of the fact they were nearly two hundred people. They were true nomads, this in spite of the fact that they had with them a few families that couldn't be left behind to fend for themselves. It was agreed that some of these families would remain in the permanent family camp with Solomon's group. This would give Diadia's group even more mobility.

At the prearranged time, they transmitted a brief message.

"Brothers in arms, White Rabbit coming in." And then, just as a teaser, which they knew the recipients would not fully understand, they signed off, "*Shalom, brothers—Shalom*, from White Rabbit." The message was accompanied by a code word, which told Sol's group that their five emissaries were safe and that all was on the up and up.

It took three days for the large group to migrate to the vicinity of the family camp. They had to move slowly because their pace was set by the elderly and children. The meeting of the two groups took place just before the beginning of Passover. On April 18, 1943, the two Jewish communities celebrated the first night of Passover together. While the Jews had their *Seder*, the few gentiles monitored the radios and took care of all the chores of the camps.

Father Peter was at his favorite post, in the radio hut. He was the first to hear a message relayed from an underground transmitter in the Jewish ghetto of Warsaw, Poland...

"Please send help! All resistance forces in Warsaw area please send help! Siege of our ghetto is imminent. Please send help..."

66

WARSAW GHETTO UPRISING...

The messages out of the Jewish ghetto in Warsaw struck me the deepest for I had many friends left behind there. Messages from or about the Jewish ghetto at Warsaw were frequent. They came over the radios in the Ukraine and Eastern Europe intermittently and with increasing frequency during the days and nights of 1943. Actual signals from within the ghetto were too weak to be heard in the Ukrainian resistance camps, but the messages were relayed by others who could receive them. Most messages were reports of inhuman treatment of the Jews in the ghetto. They told of roundups, starvation, disease and overcrowding and deportations to a place called **Treblinka.**

They also asked for help from nearby partisan groups, from governments of the free world, from the people of Warsaw...

Help never came!

But this new series of messages that came on the 18th of April of 1943 were different. They indicated that the ghetto's destruction was imminent. They were asking for supplies, weapons, ammunition. The Jews of the **Warsaw Ghetto** were going to fight. They also asked that the freedom loving people of Poland rise up against the Nazis simultaneously outside of the ghetto. They suggested that while the Germans were occupied with the attempted elimination of those Jews left inside the Warsaw Ghetto, the guerrilla forces of the area take the opportunity to attack the Germans at other points to divide their attention and forces.

The suggestions went unheeded.

After all, there had never been a major uprising against the Germans since the beginning of the war. Why expect these surrounded, half starved, unarmed Jews to cause the Germans any problems? Once the Germans started their destruction of the ghetto, it and they would be eliminated. To many of the Poles, that thought was not disturbing. Let the Germans do what many of them had wanted to do themselves — rid Poland of the Jews.

On the night of April 18ᵗʰ, the Jews of the Warsaw Ghetto were totally alone. They awaited the German attack, which they knew would come early the next morning. There were secret routes of escape from the ghetto, difficult and dangerous, but not as difficult and hopeless as the coming days would be in the ghetto. Only a few of the ghetto Jews chose to escape. In fact many Jews, who by some good fortune and deception were able to continue living outside, chose this time to enter the ghetto. They entered the ghetto through the secret escape routes so they could fight the Germans with their brothers. After all, if a Jew was outside the ghetto, he was still in a hostile territory, with no real sanctuary he could get to.

That night of April 18, 1943, Jews from outside the Warsaw Ghetto celebrated the first night of Passover with the Jews inside the ghetto. They all knew this would probably be their last Passover. They chose to die fighting the Nazis.

While the world watched in silence, **Himmler** himself decided to destroy the Warsaw Ghetto. The Germans feared that if the Jews resisted, others might be encouraged. Better raze the entire ghetto and kill every

Jew in it. Himmler intended to accomplish this in one day, so he could give Hitler a birthday present on April 20th — a message, *"Warsaw ist Judenrein!* — Warsaw is clean of Jews!"

To do the job, the Germans mobilized two thousand **SS** men and officers, three detachments of **Wehrmacht** artillery and mine experts, two battalions of German police, more than three hundred fifty Polish police and a battalion of turncoat Ukrainians who chose collaboration over prisoner of war camps. In addition, a massive force of seven thousand men was brought into the Warsaw area in case reinforcements were needed. The weapons of war to be used against the poorly equipped Jews were the most modern and sophisticated in the world. After all, the world would be watching and Himmler did not want to be embarrassed on the Fuhrer's birthday.

67

THE JEWS OF WARSAW ARE FIGHTING...

On the morning of April 19, Father Peter monitored the radio...

"The Jews of the Warsaw Ghetto are fighting. Armed uprising against the Germans..."

There was no more news than that.

The message was transmitted throughout the day. No details were given. The same message was received and relayed throughout occupied Europe and Russia. It was relayed to the free world.

"The Jews of the Warsaw Ghetto are fighting!"

68

THE GERMANS WERE BEATEN TODAY...

On the evening of April 19, Father Peter heard another message relayed to the radio receivers of the Ukraine.

"Warsaw Ghetto Jews still hold the ghetto. Germans were beaten today. Fellow freedom fighters — join the revolt!" There were messages the night of the 20th and 21st and for many more nights. Each night, the listeners thought it would be the last. Each night, they were surprised and elated that the Jews still held the ghetto. Each night there was an appeal for help. Each night the appeal fell on deaf ears.

The fighters in the Ukraine were too far away — those who were near enough didn't help. Then the ghetto fighters appealed to the allied forces to bomb the Germans, to drop supplies, to help in any way they could.

No one seemed to care.

But the Warsaw Jews were prepared to fight to the end — alone if need be.

The days and nights turned into a week — that single week into a miraculous two. Each day the Jews fought heroically against staggering odds. They suffered savage casualties but fought back with unbelievable determination. Even the Germans officers developed a silent, unspoken respect for them. The German soldiers dreaded every time they had to enter the ghetto.

There was merciless shelling and mortar barraging of the area. If the Jews had given up at any time, they would still have had the respect of those who watched — those who watched but would not help. But the Jews refused to give up. They knew surrender meant death. So did continuing the battle. But they preferred to die with weapons in hand, even when those weapons were only sticks and clubs. And each day their broadcast confirmed they still had control of the ghetto.

On May 8th, the resistance in its twentieth day, the Germans came across the headquarters of the **Jewish Fighting Organization**, a large bunker at **Mila 18**. At the time, it hid about three hundred noncombatants and just under a hundred ghetto fighters. There were five outside entrances to the bunker. The Germans surrounded it. The bunker was terribly overcrowded and if there were any chance to make a fight of it, it would have to be emptied of some people. Under the circumstances, a majority of the noncombatants chose to give themselves up to the Germans, knowing full well they were probably going to their deaths.

Those who stayed in the bunker were given what weapons there were and prepared for war literally underground. But the Germans didn't come in. They sealed the five entrances and piped lethal gas down into the bunker. With the exception of a few who were accidentally near an air source, the fighters died either of suicide or of the horrible choking gas.

That night there was no message to the outside world. Mila 18 had been the communication point from which news of the actions was transmitted. It had been the coordination center of the Jewish Fighting Organization. But even though the communication and nerve center of the revolt was struck down, the Warsaw Ghetto was still not in the hands of the Germans.

On May 16, after four weeks of fighting, there was still enough resistance from the ghetto that Germans could not enter without risk. It was rubble. A continuous black smoke rose from smoldering buildings. The resistance was no longer organized, but death greeted any German who dared enter. There had been no surrender. Nevertheless, **SS General Jurgen von Stroop** sent word to his superiors that the Warsaw Ghetto no longer existed.

69

UPRISING...

The Warsaw Ghetto Uprising was a tremendous encouragement to all partisans in the occupied territories. With this, the first major uprising against the Germans in the entire war, the myth of the German super race was shattered forever. That, along with the daily reports of Russian victories, gave guerrilla fighters all the courage they needed to take on the enemy. Sabotage, ambushes, raids, harassment and reprisals were going on all over the occupied territories. In the Kiev area, the joint coordinated actions of the two Jewish groups became intolerable to the Nazis.

Diadia Misha's group encamped themselves about fifteen kilometers from the family camp. Because of the permanence of the family camp many of the elderly and noncombatants from Misha's group joined the community. Solomon frequently traveled the distance between the camps to coordinate activities. Both were keeping radio silence now.

He enjoyed the trips through the forest during the spring and summer months. Often he would be accompanied by Rachel and then the journey would be especially wonderful. They would pretend it was a summer picnic outing, that there was no war, that they were free to pursue life. With the increasing number of reports coming in of Nazi retreats on the Russian front, they began to talk more and more of their future.

On one such occasion Solomon was particularly optimistic. The day was warm and beautiful and his mood was reflected in the brisk pace he set for Rachel as they walked. She loved it when he felt uplifted like this, but his buoyancy was wearing her out.

"Solomon darling. Please slow down. It's so lovely in the woods. Let's sit down a while and just enjoy it." She sat down on a huge fallen tree and made a place for him next to her. "Smell how fresh and sweet the air is." She grabbed at his hand and pulled him down to sit next to her.

"It really is a wonderful day, Rachel."

"It's a day when you could almost put the past out of your mind. It's a day to only think of now."

"It's better than that, Rachel." Solomon had an almost dreamy look in his eyes as he stared off into the little bit of blue sky that was allowed through the treetops. "It is a day to think about the future."

Rachel rested her head on Solomon's shoulder and hugged him gently. "Oh Solomon. There really will be a future for us. It makes me so happy to know you realize it, too. I do love you so!"

Sol was still caught up in his daydreams. "Can you imagine, Rachel, what it will be like in Palestine? The Zionists tell me it is like nowhere else in the world for a Jew. Our history began there—it's our heritage. They say it will someday be our nation again. Imagine it! Our own country—a place where we will be free—one place in this damned world where we will feel welcome, where we will be among our own people. Can you imagine it?"

"What do you mean, the Zionists tell you? Solomon, you *are* a Zionist! You know, it's all you ever talk about anymore. I think you've persuaded more of our group to go there than anyone else has."

"I guess you're right," Sol agreed with a chuckle. "But what else is there to do after the war? There's no place for us anywhere else in the world—except maybe America—and there's an ocean between there and us. To Palestine we can walk if necessary!"

"Are you sure there will be no place for the Jews in

Europe or Russia after the war? Don't you think the world will be wiser for the tragedy it has witnessed now?"

"Did the world lift a finger for the ghetto Jews of Warsaw? The same apathy that let the Warsaw Ghetto Jews die will let the anti-Semites run rampant with their pogroms again. Whenever there will be problems in a country, the Jew will again be the scapegoat. We will live in freedom *only* if we have our own country."

"When will we go?"

"As soon as the way is clear."

"That might be a long time, Solomon."

He contemplated a moment, kicking at some loose pebbles. "If what the radio broadcasts is true, it may not be as long as we think. The German defenses are breaking down everywhere now. And with England and America becoming more of a threat—and the losses in Africa, Hitler's attentions are being divided. While Russia becomes stronger, the Nazi is weakening." He paused, picking at some bark from the tree trunk they were sitting on, then added, "And we must do everything we can to weaken him further!"

In the months after the two groups joined forces, their coordinated effort took a devastating toll of the German supplies and troops. Together they attacked trains, convoys, struck at factories, fuel depots, warehouses, small German outposts, whatever appeared to be important target. The partisans lost many of their own fighters, but now with the tide of the war turning and the Germans becoming more intolerable as occupiers of the Ukraine, more and more people wanted to join the resistance.

In all the cities and towns in the occupied areas, the Germans were now rounding up civilians for forced labor camps. People who had been willing quietly to outlast the occupation were now being threatened with deportation to German labor camps to the west. People would leave their homes in the morning and never return. And no one ever returned from a labor camp. The only way to avoid deportation was to bribe someone and few had anything to bribe with. Many of the young and able who remained in the occupied lands, who were the prime targets of roundups, preferred escape into the forests to join partisan groups.

70

OBSESSION...

Over the months, Major Hans Oberman turned partisan hunting into a science. More groups formed, but at the same time it became easier to run them down. Oberman was not capturing groups faster than they were organizing, but he made sure that only he knew that. He released to his superiors only the numbers he'd captured and destroyed. Statistics favorable to the partisans he kept strictly to himself. Oberman's only frustration was that he could not pinpoint the "Jewish group." He had no idea that now there were two in his area. By midsummer, "Getting those damned Jews!" obsessed him.

He pondered for hours at a time over his problem. He went into rages if someone disturbed his concentration. It insulted his intelligence to think the *"sub-humans"* could outsmart him. He was determined to get them. He had to get them! Each week that passed deepened his obsession. He had the map of those woods memorized. There were hundreds of locations that could hide a large contingent of Jews. How can he isolate them? Where could he hide *his* troops in those forests? There had to be an answer. And he knew when he found it, it would probably be a simple answer.

I've been working too hard on this problem, Oberman finally decided. "I must get away for a while and come back to it when I'm fresh. A new approach is what I need!"

He called one of his many women companions, **Eva Kromer** and arranged to go with her to a resort area the Germans had established for their officers. Eva was perfect for his needs. If anyone could take his mind off of his problem, it would be Eva. She was a perfect distraction. She had beautiful, long, red hair — when she let it down — and she let it down often. Eva was a little taller than Oberman, but that didn't bother him. Her long legs were curved gracefully, joined to her slim body by perfectly shaped buttocks. Nature had sculptured her face to go ideally with the rest of her body. She considered her freckles a flaw, but Oberman thought they made her even more attractive, contrasting with and setting off a sparkle in her blue eyes. She was one of many German women brought to Kiev once the Germans had settled in, to bring a little of home to officers of the Reich. Her looks alone were enough to distract most men from their problems, even if they didn't know that the only thing fierier than her flaming hair was her insatiable passion.

The ride to the resort took them through heavily wooded hills. In the chauffeur driven staff car, the beautiful Eva at his right, Oberman started to unwind. The driver had a difficult time keeping his eyes off Eva in his rear view mirror. She knew he was watching her and did all she could to provoke him. Oberman didn't notice. He thought the thigh she was showing was for his benefit.

The resort was old and posh, established nearly a century earlier to host aristocracy in the days of the Tsars. Now it was a favorite German hideaway. The palatial lodge had hundreds of rooms. It boasted seven elegant dining rooms, three ballrooms, billiard rooms and a library which had been emptied of most of its good books under the Communists and which had been restocked now with German volumes. There were three kitchens to prepare gourmet meals for the officer and their guests. There were several cocktail lounges and even more sitting rooms. A long porch graced the back of the building and overlooked formal gardens that led down to a large lake where Germans swam, sunned and went boating. About half the rooms were available to officers; the others housed a rotating complement of prostitutes, some imported from Germany, some brought in from the occupied countries. The rest of the sizable staff lived in special servant quarters. It was the type of building the Communists loved to destroy or cut up into apartments for the masses. Only because it was secluded and a place the Communist Party also used for high ranking officials, did it survive.

Oberman loved this place. It fit his self image. By the time he and Eva had dinner and drinks and a walk in the gardens, they were ready to retire. With the drive up, it had been a full and tiring day and Oberman wanted to use what energies he had left for a prolonged evening of sexual pleasures. His holiday was already a success. Kiev, the war, the Jews — they were the furthest things from his mind.

Eva knew her part well, but for her it was not an act. She loved what she did best. If she could do it the way that excited her companion the most, it heightened her own pleasure. She had a knack for discovering what each of her suitors liked. Best of all she had no inhibitions preventing her from pleasing them. She even had a masochistic side to her that pleased many of the sadistic tastes of the German officers she knew.

Oberman sat down in an easy chair and lifted his leg toward Eva, her cue to start the ritual. She took his boot by the heel and with a giggle swung her own leg over his, showing as much thigh as she could in the move. This left her straddling Oberman's boot, holding the heel in her hands, her shapely posterior swaying before his eyes. Oberman placed his other boot on her backside and pushed until the boot she held came off, sending her sprawling onto the bed nearby showing as much of her thigh to Oberman as she could and still leaving something for the other boot. This brought a roar of laughter from Oberman and more giggles from Eva.

She repeated the procedure with the other boot, this

time showing off as much of her inner thighs as she could when she fell. Again laughter! "And what do you see that is so interesting, you rascal?" she asked, displaying the fact that she wore no undergarments.

Oberman roared with laughter and drew his pistol and took aim at his target. "Bang, bang. Now you have a *big* hole there."

"The better to engulf you with," she said in a low, wolfish voice. She got up and unbuttoned his tunic, belts and shirt and removed them all. She pulled off his socks and left him sitting only in his trousers.

"Now I feel self conscious with all my clothes still on. What shall I do about that?" Without waiting for an answer, she moved about the room dropping her garments in the most seductive ways she could think up. Like a stripper dancing on a stage, bumping and grinding, responding to her audience's rising ardor. She ended up directly before him in a full display of her naked beauty.

"Eva, you are one of the few women I've ever known who is more beautiful naked than partially dressed."

"Oh, Hans, you say such sweet things. I'm happy you like what you see," she giggled coyly.

"Do what else I like to see!"

He became increasingly aroused as she performed every autoerotic act she could think of for him, pleasuring herself with every variety of self stimulation. When she sensed that he was eager for her touch, she removed the remainder of his clothing and stimulated him first manually, then orally. It took quite some time before they fondled and manipulated their way to the bed. There they tried every contortion imaginable. By 10:00 PM he cuddled up to the soft, warm buttocks of his sleeping bed partner, then dozed off.

"The water!" Oberman came to a sitting position as he

shouted the words.

"My God ... what is it, Hans?" Eva woke with a start.

"That's the answer! The water! Damn if it didn't come to me in my sleep. I'll get those bastards because they need water! My God, it's so obvious! How could I have missed it?"

He jumped from the bed with no further explanation to Eva. "Go back to sleep. I'm going to take a ride around the lake and think. It's a military problem and does not concern you. Sleep a few more hours; when I return we will go to breakfast."

Oberman was at the stables in fifteen minutes. He was given a fine animal—spirited and sleek. He was an excellent rider, having been taught as a child by his grandfather who had been a cavalry officer. It was early and he had the bridle path to himself. Spirited as it was, the horse knew that the man on its back would not be intimidated. It settled down to accepting Oberman's every subtle command. There was a chill and mist in the air—it would be the better part of an hour before the sun would burn it off. Oberman's mind was free.

He mentally went over the maps he had so thoroughly memorized, seeing them as if they were spread before him. Aloud he said to himself, "It has to work, I can't miss," "Those Jews have to live near water—and it must be a sizable source. Let me see," he said visualizing the maps. "There are one, two, three"—four, five—and there is a lake—six, seven—and another lake—"yes, that's it. I'm sure—two lakes and seven streams or rivers large enough to support a large band..." They have to be along one of them. "I've got them now!"

He thought it through again, smiling broadly. "Yes, by damn, I have them!"

71

LIEUTENANT MEINHART...

As soon as he returned to his office, Oberman rechecked his maps. They were just as he'd recalled them. He sent for one of his lieutenants. In a few minutes a young, ruddy faced, blue eyed German entered the office. He snapped his heels smartly, extended his arm in a proper, "Heil Hitler! **Lieutenant Meinhart** reporting as ordered, sir."

"Heil Hitler; be at ease, Meinhart." Oberman paused. "Please sit down, Lieutenant. I have heard much about you. You are a very conscientious officer." He paused just long enough to see that his patronizing statement was sinking in. "I have a very important project—and I need a man with your qualifications."

"Thank you, sir. I try my best to do my duty for the Fuhrer."

"Meinhart, I want you to put together a mission for me and carry it out to the letter. There can be no blunders. If it is carried out properly, there will be a citation for you."

Meinhart's eyes lit up. Oberman knew they would.

"This operation is in two stages. The first stage will require seven small detachments, perhaps five men in each. They should be made up of Ukrainian or Polish collaborators and police. The second stage will depend on a large detachment of our finest men—as many as possible battle seasoned—perhaps two hundred—and well armed." Meinhart's eagerness could not be disguised, "I am honored, Major Oberman. I have been hoping for a chance like this—to serve my Fuhrer—to show what I can do. I will not let you down!"

"I know I have picked the best man for this important job. I knew it when I first heard of you. You are ambitious. That is nothing to be ashamed of. To me it means you will do this job right."

Oberman rolled out a map on his desk. He motioned Meinhart over. "Our objective is somewhere in this vast forested area. It is the headquarters of the most dangerous guerrilla group in the Kiev area. They have caused us more losses in men and equipment than all the other groups together. I estimate them to be at least two to three hundred strong."

Looking over the map, Meinhart asked, "What is your plan to flush them out, sir?"

"The first stage is to locate them. That is where the non German personnel will be used. To find the partisans we will have to sacrifice some of the men from the seven small detachments. They will be the Poles and Ukrainians—no great loss. Once we've located them—then the German troops must move in immediately before the guerrillas can escape."

Oberman took a pencil from his desktop. He motioned Meinhart to bend closer. "For a group as large as the one we are after, there must be a large water supply. We know they have been operating in the area for a long time. To me that means they have a permanent camp. That camp has to be near or on one of nine water sources."

With a broad motion, Oberman circled the area showing the potential sites. "You will note that in this area there are seven streams and two lakes that could support such a large group."

Meinhart leaned even closer to the map, squinting, concentrating, as Oberman paused to let him study each of those waterways. "Yes, they must be on one of those water supplies. But which one; and how will we send our troops there before they move out?"

"Ah, that's the beauty of my plan!" Oberman grinned with great satisfaction. "We send one detachment of

Polaks and Ukrainians up each of the streams and to the lakes. We have our troops ready for instant mobilization. Each reconnaissance unit will carry a field radio on which they will transmit a password every ten minutes. Each will have its own codeword. They will transmit only that codeword, so if the partisans are monitoring us, they will not know what we are up to."

Meinhart straightened up. "I think I understand. When one of them stops transmitting, we will know the guerrillas have taken them and where."

"I knew I had the right man in you," Oberman replied. "If a detachment is killed or captured by the guerrillas, they will miss a code transmission. We'll know immediately which area to send our troops to and within a mater of minutes, they'll be mobilized."

"You realize the patrol won't have a chance to survive."

"That is why we send Slavs."

"When do we do this?"

"As soon as you and I have our details worked out. First of all, we have to determine the best way to transport the attack force. We must assume those J... those guerrillas are going to be in the most difficult area to reach. We'll have to move a lot of men and equipment through rough terrain in a hurry. And one thing for sure – I want every one of them wiped out. No prisoners!"

"Yes, that will set an example, of course."

"Yes, they'll be destroyed and buried in a mass grave right in their camp – and the camp will be leveled. Do you understand?"

"I'll work out every detail."

"Meinhart – make sure there is no room for error. Take the rest of the week if you must."

Meinhart left Oberman's office, his assignment uppermost in his mind. Oberman looked out of his window and saw what a sunny day it was. Enough work for today. He turned and headed out the door. As he passed the desk of his aid, he said, "Give me a blank sheet of paper."

The aid handed him a sheet of official letterhead and Oberman signed it on the bottom.

"There, now type up an order for a roundup in retribution for the train derailment last night. Pick a place where we can get about two hundred of these Ukrainian dogs. Just type it up above my signature and have the roundup taken care of today. Dispose of them in Babi Yar."

He left the building to spend the rest of his day at leisure.

72

A LOVELY DAY...

Ivan and Sosha enjoyed the lovely day as they made their way into the city. They made the trip about once a week by horse cart to keep abreast of what was new in the occupation. "One could almost think there was no war on a day like this," Ivan said.

"It is beautiful today," she agreed as she looked up at the cloudless sky. The sun warmed her face and she remembered how it used to be to enjoy carefree days. A bird flew through her field of vision. "I wonder if birds know there is a war?"

Ivan looked at her and chuckled.

"I really mean it, Ivan. Do you think they know or sense a difference? After all, we share this place with them. We live in a hell on earth. Could they be indifferent to it? Are they disturbed by what we do to each other? Or are they in a world apart? If so I wish I could be a bird." Frivolous thoughts were a luxury and Sosha wanted to savor the mood.

Ivan remained silent, holding the reins out of habit, the horse making all of the important decisions of the morning. How much longer? He wondered. When will this horrible time pass? It seems an eternity since Sol came into our lives and brought the war with him. How will it all end? When?

A squirrel ran across the road ahead of the horse. The animals seemed to ignore each other completely. "Why can't people be like that?" Ivan said, nodding toward the squirrel as it vanished into the brush. "They live and let live. They only attack for survival, while man attacks for the sake of destruction—pure destruction."

"What?" Sosha asked. "I'm sorry. What did you say?"

"Nothing, it's not important."

It was midmorning when they approached Kiev. There didn't seem to be the usual turmoil as their horse took them to the marketplace by the route it knew so well. Everyone seemed affected by the weather. It was like that first day of sunshine after a dismal week of rain.

"We picked a good day to come to the city," Sosha said. "It was a lovely ride and the people will be in a mood to gossip."

Ivan was about to agree when he heard a commotion behind him. He started turning to look over his shoulder as a truck crossed the street and stopped in the intersection just ahead of them. Soldiers with machine guns jumped from the tailgate. Then he realized what the commotion behind them must be. "It's a roundup! Jump off the wagon and run back the way we came!" But he looked over his shoulder as he'd started to do a second earlier and lost all heart. "Dear God, we're caught!"

The street behind them was cordoned off.

All around them people were screaming, running for doorways that were barricaded and boarded up. The Germans, as usual, had chosen the site of the roundup well. The only escape was to charge the barricade and be shot. Some did just that. Gunners obligingly shot them down.

As things settled down, Ivan estimated that there were perhaps seventy people in the area. At precisely the same time, roundups were taking place in two other places just a block apart.

"Ivan, what can we do?"

"Stay with me, Sosha. If you see any chance at all for escape, tell me. But don't let us get separated—and don't do anything to draw their fire. Maybe they will interrogate us and let us go. Just keep your eyes open and be cautious."

The Germans advanced from both ends of the street. Ivan and Sosha climbed from the wagon. People were being herded into a compact group for easier control.

"Look, they're taking our wagon and horse!" Sosha exclaimed, watching soldiers lead the animal by his reins.

"Shh! There is nothing we can do about that. If all we lose today is our horse and wagon, I'll consider it a bargain."

The group was tightly crowded together. Two Germans with machine guns guarded them as two trucks pulled up. *"Schnell! Hinein!* Hurry, get in!" one of the Germans commanded gruffly.

The crowd was divided into the two trucks. Ivan and Sosha remained together.

73

GESTAPO HEADQUARTERS...

It was only a few minutes by truck to **Gestapo** headquarters in the old **Palace Of Labor** building at **Vladimirskaya Street 33.** It was an enormous, dark gray, almost black building; an ominous building. People were known to walk blocks out of their way not to have to pass near this structure. Its façade was almost majestic, but it fooled no one. Inside was a multitude of interrogation rooms, detention cells, torture chambers and, for lack of a better word, dungeons.

The truck pulled into a courtyard in the rear of the Gestapo building and unloaded its terrified cargo. The trucks from the other roundups were already there. The poor souls that had disembarked them were lined up in three rows along one wall of the yard. The newcomers, Ivan and Sosha among them, were shoved into three more lines in front of the first. An SS captain walked in front of the rows of captives, a riding crop in his right hand. As he walked past each person in the front row, he pointed the whip at that row and counted by sixes as he went. Ivan thought it remarkable that he knew his multiplication tables of six so fluently. How often he must do this, Ivan thought bitterly. When he got to the end there were only five in that row. He had thirty-four rows of six and one of five deep.

"Two hundred and nine of you is what I count," he said. "My orders call for two hundred."

With his whip he tapped nine of the prisoners in the first row on the shoulders. Ivan and Sosha were ten and eleven in that row. "You nine that I have tapped, get out of here — fast!"

He waved his riding crop toward an iron door in the wall of the courtyard. The fortunate nine wasted no time in going out the portal that was opened for them by a guard. Simultaneously Ivan and Sosha thought, thank God we've not been separated!

"All right," the Captain started, "last night a train was derailed by partisans. You are the price for that act." Then he said what Ivan had feared. "Sergeant, separate the men and women and take them into the male and female detention rooms." He went into the building.

Just before they were separated, Ivan quickly told Sosha, "Be careful. At least they're taking us inside. That must be a good sign. If we were just to be shot they'd be putting us back on the trucks. Watch for opportunities that..."

He was pushed on his way.

The women were taken into the building first while the men kept standing in the new lines they had formed. After about twenty minutes, a door opened and an officer called to the sergeant who had been put in charge of the men. "Get going! The first two lines — through the door! The second two lines follow next! Then the last two lines. Go! *Schnell!*"

As they entered the building, they were immediately redivided. An officer stood where he could quickly see each man as he entered. Most he sent down a hall to the right. Every once in a while he directed someone out and had him held in a new line forming along a wall of the hallway to the left.

Ivan found himself standing in the left hall along with about thirty other men, all particularly strong and healthy-looking. Ivan was among the oldest in the group, but also the biggest. All the elderly, sickly and those younger than their late teens had been sent on.

Ivan immediately decided that they had been held out for some kind of work detail. He feared for the others. But he took heart that the same sort of division was made among the women. Sosha was, after all, a strong and healthy woman.

Oh God, please let her be safe! He prayed silently.

There had been fewer women than men in the roundup—only fifty of them. They, too, had been divided into two groups. Out of the entire group, nine had been pulled out for further evaluation, all in their late teens or early twenties and all attractive.

Sosha and the others had been sent down the hall to the right. At the end of that hall, they were herded into a large, windowless room. There were two doors in one wall—a small one for people and next to it an opening with two swinging doors, large enough to unload supplies off trucks. The floor was concrete, the walls bare brick. The room was illuminated from overhead lights. It had obviously been a big storage room. As the women entered, a woman in a German uniform handed each a large envelope and a pencil and directed them to one wall of the room opposite the two doors. When everyone was in place she announced, "Each of you has an envelope and a pencil. First, write your name and your home address on the front. Then put all of your belongings into the envelope. Everything! Papers, money, jewelry, rings, bracelets, necklaces... Your name on the envelope will insure that you get it back after you are either released from custody here or when you reach your destination—if it is decided that you are to be sent for factory work." The woman's voice and demeanor was firm but pleasant. She had her job to do and she tried to do it as efficiently as possible. She was going to get these people through the unpleasantry of the day as easily as possible for everyone.

"What about our husbands, our families?" one woman asked.

"If you were picked up together, you will be reunited at your destination or you will be released together if all of your papers are in order. Those of you who are sent to work in a factory will have a chance to tell your families after processing. Now all of you do as you are told! Bring up your envelopes as soon as you've followed your instructions. And be sure! You will be searched later. If you hold out anything, it will go hard for you!"

One by one the women handed in their envelopes.

"Very well, is that everyone?" She paused to look around at the women. "Good. Now line up in two rows by the double doors here. When they open, you will be asked to get on a truck that will drive you the short distance to the old school a few blocks from here. There you will be taken into the building for further processing. Be prepared to tell them all the skills you have. Also you will have the opportunity to request that the rest of your family be notified where you are. Those of you who are to be released will get your belongings back then, also. Those of you who were picked up with husbands or family will be reunited there—as long as papers are in order and you cooperate!"

She looked once more about the room. Satisfied that everyone understood, she continued, "When the door opens, hurry along. Those who loiter will have the last choices for good jobs."

As soon as her speech was ended, the doors swung open. The women rushed forward. No one wanted to be last. No sooner were they crowded in the van of the truck than the doors were slammed shut, plunging the women into pitch darkness. The darkness itself brought terror. The truck lurched and in the blackness most of the women fell over each other. There was screaming and swearing. The smell of engine fumes started to fill the darkness. Suddenly a woman realized and cried, "It's a gassing van! They are killing us!"

For an instant it became quiet—quiet enough to hear the hissing, then pandemonium.

"Oh Ivan, Ivan, I want to be with you!" Tears burned in Sosha's eyes. She lay on the floor where she had fallen, oblivious to the panic about her. "Oh dear Ivan, oh God no, not like this!" She became nauseated and dizzy. She wanted not to vomit. She coughed out the contents of her stomach. Her head began to throb. "Please, God—no. Ivan—help—Plea .. se..." ...then passed into unconsciousness.

One by one, the screams from inside the van died out. And then there was only the hissing.

The truck bumped and bounced down a rough dirt road into the ravine of Babi Yar. It came to a stop at the front of a sand and clay cliff about five meters high. The van doors were opened. A stench of human waste and carbon monoxide filled motor fumes poured out as daylight broke in to reveal a limp tangle of female corpses, their lips all strangely red from the gas.

Four Ukrainians jumped into the van and started to throw out bodies. A few still lived, but that didn't matter—they were thrown off with the others. Once empty, the truck was driven off. It would be hosed out and cleaned up for its next load.

The four Ukrainians joined thirteen others who were already taking shoes and other garments off the dead. They placed the clothing on individual piles of coats, blouses, shoes, skirts, even underwear.

One Ukrainian checked each mouth and pulled out with pliers what valuable gold teeth he found, tossing them into buckets. His work was easy. Death by gas left the mouths gaping. Another Ukrainian pressed a finger into each anus and vagina to make sure no valuables had been smuggled that way. His efforts often produced rings, diamonds, gold coins and other small valuables.

They were an efficient crew and in minutes the bodies were being laid out neatly next to each other at the foot of the cliff. A German supervised the entire operation. He passed by the bodies and anyone that didn't seem dead he shot in the head with his pistol. Sometimes he shot just out of boredom. The Ukrainians were ready for the next truckload, which would be along soon.

After several trucks, when there were a few hundred bodies, German ingenuity was again demonstrated. To expedite the burial, large charges of dynamite would be set off along the cliff, bringing down just the right portion of it to cover the dead. Over several months this procedure had terraced the ravine in this section of Babi Yar.

74

SYRETSKY CAMP...

Ivan and the group of men he was with were taken to another large room where they, too, turned over all their possessions. No pretense was made that they would get anything back. Good clothing was exchanged for rags — their hair was cut away — they were told that if they didn't cooperate they'd be shot on the spot. Taken back to the courtyard by another door, they were herded onto open trucks under heavy guard.

As they pulled out of the courtyard, a gas van waited to enter. Seeing it Ivan's fear for Sosha turned to despair. After a few moments of driving, Ivan saw they were being taken in the direction of Babi Yar. At the entrance to the ravine, the road forked just outside the gate. The road to the right wound down into the ravine. The fork to the left, which their truck took, led around the top of the ravine's southern rim. Shortly, the truck came to a double set of barbed wire gates. An armed guard opened the first, which was situated at the foot of a machine gun tower. As soon as the truck passed through, the gate behind it closed. Another guard opened the second one. On both of the gates, as well as on the barbed wire fences, there were signs in German, Russian and Ukrainian: **"Lethal Electric Charge — Danger!"**

Once inside the second gate, the truck drove on until it stopped in what seemed to be a camp. Ivan and his companions were ordered to disembark.

Immediately they were met by a harsh command to line up and stand at attention. They were left standing that way for what seemed like an eternity. Three soldiers kept them covered with automatic weapons, while a junior officer silently walked up and down waiting. He walked up to the third man who had moved to scratch his nose, drew his pistol and at point blank range blew the man's brains right out of his head. Then he turned, smiling to the rest of the shocked but motionless prisoners and said, "You see, that is what happens when you disobey an order here. Welcome to Babi Yar."

He took a sweeping look at the prisoners, standing at a rigid attention. His smirking smile deepened. "We affectionately call this the **Syretsky Camp,** after your lovely suburb of Kiev, the **Syrets District.** This camp is on the very edge of Babi Yar. Any infraction will buy you a spot in the ravine.

"Now, continue to stand at attention until our camp commander comes."

No one moved.

Time dragged.

Ivan's muscles began to ache. He feared he might faint, so he carefully wiggled his toes, flexed and relaxed muscles to maintain circulation. At least the officer was now talking to one of the guards, not looking for the slightest motion among the captives. He had made his point—taught his lesson. No one dared move.

At last, a staff car drove up and stopped directly in front of the line of agonizing men. Ivan dared not move his head, but could see out of the corner of his eyes that the officer was driving the vehicle himself. On the front seat, next to him, sat a huge dog, a dark gray Alsatian, while in the back seat sat a junior officer, who, by all protocol, Ivan thought, should have been the driver.

The senior officer jumped from the driver's seat, not waiting for anyone to open his door. The Alsatian heeled, without command, at his side. The man looked about fifty years of age. His head was completely bald, lengthening his already long, thin face. He wore glasses through which he squinted. His uniform fit smartly, tailored to disguise his less than perfect body. The holster he wore, prominently displayed, was as polished as his gleaming boots. His voice was gruff, angry in tone. He spoke only German. The junior officer from the back seat walked with him, the dog between them. He repeated in Ukrainian everything the officer said in German.

"Well, what have we here?" the commander said, grinning down at the dead body. "Looks like you had to do some disciplining. I hope the rest of them learned a lesson from it." Then he walked down the line of men, counting until he got to the seventh — the man next to Ivan. He drew his own pistol — and without a word or flinch, shot the man in the head.

"Now that is the second lesson for you to learn today. Your lives mean nothing to me! I would as soon shoot you all. One wrong move out of anyone and all your pleading will do no good. Also, if one of you does wrong, I might have your entire barracks eliminated. We can easily replace one or all of you, so it is up to you to keep each other in line."

He paused for emphasis, then continuing spoke, "I am **Strumbahnfuhrer Paul von Radomsky**. I am the camp commander. Also I want you to know **Rex,** here."

He pointed to the animal at his side.

"Rex, as you can tell, is a very well trained dog. He is especially trained to rip the flesh off a man at my command — especially genitals. So make sure you do nothing to provoke me."

With that, he turned and strode to the car. The dog jumped into place, the interpreter into the back and they drove off.

The first officer now took over again. "All right, find yourselves places in that building over there." He pointed to the row of huts similar to those that served the Jewish resistance in their forest community. Ivan hurried to the dugout hut as quickly as he could, realizing the bunk space would be first come. As he entered, all similarity between this and the family camp ended. Here, the stench was unbelievable. It went right to his stomach; he thought he would be sick. But he couldn't turn around. He had to find himself a bunk; he took one as close to the entry as he could. That was the only source of "fresh" air in the entire dugout.

The horrible dwelling was illuminated by a solitary kerosene lamp that hung from the ceiling near the rear. It took Ivan a few moments to get accustomed to the semi darkness. The hut was only two meters from dirt floor to sod ceiling, but in that shallow area the Germans had arranged to get in three levels of bunks. The bunks were shelves on which straw had been thrown. There was a ragged blanket for each space. The odor in the stuffy room was a combination of mildew, vomit, urine, feces and sweat.

When Ivan chose his bunk, he lay down on it in hopes of getting a moment's relief from his fatigue. He lay there in misery, trying to figure out how a day so beautiful could end so tragically, when suddenly he came up off the putrid straw.

"Damn it to hell! This place is full of lice! The straw, the blankets, the entire hut is infested!"

"What did you expect, a maid to clean this dump?" a man replied out of the semi darkness.

"Everybody outside!" came a command in perfect Ukrainian.

Ivan was only too happy to get outside again. Everything about that hut repelled him. They all fell into formation outside the dugout. It was turning dusk. Ivan realized he had not eaten since he shared breakfast with Sosha. Oh God, he prayed, please see over my dear Sosha.

"My name is **Timtov.** I am responsible for you. If you cause trouble, I might suffer for it, so it is up to me to see to it that you do no wrong." He brandished a whip with leather tails, each strand tipped with metal.

"Disobey and I will be the first one you will have to

deal with. If it goes no further than that, you will consider yourself lucky. Now you may sit here on the ground until the remainder of the dugout residents return from today's work detail. Then you will be lined up with them for the roll call before you are locked into your hut.

"Tomorrow at 3:00 a.m. your day will start with roll call and breakfast. At roll call, you will bring out your dead—those who died during the night—and lay them in front of your ranks. Everyone must be accounted for or the entire group goes to the ravine. I don't care how many of you die during the night—and some of you will try to kill yourselves... That is your business. But in the morning, everyone—dead or alive—must be accounted for."

Everything seemed clear.

75

FEELINGS...

A week had gone by. The Jews at the family camp had found out about Ivan and Sosha's arrests. They had no idea about their fate, but Ivan had been seen and recognized on the open back truck headed for Babi Yar. They knew of the concentration camp at Babi Yar, but no one knew what the layout of the facility was. There had been much discussion of making a raid on the camp and freeing the inmates. It would be a risky mission and there was no guarantee either Ivan or Sosha was still alive. Besides, the men and women's concentration camps were separate. It was doubtful both could be liberated.

"We have to try," Sol argued. "Even if they aren't there... We'd still be freeing many other prisoners."

"Solomon, you are overly involved because they saved your life. Maybe you're right, but we can't let our decision be an emotional one," Yorgi warned.

"Might I suggest that we discuss the idea with Diadia's group," Father Peter offered. "They've carried out a raid on a small concentration camp once; they can speak with experience. And besides, such an endeavor would probably require a joint effort."

"A good suggestion," Yorgi agreed. "I appoint you and Solomon to go to their camp and make the inquiries. Dov, why don't you go with them and see if you can barter with them for some medical supplies. Besides, it will do you some good to get out of that hospital for a while. Rachel can handle things while you are gone."

An hour later, Father Peter and Solomon and I headed out through the forest toward Diadia's encampment. Sol was quiet, thoughtful. Traveling through the forest now, he was reminded of his own escape from Babi Yar — that flight through the woods for his life, so very long ago. He remembered few of the details but could still feel the terror as he ran blindly through those woods. Now he wanted to return to that ravine to save his friends, to avenge his people. He wanted to strike a blow at the one place that was to him a symbol of all that the Nazis stood for. Father Peter was sensitive to Sol's torment.

"I suppose that next to Rachel, Ivan and Sosha were the most important people in the world to you," Father Peter said. As soon as he spoke he was sorry he'd used the past tense.

"*Are* the most important to me..." Sol corrected, but without anger.

"Of course, I didn't mean..."

"I guess they became my second family when Ivan pulled me from that ditch and took me home to his storage cellar. It's kind of ironic, too, when you think about it."

"Ironic? How?" I asked.

"In a lot of ways; I don't think I know if you can understand them all."

We came to some rough, thickly overgrown terrain that required considerable effort to traverse, so none of us spoke. When we finally got through, they had to sit down and rest.

"Tell me what you were talking about," I reminded Solomon, "the ironies, I mean."

"Well, it's just that being in a camp of predominantly Jewish resistance fighters, I'm so close to three of the few gentiles among them. You must realize, as a Jew I have always been leery of gentiles. Now my greatest concern is to get them out of the very place where I would have perished. If anyone would have told me, when I was a boy, that someday I would have been traveling through the forest with a priest to save the lives of two gentiles —

well, I'd have considered it inconceivable."

"I guess we Christians have never done much to endear ourselves to the Jews. But there are many Christian faiths. Granted the Church — the Catholic Church — has treated the Jews badly through the centuries with expulsions, forced conversions, the Crusades, Inquisitions. It is painful for me to have to confess this — and the position of the Church in this horrible time — there are other types of Christians. And all Catholics are not in agreement..."

"Father Peter, until Ivan and Sosha took me in, my idea was that a Christian was someone to be avoided. I think most Jews feel about Christians the way mice feel about cats.

"And yes I know that there are other Christians. And when I speak of the Church I speak mostly of the Roman Catholic Church. *But* ...I've not seen too many Lutherans speaking out or Protestants or Russian Orthodox. And granted, it is risking one's own life to speak out in these times and perhaps in unoccupied countries perhaps there is an outcry against the treatment of the Jews. However, I doubt it. I only know that the Lutherans have condemned the Jews to hell since the time of Martin Luther. I know the Protestants in England burned hundreds of Jews to death a few centuries ago and then expelled us form the British Isles when that inhuman act didn't scare us off. The Russian Orthodox, I only know, to have raped, looted and killed Jews in their pogroms... seemingly their favorite way to celebrate Easter.

"I know, Father Peter, there are probably other Christian churches that are tolerant of the Jews, but in other places far away — in America perhaps. And I know there are good and tolerant Christians here too. But they are too few for any Jew to trust at random."

I had to agree. We got up and started to walk again. Solomon checked a captured German pocket compass. Without trails to follow, direction was all we had to lead us to the constantly moving camp of Diadia Misha.

"Did you still really think all Christians were anti-Semitic?"

"Aren't they?" Sol replied.

Father Peter looked at Solomon in surprise. "What do you mean, 'Aren't they?' You still feel that way?"

"It's a matter of degrees, but anti-Semitism has been drilled into Christians from infancy. I think if sufficiently provoked, ninety-nine percent would fall back on their anti-Semitic indoctrination."

"I can't believe you feel that way!" Father Peter exclaimed, shock in his voice, an expression of hurt on his face. "Do you feel that way about Ivan, Sosha—me?"

"Ivan and Sosha told me long ago that they didn't consider themselves Christians. He considered the Church a hypocrisy from the time he witnessed a pogrom that local churchmen didn't condemn. I really think he and Sosha were not anti-Semitic. But I don't think a person can embrace Christianity without embracing some degree of anti-Semitism."

"Then you must think me one," the priest said, obviously hurt."

"Father Peter, I think the world of you—and honestly could feel toward you as a brother." Solomon spoke slowly, pausing to choose the right words. "If you were captured, God forbid, I would want to do all I could to help you—would risk my life for you. And I know you'd do the same for me—and with less reservation. I know what risk you took when you helped save Jews who sought you out. You'd have laid down your life for any one of them." He stopped and looked Father Peter straight in the eyes. "I appreciate the enormous sacrifice you made when you left your parish. But in a way, you are the most dangerous type of anti-Semite—the one who doesn't realize he is one—and certainly doesn't try or want to be one."

The words cut at the priest like the slashing of a knife.

"Solomon, what are you saying? I can't believe... Is this some ugly joke? How can you say that?"

We had come to a complete stop in the forest. The expression on Father Peter's face was shock, dismay, hurt. Solomon interrupted, "Please, hear me out. Maybe the word anti-Semitic is a bad one to use, but I use it for lack of another. Let me put it differently. The difference between you and Ivan and Sosha is that they were not practicing Christians. You are. And my grandfather ...blessed be his memory — told me from the time I was a child that every practicing Christian is to some degree anti-Semitic. In my lifetime I've not seen proof otherwise."

"Solomon, how am I anti-Semitic?"

Solomon could see how his words were hurting his friend. "You are a good friend, Father Peter — and I know I could trust you with my life. I take no pleasure in telling you these things, but I think you really want to understand how we Jews feel — why we feel the way we do." He looked deep into the Christian's eyes. They held tears, as did his own. "Don't you believe that for salvation — to be accepted in the eyes of God — to keep from spending eternity in Hell — not to be damned for all time, a person has to accept your Christ?"

"Well, it is basic..."

"And didn't you teach that to your parishioners?" Solomon interrupted. "In fact, do not all priests teach that to all Christians, from infancy on?"

"Yes, but..."

Again Solomon interrupted. "And how else do you think anti-Semitism is handed down from generation to generation, from century to century? What does the Christian think of the Jew, who does not accept your doctrine? In the eyes of the practicing Christian, the Jew is an evildoer, the non believer — the damned — condemned to burn in hell. Your faith propagates hatred of the Jews. If at any point in history society has needed a scapegoat,

Christianity has helped provide it. And priests have paved the way."

Father Peter was speechless. I felt sympathy for him — his feelings, but I had to agree with Solomon. We began to walk slowly. Solomon began to realize he had been a little over zealous. He'd gotten carried away, had spilled over much pent-up hostility — had hurt a friend.

"I'm sorry, my friend. I shouldn't have said all that. God knows, you *have* done much for us. It is just that we Jews have been made to live in mortal fear of Christianity. As children, we put up with daily taunts and beatings from Christian children who always outnumbered us. As adults, we feel the oppression of the Christian community. It's not only passed from fathers to sons, but from Church to parishioners. I know there are others who deserve the blame far more than you, but, nonetheless, you must realize that most Jews are going to be forever mistrustful of all Christians and the one in a hundred like you will have to bear some of the blame, rightfully or not."

We continued a little further in silence. Then Father Peter quietly said, "I'm truly sorry for my part in this catastrophe."

Solomon stopped in his tracks and embraced his friend.

76

LOGICAL & RATIONAL...

The news of Ivan and Sosha's arrests reached Diadia's camp. What had happened and what could be done about it provoked long and serious discussions. In the end, Diadia summarized his position. "Father Peter, Solomon, I hope you will understand the only position I can take in this matter. I hope you and your group will not think we do not want to help or that we wouldn't help if there was a chance for success. But under the circumstances, the risk would not be justified. To begin with, your comrades were arrested in what has all the appearance of a retaliation roundup. That being the case, they were probably executed the same day."

Solomon bowed his head as he listened, not wanting to admit to himself that what Diadia Misha was saying was probably true.

"Now even if by some miracle one or both of them were spared—it has already been over a week since they've been interned. That is longer than the average human being can survive in such a place."

"They are not average! They are both strong, tough!" Solomon interjected.

Diadia continued ... a little deeper sadness in his eyes. "If we were successful in raiding the camp at Babi Yar, chances are we would not find them alive. Maybe we could save some others. To my knowledge that camp holds a maximum of three hundred prisoners. If we were lucky, we might be able to break out ten percent—maybe thirty. Believe me when I tell you that's the most we could hope for.

"To assault such an installation, almost in the middle of Kiev and the German army—especially since we know nothing of its layout and defenses—we would have to expect to lose almost twice as many of our people as we could contemplate saving. It would have to be a major assault." He paused a moment, looking at Solomon, his head still bowed.

"And after the raid—the Germans would probably kill everyone left in the camp and pick up a thousand more people in Kiev as reprisal." Diadia didn't like having to turn his friend down and paused to give the matter a last thought. "No, there is no way I can see to justify such a mission. It would be suicide. Only my emotions tell me to do it—and they are clearly wrong this time."

Solomon and Father Peter and I knew he was right. They didn't argue the points Diadia made, but Sol asked, "What would you say to a small party—all volunteers— trying to break in, sneak in, under cover of darkness and try to steal them out?" He knew as he asked it was foolish, but he had to cover all possibilities.

Diadia thought long on the question then asked, "Solomon, if you were the prisoner in the place of Ivan or Sosha—would you want anyone to risk such a mission to get you out?"

"No." His voice could hardly be heard.

"How can you ask anyone else to join you in such a hopeless effort? Who of these people or of your group would you commit to the action?"

It was late. We spent the night in Diadia's camp. We started back the next morning. I was able to barter some needed medical supplies. It was actually mid-morning before we started back to our own encampment. The day was warm, but the forest kept us comfortable. We forced ourselves to make the best possible time the day before as we were going to Diadia's camp. Now that we had resigned ourselves to the fact there was nothing we could do for Ivan and Sosha, we made our way back home in an almost leisurely pace, depressed at the situation. The forest quiet was disturbed only by the chatter of squirrels, the incessant chirping of the birds and the sound of our own footsteps on the leafy floor.

We were still a long way from home, perhaps three hours at this slow pace through the difficult terrain, an estimated eight kilometers yet to walk. We sat down by a small spring to rest, refresh, to take some pleasure from the forest and its sounds and the intermittent silence.

"I feel bad about yesterday," Sol said to Father Peter. "I hope it won't destroy our friendship."

"Nonsense, your points were well taken. I had never really understood before. It was something that needed saying—especially between friends."

"But I feel I let out a lot of pent up anger on the wrong Christian. Actually..."

"Shh!" Father Peter interrupted. "Did you hear that?" He had his ear cocked to the wind.

"What? I don't hear a thing." Solomon said. He automatically drew his pistol which had been untouched in his belt for the past days.

"Yes, I hear it. Explosions ... gunfire!" I agreed, "From that direction." And I suddenly realized I was pointing in the direction of our camp.

"Listen! It's that horrible sound that haunted me in Kiev. I haven't heard it in all these months—that terrible sound of gunfire from Babi Yar. The wind must be carrying it all this distance."

Solomon slipped the pistol back into its place. He cocked his ears as the priest had done and concentrated. "Yes, I do hear it. But that wind is from the wrong direction. Babi Yar is southeast of us. That wind is from due south."

We all listened carefully. There was no question; the

wind carried the sound of gunfire.

"That's not only gunfire—there are explosions. Grenades! Mortars! It sounds like a battle," Solomon speculated.

Suddenly Solomon voiced it; the same conclusion I had come to seconds earlier, "Dear God, that's the direction of the family camp!"

We came to our feet and started running and stumbling through the thick underbrush. We ran several minutes, the trees and scrub tearing at our clothes, scratching our skin. We tripped, fell, got up and ran further in the direction of the camp. Finally, we were stopped by a small cliff we would have to climb and our exhaustion caught up to us.

Our breathing was labored. I could hear nothing over the pulsing of my blood. We slipped silently to the ground as we tried to get our breath back.

"This is insane," I eventually found the strength to say, between panting. "We'll never—get back this way... We—must use our heads. We're wasting—too much energy. A deliberate, forced march will get us there quicker." Breathing was painful. "We must pull ourselves together."

"I don't hear—the sound any longer. Do you think— oh my—I can't get my breath! Do you think we—just imagined it?" Solomon asked.

"Not unless 'we' were sharing the same nightmare." Father Peter said. We lay silently a minute, strength returning now. Father Peter continued his opinion, "Perhaps when we get to the top of this ridge. It'll protect us from the wind. It might carry the sound over our heads."

We climbed the steep but short incline and at the top carefully listened...

"Silence," I whispered with some relief.

"I don't hear it either," Father Peter agreed. "All right, with a steady and forced pace we ought to make it back in about two hours, maybe one and a half. Running through this terrain will only slow us down—and we risk injury. Let's be rational. And when we get near the camp, let's use caution. If there's trouble back there, we'll be unable to help anyone if we just blunder into the same situation."

74

WHY ME...

It took only one hour and forty minutes to get back to the family camp. When we reached familiar territory we slowed our pace, using extreme caution. The sounds of battle had no longer been heard since the time we first heard them almost two hours ago. We felt some cautious relief.

At half a kilometer from the camp we stopped. We remained hidden from anyone who might happen by and listened.

Silence.

The wind, though mild—more a light breeze—still came from the direction of the camp.

"We should be able to hear some sounds from the camp at this distance," Sol whispered.

"I agree. I smell smoke on the breeze—and gunpowder!" I said.

"Yes, I smell it too. I'm afraid to think about what it means. God, I wish we could hear something!" Solomon said with concern in his voice.

"We should hear something!" Father Peter repeated. "Either our people or the enemy. Do you suppose they've all been captured and taken off?"

"Let's go in and see," I said. "Careful, they may have posted guards or snipers."

"Let's separate, just in case; no point in all of us getting caught." Solomon added.

"You're right, Solomon. You go left—I'll go around to the right. Dov go straight ahead—*carefully!*"

As I crouched and creeped the last half-kilometer

toward the camp, I listened for any sound that would betray some form of life in the area. Even the forest animals were still. I constantly looked about and up into the trees, wary of ambush. When I'd worked my way to about thirty meters from where the first dugouts of the family camp were, I stopped and raised my head above the low shrubs.

"Oh, dear God, no!" I stood up, grief expelling caution. Where I had expected to see the first of the dugout huts I saw it collapsed into a crater, smoke rising from its smoldering timbers. I walked forward, not caring for my safety anymore. Not a single hut was left standing. Smoke filtered up through the trees, carried on the mild breeze into the direction from which we'd come. It lay on the ground in places like a early morning haze, giving an eerie, mystical, unreal look to the destruction. "Am I dreaming? Please, God, let it be a bad dream!"

Suddenly I saw someone walking toward me through the smoke. I was about to drop back into cover of the shrubs when I recognized Father Peter. He recognized me and called out loudly, "Come in, Solomon! Come in, there's no one here; just Dov and me."

Sol came in and to Father Peter's side. There was not a building standing, not a body in sight, not a single person to be seen. Small trees were uprooted, broken off at their trunks by what must have been explosions. The larger trees were badly scarred by shrapnel and bullets. "Whatever happened here was devastating. But there are no dead. Not ours, not theirs. What do you make of it?" I asked.

Sol was white with trepidation. "Only one thing — they found the camp. They must have surrounded the area and surprised us before we could make a move. They must have rounded everyone up — taken them prisoners — then just destroyed the camp so it could never be used again."

"That makes sense. Or maybe we had warning. Maybe there was time to get away into the woods and they destroyed an empty camp ... maybe?" Father Peter hopefully speculated.

Sol replied, "I'd like to believe that. But we have to assume the other. We must try to stop them. They'll have to move slowly with so many prisoners. If they get them out of the forest, they'll execute them all, either at Babi Yar or, more likely at a public execution in Kiev. God, what can we do?"

"I don't know. Do we have time to contact Diadia? We need help!" I interjected.

"We have to think, fast," Sol said. The problem was overwhelming. "Maybe we can find a radio intact in the rubble of the main hut. It would be too lucky, but let's look."

Together we started to walk through the area, kicking over large planks and rubble that might be hiding something we could use. When we reached the spot where the radio shack had been, we came to a sudden stop.

"Oh, tell me I don't see it," I said, all hope leaving me.

Solomon was silent. He couldn't move. His heart beat furiously in his chest. His throat went dry. Nausea and a cold sweat swept his body. His mouth opened as if to cry out, but no sound came forth. He put his hand over his eyes.

"We have to check. We have to look." Then Father Peter, too, was overcome. "Oh, dear God in Heaven, don't let it be..."

Gathering our courage, we walked to a large area of fresh-turned soil. It was about ten meters by about fifteen meters. There was fresh dirt scattered all around its edges and the black earth mounded gently toward the center. "How could they have dug such a large pit?" Father Peter asked. "They couldn't have had much time."

"They had our people dig it themselves. It can't be very deep."

"Solomon, we have to be sure. You know what we

have to do. Solomon, we have to check!" I said.

"I know. Oh please, Rachel, don't be there."

Slowly — filled with dread — we approached the turned earth. At its edge we dropped to our knees and with our bare hands began to dig in the cool, soft, loose dirt. We'd not dug more than a few inches when Solomon felt a hand. Withdrawing his own, he beat at his chest and cried out. "They're all in there, God, aren't they? All but me!

"Why?

"Why me?

"Why not me?"

78

INSATIABLE FURY...

The disaster was too huge to fathom.

There was nothing to do but return to the camp of Diadia Misha.

As we made our stunned way back through the forest, Solomon's pain was almost more than he could bear.

By the time we arrived at the camp, the group already knew of the disaster. The Germans wasted no time in broadcasting their triumph over the radio. They described the action in full detail and boasted that every man, woman and child at the "Partisan Camp" had been killed. The only fact omitted from the broadcast was that the great majority of the group was Jewish.

Solomon kept his grief to himself.

Outwardly, he displayed hate and confusion. He again insisted on going out on almost every mission. His new comrades could not decide whether he was determined to kill every German in the Ukraine or was seeking death himself. In any case, he became a fighter with an insatiable fury. No action was too dangerous. The greater the odds against him, the more eager he was to go on the mission. Any Nazi or anyone collaborating with the Nazis was marked for death in Solomon's mind. Some of his friends hesitated to volunteer for missions with him, feeling his eagerness for revenge might jeopardize the safety of others in the operation.

But Solomon always returned; never as much as

received an injury. In time, the others realized he had no intention of throwing his own or anyone else's life away. In conversation one evening, he replied to a comment with, "I cannot kill the enemy if I'm dead. I have every intention of going on living until there are no more of those bastards left to kill!"

By the end of the summer, it became quite clear that the days of the German occupation of the Ukraine were numbered. The resistance started to make plans of how to reach the advancing Russians and join forces with them against the Germans on the front lines.

71

DIMITRI...

Ivan learned quickly.

He became an expert in survival.

Anyone less than an expert was dead in a week. Two things were necessary to cheat death at Babi Yar—expertise and luck. On the average, twenty percent of the prisoners at Babi Yar camp died daily. Some died from exhaustion, some from disease and some from being shot for minor infractions. Others were just murdered at the whim of von Radomsky or other camp personnel. Even the *Kapos*—prisoners used by the Germans to keep order in the camp—held the power of life and death over their fellow prisoners. In fact, many of the Kapos were more brutal than some of the German guards. They were certainly hated more by the other prisoners than the German guards were.

Camp commander Paul von Radomsky had a favorite game, which contributed significantly to the mortality of the prisoners—and to the morale of his soldiers. He would walk among the inmates after the daily evening roll call—up and down the rows. He had his daily lucky number, as he liked to call it. Some days the number was chosen at random; other days it was determined purposely low so more prisoners would be selected to compensate for overcrowding in the camp. It was just another efficient way to reduce the number of prisoners ... and entertain the guards. If the attrition rate of the inmates did not keep up with the number coming into the camp, the lucky number would be a low figure. After each day's roll call in the late afternoon, von Radomsky would drive up in his car, his interpreter in the back and his trusted dog in front. He would get the evening count from the officer in charge. He'd make a quick mental calculation, then announce for all to hear, "Today's lucky number is eight!"

Then he would casually get out of his car, dog and interpreter following. He'd walk to the first row of prisoners, to a random spot. Unholstering his Luger pistol, he would start down the line of men counting, "One, two, three, four, five, six, seven..." and the next man would be shot.

Without even breaking stride he would continue up and down the rows — counting and killing — counting and killing — every eighth man — counting and killing. He used two pistols for this game. When one was empty, he'd hand it back to the interpreter who would reload as they walked. This went on until they became bored. Then, so as not to stop anticlimactically, the next unfortunate "winner" of the lucky number was told, "Run! Run or be shot!"

Not all ran, but most did. With an inaudible command, the Alsatian would pursue the terrified victim and bring him down, clamping his genitals between powerful jaws. The downed runner would scream horribly, producing cheers and laughter from most of the camp personnel. It was the highlight of their otherwise tedious day.

If the dog didn't finish the victim off, which was rare, he would usually be taken to the ravine and left to die. Fortunately, death was far more merciful than the Germans and usually came quickly.

But even with all the daytime help death had from the Germans, many inmates died during the night. They fell, exhausted and weak, sick and starving onto their lice-infested straw at night and were found there, dead, in the morning.

For morning roll call, the dead were taken out by those who had shared the huts with them and were laid on the ground, in ranks, to be counted with the living. Or were the living counted with the dead? Each morning, after roll call, the daily meal was given. It consisted of weak, muddy brown liquid cynically called coffee and dry bread made of potato peels and sawdust. A few days of this diet followed by sixteen hours of hard labor led to death for most of those not skilled in the art of survival.

Ivan made a point of associating himself with those who had lived the longest in the camp. There were some who had actually survived for months. It was from these, Ivan reasoned, he would learn what he'd need to know.

The morning after he arrived at Babi Yar, after the first meal, Ivan asked a man who looked better nourished than the others, "How have you kept from starving? No one can stay alive on this. You've been here weeks and you look as well fed as anyone here."

He looked at Ivan disdainfully. Ivan wondered if he was going to answer. Then he said coldly, "Are you willing to eat rats, cats, mice and other vermin?"

Ivan didn't even hesitate, "If that's what it takes to stay alive – but how do you get them?"

The man's expression changed, warmed. He smiled. "I don't know why I should show you – but I like you. You've got guts. Maybe someday you'll be able to help me. You're the one they call Ivan?"

Ivan nodded.

"Me, they call me **Dimitri.** Stay with me, it's the only way I know to get enough food to keep going."

After the brief feeding period of the day and before the work of the day was begun, the inmates were made to police the grounds.

"Stay near me, Ivan," Dimitri said in almost a whisper. We'll police the area nearest the fence. Remember that there are 22.000 volts in this fence. Don't touch it, but collect all the rats, mice, weasels, rabbits and other animals that have. In twenty four hours, a lot of creatures meet death on those wires. Carry a stick to pull them away from the bottom of the fence and put the animals in your clothes. When they try to go under the bottom wire, they ground it and poof, our meal!"

Ivan was surprised to see how many of the survivors were doing the same thing. Mostly, the fence held dead rats, mice and occasionally squirrels. The prized larger animals were rare.

"Keep what you can scavenge until lockup tonight. It is up to you how you prepare it for eating. They can be cooked on the wood stove in the huts. If you are at a job where there is fire, you might even be able to eat them during the day, but that is a little risky. Some German might think that an infraction and shoot you on the spot. Most of them get a laugh out of watching us eat vermin, though."

80

WORK DETAILS...

Ivan was assigned to a variety of jobs. Almost every day, he would be sent out on a different work crew. There seemed no pattern or logic to the way jobs were distributed. Some prisoners were sent to the same workday in and day out, while others never did the same job two days in a row. Ivan was glad he did different work each new day for two reasons. If Sosha was still alive—and he made himself believe she was—he'd have a better chance of maybe seeing her if he was moved around a lot. The more different places he was sent, the better the chance to find an opportunity to escape.

On his first day, Ivan was taken on a work detail dismantling some old Russian barracks. Each board was salvaged, each nail withdrawn, straightened and placed in containers according to size. The second day, he was assigned to cut down trees and dig out roots. Any tree in the vicinity of the camp that offered cover to a potential enemy or escapee was removed. For this, they had to go outside barbed wires and they went under heavy guard. They were told that any escape attempt, even by one individual, would get everybody in the party shot on the spot. He went back to dismantling barracks on his third day. On the fourth, he was put to work as a beast of burden. He and several others were harnessed to a heavy wagon and all day they pulled that wagon around the camp while other prisoners loaded it with trash, sewage, garbage and other refuse.

There were other jobs, but Ivan was never assigned to those. There were jobs from which prisoners never returned. Those who were taken to work on secret projects at one end of Babi Yar never returned. Once there, they would know too much of what was going on. They were kept at the project until their usefulness was exhausted; then they were shot, only to be replaced by others who knew they would never return.

Even with this security, information had a way of filtering back. Before long everyone in camp knew that the project was construction of a factory—a factory that would make industrial soap of human corpses.

The worst part of Ivan's jobs was that they used only his body, leaving his mind to think—to worry about Sosha and his son, his daughter in law, his grandchildren. There was still so much he wanted to tell them, do for them, to enjoy them. How was the war treating them? There had been no communication since the occupation. Had they been able to stay safely out of occupied territories? How he wished he could see them, if only once more. The only hope of that would have to include escape. It was, he knew, the only way out of Babi Yar alive.

But most of the time he thought of Sosha. My God, how I wish I could be with her—even if she... He couldn't think it. She has to be alive. God, please let her be alive. Is she eating vermin to survive? Does she know how to live in the face of this horror? I'd like to kill every Nazi in this mad world. How can anyone condone this inhumanity? She's strong. She'll survive. She's smart. She's alive. I know it. She'll live. I'll find a way...

For Ivan and ninety nine other prisoners, all this ended on August 14, 1943. This group was selected for the most inhuman job any person could possibly devise—and the Germans devised it.

"What have we been selected for?" Ivan asked Dimitri, standing next to him in line.

"I don't know. No one seems to know. It must be very secret."

"That's what worries me," Ivan replied.

"What do you mean?"

"People never come back from secret assignments!"

Just then, von Radomsky drove up with his two constant companions, his best friend Rex and the interpreter. "Good morning, men. I presume you all slept well last night!" von Radomsky grinned at his own humor. "You are surely wondering why you have been picked out of all our guests here? Well, you are a very special group," he explained sarcastically. "You are the strongest and hardest workers – and for this you are to be rewarded." At that he started to laugh hysterically. The interpreter spoke with a stupid smirk on his face, not knowing if he should laugh, too. After von Radomsky regained control of himself, he went on with his little speech. "I want to remind you that any infraction or escape attempt will end in the usual manner. Any hesitation to do your assigned work will be punished with a very special, painful death."

"It is obviously our end," the man on the other side of Ivan whispered through his teeth.

"I think you're right. I just wonder what he has planned for us between now and the end."

In just a moment later, Ivan and his group found themselves marching to the single gate of the concentration camp. Timtov, the leader of Ivan's dugout hut, was in charge of the group, along with seven other Kapos. Two Kapos for every twenty five of us, Ivan noted. We've never had such supervision on a work detail before. What can they have in mind for us?

They were marched out through the double gates and up the road by which they'd been trucked into the camp. When they reached the fork in the road, they turned into the ravine.

"Oh, shit," Ivan heard Dimitri say.

For the prisoners of Babi Yar, this had always been a one way road. "Today I join my Sosha," Ivan heard himself say and felt shock as he said it. He realized it was the first time he let himself admit what he feared was true; she was most probably dead.

It was a long hike into the ravine. The men walked in silence, each with his own thoughts — thoughts that surely he considered among his last. Strange, Ivan thought, how often during one's life one wonders what the end will be like. Now it is here. God, I don't even know the date. I hope they make it quick. Why aren't I upset? Damn these Germans. Why did they have to come into our lives? So this is really the end. How many have gone ahead of me here? I'm afraid Sosha did — that first day we were arrested. A tear rose in his left eye. I hope she didn't suffer. I hope she was brave. I hope she felt at ease about it as I do now. I can't understand why I'm so calm. I guess they've worn me down. I guess I just don't give a damn anymore.

"Halt," Timtov ordered.

The procession halted.

They had marched to a far end of the infamous ravine. The ground was sandy, mixed with clay. Looking around, Ivan noted shovels being counted out by German soldiers at the back of a truck some thirty meters away.

Dirty bastards are going to make us dig our own graves, he thought.

"All right, men," Timtov started, "we have a big job to do. Each of you will be given a shovel. You will dig in groups of ten or fifteen. You will unearth bodies that have been buried here. The Germans have decided that all who have been buried in Babi Yar must be unearthed and burned!"

No one could believe his ears. It was absolute madness. Surely this was some insane joke, a ruse to get them to dig their own graves without suspicion. Everyone knew that there must be more than a quarter million dead in the ravine. Every day they could hear the gunfire from dawn to dark. They had heard it every day in Kiev since the end of September 1941, when they rounded up all the Jews. They heard it every day at the concentration camp. It never stopped while daylight lasted. From another part of the ravine the sound of gunfire could be heard. They were still killing!

How many days had there been since September of 1941? This was August 1943. How many days, how many thousands of bodies? Now these madmen expected them to be dug up and burned?

"Get started. Everyone take a shovel and start to dig!"

It was no joke. It was no ruse. It soon became evident the Germans were expecting them to dig up bodies. All day they dug; first in one place, then in another. By noon, they had dug up enough ground to make mass graves for themselves several times over. The Germans were really looking for the dead. And the humor of it was, if one could call it humor, that in this ravine of death they could find no bodies. Could it be that they had started digging in one of the few undefiled places?

After twelve backbreaking hours, the only dead were those of their own that had died of exhaustion or shots in answer to some infraction. At dusk, seventy three men, those who had not died that day put down their shovels for the night. An extra ration of food was given them. It was a real meal with *real* bread and a bowl of soup that had potato and a bit of meat in it. It was real potato, not just the peels and real meat — horse meat, to be sure, but real meat. For the first time that day they realized they were not to be shot at sundown. They'd not get their stomachs filled for that.

That night they slept where they had been digging, in the ravine. They were exhausted, but for once with something in their stomachs. They slept like the dead they were searching for. They were awakened at the first light of dawn. Again they got bread, real bread and coffee that resembled the real thing, strengthened by chicory. By the time they were ready to start digging again, a truck had come with replacements for those who had died the day before. Again they dug all day, this time sixteen hours. Again they had only their own dead to show for it at day's end. Thirty nine died that second day.

On the third day, replacements came again. By noon, they still had not unearthed any dead. At about 1:00 p.m. a staff car rolled up, two officers in the back seat. One was a member of the present staff at Babi Yar and the other had been at Babi Yar in the beginning, when the Jews were slaughtered there.

It was a quirk in the systematic German mind that made them insist on digging up the dead in the same order that they had put them into the earth. They were determined to dig up the first Jews they had slaughtered, but they couldn't find them. "You damn fools!" the visiting officer called out. No one knew for sure if he was addressing the diggers or their supervisors, but no one really cared. "You are digging in the wrong place! This is where we had them undress." Then he added, pointing to an adjacent area, "That is the place." He got out of the car, walked about sixty meters with determined strides and then with his heel made a mark in the ground. "Dig here!"

The prisoners were brought over and the next few shovels full of earth revealed the ghastly remains.

81

EXHUMING THE DEAD...

There was little dirt over the dead and the pits gave them up by the thousands. The first bodies were in such advanced state of decay that they came away in parts. The stench was unbearable. The prisoners were sick from the sight and smell. They vomited. The Kapos vomited. When even the German guards began to vomit, they started guarding the diggers from a greater distance.

As Ivan worked he came to the horrible realization that this first pit was the one Solomon's family was in. He wondered if he were lifting the very bodies of his parents, brothers, sister, his grandfather. Then an even more horrifying thought crossed his mind. If I survive long enough might I come across? He couldn't make himself think her name in that regard.

Ten meter square areas were marked off on the ground. The bodies and parts were laid out in the spaces. On each layer of the dead was placed a layer of wood and on that, another layer of the dead. Those diggers who died that day were also placed on the pyre. Thus they were placed until the pyre was about two meters high. Then petrol was poured over the entire pile and ignited.

Flames licked at the sky beneath a thick black cloud of smoke. A new disgusting smell was added to the already existing stench. But after a short time, the flames died. The petrol and the top two or three layers had burned, but the mass below was packed too tight. There was insufficient draft to let the pyres burn.

By dusk that day, there were six partially burned, smoldering piles. When their food came, no one could force himself to eat. They escaped the horror in sleep.

Again the German's ingenuity came to the rescue. The next day the replacements were accompanied by two hundred additional prisoners. The newcomers' shock was evident on their faces. While two hundred prisoners dug and carried the dead out of the pits, the remaining hundred or so were put on trucks. Ivan was among the latter. It was still in the early morning and already the sun was hot. Dimitri said to Ivan, "The heat will take its toll. Many of us will die today."

"It will make little difference which day we die," Ivan replied. "Do you have any guess at where they are taking us?"

"None."

They drove only a few minutes when the truck stopped just outside the old Jewish cemetery at the entrance to the ravine. "Good Lord, you don't suppose they want us to dig up these dead, too?" Dimitri asked, half-joking.

"Well, at least we'll know where to dig, if so," another answered.

"Get out! Hurry! Everyone out into the cemetery," Timtov commanded.

"I can't believe it," Ivan said. "I think they really are going to have us exhume those corpses. They won't even leave the Jews at peace in those age old graves."

Once inside the graveyard, Timtov gave them instructions. "At once, start taking down the grave markers. Take down each headstone and carry it over to the main gate where I want them neatly stacked. Now, you four," he said, pointing to the largest and strongest men he could see, "you will take them from that pile and stack them on the trucks. Two carry to the trucks while two of you work on the truck stacking.

"Four more of you are to take down the iron fence that is on top of the brick wall. Four volunteers, quickly!"

Ivan and three others stepped forward. Ivan wanted

no part of desecrating these graves. He thought it strange after all that he had been through the previous day, but the thought of taking down headstones left him with an uncomfortable feeling.

The work was hard, but a pleasure compared with the work in the pits the day before. By noon, the sun burned down without mercy. The temperature was well over a hundred; there was no refuge from it. Even the Germans realized that to get the work done they'd have to indulge the workers in an unprecedented act of kindness — they brought in a water truck.

As the men took their unusual break, they noticed a strange, muffled explosion. A few minutes later another, then another, puff, puff, puff after puffing. As the temperature rose, the explosions became more frequent.

"What in the hell is that?" Ivan asked Dimitri, not really expecting him to know the answer.

"I've never heard anything like it. It's too muffled to be a very big explosion. I can't imagine what it could be. But with the Germans, there are a lot of things I can't imagine!"

"I can't guess what they want these headstones and iron fences for," Ivan added.

All day they worked. Truck after truck was filled with materials, which were driven back into the ravine. By dusk, the cemetery had been denuded. It looked eerie, a field of unmarked graves, unkempt and overgrown with weeds. No one will ever be able to find a loved one's grave in here again, Ivan thought, then he realized there was no one left to return to those graves.

The trucks returned once more to take the prisoners back to their temporary living area in the ravine. As the sun set and the air-cooled, the muffled explosions had ceased. When they arrived back at the area, they saw what their labor had been for. Makeshift open furnaces were being built of the headstones and the iron fences were being used as grates, letting the pyres draw air from underneath.

The pyres from the day before had been restacked on the grates. They were packed more loosely and three were ready for ignition. One of the Kapos was given a torch, which he put to the stacks of dead bodies. It went up in roaring flames. The same horrible stench filled the air.

Humans can get used to anything, Ivan thought; that night when the food came, almost everyone ate.

Ivan sat near one of the men who remained behind on the pit detail. "What was that noise we heard all day? Sounded like muffled explosions, all-coming from inside the ravine. Do you have any idea?" Ivan asked.

"They were just that, explosions. We could see them. Never saw such a thing and hope never to again. We were working in the terrible heat, when suddenly we started hearing those sounds. They came more frequently and we could see puffs of dust rise from the ground with each report. They were over there by that cliff." He pointed over his shoulder without looking himself.

"Well, what was it?" Ivan asked impatiently.

The man shrugged. "It appears the Germans used that area for their slaughter last week. The earth over the dead is very shallow. The sun reflecting off the cliff raises the temperature over there much higher than it does here. The heat beating down on the dead causes gasses that form in the corpses to burst. Those bodies were actually exploding under the ground. Each time one exploded it made a loud puff and raised a little dust."

The thought of it ended Ivan's meal. He gave his bowl to the man who had related the story. He was glad to take what was left of Ivan's food.

Ivan rolled over on his side right where he had been sitting and went to sleep.

82

BURNING
THE EVIDENCE...

The bringing up and burning of bodies went on for almost six weeks—seven days a week, sixteen hours a day. The number of workers was increased to five hundred. And all the time that Ivan and the other prisoners were made to dig up and burn old corpses, new corpses were being added by the Nazis. Each and every day the shootings continued as the Germans brought in new victims.

Each pyre had a hundred bodies in each layer and sometime there were twenty layers to a stack. The Germans decided two thousand bodies made the most efficient blaze. It took about two nights and a day to burn out one pyre completely. The prisoners worked all day to stack as many pyres as possible and that night would ignite them and the next day, while they still burned, new pyres would be stacked for burning that evening.

After a burning, when the ashes heaped under the grates, a crew of prisoners sifted through them for any gold or precious stones that might have escaped detection at the time of execution. What bones were found were brittle and another group of prisoners was put to work crushing them. Then the bone ash was bagged to be used as fertilizer.

Ivan estimated that each day, they burned about ten thousand corpses; bodies, people, humans. There were usually at least five pyres stacked each day, sometimes as many as eight. This pace continued for forty one days—

from August 19, when the efficient burning plan was accomplished, to September 28, when the digging was finally stopped. And there were untold bodies still in the ground.

The nights were getting cooler in September and after the first week of that month the Germans started taking the workers back to the dugout huts in the concentration camp for the nights.

As they rode back to the camp one evening toward the end of September, a relative newcomer to the work crew said to Ivan, "Do you know what I just calculated?"

"How many days to Christmas?"

"No! But do you know how many bodies have been raised and burned since you started this work?"

"Yes, about four hundred thousand bodies to date. The question I have is how many are still left in the ground?"

Ivan wondered if Sosha's body...

"How could they have murdered so many?" the young man asked.

"How? For them it was easy. They just sat day in and day out and pulled the triggers and released gas in their vans. In the first week of their slaughter, they murdered a hundred thousand Jews."

"Are you serious? In the first week?"

"That's the estimate I heard and I believe it. The first pit we emptied was filled with their remains. When we had them all out, the bare pit was ten meters deep, twenty meters wide and over eighty meters long. The weight of the corpses on the top had so compressed the ones on the bottom that we had to hack them apart with shovels and axes to get them out. In a few cases, the Germans went down and set small charges of dynamite to blow the bodies apart."

"Oh God!"

"Oh God, hell! Better ask, 'Where was God then? After that first week, they imported more Jews—then Gypsies and Russian prisoners—then Communists and partisans — then just innocent men, women and children who happened to be on the wrong street at the wrong time." He paused, remembering his own arrest with Sosha. "Anyway, by now they've killed so many we'll never get them all out. I'd bet we haven't taken out half. And the killing hasn't stopped yet." His bitterness was overflowing now. "And the last pyre will be ours, because we are witness to it all and we can't be left behind to give testimony to this — this..."

"How much longer do you think it will last?"

"Not long. When the wind blows from the east, it carries the sound of battle. The Russians are advancing. But rest assured, the Germans will get rid of us before the front passes back through Kiev."

83

ANNIVERSARY...

It was a coincidence that the last bodies to be exhumed were taken from the ground on September 28, 1943, exactly two years to the day since the first Jewish roundup in Kiev. As the last pyre was ignited, Ivan and the other survivors of the forty-one day ordeal knew that tomorrow would most likely be their execution date. That knowledge encouraged the only known mass escape attempt at Babi Yar.

There was nothing to lose.

They would try an escape during the night. It would have to be spontaneous. It was too late to make definite plans. When they were locked in for the night, the men in Ivan's dugout considered their best course. Like prisoners everywhere, the men had over a period of time collected things that might come in handy. This night each brought out his secret treasures. There were some pliers stolen by the men who had been assigned to pull teeth from the dead. One had found a small hammer that some poor soul had taken to his grave with him in the ravine. There were pieces of wire, nails and needles, bits of string, a broken knife blade—but no weapons and little that would be of much help in an escape.

"Give me that piece of wire," one of the men said. "Maybe I can work the lock with it."

He went to the single door in the dugout and pulled the lock, which was outside the wire mesh door, to where he could manipulate it. To everyone's surprise but his own, the lock snapped open with ease.

"Don't tell anyone what you just saw!" he said with a

chuckle. "They might get the wrong idea of my past life." To everyone's further surprise, he snapped the lock shut again.

"What the hell did you do that for?" someone asked.

"I just wanted to see if I still had the touch. It's too early yet. We must go after midnight when they least expect it. If the guard comes around and sees the lock off before then, we'll all be shot right in our bunks."

The next four hours were the longest Ivan could ever recall.

While they waited, a fog set in. It lay heavily on the ground to a depth of about a meter. The lock picker volunteered to crawl in the fog to the other dugouts and unlock their doors. "I've done riskier things in my life," he said. "I think I can do it. These fogs usually last the night. Just give me five minutes after I leave the hut; the more people who break for it, the better our individual chances."

"And once we're out of the hut, what do we do?" someone asked. It was a reasonable question.

"All I can think to do," Ivan volunteered, "is to surprise the Germans. Overpower them and hope we can bluff our way out."

"That's crazy!" A voice came out of the darkness.

"Does anyone have a better idea?"

Silence.

"Okay. We outnumber the Germans ten to one at least. If we can eliminate a few before they give the alarm and get their weapons, we may be able to shoot our way out. If we can get lucky and get a few grenades, we might even be able to blow an escape route through the fences." Ivan paused. He knew it had little chance. "Besides, it beats just waiting to be shot tomorrow."

"Maybe they won't shoot us tomorrow. If that's all they have planned for us they wouldn't have brought us back."

Ivan thought. It made sense. "True. So it will be the

next day. Only the agony of waiting will be prolonged. I want out tonight—I want to be free one way or another..."

The camp had been quiet for more than an hour. The guards were at the daily minimum.

"Now's the time, now or never." announced the lock expert. He slipped from his bunk and had the lock off in a few seconds. "Five minutes!" He was gone, somewhere in the deepening fog. It was hard for the men to contain themselves. They had no watch. Several of them counted seconds. Five times they counted to sixty, slowly, precisely. Five minutes are hard to estimate, especially when every nerve and muscle wants to go. It may have been five minutes—it was probably a little less. It seemed more.

Suddenly prisoners ran crazily in every direction.

The alarm was sounded.

A few Germans were downed by blows, but in the panic no one got any weapons. The Germans in the gun towers were, at first, helpless to fire. In the fog, they couldn't see who their own men were or who were prisoners. The dogs were set loose and barked from under the fog. They tore Germans and prisoners alike.

The other dugouts had been opened and three hundred and thirty prisoners ran crazily among dozens of equally confused German guards. Finally the guns in the towers in the towers started to fire—first at specific targets, then they just raked the area blindly. Screams, shouts, swearing and gunfire mingled with the yelping of dogs and sirens.

The Germans made only one mistake in their surprise and confusion. They opened the gates to let in reinforcements, a truck and several motorcycles. The cyclists could barely see over the fog. In the few moments, those two gates were open and fifteen prisoners escaped by running against the traffic. They were out before the Germans knew what they'd done.

Out of the three hundred and thirty prisoners in the

camp on the morning of September 29, 1943, fifteen got out. For Ivan, the waiting was over. He had been killed by the first blast of machine gun fire from one of the guard towers. He was finally free—reunited with his beloved Sosha.

84

FREE & ALONE...

By the first week in October 1943, Russian guns could be heard almost daily in the Kiev area. Constant radio transmissions from Russian broadcasters encouraged all partisan groups to step up their activities against the Germans. They invited guerrilla groups to try to break through and join Russian forces where they could. In isolated areas, partisans actually took over small towns and villages, running out the Nazis and setting up their own governments. This created little islands of freedom inside occupied territories.

Diadia Misha and his group remained in the forests, but they started to move eastward in hopes of joining the Russians. There was special motive on their part. Not only would this give the fighters a chance to join the Russian troops, but also it would offer the non combatants among them sanctuary. The elderly, children and non fighting women would for the first time since the occupation be able to leave the forest and live in towns.

Cautiously, the group migrated through the forests north of Kiev. Then they turned in the direction of the nearest gunfire and in the third week of October they passed out of occupied Ukraine into regained Russian territory. Two hundred and eighteen Jews and seventy seven gentiles walked into a Russian encampment. As soon as the Russians realized who this group was, they were received with enthusiasm.

But, strangely, those who had just regained their futures, a new prospect for living out their natural life spans, who just walked out of the threat of eventual annihilation by the Germans, those who had just become survivors, showed little joy.

That evening Solomon wrote in his diary:

"Today I walked out of the German occupation. I'd thought—on those few occasions when I allowed myself to think I might survive—that this day would be a day of celebration. It is not. Physically I am alive, but I fear I'm dead inside. I think that part of me which feels, died with all those others who were torn from life.

"I have nothing to celebrate. Today I came to the realization that I am again alone in this world. I felt it almost the instant we walked into safety. I think we all felt it. Almost all of us have lost all those most dear to us. Of the two hundred ninety five of us, there were only three family parties intact. Diadia Misha has his son, Simcha, but no one else left...

"People who still had someone left from their past showed emotion. Many cried; for the rest the past has been slaughtered. We are alone with unknown futures. Our gentile comrades are much more elated over their liberation. Many of them have lost family, too, but most have someone to go back to, families, after the Germans are pushed out completely. They will probably have homes to go back to, communities that will welcome them. They worry about their families who still live under Nazi occupation, but at least they have hope of finding loved ones. They are victims of oppression and political tyranny, but only we Jews are victims of genocide. We have no loved ones to return to, we have no home. We are adrift. I feel more uncertain today than I did yesterday. Yesterday I had a goal. Today, I don't know...

"What will tomorrow offer me? Yesterday I knew I had to fight against the Germans—tomorrow what do I do?

"Suddenly I realize that today we were liberated by the very people from whom we thought the Germans were liberating us two years ago. Am I back among the same anti-Semites who for centuries have slaughtered my people with their pogroms? Will they now be different? Has their inbred hatred changed? What will it take to reawaken it? How soon?

"Already our fighters are planning to turn back to the west and chase the Nazis out of our lands with the Russian troops. Somehow, I no longer feel it my homeland, but I'll join them. I may not have a country, but I still have my hate. Vengeance still tastes sweet."

85

BARBED WIRE AGAIN...

Solomon sat in dusty confinement behind barbed wire. His face showed abysmal depression. Incarcerated with him were thousands of other Jews who shared his feelings or had by circumstances been pushed beyond to indifference. Many of those committed suicide. Then there were those who didn't take their own lives but died from sheer lack of will.

Solomon just sat there. No reason to move. Staring at barbed wire and the armed guard on the other side, he recalled the utter helplessness that he had not felt since the night of September 29th, 1941, when he and his family were being held under armed guard on the way to Babi Yar. There was no way out then either.

Just a few weeks earlier he'd thought he would have a new life. But now — hell, what's the use? At that moment, Solomon was sure of only one thing, there is no place for Jews in this Christian world except under their thumbs, behind barbed wire or in the ground.

A group of seven children walked by, supervised by a girl in her early teens. Solomon guessed the younger ones at four or five years old. It was hard to be sure — malnutrition left many of these little ones small for their age. They should be in kindergarten — not behind barbed wire. Barbed wire was invented for animals, not children. They know only survival and fear. They have succeeded where their families have failed. Now I'm a fellow inmate with them and thousands of other Jews. Why, for God's sake, why? Why can't this damned world leave us in peace? Free to live and believe as we please.

A few weeks ago, he thought he understood at least part of the answer.

"Why me?" He thought he understood.

"Why not me?" It was his job, he thought; he was convinced it was his obligation to all those who died — to make sure the world knew. But now, he doubted that anyone in this world will care or be willing to listen.

Jews came together in this camp from all the death camps of Europe and from the forests, basements, attics and hiding places where the more fortunate evaded capture. Atrocities were coming to light. Babi Yar, in relation to some of the others, was a minor offense. The early first figures were in: eight million gentiles, six million Jews.

Out of every ten Jews in the world, the Nazis murdered four. Of the eight million gentiles slaughtered, some were political enemies of the Third Reich, some partisans and saboteurs and some refused the immoral, unprincipled occupation governments or spontaneously acted on conscience. Only the Jews and the Gypsies were slaughtered because of their birth.

And there was that inevitable question, "Why did God do it?" And there was an answer, "God didn't do it — man did it." And that left Solomon asking, "God, why did you let man do it? Why six million Jews; why all those others?" Nothing would ever placate Solomon's bitterness toward the Nazis or toward the German people who let the Nazi ideology take root. He was bitter toward all the anti-Semites of the world. And he was bitter toward the rest of the world, the "good Christian world," because after all the crimes against the Jews. The "free world" apparently didn't give a damn. How could a world that gave a damn about what happened to the Jews under Hitler allow this further incarceration of Jewish survivors? These children still had never experienced freedom. How could a world that cared keep people who had suffered so much behind barbed wire? Hadn't the world learned anything?

Solomon wanted to scream the question at the British soldier on the other side of the barbed wire. While the rest of the world was free, *including most of the Nazis,* the Jews were still behind barbed wire, this time prisoners of the allies. How could the British hold them on the island of **Cyprus,** like this? Non-Jewish refugees were not put to this outrage—this humiliation—this incarceration.

Three years had passed since Solomon walked out of the German-occupied territory to fight alongside the Russians. There was still no place for the Jews. Of course, it really is different, he thought. There was no gas chamber. No crematoriums. And now the guards are supposedly our friends. But "our friends" still will not let me have my freedom. I cannot breathe free air.

Solomon reflected on the years since he and Diadia Misha walked out of the Ukrainian forests in October 1943. They'd fought their way back to Kiev and liberated the district from the Germans on November 5, 1943. "I can remember so clearly when Dov, Father Peter and I went together through the city and its surroundings." Solomon said to himself. Father Peter found many of his old parishioners and acquaintances who greeted him with open arms.

"I found no one!"

The city had no Jews left. There was no one nor anything left to attest that a hundred and ten thousand Jews who once lived there had ever existed. Their property had been confiscated by either the Nazis or the Ukrainians. A few gentiles from the Podol area where Solomon and his family had lived remembered him. One or two talked to him, but most preferred not to linger in conversation.

"Tell me, Father Peter, is it my imagination or do they

really try to avoid me?"

"I have to admit, you cause them obvious discomfort."

"What is it that bothers them?"

"I think their consciences. After all, they probably think you blame them."

"I think I do."

"I guess I can understand that, too; but they also probably fear you a little. After all, we have come back with the liberating forces, armed to the teeth. They have known nothing but oppression from all their previous liberators. Who knows what they expect you to do? After all, you carry a machine gun slung over your shoulder. Maybe they think you plan to loot their homes."

"As they looted Jewish homes?"

"I'm sure some of them did that. Maybe they fear your revenge."

Father Peter's parish had no priest. At the request of his congregants, he unofficially took over the leadership of his flock. He wrote his superiors, but could not get an answer. Each noncommittal reply suggested his letter would be forwarded to someone in a position to take the matter under advisement. It embittered him. The Church would not back him when the Nazis were occupying the district and now would not commit itself. It occurred to him that the Church didn't really care what was right. Perhaps it wanted to wait to declare its stand until it was certain which turn the war would really take.

After a few depressing days in Kiev, finding no one or anything from the past, Solomon decided to move on with the Russian forces. He stayed with them until they pushed the Germans beyond the Ukrainian borders. His decision was made when he went to the old Jewish cemetery and could not find his grandmother's grave. He could not bring himself to go into the ravine to the last place where he saw—was with his family.

Kiev held nothing for him anymore.

86

OBERMAN'S FATE...

Major Hans Oberman left Kiev along with the rest of the staff officers, just the day before Solomon, Father Peter and I and the Russian troops broke through the faltering German defenses. To the other officers, it seemed a strategic retreat. To Oberman, it was the beginning of the end of the Third Reich. Oberman was no fool; he was wise enough to keep his options to himself. No German could be trusted. The only intelligent thing to do was to keep his eyes open for opportunities that would save him in the future — the not-too-distant future.

Good fortune was familiar to Oberman. He was a man who knew how to make the most of his breaks. He had built a reputation for his superior, the Colonel, was a master at destroying resistance movements. It was quite natural that his Colonel should be transferred to an area where there was a hotbed of resistance activity. It was also natural that the Colonel would request his chief aide, Oberman, be transferred with him. It pleased the Colonel that Oberman was perfectly willing to let him take all the credit for their successes. Oberman, of course, reaped other benefits, more important to him than fame. Oberman's philosophy was: If anyone screwed up, the man with the reputation would hang first.

The hotbed of resistance to which the "team" was transferred proved to be Holland. Major Hans Oberman was delighted. He looked forward to getting out of the Ukraine. Let the Bolsheviks have it back with its uncultured slobs, these people. How I long to get back to real people — Europeans.

Oberman thought of other things beside good company. He contemplated how to insure his future. He knew that no matter what the future held, wealth was going to help. His family wealth was considerable but not easily moveable. If he could liquidate his property, turn it into currency in Holland, he could change cash into diamonds. Easily transported, they were an international currency with a much surer future than the German Reich's marks. Besides, these Ukrainians had nothing of any real value. Perhaps in Holland, he could increase his wealth. Extortion was a game he was in a good position to play. In Holland, the stakes made it more worthwhile.

Amsterdam was the city to which the Colonel and Oberman were assigned. "God, it's a whole different world," Oberman said to his Colonel. "I had forgotten what civilization was like."

The Colonel had a blank expression on his face, and stared out the window of the staff car as it drove past the Dutch city's canals. Oberman doubted his superior noticed the difference.

The old fool is little better than the Ukrainians, he thought. Oh well, that is part of my advantage. Oberman found himself a comfortable, spacious apartment with an abundance of old-world charm. He furnished it with his favorite things and then set about selling everything he didn't need. Whenever he could, he traded for diamonds and precious gems. When he had to take money he quickly converted it into the little stones elsewhere. When he had sufficient small stones, he traded up for larger, more precious gems. It would be easier to carry the larger stones than a large number of little stones. He kept a number of smaller stones to bargain with, but his real fortune was in rare large stones, prized by buyers of quality anywhere in the world. By mid-summer of 1944,

Oberman had turned almost his entire fortune into easily transported and negotiable jewels, true pirate treasure.

He had also been doing well at his job, ferreting out resistance groups. But now he was turning his back on as many as he was arresting. Where he could, he took extortion in exchange for opportunities to escape. The resistance movement in Holland was altogether different from that in the Ukraine. Here, in Holland, it was almost universal. In the Ukraine, the Germans looked down on the people; here the Dutch looked down on the Germans. These people had courage. They were not anti-Semitic. They didn't give up their Jews to the Germans if it in any way could be avoided. They suffered, but with pride; even the Church resisted in Holland, despite the stand of the Vatican.

As time passed, Oberman was more certain that Germany's chances of winning the war were approaching zero. To express such feelings was considered by many as treason, so he kept his thoughts to himself. But he started thinking seriously about how to get out of Europe. He didn't know what repercussions there might be after the war, but he'd take no chances. He was quite certain that any Germans taken by the Russians would pay dearly for their part in the war. He figured the Americans, English and other powers would be a little more forgiving, but he thought it would be wiser to observe this from outside of Europe. He would always have the option of coming back if there was to be no retribution. If he stayed, he might not have any options.

His occupation now would be to make proper arrangements so when the time came he would be ready.

87

VATICAN LOYALTIES...

Oberman did not speak out. He listened. By the beginning of 1945, the Germans withdrew on all fronts. Oberman returned to Germany. Now there was considerable talk of ways to escape the advancing enemies. Oberman kept his mouth shut. He listened and gathered information. His fortune was in a pouch hidden where he could get it quickly. The more he heard, the more he realized that for him and other Nazis, salvation would come from the Church.

There was little question in Germany where Vatican sentiments lay. The Vatican had remained silent through the years. Never did the Holy See cry out against the policies of the Third Reich. Atrocities were never criticized. The Nazis were allowed to do their work without any show of indignation. But though the Vatican didn't speak out for or against Hitler's policies, it showed support in other ways.

Oberman heard that when Germany occupied **Rome** on September 10, 1943, the Nazis ordered the roundup of all Jews trapped in the city. The world waited for the Vatican to protest the arrest of eight thousand Italian citizens. There was a resounding silence. In spite of Vatican indifference, many of Rome's clergy gave refuge to condemned Jews, hiding as many as they could. The less fortunate were sent to **Auschwitz** or were shot right there in Rome. Because of the outrage around the world at the Pope's silence, the Vatican later issued a statement that three thousand Jews were hidden from Germans in the Vatican itself. Actually, of the eight thousand Jews threatened by the Nazis in Rome, some two or three dozen did find refuge in Vatican City.

Though the Vatican made no official statement, **Archbishop Constantini** voiced Vatican sentiments in 1943 when he said, "We wish with all our hearts that the Germans will bring final victory and the fall of Bolshevism." He hailed the brave soldiers who were fighting "Satan's deputies in Russia." Oberman kept in mind this statement by a leading churchman, a confidant of the Pope.

Christian support for the Nazi policies was further demonstrated by what Oberman recognized as previews of how the Church would help in his future. After the Americans and British landed forces in Europe, many German soldiers and officers were helped back to their own lines or hidden by priests. Many were smuggled back to their troops disguised as Jesuits and Monks. Oberman was quite sure the Church was pleased with the job the Nazis had done to combat Communism and destroy Judaism in Europe. He was quite sure that the Church would show its gratitude by helping Nazis escape prosecution after the war.

He set about to avail himself of its services.

88

THE VATICAN
RESCUE MISSION...

In the first week of April 1945, about a month before **VE Day**, Major Hans Oberman took off his uniform for the last time. Dressed as a middle class German citizen, false papers in his pocket and the pouch of diamonds and other gems under his clothes, he left his apartment to go to *"confession."* He closed the door, not bothering to lock it.

There was no staff car awaiting him at the door this time. Casually, he walked the three kilometers to a small church in the outskirts of bomb-shattered Berlin. Upon entering, he strode straight to the confessional. After a short wait a priest appeared.

"You wish to confess?" the voice of the elderly priest trembled through the screen.

"I seek salvation only this sanctuary can give to the misjudged," Oberman said, speaking each word deliberately.

The old priest immediately recognized the code phrase.

Two days later, Oberman was hidden away in a monk's cell at a monastery in the **Austrian Alps**. He remained at the monastery for eight weeks. He spent his time reading and relaxing and growing a beard. He found it boring after only a few days, but there was no alternative. He showed no surprise at the announcement of Germany's surrender during his third week at the monastery. Each day at the cloister, more and more German officers came to be hidden by the monks. They were kept separate—no one was told identities of the others. Since most of the Nazis passing through the monastery now were very high ranking officers, they were sent through quickly. It meant Oberman was kept at this first refuge for weeks longer than most. It couldn't be helped. Those of high rank, wanted for war crimes, had to be moved out first. Never was Oberman asked to make payment for the services he received from the Church. It was, after all, Christian charity.

The war in Europe had been over for about four weeks when one morning a knock came earlier than usual at Oberman's cell door.

"Please come in. I am awake."

The door opened. A monk, robed in brown, entered the humble quarters. "Today is your day," the monk announced. He placed a garment similar to his own on the table next to Oberman's bed. "Please dress in these today. Later you will get new identity and proper papers."

"Where will I be going?"

"You will be told what you need to know when you get there. It would not do for you to know the next point on the escape route in case you were picked up."

At mid-morning, Oberman set out with seven other refugee Nazis along a country road in the direction of **Innsbruck.** A group of monks sworn to a vow of silence accompanied them. The walk would take three days at an easy pace. The nights were spent in safe houses established along the way.

They had no difficulties on the road to Innsbruck. Once there, they met a mountain guide. For another week, they hid in a third rate boarding house. At the end of the week, they walked to a small village near the border. There the guide had provisioned the party for the most difficult portion of their *"pilgrimage"* to Rome. For the next few days, they crossed the rugged **Brenner Pass** to an inn on the Italian side of the border. There they would rest from the ordeal.

Two days later, they were all safely hidden in a convent in **Northern Italy**. From there, the Nazis were taken out, one or two at a time. They received new identities and were driven to Rome. Again Oberman was the least important, so he was not taken to that city for almost three weeks being bypassed by more important, more desperate Generals and Colonels marked for *war crimes.*

Christian charity again took care of all expenses.

In Rome, he was passed on to **Collegio Croatto**, a seminary operated by a group of **Yugoslavian priests**. From there, contact was made with the **Titular Bishop of Aela,** a close friend and confidant of **Pope Pius XII.** That Bishop was a last contact before the infamous **Bishop Alois Hudal,** who operated the **Vatican Rescue Mission.**

In years to follow, Bishop Alois Hudal would make possible the escape of more than *fifty thousand* Nazis, among them **Martin Bormann,** right-hand man to Adolph Hitler. Bishop Hudal moved the fleeing Oberman along with other Nazis into **Teutonicum Monastery,** *within the walls of the Vatican.* There Oberman received yet another identity and a matching **International Red Cross Refugee Passport.**

In two days, Oberman found himself on an **Argentine** ship. While on board, he was given a choice of **South America** or **Syria.** Oberman chose Syria. He wanted to stay nearer Germany and the continent he knew. The thought of going to South America distressed him. He imagined it a primitive land of natives and jungles. He further suspected that in a few years, all would be forgotten and he would be able to return to his homeland. Besides, he wasn't even sure yet that he would be among those wanted for prosecution. He figured that he could make some investments in the Middle East and parley his fortune while in exile.

He disembarked the Argentine ship in **Barcelona, Spain.** When he got off, he had yet another identity and a new passport—this one, the most valued and versatile in the world—a **Vatican Refugee Passport.**

He was put aboard a ship for **Lebanon.** In Lebanon he was met by a priest of a church in the Christian sector. That priest was assigned to transport fugitive Nazis across his country into Syria. He also offered those Nazis positions as consultants to the Syrian army.

Oberman accepted an advisory position in guerrilla warfare and terrorism.

89

ONE FRIEND
IN ALL THE WORLD...

Immediately after Solomon decided to leave Kiev, he rejoined the Russian forces chasing the Germans out of the Ukraine. Many of the partisans actually enlisted in the Russian army. Diadia Misha joined, went to Officer's Training School and received a commission of captain. Many of the Jews preferred not to sign up. Before World War II, Jews were made to suffer terribly in the Russian army — and the reputation of their mistreatment lived on. Jews had been conscripted for periods as long as twenty-five years and most never lived to see discharge. So Sol and several of his Jewish comrades were satisfied to fight alongside the Russians as civilians, able to walk away as soon as the war was over.

Originally, Solomon intended to fight only until the Germans were out of the Ukraine, but he fought through the winter of 1943 and into the summer of 1944. Then he felt compelled to return once more to Kiev. He really didn't understand why. Perhaps it was homesickness, though no one was left who meant anything to him except Father Peter. He recalled the emptiness he'd felt when he'd returned there in November and asked himself, "Why should it be different now?" He had no answer. But he had to return — perhaps just to be absolutely sure before he closed that door behind him forever.

In November, the city had been freshly liberated; maybe now things would be more normal. Though almost everyone he cared about was dead, their memories lingered in the Kiev district. He reached the city in the last week of June 1944. Hardship and poverty were evident everywhere. A few Jews were now returning, coming out of the forests, out of hiding. Two or three thousand out of a pre occupation population of over a hundred thousand had come home to salvage what they could of their lives.

"Look how many have returned!" could be heard in street conversation everywhere.

"How come so many survived? I suppose they want to move back into their homes now."

"I thought they killed them all!"

"They're lucky to be alive. Why do they come back here now?"

There were certainly those who felt compassion for the survivors and wished them no further harm or hardship, but they were a silent minority.

"It is not up to us to give them back their property," the majority complained. "The Germans ran them out. To the victor go the spoils and we are the victors!"

Anti-Semitism was growing, flourishing.

"Damn Jews. Want to take over everything, again!"

Of the few Jews who returned to the city, Solomon knew none of them before. He went to the only friend he knew, Father Peter. As he approached the little parish church he wondered whether his friend still held the pulpit there. "Solomon! Welcome home, Solomon! Dear Solomon," he heard as he turned into the walk. Father Peter came around the side of the building.

"Father Peter! It's good to see a familiar face. Thank God you're still here."

"I was tending my garden. I saw you walking up the road but couldn't believe it was really you. When did you return to Kiev?"

"Only yesterday, but I couldn't stand it any longer. The city's terrible! I had to get away."

"Why didn't your come sooner? You are always welcome here, you know. Don't you, Solomon?"

"I was sure I'd be welcomed, but I wasn't sure you'd still be here. I'm so glad you are." The two men embraced.

"Solomon, come in. Let me make some tea and lunch. You must be hungry. I haven't anything fancy to offer, but my parishioners do keep me from starving. We have so much to talk about."

Sol had forgotten what a welcome was like. Not since leaving the forests had he felt it. It made him realize how very alone he was. Father Peter filled a *chinik* with water and put it to boil.

"Well, what have you heard from the Church? Will they let you keep the parish?"

Father Peter answered as he went to a shelf to take down two glasses, "I've heard nothing. I'm doing my work here. My parishioners need me, but I don't know if I'm working officially. I don't know if the Church wants me."

"They're noncommittal?"

Father Peter measured some tea into a perforated container. "They're silent!"

"What will you do?"

The priest sat down to wait for the water to boil. "I don't know. I can't go on like this much longer, though. Soon I'll have to make a decision." He paused. He looked sad, "But enough about me. What are your plans?"

Sol sat silently for a moment. He, too, looked sad. "I'm not sure either. I felt I had to come back here once more before I could decide anything. Don't ask me why? Kiev is as dead as my past. Still, where will I find it better? We Jews have had no real home since the year 70, when the Romans ran us out of Palestine."

"I remember you talked of going to Palestine when we were in the forests. What happened to that idea?"

"It died with—all the others. Things were different then." Sol choked up a little. The chinik began to whistle, signaling that it was ready. Father Peter busied himself finishing the tea. He let is steep as he brought the small pot to the table. Solomon slipped deep into his thoughts and the priest let him daydream while he tested the brew in his own glass. He let it steep a few moments more, then filled both glasses full.

Sol sipped. He still had to fight back tears whenever he thought of Rachel. "Things were different then," he repeated.

"Give yourself time. When the war is over, then it will change. The world will surely have learned a lesson." Father Peter didn't speak with full conviction.

"What I have seen and heard in the city since yesterday—well, I assure you not. At least not here."

"I've heard it, too, but things are still difficult now. When things improve, the atmosphere will be better."

"But we Jews can't go through life waiting for good times! We can't live in constant fear that hard times will return—because they always will. And there aren't enough of us left to withstand another pogrom."

"Pogrom, you can't believe that will ever happen again?"

"Pogroms are our destiny."

"If so, then all our struggles have been in vain."

Solomon answered dejectedly. "What is, was—what was, will be. It *is* our destiny."

90

PALESTINE...

Solomon stayed at the church with Father Peter.

Most Jews who returned to Kiev found the corners of destroyed buildings to dwell in. They lived in rubble while trying to reclaim, trying to start anew. As more and more Jews returned to the city, the anti-Semitism became more organized. Through some of the congregants of Father Peter's parish, Sol heard that a pogrom was actually being planned by a radical group of organized Jew haters.

"They intend to finish what Hitler started," Solomon told Father Peter.

"But they are a minority! The rest will not let it happen."

"Like they stopped the slaughter in Babi Yar?" Solomon snapped back.

Father Peter was stymied.

Sol continued, "A small minority is all it takes. Then the masses come out to see what's happening and the next thing you know there's a mob. The mob will kill. Once a pogrom starts, they don't care who they kill. The smell of blood makes them wild as a pack of dogs."

"I'll go to the commander of the city," the priest said. "I know him. Perhaps he'll help."

"I doubt it — he's a Russian."

"What else can I do?"

To Solomon's surprise the commandant was an understanding man. Furthermore, he was aware of the problem and had already taken steps to break up the threat. The pogrom did not materialize, but there were numerous incidents of confrontation and many fights, all spontaneous between individuals.

In September 1944, Father Peter received a letter from a priest he'd gone to school with. At the time Father Peter returned from his schooling to start his work, his friend took over a small parish in **Polish Kielce.** They had corresponded infrequently through the years. This was the second letter since the two cities' liberation. He let Solomon read that piece of mail in his rectory. From the letter Father Peter and Solomon discovered the relative good fortune of the Jews of Kiev.

In 1939, before the German occupation of Kielce, twenty five thousand Jews lived in that city. Like Kiev, Kielce was devoid of Jews at the time of its liberation. As in Kiev, a few Jews drifted back to the city that had been their home. Only two hundred returned from the forests, from the interior of Russia and from cheating the death camps. But even two hundred were too many for the Polish anti-Semites. When the Jews tried to reorganize their community the Jew haters also organized. Their efforts culminated in a full blown pogrom. Jews who survived the Nazi occupation died at the hands of Poles who also thought the Germans were inhuman animals.

"You see? Nothing has changed," Solomon said shaking his head dejectedly. "It's not only here in Kiev or in the Ukraine. It's everywhere in Europe and Russia! We'll never be free as long as we have no country of our own."

"Solomon, my dear friend, I fear you're right," Peter admitted.

Over the next few months into 1945, conditions grew worse for the Jews of Poland, the Ukraine and in the liberated areas of Europe. There were few left after the Holocaust, but their minority position only encouraged harassment. Father Peter's disillusionment with the Church was deepened. He could get no meaningful response from anyone.

"They'll make no commitment until the war is completely over," Solomon kept saying, "Though to tell the truth, I can't believe they could still think about a Nazi counteroffensive anymore."

"I just don't understand it," Father Peter said. "But I know I can't continue like this. Even if I get Church support, I'll no longer respect the hierarchy. Such hypocrisy! Too much has happened. Too much has changed."

"What else can you do?"

"I can teach. I could teach history. I would like teaching. But that has its problems, too."

"Which are?"

"I certainly could not teach in a communist state." Father Peter shook his head and laughed bitterly. "I am still Catholic. I can't give that up!" He paused, "I'm intolerant of both and for the same reason. The Church and communism—they both make the same intolerable demands of dogma!"

"What if you were to move to a non-Communist country?"

"I have considered it. A big step, there are language problems—and I would have to leave everyone I know."

"Have you ever thought of going to Palestine?" Sol asked.

"You mean on a pilgrimage? Of course."

"No, I mean to stay!"

"To stay? Of course not!"

"Well, think about it now. After all, your faith began there! Surely there must be opportunities for a man like you—to teach—to do research—to write... I think it might be your answer!"

91

TRAVEL COMPANIONS...

By the time the war ended in mid 1945, the idea of leaving totally absorbed Father Peter. He'd talked it over with his friends and several reluctantly agreed he should make the move. Father Peter would accompany Solomon to Palestine.

The first problem facing them was getting out of the Ukraine. Exit visas were not easy to come by. Even applying for one was risky because it alerted authorities and put one on a list of possible enemies of the state. Finally, Father Peter and Sol agreed to slip out of the country secretly. One advantage they had was that much of the country was in transit. Soldiers and refugees were returning, displaced persons were trying to find places to settle. The Jew and the priest joined the flow of transients toward the border towns of the Ukraine.

They made for the mountain town of **Glybokaya** in the south. From there, they crossed the border at night to the Romanian Mountain town of **Putna.** Father Peter had several priest acquaintances, friends who willingly helped them to cross the country. Security was not strict and they had no problem getting into **Hungary.**

As they traveled west, the number of people in transit increased and security was even more lax. The two men traveled now as priests — as members of the clergy, they escaped scrutiny. They left Hungary and crossed into **Austria** under the protection of the forests. Once in Austria, they considered their problems behind them.

The first thing they did was present themselves at the headquarters of the U.S. and British occupation forces.

They had no difficulty proving their identities from papers they had brought with them out of the Ukraine. They were given asylum when they announced they were defecting. They received new papers allowing them to stay in the west, work permits and a list of all available aid societies that had been set up for refugees and displaced persons. They were sent to a special office for those who wanted to resettle in other countries of the non-Communist world. Austria was the major staging area for resettlement.

"Your papers, please," the official requested, "You want to go to Palestine? You wish to live in the Holy Land, Father?"

"Yes, we seek a new life in the place of our beginnings," Father Peter replied as he handed the man his own and Solomon's papers.

"Let's see — you're from the Ukraine — the Kiev district. That should be no problem. We have few requests from Ukrainians to enter Palestine. The quota should be far from filled." He searched a loose-leaf book before continuing. It contained columns of countries and figures. "Ah, here it is. Oh my, they have never filled their quotas. Since the war not even two percent of it. You'll have no problem at all." The man seemed to develop an immediate rapport with the priest and addressed all his comments to him. Father Peter took over the role of spokesman.

The official took some papers from a drawer in his desk and handed them to Father Peter. "Each of you must fill out one of these forms completely — accurately — then bring them back to me. We'll process you together so you won't be separated."

"Thank you," Sol replied. "You're a great help. I never dreamed it would be so easy."

The form asked a multitude of questions: date of application, place of birth, date of birth, family name, given name, middle name, father's name, mother's maiden name, citizenship, race, religion, education, profession, skills, political convictions, criminal history. There was a section on health history, family history, personal history and a section on the whys of wanting to resettle.

When both he and Solomon finished the chore, Father Peter gathered all the papers and returned to the room where *"their"* official worked. He'd just finished a family group, so he turned his attention immediately to Father Peter and Sol.

"Ah, you are finished. Let me see your forms. This is only the first in a tedious series of steps, but it is the most important of all — and if it's not properly done you'll have difficulties later." He scrutinized each form, point by point and gave an affirmative nod after almost each item. He mumbled, "Fine — fine — very good — fine..." intermittently and, "Seems in order..." and initialed each page in the proper box — until he came to one answer on Solomon's. His face grew stern.

"Oh my!" he shook his head, reopening his book of countries and figures, "Oh dear me!" He turned a few more pages and checked in another place. "This presents a problem. Mr. Shalensky — being with the priest, I assumed — well — I assumed you were with him."

"I am!" Sol said with some irritation.

"Well, yes, of course. But I mean to say, of his religion — aaaah — his religious conviction."

"What are you getting at?" Father Peter demanded.

"Well, Father Rochovit, Mr. Shalensky comes under another quota list. It is the way the British have set up the quota. Jews are under a different quota listing!"

"What are you saying? We are Ukrainian! We are both from Kiev!" Father Peter was almost shouting. "You yourself said the Ukrainian quota was far from filled!"

"For Ukrainians, yes, but not for Jews. I am truly sorry, but I have no control over the matter. Jews are under a separate quota system. The British will not let you in, Mr. Shalensky. The Jewish quota is small ...filled — and the waiting list is very long."

Solomon was disappointed, angry, but not surprised. "It is as I said, nothing has changed. We are separate in the eyes of the non-Jewish world. You distinguish between Ukrainians and Ukrainian Jews. The Nazis did, too."

"I don't," the official quickly pointed out, "the system does. Your friend can be on his way within the week — but you — as a Jew — well, that will take a long time, I'm afraid."

"Just how long, specifically how long?" Solomon demanded.

Father Peter couldn't restrain himself any longer. "This is not possible!" he shouted. "We — the whole damned world just suffered a war because of this same bigoted attitude and you have the audacity to..."

Solomon put his hand firmly on Father Peter's shoulder to calm him and redirected his question to the intimidated official, "How long?"

"They take a few thousand a year," the man shrugged. "And the waiting list seems endless."

"My God! What madness this is!" Father Peter raged. "It's the Jews who need the refuge of Palestine! There is no place for them in Europe or Russia. I can go there — I who could go anyplace — and the Jews who have nowhere... Now the British tell them they can't enter Palestine? What are they to do?"

The official's face colored. "There are displaced person's camps where they will be taken care of until something can be worked out."

"Displaced person's camps? Something worked out?" the priest screamed.

"Please, I understand that you are upset, Father..."

"You understand?" Solomon interrupted, "you don't understand shit!" He leaned across the official's desk and looked him straight in the eyes. "How long will it take the non-Jewish world to learn? It's quite obvious why we no longer want to stay in Germany, Austria, Poland or the Soviet Union. How can anyone ask us to stay where our families were butchered, gassed and burned — turned into soap and fertilizer — their corpses raped of gold teeth and hair to further the economy of what you called civilized nations? You're shocked that the Nazis could have done such things — but there are an awful lot of you who are at the same time sorry the job wasn't finished!"

"You can go, but not to Palestine!" the official muttered uncomfortably.

"All right, where can I go?"

The official's face became even more florid. He picked up his book and leafed through it as if looking for an answer. "Well," he stated finally, "except for returning to the Ukraine, where they have to accept you back, there's no place that will take you right away. However, there are a number of countries, which have much shorter waiting lists. You could go to Holland, Denmark or Sweden in a shorter time. Maybe even America. Canada!"

"But what about this week? Or next?"

"No place."

"And if I did go to one of those countries, could I then go to Palestine?"

"Not as a Jew."

There was nothing left to be said. Solomon turned and walked away from the desk, bitter, frustrated.

Father Peter picked up all the forms and began to follow Solomon out of the office.

"No," Sol said, turning back to the sound of the priest's following footsteps, "complete your paperwork. This is my problem. You must make your arrangements to go to Palestine. I insist. I'll wait for you in the hall."

Solomon's tone told Father Peter that he best finish. The more I see how the world treats the Jews, Father Peter thought, the more I realize that no gentile will ever know just how it feels to be Jewish. After his paperwork was complete, Father Peter met Sol where he waited in the hallway.

"You want to know something funny, Father Peter? All my life I have wondered about something and the answer has always eluded me. I remember my grandfather saying that the most precious thing we had was our birthright. Well, I understood that we were Jews by birth, but he spoke of *'birthright'* – *'birthright!'* – implying it to be a privilege.

"As a child, growing up, I wondered what privilege he saw in it. Was it a wonderful privilege to be everyone's scapegoat, to be spat on and beat up by the goyim? Was it a privilege to have lived in ghettos and worry about every drunken group of goyim starting a pogrom — or just having fun breaking our windows and looting our stores, raping our sisters and mothers?

"Well, now it all comes clear to me. Finally, when my birthright allows me to spend my days in a displaced person's camp, I realize what my grandfather understood so long ago.

"My birthright allows me to live with a clear conscience! As a Jew, I don't have to carry with me the gentile's guilt! I haven't the shame of contributing to the bigotry, bloodshed and hate that has contaminated this planet for the last twenty centuries. It is my birthright to be oppressed throughout history — but I think that is easier to live with than the guilt of being the *oppressor!*"

92

THE DISPLACED PERSON'S CAMP...

That evening, tempers cooled, perspective regained, Solomon persuaded Father Peter that the only thing for him to do was to go ahead to Palestine. "It would be pointless for you to stay here. Go ahead! Get settled in your new homeland. Write me about it. At least I'll know from you what it's really like. And when I do get there, I'll have a settled-in friend to help me out."

There really was no alternative. By the end of the week, Father Peter headed toward Palestine and left Sol considering life in a displaced persons camp. It was not easy for a Ukrainian Jew to find a place and a way to make a living in postwar Austria. At least in the displaced persons camp, he would be among his own people. He would have shelter, food, medical aid should he need it. And unlike the concentration camps, he could always leave if things didn't work out.

The displaced persons camps were really far different from concentration camps, but for those who had survived concentration camps — especially the children — they kept the nightmares alive. Any form of confinement and regimentation, however lax, was a reminder. But for the displaced Jews the DP camps were the best alternative. The DP camps came under the auspices of the **United Nations Relief and Rehabilitation Administration.** At war's end, only 50,000 Jews came out of the death factories alive. At first, they joined the streams of refugees returning to their places of origin, but before long they found that, unlike the non-Jewish refugees, they had no place to return to. In addition, there were those who had survived the war in hiding, in resistance groups and a few who had succeeded in posing as *"Aryans."* The DP camps brought all of these Jews together.

Since Jewish communities were prevented or discouraged from re forming in postwar Europe and Russia, they began to form in the DP camps. There the universal problem was recognized and out of that universal problem grew a universal Jewish purpose — to open the doors of Palestine and re establish it as their rightful homeland — the Jewish **State, Israel.**

President Truman, on June 22, 1945, appointed **Earl G. Harrison** to report on the conditions and needs of the displaced persons in Germany — particularly the Jews. On August 1, 1945, Truman received the report. It described the harsh and crowded conditions. "The first and plainest need of these people," the report read, "is recognition of their status as Jews. Refusal to recognize the Jews as such has the effect of closing one's eyes to their former persecution.

"For reasons that are obvious, most Jews want to leave Germany and Austria. The life which they have been forced to lead has made them impatient of delay. They wish to evacuate to Palestine now. I come to but one conclusion: the only real solution to the problem lies in the evacuation of all non repatriable Jews in DP camps, who wish it, to Palestine."

President Truman transmitted the report to **General Eisenhower, Supreme Commander of the U.S. Forces in Europe,** to be acted upon. Conditions in the camps were immediately improved. **UNRRA** appointed Jewish refugees to posts in the administration of the camps. Most importantly, President Truman recommended to the British Government that one hundred thousand immigration certificates be issued, allowing Jews in the DP camps into Palestine.

The British refused.

93

MILTON FELDMAN...

By the time Solomon made his way to a DP camp—it was on the German side of the German Austria border—the improved conditions were already being enforced. He found a highly organized society within the camp. A kindergarten was being operated for those too young for regular school. School-age children were being taught in **Hebrew** and **Yiddish** as well as in the language of their origin. For most, it was the first formal schooling they'd ever had. There were also **ORT vocational schools for adults,** teaching skills needed in Palestine. Agricultural schools were also established. Anyone who didn't know the languages tried to learn conversational Hebrew and Yiddish, which would become their native tongues.

Newspapers were published by the DPs themselves and the **Zionist Organization** actually set up an office in the camp to help Jews prepare for their future. In an extensive survey carried out by UNRRA, it was found that 96.8 percent of the Jews desired to go to Palestine. There was only one problem—the British refused to let them in!

On December 5, 1945, the British closed the doors of their European occupation zones to refugees. The ban was for *all* refugees; almost all other DPs had found places to settle and start anew. Only the Jews had no place to alight. Of course, this placed added burden on the DP camps in the American zone. Also, more and more Jews came out of the Polish and Russian zones because of renewed anti-Semitism in those countries. In the first few months of 1946, one hundred forty thousand Jews fled Poland alone—after the bloody pogrom in Kielce, on July 4th of that year, ninety thousand more Jews abandoned their homes in terror. The pogrom in Kielce murdered nearly one out of every four Jews resettled in that city — and most of the others had been severely injured.

International opinion and pressure did not impress the British. They barred the door to Palestine and that was all there was to it.

Sol had been attending one of the ORT trade schools in the DP camp. He was learning auto and tractor mechanics. He thought that when he got to Palestine it would be a valuable and needed skill on a *Kibbutz*. Though the work had its challenge; it not only enabled him to make a contribution, but it gave him time to himself when he could think. One morning in the spring of 1946, a young man approached Sol's workbench. "You are Solomon Shalensky?"

"Yes. What can I do for you?"

The man looked about Sol's age, twenty two or twenty three years old. He spoke Yiddish, the language understood by most DPs, allowing communication between people from all over Eastern and Western Europe, as well as those helping from other parts of the world.

"My name is **Milton Feldman**. I'm an American with the **Jewish Committee**. We are making inquiries into the conditions in the various camps. Could we talk — privately?"

"What can I tell you?"

"I have been lent an office upstairs. Do you mind if we go there to speak?"

"Not at all," Sol replied, putting his tools away and wiping the grease off his hands. There was something about this young man that did not quite ring true. He wore a short sleeved shirt without tie or coat. He was neat, but certainly not dressed in the business attire of most officials. He seemed to have something else on his mind beside the conditions of the camp. Sol didn't know why he sensed that, but the feeling was strong. There was no conversation on the way to the office. When they got there Milton ushered Solomon in. It was more a storage room than an office. Milton closed the door behind him. The room contained a table and two chairs — nothing else.

"What do you want of me?" Sol asked. "Who are you really? I feel it is something other than camp conditions."

The stranger smiled. "Of course I'm not interested in the camp conditions. I can see all I need to know about the camp conditions. I am interested in emptying the camp! The Jewish Agency provided us with a front — and an excuse to enter these camps. I am really an American, but I come via Palestine. I'm with the **Haganah.**"

"Haganah? The Jewish army of Palestine? You are really with Haganah?"

"Yes, with a special section assigned to bring *'illegals'* into Palestine."

"Illegals?"

"Yes, illegals. It is the British name for those who enter Palestine without *legal* papers."

"You are making an overture? Recruiting me to enter Palestine illegally?"

"You come to the point quickly, don't you?" Milton Feldman grinned.

"Why wouldn't I go? What fool would turn down such an invitation?"

"It's not without risk, Solomon. Many get caught. If that happens, you will most likely be interned in a British prison camp on **Cyprus.** Believe me, the conditions here are much nicer than on Cyprus. Also, you will be taken off the quota lists. It may end your chances forever getting into Palestine legally. It is something to think about."

"I have just given it all the thought I intend to. I want to go. What must I do?"

"You just did it!"

Solomon laughed, "I did?"

You will be contacted," Milton told him. "Now go back to your work and say nothing of this to anyone!"

"May I ask why you came to me for this privilege?"

"There will be time for that later. Just return to your work and say nothing. If anyone asks you, you just told us of the general conditions here and how much you love it."

94

THE SURVEY
RESULTS...

Nothing happened.

Nothing more was said.

Several weeks passed and Solomon began to think he'd imagined the whole thing, except he knew of several other DPs who had been interviewed about *"camp conditions."* But none spoke to each other about the incidents. They all did as they were told and said nothing. Sol knew of at least seven who had been interviewed. Could it all have been a cruel joke? He wondered how many others had been asked. He was dying to talk to someone about the matter, but too much was at stake. He was not about to spoil his or others' chances.

At long last, another stranger came to his bench one morning and asked, "Solomon Shalensky"

"Yes!"

"We finally have the results of the survey on camp conditions you took part in. You remember the survey, don't you?"

Sol's heart began to pound. "Yes, of course. What's become of it?"

"That is why I'm here. All those who are interested can hear the results. I assume you're still interested?"

"Absolutely!"

"Good. Tomorrow morning, leave the camp as if you were just going to town. Take only what you consider essential. No luggage—only the clothes you wear. Come to this address before seven in the evening, but not before noon." He handed Sol a folded piece of paper. "Again, say nothing to anyone."

Solomon arrived at the address in the early afternoon. It was a bookstore. Milton Feldman was there, greeting each DP as he or she entered the store. They came throughout the afternoon. As quickly as they arrived they were taken away by another Haganah member. The DPs came from several camps so that not any one camp would turn up with a large number missing in any one day. A few absentees per day were considered normal attrition in most camps.

From the store, Solomon and two others were taken to a farm just on the other side of the Austrian border. It was a safe house run by the Haganah. The tight security was not so much for fear of local authorities, for the DPs had every right to move about the country. Security was kept strict so that the British wouldn't be on the lookout for a large group of 'illegals' getting ready to run past their patrols off the Palestine coast.

Solomon and the growing group stayed three more days at the farm. When the last of their numbers arrived, they totaled thirty nine; just enough to fill a bus which the Haganah simply chartered to take the DPs to the Italian port city of **LaSpezia.** Numerous other groups of DPs were waiting there and others were yet to come. The Jews were hidden on several nearby farms.

On the evening of the third day after Sol's group had arrived at LaSpezia, a dilapidated Greek freighter steamed into port. It off loaded its cargo and moved to another pier to await its turn for a dry dock overhaul. Its crew was given a two day shore leave; only the captain and a skeleton crew of handpicked men remained aboard. A messenger was sent to a member of the Haganah with the code phrase, "Awaiting new manifest."

That night, seven hundred and sixty seven Jews of all ages and nationalities were loaded onto the waiting ship. They were stuffed into cargo holds, crew quarters, officers' cabins and any place where people could be put below decks. At a quarter past midnight the skeleton crew fired up the boiler and the engines began to crank. As soon as the ship had cleared the harbor the Jews were allowed on deck.

A message to the port authorities had informed them that the ship had been given clearance to another dry dock which would save several days and the captain had found a cargo at that other port. By dawn, the ship was well out into the **Mediterranean Sea** on its illegal voyage.

The ship did not head directly for Palestine but churned toward **Lebanon.** Vessels headed in the direction of Palestine were watched by British patrols from the air. Once sighted, the ship's progress was charted daily. The crews and passengers watched for aircraft, but fortunately none was sighted. As they approached the waters off Palestine, the Captain started to run an erratic course, which slowed their progress but would confuse any British that did happen upon them. Slowly he worked his vessel into position to run the British blockade that night. At nightfall he dropped anchor and waited. They were still out of sight of land. The next two hours seemed an eternity.

"I don't like it. It's been too easy," the Captain said to his chief. "I've done this several times now, but I feel very uneasy tonight."

"Perhaps we shouldn't try tonight," the second officer replied.

"No. The longer we are in these waters, the greater the risk. We go in thirty minutes. But I still feel uneasy."

Thirty minutes later, the anchor was hoisted and the ship's crews began their struggle against the current. The Jews were headed home.

In another hour, a light flashed from the shore at a predetermined location and the captain set his bow in that direction. Fifteen minutes later, the signal flashed again and the captain knew he was still on course. They were minutes from their destination when a crewmember on watch yelled out, "Patrol boat closing in from starboard!"

No sooner had he called out than the approaching vessel turned on its powerful searchlights. Pandemonium broke loose on deck.

"I'm going to make a run for it!" the Captain shouted. "Full ahead!"

"We can't outrun her!" the bewildered second officer exclaimed.

"No, but I can damn well ground her. These are shallow waters with a sandy bottom. As soon as we hit, lower every lifeboat loaded full. A few of these tormented souls may get to shore. The rest are headed for Cyprus anyway. What the hell do we have to lose?"

As soon as the ship grounded on the sand, six lifeboats were put into the water. The patrol boat started after them but could only stop one before the others were in water too shallow for it to follow. The five successful, overloaded boats landed nearly a hundred-thirty lucky Jews on the sands near the ancient town of **Caesarea.** There they were met by Haganah members who whisked them off under cover of night.

A few Jews jumped off the grounded British ship and swam for shore. No one knew just how many tried that or what their fates were. The Greek Captain and his crew were incarcerated in Palestine at the old prison of **Acre.** The remaining DPs were taken to the internment camps on the island of Cyprus. Solomon was among them...

95

CYPRUS...

Solomon's eyes lifted briefly to the barbed wire. His gaze fell back to the ground. His thin face was worn. Barbed wire confined him. A British soldier guarded him and fifty thousand other Jews. How quickly they've forgotten.

These are our liberators?

They liberated us from the Nazis. They imprison us here on Cyprus. God, why can't we just be allowed to live our lives in freedom? There are Jews in this camp who have faced death at the hands of the Nazis every day for the past decade. Now they are thrown into this hellhole by our 'allies.' There are children here who have not known a day free of fear in their entire lives.

The sun burned down on the island. There wasn't even a breeze. The internment camp was a tent city quickly thrown up to hold the prisoners. Palestine was their only hope. But Palestine was in the hands of the British—and the British had closed the doors to the only country that would take the Jews of Europe.

Now Cyprus was their concentration camp.

For many who finally gave up hope, Cyprus became their death camp. Attempted and successful suicides were commonplace. Some of the elderly who had survived Hitler could no longer struggle against this last disappointment. Without hope, the soul died—shortly after, the body.

"They have already forgotten..."

DOV...

I have tried not to dwell too much on my own story because there were so many others who suffered far more, fought more bravely, made greater sacrifices, lost everything even life itself. There were many heroes in World War II, many of them Jews. Few have received any recognition at all. Those who died are remembered, perhaps only because *we* won't let the world forget. But what of those who lived? Our ordeals have been mostly forgotten. *"They went to their deaths like sheep to the slaughter!"* That they remember. Before the war was over, the ordeal of the living was forgotten, pushed from the minds of the guilty and the complacent. Not until the formation of the State of Israel did those Jewish displaced masses find a welcome in this world.

In 1948, Israel achieved statehood and the displaced persons camps all over Europe and those internment camps in Cyprus emptied. Their multitude finally allowed the freedom to go home to the only country that truly welcomed them in nearly two-thousand years.

Solomon finally found the freedom he'd fought so hard for.

I moved to Israel as well, but I'd not been interned in a camp. After we arrived in Kiev with the Russian army, I bid my friends, Sol and Father Peter, farewell and continued with the Russian Army as they made their way west. I had no one anywhere in Eastern Europe. I worked as a battle field physician attending to the casualties where they fell. We did what we could to stabilize them for their trip back to the hospitals.

When we crossed over into Germany and the number of Russian casualties dropped precipitously, I left the army before they had a chance to send me back to Eastern Europe. I made my way south to Austria where I made contact with members of the Jewish Committee and also the Haganah. I was given a job traveling from DP Camp to DP Camp all through Europe making sure that our people were getting the best treatment possible and, more important, surveying the health status of the recovering survivors from Hitler's death camps. During my travels, I learned of horrors that shocked me even after all I'd been through. Then I vowed to do my part never to let the world forget. But for years I tried to forget. Remembering was too painful. I actively tried to put it out of my mind. My nightmares would not go away.

In 1948, I too moved to Israel. Solomon and I were reunited. We met on the field of battle in the effort to break the Arab siege of Jerusalem. But that is another story.

After the 1948 War, I became a staff physician in a hospital in **Afula** a town North of **Jerusalem** and East of **Haifa**. Solomon moved to a kibbutz near the town of **Ramat-Yishay**, not half an hour's drive from me. We have become even faster friends than we were in the forests. Shortly after Solomon joined his kibbutz he met a **Sabra**, an Israeli born, ironically by the name Rachel. They married and have four wonderful children—three boys and a girl, named for his departed brothers and sister and grandfather.

Father Peter became a professor of religious history and philosophy. He never was able to resolve his discord with his Church, which he'd dearly loved before Babi Yar. He died in 1956 of a myocardial infarction. His Church did put him to rest in hallowed ground. I hope he found his peace and reunion with his beliefs.

I, too, found my love and marriage. We have three wonderful *"children"* grown up to have given us seven grandchildren. Since 1948 life has been good.

After my retirement, my family insisted I put down on paper the memories that have haunted me all these years. And now that I have done it, nightmares of my memory are finally leaving me. If nothing else this writing has been a catharsis. But I hope it will be more than that. Though it has given me some peace, I hope it gives the rest of the world outrage enough to insist on remembering after we are no longer here to remind.

ABOUT THE AUTHOR

OTHNIEL J. SEIDEN

Othniel J. Seiden, or Otti as he prefers being called, typically takes on an interesting historic subject and studies it to find the most fascinating storyline.

When doing the research for "The Remnant," however, Otti found that it wasn't just one story, but the mixture of the stories of the survivors and their resistance work that really told the true story of the 'Free Jews of World War II' and the part they played in bringing down the Third Reich.

After researching the transcripts of the Nuremburg Trials and interviewing 'The Remnant' or Jewish survivors of the holocaust; Otti was compelled to write their startling and remarkable stories of World War II while the remaining members of "The Remnant" were still alive.

It is a stunning and compelling novel made of up the collection of stories of the Jews who were able to remain free and fight. Otti documents their escapes, their survival, their sacrifices, their suffering, their missions and their guerrilla warfare tactics against the Nazi occupation forces.

Otti tells most of this story in the shadow of the atrocities of the now infamous Babi Yar ravine where it is thought that nearly a million people, Jews and non-Jews alike were massacred. Its existence was kept hidden for many years after the war by both the German and Russian interests. The brave few who escaped certain death here did so by acts of amazing bravery and sheer determination to live.

Otti in this book, with these stories based on real

people and historical transcripts, should dispel the myth that the Jewish people *"went to their deaths like sheep to slaughter..."* The Remnant and their incredible stories will erase that perception forever!

The Remnant is Othniel Seiden's fourth historical novel following *The Survivor of Babi Yar, The Capuchin,* and *The Cartographer – 1492.* All of Otti's books current are available on the website BoomerBookSeries.com.

More From Othniel

Health

5 HTP The Serotonin Connection:
The Natural Supplement that helps
you be in control of your mind and body!
ISBN: 1519148445
5-HTP and Depression Management:
Available in Kindle Only
5HTP and Memory Loss Management with:
Available in Kindle Only
5 HTP PMS and Menopause:
Available in Kindle Only
Coping with Arthritis:
ISBN: 151941353X
Coping with BPH:
Benign Prostatic Hypertrophy
Male, over 45, you probably have it!
Available in Kindle Only
Coping with Colorectal Cancer:
Prevention and Cure of theSecond Leading
Cause of Cancer Deaths
Available in Kindle Only
Coping with Fibromyalgia:
It's not in your head, it's a disease!
ISBN: 1519438311

Coping with Prostate Cancer:
*Prevention and Cure
of Man's Most Common Cancer*
ISBN: 1519438737

Heart of a Woman:
Prevetion and Cure of the #1 Killer in Women
ISBN: 1519441533

Heavy and Healthy:
Forget Your Weight and Get Fit!
ISBN: 1519495412

Quit Smoking Now!:
*The Program to Help You
Quit Smoking Now and Forever!*
ISBN: 1519495781

Sharpening the Aging Mind:
*Methods, Tricks & Tips to
Keep Your Mind Super Sharp*
ISBN: 1519496028

Sleep Disorders Management:
Available in Kindle Only

The Second half begins at 50:
Your Longevity Handbook
ISBN: 1519496389

Walk!:
Walk Your Way to Great Health & Long Life
Available in Kindle Only

Weight & Appetite Management:
Available in Kindle Only

Relationships:

Adultery Case Histories:
> *Why People Cheat on Their Partners*
> **Available in Kindle Only**

Communing with the Dead:
> *Death Needn't Part You*
> **ISBN: 1519190085**

Foreplay:
> *The True Focus of Great Sex*
> **ISBN: 1519440979**

Sex in the Golden Years:
> *The Best Sex Ever, Stay Sexually Active for Life*
> **ISBN: 1519495927**

The Big O:
> *Male & Female Multiple Orgasms*
> **ISBN: 1519496109**

The Hospice Experience:
> *Making Your Most Important Final Decision*
> **ISBN: 1519496281**

When Your Spouse Dies:
> *A widow's & widower's handbook*
> **ISBN: 151949646X**

Jewish Fiction

Padre Pio:
> *The Capuchin – the life of Padre Pio -*
> *St. Pio of Pietrelcina*
> *Sex, Horror & Violence vs. Unyielding Faith!*
> **ISBN: 1519495684**

Seed of Avraham:
A 4000 Year History of the Jewish Family...
ISBN: 1519495811

Shtetl:
The Story of a Life No More...
As told from the hereafter
ISBN: 1519496036

The Cartographer:
1492
ISBN: 151949615X

The Condemned Voyage:
The S.S. St. Louis - 1939
Available in Kindle Only

The Crusades:
The Jewish World of the 12th Century
Available in Kindle Only

The Death of Berlin:
A Story of Hollocaust Survival and Revenge
Available in Kindle Only

The Remnant:
The Jewish Resistance in WWII
ISBN: 1519496346

The Uprising of Babi Yar:
The Syrets Deathcamp
Available in Kindle Only

Miscellaneous

Guaranteed Routes to Success for Writers:
A Road Map Through Today's
Dramatic Changes in Publishing
Available in Kindle Only

Joy of Volunteering:
Working and Surviving in Developing Countries
ISBN: 1519495587

So You Want to Write a Book:
ISBN: 1519496079

If you liked

The Remnant

Please leave a review on Amazon.com

Also available in Kindle

Made in the USA
Middletown, DE
02 August 2019